#1

# THE WANDERER

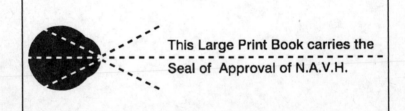

This Large Print Book carries the
Seal of Approval of N.A.V.H.

# The Wanderer

## Robyn Carr

**WHEELER PUBLISHING**
*A part of Gale, Cengage Learning*

GALE
CENGAGE Learning·

Detroit • New York • San Francisco • New Haven, Conn • Waterville, Maine • London

GALE
CENGAGE Learning®

Copyright © 2013 by Robyn Carr.
Thunder Point Series.
Wheeler Publishing, a part of Gale, Cengage Learning.

Wheeler Publishing Large Print Hardcover.
The text of this Large Print edition is unabridged.
Other aspects of the book may vary from the original edition.
Set in 16 pt. Plantin.

LIBRARY OF CONGRESS CATALOGING-IN-PUBLICATION DATA

Carr, Robyn.
    The wanderer / by Robyn Carr.
        pages ; cm. — (Thunder point series) (Wheeler Publishing large print hardcover)
    ISBN-13: 978-1-4104-5713-4 (hardcover)
    ISBN-10: 1-4104-5713-3 (hardcover)
    1. Large type books. I. Title.
PS3553.A76334W36 2013
    813'.54—dc23                                        2013003370

Published in 2013 by arrangement with Harlequin Books S.A.

Printed in the United States of America
1 2 3 4 5 6 7 17 16 15 14 13

To the magnificent Kristan Higgins,
who is beautiful inside and out.

# ONE

It took Hank Cooper almost eight hours to get from Virgin River to Thunder Point, Oregon, because he was towing his fifth wheel, a toy hauler. He pulled to the side of the road frequently to let long strings of motorists pass. Just prior to crossing the California/Oregon border, he stopped at a redwood tourist trap featuring gardens, souvenirs, wood carvings, a lunch counter and restrooms. Skipping the garden tour, he bought a sandwich and drink and headed out of the monument-size trees to the open road, which very soon revealed the rocky Oregon Coast.

Cooper stopped at the first outlook over the ocean and parked. His phone showed five bars and he dialed up the Coos County Sheriff's Department. "Hello," he said to the receptionist. "My name is Hank Cooper and I'm on my way to Thunder Point following a call from someone saying my friend, Ben Bailey, is dead. Apparently he left something for me, but that's not why I'm headed your way. The message I got was that Ben was killed, but there were no details. I want to talk to the sheriff. I need some answers."

"Hold, please," she said.

*Well, that wasn't what he expected.* He'd figured he'd leave a number and eat his lunch while he waited.

"Deputy McCain," said the new voice on the line.

"Hank Cooper here, Deputy," he said, and in spite of himself, he straightened and squared his shoulders. He'd always been resistant to authority, yet he also responded to it. "I was hoping to speak with the sheriff."

"I'm the deputy sheriff. The county sheriff's office is in Coquille. This is a satellite office with a few deputies assigned. Thunder Point is small — there's a constable but no other local law enforcement. The constable handles small disputes, evictions, that sort of thing. The county jail is in Coquille. How can I help you, Mr. Cooper?"

"I'm a friend of Ben Bailey and I'm on my way into town to find out what happened to him."

"Mr. Cooper, Ben Bailey's been deceased

for more than a couple of weeks."

"I gather that. I just found out. Some old guy — Rawley someone — found a phone number and called me. He was killed, Rawley said. Dead and buried. I want to know what happened to him. He was my friend."

"I can give you the details in about ninety seconds."

But Cooper wanted to look him in the eye when he heard the tale. "If you'll give me directions, I'll come to the Sheriff's Department."

"Well, that's not necessary. I can meet you at the bar," the deputy said.

"What bar?"

"Ben's. I guess you weren't a close friend."

"We go back fifteen years but this is my first trip up here. We were supposed to meet with a third buddy from the Army in Virgin River for some hunting. Ben always said he had a bait shop."

"I'd say he sold a lot more Wild Turkey than bait. You know where Ben's place is?"

"Only sort of," Cooper said.

"Take 101 to Gibbons Road, head west. After about four miles, look for a homemade sign that says Cheap Drinks. Turn left onto Bailey Pass. It curves down the hill. You'll run right into Bailey's. When do you think you'll get there?"

"I just crossed into Oregon from California," he said. "I'm pulling a fifth wheel. Couple of hours?"

"More like three. I'll meet you there if nothing interferes. Is this your cell number?"

"It is," he said.

"You'll have good reception on the coast. I'll give you a call if I'm held up."

"Thanks, Deputy . . . what was it?"

"McCain. See you later, Mr. Cooper."

Cooper signed off, slipped the phone into his jacket pocket and got out of the truck. He put his lunch on the hood and leaned against the truck, looking out at the northern Pacific Ocean. He'd been all over the world, but this was his first trip to the Oregon Coast. The beach was rocky and there were boulders two stories high sticking out of the water. An orange-and-white helicopter flew low over the water — a Coast Guard HH-65 Dolphin, search and rescue.

For a moment he had a longing to be back in a chopper. Once he got this business about Ben straightened out, he might get to the chore of looking for a flying job. He'd done a number of things air-related after the Army. The most recent was flying out of the Corpus Christi port to offshore oil rigs. But after a spill in the Gulf, he was ready

10

for a change.

His head turned as he followed the Coast Guard chopper across the water. He'd never considered the USCG. He was used to avoiding offshore storms, not flying right into them to pluck someone out of a wild sea.

He took a couple of swallows of his drink and a big bite of his sandwich, vaguely aware of a number of vehicles pulling into the outlook parking area. People were getting out of their cars and trucks and moving to the edge of the viewing area with binoculars and cameras. Personally, Coop didn't really think these mountainous boulders, covered with bird shit, were worthy of a picture, even with the orange chopper flying over them. *Hovering* over them . . .

The waves crashed against the big rocks with deadly power and the wind was really kicking up. He knew only too well how dicey hovering in wind conditions like that could be. And so close to the rocks. If anything went wrong, that helicopter might not be able to recover in time to avoid the boulders or crashing surf. Could get ugly.

Then a man in a harness emerged from the helicopter, dangling on a cable. That's when Cooper saw what the other motorists had seen before him. He put down his sandwich and dove into the truck, grabbing for the binoculars in the central compartment. He honed in on a boulder, a good forty or fifty feet tall, and what had been specks he now recognized as two human beings. One was on top of the rock, squatting to keep from being blown over in the wind. The other was clinging to the face of the rock.

Rock climbers? They both wore what appeared to be wet suits under their climbing gear. Thanks to the binoculars, he could see a small boat bouncing in the surf, moving away from the rock. There was a stray rope anchored to the rock and flapping in the breeze. The man who squatted on top of the boulder had issues with not only the crosswind but the helicopter's rotor wash. And if the pilot couldn't keep his aircraft stable, the EMT or rescue swimmer who dangled from the cable would slam into the rock.

"Easy, easy, easy," he muttered to himself, wishing the crew could hear him.

The emergency medical tech grabbed on to the wall of the rock beside the stranded climber, stabilized himself with an anchor in the stone, and held there for a minute. Then the climber hoisted himself off the wall of the rock and onto the EMT, pig-

12

gyback to the front of the harnessed rescuer. Both of them were pulled immediately up to the copter via the cable and quickly yanked within.

"Yeah," he whispered. Good job! He'd like to know the weight of that pilot's balls — that was some fancy flying. Reaching the climber was the hard part. Rescuing the guy up top was going to be less risky for all involved. The chopper backed away from the rock slightly while victim number one was presumably stabilized. Then, slowly edging near the rock once more, hovering there, a rescue basket was deployed. The climber on top waited until the basket was right there before he stood, grabbed it and fell inside. As he was being pulled up, motorists around Cooper cheered.

Before the climber was pulled all the way into the chopper, the boat below crashed against the mountainous boulder and broke into pieces. It left nothing but debris on the water. These guys must have tried to anchor the boat to a rock on a side that wasn't battered by big waves, so they could climb up, then back down. But once the boat was lost, so were they.

Who had called the Coast Guard? Probably one of them, from a cell phone. Likely the one on top of the rock, who wasn't hanging on for dear life.

Everyone safely inside, the helicopter rose, banked and shot away out to sea.

*And that, ladies and gentlemen, concludes our matinee for today. Join us again tomorrow for another show,* Coop thought. As the other motorists slowly departed, he finished his sandwich, then got back into his truck and headed north.

It was a good thing Cooper's GPS was up-to-date, because Gibbons Road was unmarked. It was three hours later that Coop found himself on a very narrow two-lane road that went switchback-style down a steep hill. At a turnoff, there was only a sign that read Cheap Drinks, and an arrow pointing left. Very classy, he found himself thinking. Ben had never been known as what Cooper's Southern grandmother had called "High Cotton."

From that turnoff, however, he could see the lay of Thunder Point, and it was beautiful. A very wide inlet or bay, shaped like a *U,* was settled deeply into a high, rocky coastline. He could see Ben's place, a single building with a wide deck and stairs leading down to a dock and the beach. Beyond Ben's place, stretching out toward the ocean, was a completely uninhabited promontory. He sat there a moment, thinking about Ben's patrons taking advantage of those cheap drinks and then trying to get back up to 101. This road should be named Suicide Trail.

On the opposite side of the beach was another promontory that reached out toward the ocean, this one featuring houses all the way to the point. Cooper could only imagine the drop-dead-gorgeous view. There was a marina on that promontory, and the town itself. Thunder Point was built straight up the hill from the marina in a series of steps. He could see the streets from where he was parked. Between Ben's place and the town was only the wide, expansive beach. Looking down, he could see a woman in a red, hooded jacket and a big dog walking along the beach. She repeatedly threw a stick; the dog kept returning it. The dog was black and white, with legs like an Arabian colt.

The sun was shining and Cooper was reminded of one of Ben's emails describing his home. *Oregon is mostly wet and cold all winter, except for one part around Bandon and Coos Bay that's moderate almost year-round, sunny more often than stormy. But when the storms do come into Thunder Point over the ocean, it's like one of the Seventh Wonders.*

*The bay is protected by the hills and stays calm, keeping the fishing boats safe, but those thunderclouds can be spectacular. . . .*

Then he saw not one but two eagles circling over the point on Ben's side of the beach. It was a rare and beautiful sight.

He proceeded to the parking lot, not entirely surprised to find the Sheriff's Department SUV already there and the deputy sitting inside, apparently writing something. He was out of the car and striding toward Cooper just a few seconds later. Cooper sized him up. Deputy McCain was a young man, probably mid-thirties. He was tall, sandy-haired, blue-eyed, broad-shouldered — about what you'd expect.

Cooper extended a hand. "Deputy."

"Mr. Cooper, I'm sorry for your loss."

"What happened to Ben?"

"He was found at the foot of the stairs to the cellar, where he kept the bait tanks. Ben lived here — he had a couple of rooms over the bar. The doors weren't locked, but I don't think Ben ever locked up. There were no obvious signs of foul play, but the case was turned over to the coroner. Nothing was missing, not even the cash. The coroner ruled it an accident."

"But the guy who called me said he'd been killed," Cooper said.

16

"I think Rawley was upset. He was kind of insistent that Ben couldn't have fallen. But Ben had had a couple of drinks. Not nearly the legal limit, but he could've tripped. Hell, I've been known to trip on no alcohol at all. Rawley found him. Ben kept the money in a cash drawer in the cooler, and the money was still in its hiding place. The one strange thing is," the deputy said, scratching the back of his neck, "time of death was put at two in the morning. Ben was in his boxers, and Rawley insisted there's no reason he'd get out of bed on the second floor and head for the cellar in the middle of the night. Rawley might be right — except this could have been the night Ben heard a noise and was headed for the beach. Just in case you're wondering, there is no surveillance video. In fact, the only place in town that actually has a surveillance camera is the bank. Ben has had one or two characters in his place over the years, but never any real trouble."

"You don't think it's possible someone who knew the place decided to rob it after midnight? When Ben was vulnerable?"

"Most of Ben's customers were regulars, or heard about the place from regulars — weekend bikers, sports fishermen, that sort. Ben didn't do a huge business, but he did

17

all right."

"On bait and Wild Turkey?"

The deputy actually chuckled. "Bait, deli, small bar, Laundromat, cheap souvenirs and fuel. I'd say of all those things, the bar and deli probably did the lion's share of the business."

Coop looked around the deputy's frame. "Fuel?"

"Down on the dock. For boats. Ben used to let some of his customers or neighbors moor alongside the dock. Sometimes the wait at the marina got a little long and Ben didn't mind if people helped themselves. Since he died and the place has been locked up, the boats have found other docks — probably the marina. Oh, he also had a tow truck that's parked in town, but he didn't advertise about it. That's it. There was no next of kin, Mr. Cooper."

"Who is this Rawley? The guy who called me?"

The deputy scrubbed off his hat and scratched his head. "You say you were good friends?"

"For fifteen years. I knew he was raised by his dad, that they had a bar and bait shop here on the coast. We met in the Army. He was a helicopter mechanic and everyone called him Gentle Ben. He was the sweetest

18

man who ever lived, all six foot six of him. I can't imagine him standing up to a robber — not only would he hand over the money, he'd invite the guy to dinner."

"Well, there you go, you might not have the more recent facts, but you knew him all right. That's the thing that makes everyone lean toward accident. That, and the lack of evidence to the contrary. No one would have to hurt Ben for a handout. You don't know about Rawley?"

Cooper just shook his head.

"Rawley Goode is around sixty, a vet with some challenging PTSD issues. He lives down the coast, where he takes care of his elderly father, sort of. He's not real good around people. Ben gave him work. He helped out here, cleaned, stocked, ran errands, that sort of thing. He could serve customers, if no one expected conversation. People around here were used to him. I think he might've been homeless when Ben met him, but his father has lived around here a long time. Interesting guy, not that I can say I know him. Rawley found Ben."

"Are you sure Rawley didn't push him down the stairs?"

"Rawley's a skinny little guy. The coroner didn't find any evidence to suggest Ben had been pushed. And Rawley . . . he was dependent on Ben. When Ben died, there wasn't anyone for us to contact. But don't worry — the town gave Ben a decent send-off. He was well liked. There are better bars around here to hang out in, but people liked Ben."

"Yeah, I liked him, too," Cooper said, looking down. "There must've been a will or something. Rawley wasn't the most articulate guy on the phone, but he said Ben left something for me. Could be old pictures from our Army days or something. Who do you suppose I should see about that?"

"I'll make a few calls, check into that for you."

"Appreciate it. And maybe you could suggest a place to hook up the fifth wheel?"

"There are several decent spots along the coast for tourists — Coos Bay is a nice area. You planning to hang around?"

Cooper gave a shrug. "Maybe a few days, just long enough to talk to some of the folks who knew Ben, pick up whatever he left for me, pay my respects. I just want people to know — he had good friends. We didn't get together a lot, and it sounds like I didn't get a lot of inside information from Ben, but we were always in touch. And since I came all this way, I want to hear about him —

about how people got on with him. You know?"

"I think I understand. This place is locked up. No one would care if you sat here for a while, while you look around at other possibilities. No hookup for your trailer, but you'd be fine for a couple of days."

"Thanks, maybe I'll do that. Not a bad view."

The deputy put out his hand. "I gotta run. You have my number."

"Thank you, Deputy McCain."

"Roger McCain, but hardly anyone remembers that. Folks tend to call me Mac."

"Nice meeting you, Mac. Thanks for helping out with this."

Sarah Dupre walked with Hamlet, her Great Dane, down the main street in Thunder Point to the diner. She looped his leash around the lamppost and went inside, pulling off her gloves. This was one of the things she loved about this little town — there was always somewhere to stop and chat for a few minutes. She wasn't well-known around here, had only lived here a few months, but considering the way she was treated by her new friends, it was as if she'd been here quite a while. If she wasn't working, she liked to take Ham down to the beach and

21

stop off at the diner on her way home. Apparently she wasn't the only one — there was always a large bowl of water for dogs by the lamppost. Twin benches on either side of the diner's front door frequently seated one or two old guys, passing time.

Gina James was behind the counter of the diner. Gina took care of almost everything at the diner except the cooking. There was another waitress at night and a couple of part-time girls, but it was a pretty small shop. Gina's mother, Carrie, was sitting on a stool at the counter, her friend Lou McCain seated beside her. Carrie owned the deli across the street. Lou was a schoolteacher who helped out with her nephew Mac's kids when she wasn't teaching. Two of said kids were in a booth, eating fries and drinking colas, an after-school treat.

Sarah said, "Hey," and all three women said, "Hey," right back.

"Something to drink? Eat?" Gina asked her.

"Could I have a water, please? How is everyone?"

"What can I say, it's Friday," Lou said. "I won't be seeing the little bast—er, darlings till Monday morning."

Sarah laughed at her. "You're going to heaven for it."

"If I died and went to hell, they'd have me teaching junior high," Carrie said.

"And if I go to hell, I'll be making pies and cakes," Lou said.

"You have a day off?" Gina asked Sarah.

"For Landon's football game. I'm sitting alert Saturday and Sunday, that's the price I pay for it."

"But no one gives you any trouble about it, do they?"

"Nah. They like weekends off as much as anyone. And I'll gladly fly weekends if I don't have to miss Landon's games. It's not as though I have any other social life."

Carrie leaned her elbow on the diner. "Wish I had an exciting career like you, Sarah. Being a pilot beats my job, any day."

"Tell me about it," Lou said.

Before Gina could weigh in, the door to the diner opened, the bell tinkling. Ray Anne appeared in her version of a Realtor's business suit — too short, too tight, too much boobage. She scowled. "Sarah, that dog should be on a leash!"

"He is, Ray Anne." She leaned back on her stool to look out the glass pane in the door. "He's all hooked up."

She wiped at her purple skirt. "He still managed to get me with that awful mouth of his."

23

"Well, Ray Anne, you're just so edible-looking," Lou said.

"Ha-ha. Well, you'll never guess what I just saw! The most gorgeous man, out at Ben's place. He was built like a brick you-know-what — worn jeans, torn in all the right places, plain old T-shirt under a leather jacket. One of those flying jackets, you know, Sarah. Driving one of those testosterone trucks, pulling a trailer . . . Handsome face, maybe a dimple, scratchy little growth on his cheeks and chin. He was talking to Mac. It was like an ad for Calvin Klein."

"What were you doing out at Ben's?" Lou asked.

"I was checking on a rental up the hill two blocks. You know, that old Maxwell place."

"Then how'd you see the tears in his jeans and his stubble?"

Ray Anne dipped a manicured hand into her oversize purse and pulled out her binoculars. She smiled conspiratorially and gave her head a toss. Her short blond hair didn't move.

"Clever," Lou said. "Man-watching taken to the next level. How old is this hunk of burning love?"

"Irrelevant," Ray Anne said. "I wonder what he's doing here. I heard Ben had no next of kin. You don't suppose cuddly old

24

Ben was hiding a handsome brother? No, no, that would be cruel."

"Why?" Sarah asked.

"Because Ray Anne would love a shot at selling that property of Ben's," Carrie said.

"That's not true," Ray Anne protested. "You know me, I only want to help if I can."

"And bag a single man or two while you're at it," Lou said.

Ray Anne stiffened slightly. "Some of us are still sexual beings, Louise," she said. "A notion you might not be familiar with." As the Sheriff's Department patrol car passed slowly down the street, Ray Anne said, "Oh, there's Deputy Yummy Pants — I'm going to go ask him what's going on. If I can get past the dog!"

Out the door she wiggled.

"Deputy *Yummy Pants*?" Sarah asked with a laugh in her voice.

"The teenage girls around town call him that," Lou explained drily. "I don't recommend it. He hates it. Gets him all pissy. I should tell you what kind of pants Ms. Realtor of the Year has. Maybe Busy Pants."

Carrie's lips quirked. "She suggested you don't quite get the whole sexual pull. *Louise.*"

Lou had a sarcastic twist to her lips when she said, "If she turns up dead, can I count on you girls for an alibi?" Then she turned and called to her niece and nephew. "Hey, kids. Let's make tracks." To her friends she said, "I'm going to beat Yummy Pants home. Betcha I get more out of him than Busy Pants does."

Sarah hung her red slicker on the peg in the mudroom just in time to see her younger brother, Landon, coming toward the back door of their house with his duffel full of football gear. "Hey," she said. "I didn't expect to see you."

"I came home to get a couple of things and grab a sandwich," he said. He bent to pet the dog. He didn't have to bend far — Ham was tall. "Gotta get going."

"Wait a sec," she said.

"What?" he asked, still petting the dog.

"For Pete's sake, can you *look* at me?" she asked. When he straightened, heavy duffel over one shoulder, she gasped. There was a bruise on his cheekbone.

"Practice," he said. "It's nothing."

"You don't practice on game day."

"Yeah, well, I hope I don't get in trouble for that. A couple of us went out to run some plays, some passes, and I got nailed. It was an accident."

"You were practicing without a helmet?"

she asked.

"Sarah, it's nothing. It's a small bruise. I could've gotten it running into an open locker. Lighten up so you don't make me look like a girl. Are you coming to the game?"

"Of course I'm coming. Why couldn't you be into chess or something? Choir? Band? Something that didn't involve bodies crashing into each other?"

He grinned at her, the handsome smile that had once belonged to their deceased father. "You get enough sleep without me boring you to death," he said. "Why couldn't you just be a flight attendant or something?"

He had her there. Sarah flew search and rescue with the Coast Guard. There were those occasions that were risky. Edgy. And admittedly, that was part of what she loved best about it. "I trust you'll be wearing your helmet tonight?"

"Funny. It should be a good game. Raiders are a good match. They're a good team."

"Does it hurt?" she asked, touching her own cheek.

"Nah, it's really nothing, Sarah. See you later."

She suppressed the urge to beg him to be careful. It was just the two of them; she was his guardian and family. She sometimes

27

wanted to simply enfold him in her arms and keep him safe. Yet watching him play was thrilling. He was a great athlete, already six feet tall and muscled at sixteen. She'd heard he was the best quarterback they'd seen in a long time here in Thunder Point.

For the millionth time she hoped bringing him here had been a good decision. He'd been happy in the North Bend high school last year. He'd barely found his footing, his friends, when she'd moved them here. But she couldn't bear to stay in the same town as her ex, in the home they had shared. It was bad enough that they still worked together.

She'd moved them so often. . . .

She reached out as if to hug him, then retracted her arms. He didn't want mush, not now that he was a man. So she held back.

"All right," he said patiently. "Get it over with."

She wrapped her arms around him and he gave her a one-armed hug back. Then he grinned at her again. He had absolutely no idea how handsome he was, which made him even more attractive.

"Play your little heart out, bud," she said. "And do not get hurt."

"Don't worry. I'm fast."

"You going out after the game?" she asked.
"I dunno. Depends on how tired I am."

Sarah looked at him. "When I was your age, I was never too tired to go out. If you go out, getting home by midnight would be nice. No later than one, for sure. Are we on the same page here?"

He laughed at her. "Same page, boss."

But as she knew, he seldom went out after a game.

# TWO

Roger McCain headed home for the day. He lived in a large house he couldn't quite afford with three kids and his aunt Lou. He was thirty-six and his oldest, Eve, was sixteen. Ryan was twelve, and Dee Dee was ten. When he got home, his first stop was the gun safe in the garage. He locked up his guns before going into the house. Though his kids had been both lectured and trained, guns did not enter his house.

It was about five-thirty when he walked into the kitchen from the garage. Lou stood at the sink, rinsing dishes. Lou was not Aunt Bee to his Andy of Mayberry. She was sixty, but didn't look a day of it. She wore fitted jeans, a white silky blouse, leather vest and boots on her young, trim body. Her curly, shoulder-length hair was auburn with some gold highlights and her nails were manicured in bright colors. She complained of crow's feet and what she called a wattle

under her chin, but he didn't know what she was talking about. Lou called herself his old-maid aunt — she'd never married or had children of her own — but in truth she was young, energetic and feisty, exactly what he needed, even if it did drive him crazy at times.

Without even turning around she said, "There are tacos. The kids have eaten. Eve is going to take the van to the game tonight. She's meeting a couple of her friends. That leaves you and me and the kids to go together. In less than an hour."

Friday night. High school football. Eve was a cheerleader. A gorgeous, young cheerleader who resembled her mother and caused him to quake in fear every time he looked at her.

"Did it occur to you to ask me if I was all right with that — Eve taking the van?"

She turned from the sink. "It did," she said, giving him a sharp nod. "It always occurs to me. But you say no and argue and then give in so you can pace and grumble. She's sixteen and a good girl. She's earned it."

He nodded, but he hated it. His ex-wife Cee Jay — short for Cecilia Jayne — had been a cheerleader; he'd been a football player back in Coquille. Cee Jay had gotten

31

pregnant at sixteen. By nineteen, he'd been a brand-new husband with a baby on the way.

Cee Jay left when Dee Dee was nine months old; that's when they had moved in with Lou. Cee Jay had been so young when she left — only twenty-three. Mac wasn't sure why he'd felt so old, as he'd been only twenty-six. But he'd been pretty busy, trying to support his family on two jobs. He was a rookie deputy, working nights, and by day he worked security on an armored car.

His dirty little secret was that sometimes he didn't mind the two jobs. But Cee Jay, left alone too much, scrimping to get by and buried in small children, complained a lot. There wasn't enough money, the house was small, old and falling apart, the kids were out of control, there was no fun in her life and very little attention from her husband, whom she accused of showing up only long enough to throw food down his throat and take off for the next job. She needed more money but hated that he was always working.

And then one day Cee Jay snapped. She packed a big suitcase, put the kids at the neighbor's house and waited for him to get home from his day job. "I can't take it anymore," she told him. "I'm sick of getting

puked on, sick of the diapers and noise, sick of this dump we live in, tired of not being able to get out of the grocery store with ten cents left in my purse. I've had enough. I'm leaving."

For the past nine years, he had asked himself why he'd been stunned. Her complaints hadn't changed, they'd just been accompanied by a suitcase. "L-leaving?" he had stuttered.

"The kids are next door," she said. "I'm taking my clothes and two hundred dollars."

His entire body had vibrated with fear. Dread. Pain. "Cee Jay, you can't do this to me."

"Yeah, well, you did it to me first. I was sixteen, Mac. Sixteen and pregnant!"

"But you were happy! And you wanted Ryan — you argued for Ryan! Dee Dee was an accident, but you —"

"And you thought that I had a clue, at sixteen or twenty-two?"

"Listen, I was only nineteen! So — we were too young, you think I don't know that? You can't just leave your children!"

"I have no way to support them and I can't take this anymore!"

"Cee Jay, how'm I supposed to work and take care of the kids?"

He remembered the sound of a horn

honking. She zipped her bag. "I don't know, but you'll figure it out. Call your aunt — she always hated me anyway."

He had grabbed her by the shoulders and shaken her. It was the harshest hand he'd ever laid to a woman. "Are you *crazy*? What is this? Is that some guy picking you up?"

When he stopped shaking her, she said, "There's no guy! That's a cab! You want me to call the cops? Let *go* of me!"

Of course there was a guy. It took him all of three weeks to figure it out — some pro golfer. At first, the mystery was how she had found the time to have enough of a relationship with him to talk him into taking her away. But he caught on — girlfriends. Young mothers like Cee Jay, running around, swapping kids, stealing time for themselves. Once Mac learned his name and began following his movements through the news, the second mystery followed: why she didn't come home to her family once the relationship was over, which took only a month or so.

He fantasized how he wouldn't make her beg much, just enough to be sure she had had a change of heart and was ready to commit, ready to promise never to do it again. No one could ever know the depth of humiliation at not being able to hang on to the mother of your children. At the time he

had lived in Coquille, and it took roughly forty-eight hours for everyone who'd ever heard of him to be talking about how Cee Jay McCain left her young husband and three small children to run off with a golf pro. He spent the next five years nurturing a fantasy that she'd eventually come to her senses and be back, if only to see her children. Then it finally dawned on him to be afraid of that very scenario — that once he'd figured out how to manage, she'd stalk back in and stake some kind of claim. So he got himself a divorce. He had to locate her to do that — she turned up in Los Angeles. They didn't communicate. She signed the papers, relinquished custody and he let go except for a couple of tiny threads. He hated her for what she'd done to their children. And he was terrified of ever getting involved with a woman again.

It was with the divorce that they moved to the outskirts of Thunder Point, about thirty minutes east to Coquille, the sheriff's office. Even if Mac had to go back to the central office, he could commute. It was here, in a down economy, that he managed to find a larger home, one big enough for his family — three kids, Aunt Lou and two Labs.

Since Mac had lost his parents young and had lived with Lou during junior high and high school, you'd think she'd be as terrified as he was that Eve would slip and fall into some horny football player's lap and end up with the mess of a life her mother had. They had never talked about it; it had never been voiced. But they both knew what was eating Mac. He wanted Eve to be twenty-seven, settled and safe. Real. Fast.

And just then his daughter dashed through the kitchen, wearing her barely there cheerleading uniform. Short, pleated skirt, V-neck sweater, letter jacket, long, beautiful legs, and a head full of thick dark hair she wore down most of the time. She had the biggest blue eyes. Her smile was positively hypnotizing; he'd barely paid off the orthodontist's bill, just in time to start on the next two mouths. Blue eyes ran in their genes but not perfect teeth. If not for the dental benefits offered by the Sheriff's Department, his kids would have teeth growing out of their ears.

"I'll wave to you at the game, Daddy," she said, rising on her toes to kiss his cheek. "We're going out after," she said.

"Midnight, Eve," he reminded her. As if she couldn't get into trouble before midnight. It wasn't that. It was just that it was all he could take. He needed his kids home and tucked in so he could relax.

"How often have I been late?"

"A few times," he said.

"Well, not very late," she reminded him. Then she beamed. "I think we're going to kick some Raider tail tonight!"

And he grinned at her. She was his doll; he'd die for her, it was that simple.

When she was out the door, Lou was shaking her head. "I wish you'd get a life," she said.

"This *is* my life," he said, and sat at the table, commencing to build himself some tacos.

"You need a little more going on. Like a woman."

"Why? You have somewhere to go?"

"I just might," she challenged.

"Well, knock yourself out," he said. "I can manage."

She laughed at him. "I'd love to see that," she said. She pulled a cold cola out of the fridge for him and sat at the table with him. "Tell me about the crime in Thunder Point, Mac. I haven't heard anything interesting all day."

"Well now," he said, sprinkling cheese on top of four large tacos. "No interesting crime, but an old friend of Ben Bailey's came to town, wanting to know what happened to him. He's sitting in his fifth wheel

37

out at the bar. Says he's going to hang around a few days."

"Ray Anne mentioned something about that. She's not one to miss a new man in town." Lou clucked and shook her head. "Still can't believe Ben's gone."

"No one can believe it," Mac said. Then he dove into his first taco.

Cooper moved his trailer around to the far side of Ben's bar on the parking tarmac, pretty much out of sight of the road to 101. The small parking lot could only accommodate twenty or thirty cars, but he discovered a road toward the front of the structure that led to the beach. More of a downhill driveway, really. The road to the beach looked much kinder than that trip up Bailey Pass and Gibbons to the highway.

He roamed around the locked-up property, peeking in windows. The newest and nicest part of the whole structure was an impressive deck, complete with tables and chairs surrounding the two sides of the building with a view. But a look through the windows revealed what he considered a dump. There was a long bar lined with stools, liquor bottles on the shelf, but only a half-dozen small tables. Life preservers, nets, shells and other seaside paraphernalia hung from the walls. A few turning racks of postcards and souvenirs sat about. The place looked like it hadn't been improved in years. He could see the dust and grime from the window. This came as no surprise. Ben had been kind and generous to a fault, good with engines and just about anything mechanical, but he wasn't exactly enterprising. He could be a little on the lazy side, unless he had an engine maintenance job to do. And he hadn't been too good with money; he spent what he had. When Cooper first met him, he was living a cash existence, just like his father had. He sure hadn't been classy. *Cheap Drinks.* Just a kindhearted good old boy.

Cooper unloaded the WaveRunner, his all-terrain vehicle — the Rhino — and his motorcycle. There was a large metal shed at the end of the parking lot, up against the hill, but it was padlocked. He stored his toys under a tarp, locked up in chains so they couldn't be stolen without a blowtorch and trailer.

He wandered down to the beach to the dock. There was a fueling tank perched on the end and a paved boat launch. He wondered if Ben had a boat in the shed, which was as big as a garage. The sun was lowering and it was getting damn cold on the water, unlike the Southern climate he'd come from. He encountered a few people out walking or jogging and gave a nod. He was glad he carried a Glock in his back waistband, under his jacket. After all, he was alone out here, no one knew him, and he still had reservations about Ben falling down the stairs. Big man like Ben, you'd think he'd have survived even a steep fall with only some bruises. Worst case, a broken bone.

With night beginning to fall, he headed back to the toy hauler. He'd have time to explore Thunder Point tomorrow. He figured he'd relax, get a good night's sleep and get to know the men and women who'd been Ben's friends in the morning.

But at around eleven, he heard the noise of people talking. He put on his jacket, gun tucked in his waistband, and went outside. He brought the binoculars from the truck, wandered around the deck. The waterfront had come alive. He saw kids on the beach, partying around a couple of campfires. From the shouts and squeals, they were teenagers. A set of headlights from clear on the other side of the beach near the town brought it all together. Ben's place was probably most often accessed from the beach side, especially at night. Sure enough, the headlights he saw pulled right up on the sand, next to a row of all-terrain vehicles — Rhinos, quads, dune buggies.

Yep, this was a beach bar. Complete with Laundromat, bait and gas for boats. It all made sense now — in winter and bad weather, Ben likely had moderate sales, but in summers he probably did a brisk business. Folks from Thunder Point, on the other side of the beach, stopping for a soda or morning coffee when they were out walking their dogs; people from the town driving over in beach buggies to have a drink on the deck at sunset. Sport fishermen or sailors could start or end their days here.

Cooper was a little bit sorry he wasn't going to be around to watch the summer storms roll in over the Pacific. Or the whales migrating in spring and fall. Whales wouldn't be in the bay, but he was willing to bet the view was great from either the far edge of the cliff or the point on the opposite side of the bay.

This would have appealed to Ben for a million reasons. It was his father's and he'd spent years here. The view was fantastic, and no one liked to put his feet up and relax more than Ben Bailey.

There was some loud popping and shrieking on the beach and he automatically reached for that Glock, but it was followed by laughter. Firecrackers. Then there was some chanting. *Go, Cougars, Go. Go, Cougars, Go. Go, Go, Get 'Em, Get 'Em, Go, Get 'Em, Go!*

Cheers. That's what was going on. It was October. Football and teenagers. This was what coastal kids did after a game and probably all summer long. Coop had spent many of his early years on the Gulf, but by the time he was a teenager his parents had moved inland, away from the water to Albuquerque, New Mexico. Cooper and his friends often went out to the remote desert, away from the prying eyes of adults where they could build a fire, drink a few beers, make out with their girlfriends.

What a perfect setup. There was a whole coastline all the way to Canada, but this little piece of it didn't have easy access. You either came at it by way of Ben's or from the town, on foot or armed with a beach mobile. There wouldn't be many strangers around.

He went back to his camper and settled in — door locked, gun handy. He let the TV drown out the noise from the kids until it faded away. In the morning he brewed coffee and took a cup with him to the dock, then the beach. Although he had no investment in this place, he found himself hoping they had cleaned up after themselves and hadn't left trash all over the beach.

And what do you know? There were a couple of big green trash cans with lids up against the hill, full of bottles, cans, snack wrappers, spent firecrackers. The tide had taken out the remnants of a fire. Except for being raked, the beach was cleaned up. Who were these kids? The Stepford teenagers?

He took a deep breath of foggy sea air and decided he'd shower and hit the town. He'd like to know a little more about this place.

Cooper thought about taking the Rhino across the beach to the town, but instead he took the truck back up to 101, just to check out the distance. The freeway curved east, to the right, away from the town, and it was five miles before he saw a small sign for Thunder Point. Then it was a left turn and another five miles to access the town. He was about a mile, maybe mile and a half across the beach, or ten miles on the road.

Heading into Thunder Point from 101, he passed the high school — circa 1960s — on the edge of town. Not too big, he noted. Then he came to the main street, Indigo Sea Drive.

He had passed through a hundred towns

43

like this, maybe a thousand. There wasn't a lot of commerce — dry cleaner, bakery, diner. There was a very small library at the end of the street. Next to it, the elementary and middle schools sat side by side. He spotted a secondhand clothing store right next to a thrift shop and wondered what the difference was. There was a grocery, liquor store, pharmacy, gas station, hardware store and small motel. There was a dingy-looking bar, Waylan's. And yes, Fresh Fish. There was also McDonald's, Taco Bell, Subway and Carrie's Deli and Catering. The Sheriff's Department was a small storefront that sat between the deli and a boarded-up store, although a man was tearing the boards off one large window. New business moving in? Cooper wondered.

Driving around, he discovered four roads that ran downhill to the beach or marina, through the neighborhoods that surrounded the main street. The beach and the bay were like a basin dug out of the land. All roads seemed to lead either up or down — down to the marina, up to the main street, down to the beach, up to Bailey's.

It appeared the main street and marina were the life of the town. Most of the slips were empty — fishing boats, out early in the morning, he assumed. He saw two boat-launch ramps and a fueling station. There were a number of small fishing and pleasure boats still tied up and one big cabin cruiser. There was a restaurant — Cliffhanger's, which also advertised a bar — at the far end of the marina, far enough up the hill to avoid high tides and flooding.

He went back to the main street and drove west, out onto the point. There were houses out there, as well. On the end of the promontory was a very large home with a gated driveway. Whoever owned that house got the best view imaginable, as the point was a high, rocky cliff. From Ben's deck he had noticed a small lighthouse, somewhere below this mansion.

It wasn't exactly a cute little town, but there were some nice touches, like big pots of flowers in front of some businesses, old-fashioned lampposts, benches here and there along wide sidewalks.

He reasoned the best places to perch for local news would be one of the bars or the local diner. Cliffhanger's wasn't open yet. Waylan's probably was, but he wasn't in the mood for a seedy bar. He went to the diner and sat at the counter. It was either designed to be retro or it was fifty years old. By the cracks in the linoleum floor, he guessed it was all about age. The waitress was there in a flash, with a coffeepot in her hand. Her blond hair was in a ponytail and she wore a black-and-white-checkered blouse. Her name tag said Gina.

"Good morning, Gina," he said.

She filled his cup. "And good morning, strange man. Hungry?"

"As a matter of fact, I am. What have you got for eggs?" Cooper asked.

She put down the coffeepot and leaned both hands on the counter. With a wide smile, she said, "It's the darnedest thing, we have eggs for eggs."

He couldn't suppress a grin. "Mess up a couple for me. Toast, too, and . . . you have sausage for sausage?"

"Link or patty?"

"Patty," he said.

"Whole wheat or whole wheat?"

"Why don't I live recklessly? Whole wheat."

"Good choice. It's better for you. Now drink that coffee slow so I don't have to keep coming back here."

"Could I have some ice water?" He looked around. The small diner was empty of customers. "If it's not too much trouble?"

"It's extra," she said. She turned and slapped the ticket on the cook's counter.

"I can afford it," he said. "But it might

46

cut into your tip."

She fixed up an ice water and placed it before him. "If it's going to cut into my tip, I won't charge you for it. You think I work here for the wages?" She gave the counter a wipe. "I know you're not just passing through — there's only two ways into this town, and both are inconvenient."

"Two ways?" he asked, confident she was going to tell him about Gibbons to Bailey's, down the hill, or Indigo Sea Drive, right through the heart of town.

"By land or by sea," she said. "We are en route to nowhere."

"I am, though. Passing through. Ben Bailey was a friend of mine and I just heard —"

She got a stricken look on her face. "Oh, I'm sorry! Man, we miss Ben around here."

"That's why I'm hanging around — to meet some of his friends. Ben and I met in the Army, a long time ago. We stayed in touch, but I've never been up here before."

"Ben was such a nice guy — the last person I could imagine losing."

"Who were his closest friends?" Cooper asked.

"Oh, hell, no one and everyone," she said with a shrug. "Ben kind of watched over the whole town, but I don't know of any one or

47

two people he was best friends with."

The door opened and Mac came in. He wasn't in uniform this morning and looked just as comfortable in jeans, boots, plaid shirt and jacket.

"This is the guy you should probably ask," Gina said. "Hey, Mac."

He pulled off his cap and sat next to Cooper at the counter. "Ask me what?"

"This guy was a friend of Ben's —"

"We've met," Mac said, sticking out a hand. "How's it going, Mr. Cooper?"

Cooper laughed. "Every time you call me Mr. Cooper, I wonder if my father just entered the room. My name's actually Hank, short for Henry, but people call me Cooper."

"Is that a military thing? Last name?"

"It started way before the Army. I'm a junior — Henry Davidson Cooper, Junior. My dad goes by Hank, but no one went for Henry or little Hank so I got saddled with Little Cooper until I wasn't so little, then just Cooper. Sometimes Coop. Take your pick. It's going all right. That beach can get busy at night."

"Kids," Mac confirmed. "They behave?"

"Not only did they behave, they cleaned up."

"Yeah, you can give Ben credit for that.

48

That whole stretch of beach right up to the town and marina is . . . *was* his. He let it go public. He'd walk down there from time to time when it was real active, a bunch of kids, and inform them in his way that the minute he had to clean up the beach after campers or partiers, he'd have a fence erected and close it. He put out trash cans and once a week or so he'd check to see if they needed emptying. He had rules for his beach."

"He policed the beach?" Cooper asked.

"Yeah, but it was more about the wildlife than saving him work. He didn't want things like plastic bags or rings from six-packs left in the sand or washing out with the tide, killing fish or getting picked up by a bird and causing harm, like strangling it. Or choking it. About once a year he'd post a couple of Private Property signs, kind of a warning or a reminder. Word spread about his place, his beach. He had regular motor-cycle or cycling groups come through in summer, he called them his weekend war-riors. He had a real scary-looking gang camping on the beach once but he con-fronted them, told them it was his property and they were welcome to use it if there were no firearms, no underage drinking, no drugs, didn't give the town any trouble and if they threw away their trash so it wouldn't harm wildlife." Mac shook his head as he laughed. "He never bothered to call in reinforcements — I heard about the riders the next day, but Ben never called me. The riders kept it cool, threw away their trash and thanked him for the use of his beach. He had a way about him, you know? That incident was a long time ago and according to Ben and folks in town, in the end they were a docile bunch. Ben's place usually attracted more graybeards, out for the weekend."

"Graybeards?"

"Older riders — minimum age fifty or so. Ben was a pretty easygoing guy and nothing scared him. He always got along with anyone."

"I know," Cooper said.

Gina put Cooper's breakfast in front of him and refilled his coffee cup.

"Good call on the eggs," Mac said. "You tell him?" he asked Gina.

"Nope. It was his first choice."

"Burgers here are great," Mac said. "Sandwiches are pretty good, soup has good days, meat loaf is terrible — don't know why Stu keeps making it, no one in this town is fool enough to eat it. It's god-awful. He just fries the hell out of eggs, so either get 'em

50

scrambled, over hard, omelet or hard-boiled. In fact, anything he can just fry to death or broil is pretty good."

"Why doesn't the owner get a better cook?"

"The owner *is* the cook, that's the primary reason," Gina said. Then, looking at Mac, she asked, "Everyone get to where they're going?"

"Eve and Ashley are at cheerleading practice, Ryan's at football and Lou took Dee Dee to dance. Just so you know, Eve and Ashley went in your mother's car."

Gina nodded but had a grave look on her face.

"You two . . . ?" Cooper started to ask.

"Single parents," Gina said. "Our daughters are best friends. Most of the time."

"So you back each other up?" Cooper asked, shoveling some eggs in his mouth.

"Lotta back up," Mac explained. "My aunt lives with me, Gina's mother lives with her. It takes a village . . . where have I heard that before. You married, Cooper?"

"Nah. No one would have me."

"Maybe it's because you live out of a toy hauler, ever think of that?" Mac asked.

Cooper grinned. "Could be. Well, now that I have the lay of the land, I can get eggs and coffee a lot easier. Straight across the beach in the Rhino. Except, I think I got what I came for — I wanted to know what the hell happened to Ben. Have I heard everything I'm going to hear?"

"The coroner ruled on it, but I'm keeping my eyes open. It's not an open case, but this is my town and Ben was a good guy. If I hear anything suspicious, I'll be investigating myself," Mac said.

"What about this Rawley Goode?" Cooper asked.

"Weird Rawley?" Gina asked with a curl of her lip.

"Aw, Rawley's got his troubles," Mac said. "I just hope he doesn't wander off, now that Ben's gone and the place is closed."

"I was kind of hoping he would wander off," Gina said.

"You have a problem with Rawley?" Cooper asked.

"I have a problem with the way he looks you in the eye like he can see straight through you and says ab-so-lutely nothing. It's creepy."

Mac chuckled. "That's pretty much why Ben gave him a dishrag and a broom and some kitchen chores. They seemed to understand each other."

"This place — everyone works together, understands each other, cleans up after each other, a regular Stepford . . ."

"We have as many idiots, assholes and troublemakers as any town, but you know what the difference is between this town and any other town?"

Cooper leaned his head on his hand. "I can't wait. What's the difference?"

Mac pushed his coffee cup toward Gina for a refill. "I know who they are."

# THREE

Cooper learned a few things about the town and Ben. Ben had helped Gina keep her old Jeep running, for one thing, and never charged her except for parts. He'd bought ads for the backs of kids' soccer and Little League team jerseys — Bailey's Bait Shop. He had a bird sanctuary on his land that stretched all the way out to the high, rocky cliffs above the ocean. In addition to the eagles, there were seabirds who lived off the water but returned inland to nest, mate and lay eggs. Cooper remembered Ben emailing him something about that, more than once.

Ben apparently hadn't done particularly social things, like volunteer as assistant coach for kids' teams, but he attended town gatherings and meetings and ate out at the diner and Cliffhanger's. He contributed a lot, not the least of which was the beach. This was the Ben that Cooper had known — not shy or antisocial, but satisfied with his own company. He hadn't had a long career in the Army, just a few years. As Coop's helicopter mechanic at Fort Rucker, he was meticulous and verged on extraordinary, but he had issues with rules, probably one of the reasons Cooper took to him. *"Bailey, where's your hat?" "In my pocket, sir!" "Why isn't it on your head?" "Because I can't get my head in my pocket, sir!"*

He learned the marina was small in comparison to others in the region. The crabbers and fishermen who docked there lived in the town, but took most of their catch to larger harbors, although they kept some of it to sell to locals or to Cliffhanger's. Some of the commercial fishermen had been in business for generations. The marina also held sport and pleasure boats, mostly used by Thunder Point's residents. The bay was a safe, quiet place, protected by the promontories from hostile weather.

When Cooper parted ways with Mac after his breakfast, he said, "I don't think there's much reason for me to hang around, except maybe the view from Ben's deck. What will happen to his place?"

Mac shrugged. "Not sure. Maybe there will be a search for a next of kin, or maybe it'll sit until it's in default of liens or taxes, then auctioned. That's not Sheriff's Department business. Damn shame, though. People enjoyed the beach, the bar."

"It's pretty run-down," Cooper pointed out.

"If you think the outside is a little tired-looking, you should see inside. Well, people didn't have real high expectations of the place, but it served a purpose. You may have noticed, it's not a fancy town."

Mac already had Cooper's cell number, but in a gesture of friendliness, he gave Cooper his before they said goodbye at the diner.

Since Cooper had no plans or pressing business, he spent a couple of days just driving around the area — up to Coos Bay, into the hills, to the casino in North Bend — keeping his trailer as a home base. One sunny afternoon, he got out his laptop and found a chair on Ben's deck, facing the bay. In just a few days, he'd come to the conclusion the damp, foggy morning was typical of the Oregon Coast. Sunshine usually arrived midmorning, at the latest, but it was cold enough this October afternoon to require a jacket. Before he opened his laptop and logged on, he saw her again — the woman and her dog. She threw the stick and waited for the large black-and-white dog to bring it back. The dog had the longest legs; he was half as tall as the woman. It was the same woman — red slicker with the hood up, black knee-high rubber boots, hands plunged into her pockets while she waited for the dog. She was walking toward his end of the beach, but before she was close enough for him to get a glimpse of her face, she turned and headed back toward the town.

He logged on, checking his email, looking up from time to time to watch the progress of the woman and dog. She was too far away for him to be taken by her looks, but he was intrigued nonetheless. There was something about her that was so . . . lonely. They probably had that in common. Cooper had no trouble getting to know people or making friends, yet he rarely did. He was a loner; he knew that about himself. It didn't take much to turn a man solitary — being the new guy too often, being controversial now and then, a couple of unsuccessful attempts at a lasting relationship with a woman. . . .

He sent a note to Luke Riordan — they'd been a scrappy pair of combat-ready helicopter pilots fifteen years ago and Ben had been their mechanic. Not too surprisingly, Ben had been the most stable of the threesome. So Cooper filled Luke in on the details of Ben's death. Cooper described the property, the beach, the town and the fact that Ben's place might end up just being auctioned.

Then he emailed his father and his oldest sister, Rochelle, to tell them where he was, although his cell was working just fine and they could reach him if there was any family business. His parents and three married sisters lived in or near Albuquerque. When he could, he made short visits to New Mexico, but he didn't spend a lot of time there. Cooper was close to his family, but their relationship was complicated. There was a part of him that felt he'd failed them by never settling down, marrying, having a family and a stable career . . . and there was a part of him that thought they'd had unreasonable expectations and tried to push him in directions he wasn't capable of going.

He heard an engine from the highway far above. He shut down and closed his laptop. Leaving it on the chair, he walked around the deck and witnessed an old pickup come down the road from 101. Even before he saw the driver, he knew this must be Rawley. The truck was ancient enough to be a classic, but the engine ran smooth. That had to be Ben's work. The tires were new and shiny, cleaned and buffed to new-car life.

Then the guy parked and got out — yes, had to be Rawley. He was a skinny, balding, grizzled man in his sixties, looking pretty worn-out, and he wore an American flag shirt with his old jeans. He had a scarf or rag bandanna tied around his head and a gray ponytail, circa the sixties. He walked right up to Cooper.

Cooper stuck out his hand. "Rawley?" he asked.

The man's expression didn't even change. Rather than shaking Cooper's hand, he put a thick envelope in his grasp. Then he turned to go back to his truck.

"Hey," Cooper said. "What's this?"

But Rawley kept walking and Cooper kept watching him. When Rawley got back to his truck, he didn't get in. He leaned against the passenger side, crossed his legs leisurely, arms folded over his chest. He gave a nod and waited.

Cooper opened the envelope and pulled out a thick document, folded in thirds. When he unfolded it, he found a will that had been drawn up by Lawrence Carnegie, Attorney-at-Law. It was pages long. But on top was a lime-green sticky note that said, "Take care of things, Coop."

He looked up at Rawley. "He wants me to take care of this?"

Rawley rolled his eyes as if to say, *Right, stupid. What did the note say?*

Cooper glanced through the document quickly. He'd assumed that Ben wanted him as executor, but it took about two seconds to see that Ben was leaving this place to *him.* Looking a little further, it appeared that included the structure and the land. And the beach? The document was four pages of legalese. There was probably something in here that explained special conditions of some kind, but that was going to take a closer, slower look. Meanwhile, he became aware of a key inside the envelope.

"To the bar?" he asked Rawley.

Again Rawley rolled his eyes, saying nothing.

Cooper almost eye-rolled him right back. But he took the key in one hand and the document in the other and walked around the deck to the ocean side, where he slipped it into the lock on a set of double doors that could open wide onto the deck. The seal on the doors was good, probably to protect against heavy storms or tsunamis. He pulled open the door and was immediately assaulted by the foulest smell he'd ever encountered. Hadn't they said Ben had been buried? Because this smell was worse than a rotting body. It took about three steps into the bar/bait shop to realize they had septic issues, combined with what smelled like rotting fish and maybe garbage. The electricity had been turned off. He yelled, "Rawley!"

The response he got was the sound of a truck. Departing.

An hour later, Cooper placed a call to Mac's cell phone. It was late afternoon now and the sun was shining, which did not cheer Cooper. It not only helped cook the smells in the bar/bait shop but also brought people out to the beach, walking dogs, nosing around or jogging. It was too chilly for swimming or picnicking. At the sight of someone opening doors and windows at Ben's place, a few brave souls came close, curious. By the time they made it to the deck, they covered their noses and retreated. Quickly.

"Mac," Cooper said into the phone. "Boy, do I have a situation."

"What's up?"

"Start with, Rawley brought me what seems to be a will. It'll have to be verified, but it looks in order. Ben left this place to me."

"Whoa. Did you see that coming?"

"He never even hinted at such a thing.

61

Second, there was a key and I went inside. Holy mother of God, there are too many rotten things in there to count. The electricity was turned off and his bait tank is full of dead fish, stagnant, moldy water and God knows what all. And I'm pretty sure I smell septic backup. I have the doors and windows open, but the place is impenetrable. Do you know anyone? Like maybe a crime-scene cleanup crew? Or something?"

"There's a flood and environmental cleanup company up in North Bend. Also a hazardous chemical cleanup crew up there."

Cooper couldn't stop a cough. "Oh, yeah, definitely some hazardous chemicals in there. Got a number?"

"Let me call 'em," Mac said. "I'll book the first available slot for an estimate. You planning on cleaning it up?"

"It's not how I planned my week, but someone has to do it. I wouldn't count on Rawley. He handed me the will and a key and took off like a bat out of hell."

Mac laughed.

"Come out here and take a deep breath and then laugh, sucker," Cooper said. "We might need a wrecking crew if the smell can't be conquered."

"I think I will come out. I mean, I'm curious. Let me make a couple of calls on the way."

To keep from inhaling poisonous gases, Cooper took up residence on the dock. Even there, he could smell it. He was not entirely surprised when he caught sight of the Sheriff's Department SUV coming at him, not from the road but right across the beach.

Mac pulled up to the dock and got out. He was wearing his uniform.

"You working?" Cooper asked.

"I'm pretty much always working, but I don't drive the company car unless I'm in uniform. It's for official business only. We have rules." He looked up the steps to the bar and wrinkled his nose. "Hoo, boy."

"Tell me about it. I never took Ben for a prankster. 'Here, I'm leaving you all my worldly goods, but you might have to torch it all.'"

"You think the will is legit?" Mac asked.

Cooper pulled a thick document folded into thirds out of his back pocket and handed it to Mac. "You know Lawrence Carnegie?"

"Yup. He's a lawyer in town. He takes care of some local stuff. I guess Ben hired him."

"Appears so. I gotta say, I never expected anything like this. Don't you tell someone if you're planning to do something like this?"

Mac shrugged. "I have a will and I haven't told anyone the details, mainly because I don't want my kids thinking if they kill me in my sleep they'll get a car or something. My aunt Lou, who's in charge anyway, is the executor. And hell, I don't even have anything worth leaving. Do you have a will?"

"Nothing fancy," he said. "I have savings. It'll be divided between my nieces and nephews if there's anything left when I go — I was thinking it could help with college. And no, I never told anyone."

Mac was flipping through the few pages. "I think I can explain Ben's reasoning, or at least the history behind this place. Ben's father was kind of old when Ben came back to Thunder Point. He was sick, had a stroke. That was right before I was transferred here. He was failing."

"I remember, Ben got out of the Army ten years ago or so to help his dad," Cooper said. "I heard something about a store here. Obviously he wasn't real specific. . . ."

"Well, everything was transferred into Ben's name so that several years later, when his dad passed, there was no will, no probate, and most important, no tax issues."

Cooper put his hands in his pockets.

"How would you know something like that?"

"Purely gossip, I'm afraid," Mac said. "The talk is that when the old man passed, there were a lot of interested buyers who assumed these hicks who ran a run-down bait shop and bar hadn't prepared for the worst. The land is worth some money, Cooper. If there hadn't been a trust or a transfer, the inheritance tax alone could've foreclosed Ben, forced him to sell. You know, there are a bunch of little moth-eaten towns around here, but we also have big resorts, the kind that host PGA tournaments or world-class hunting and draw some big money. And this area, oceanfront and five miles of natural beauty to the freeway, is prime for something like that. Something that could improve local economy. There are lots of people in town who wanted Ben to let it go. And, hey, you coming into the property . . . that might make people happy, assuming you'll just sell it."

Cooper reached into his pocket and pulled out the sticky note that had been attached to the will. *Take care of things, Coop.* He passed it to Mac. "That sound like he wants me to sell it?"

Mac handed it right back. "Listen, Cooper, I know he was a friend, but unless the two of you had some kind of understanding, you gotta do what you gotta do."

"Why didn't he just leave it to Rawley?"

"Oh, I think that's pretty obvious. Rawley's a little off-kilter, if you get my drift. Besides, I don't think they were like brothers or anything — Ben was helping him out, that's all. Ben did more for Rawley in the past few years than anyone has done for him in the last twenty-five."

"Well, jeez. This just keeps getting more complicated. Do you suppose he's one of the things I'm supposed to take care of?"

"No telling, pal. But I've got a cleanup crew coming out first thing tomorrow to give you an estimate. If you like the price, they can start right away."

Cooper gave him an incredulous look. "Did you *smell* that place? Is it even possible the price could be too high?"

Mac laughed. "My aunt Lou is getting ready to burn some dinner. Why don't you lock the place up and join us. You can't get anything done around here tonight."

"Dinner?" Cooper asked. He gave a long, dubious look at that road leading up to 101. It was bad enough in daylight.

"I'll give you a ride across the beach. And bring you back tonight."

"I thought you had rules," Cooper said.

"We do. If anyone stops me or asks questions, you'll have to act arrested."

"Well, hell, you just stumbled on one of my special talents."

Dinner at the McCain house was served in a large, warm kitchen. Three kids, three adults sat at a big round table, two Labrador retrievers standing watch near the back door. Cooper shoveled the last of his spaghetti into his mouth and then wiped his plate with a piece of garlic bread. As it was on its way to his mouth, he noticed that five sets of eyes were on him. He realized he'd eaten like a starving man, chuckled and tossed the bread onto his plate.

"There's more," Lou said.

"Sorry. But that was seriously delicious."

Lou laced her fingers together and, elbows braced on the table, said, "I guess you don't get out much."

"I eat real well. It's Mac's fault. He tried to lower my expectations by saying you were burning some dinner."

"Isn't he cute? That he thinks he has a sense of humor?" Lou said, lifting one shapely eyebrow.

"May I be excused?" Eve asked. "Ashley is coming over."

"Sure," Lou said. "Ryan and Dee Dee, your night for cleanup. I'll give your dad and Mr. Cooper coffee in the living room."

"Aw," Ryan whined. *"Prison Break* is on! Come on, Aunt Lou . . ."

"Sorry, I have *Designing Women* reruns to watch in my room." Then she looked at Mac. "When did he outgrow cartoons?"

Instead of answering, Mac leaned toward Ryan. "You boning up for a prison break or working yourself into a corrections officer's slot?"

"It's awesome, Dad, they're just so stupid."

"I know. It's my job security," Mac said.

"Dishes," Lou said, standing with a plate in each hand.

"I'd be glad to help," Cooper said quietly. "I'm much better at dishes than cooking."

"Shh, we're getting out of here." Mac stood up and poured two cups of coffee, throwing a look over his shoulder at Cooper. He lifted his eyebrows in question.

"Black," Cooper said.

Carrying two mugs, Mac left the kitchen and Cooper followed. The Labs, one black and one yellow, followed Cooper. In the living room, where there was no TV, Mac flipped a light switch with the brim of a coffee cup and the fireplace came to life. Then he waited for Cooper to choose his spot.

It was obvious where the deputy liked to roost from the shape of the cushions on the recliner. Cooper took a corner of the couch and watched as the dogs lay down, one on each side of the deputy's chair. "I guess you spend a lot of time in here," he said.

Mac handed him a cup. "There's no TV or computer in here, ergo — not a place the kids like to be. I sometimes have to compete with cheerleaders or dance practice, but they don't want my audience. I had the piano delivered straight to the basement. A man's gotta have a room, and hiding out in your bedroom? That's weird."

Cooper laughed. "Is it now?" he asked, sipping.

"Not for a woman. They do it all the time. Lou can't wait to get away from us and close that door. But every time I go out on some strange call — disturbance or domestic or hinky sexual assault — the suspect is hiding out in his bedroom. Don't ask me why. It's just weird."

"That's kind of perverted," Cooper said with a laugh.

"Tell me about it. Few years ago, some lunatic got in a big brawl with his mother and sister, then shot at a deputy. He was totally unbalanced, just over eighteen years old and living with his parents, hiding in his bedroom where he had fifteen assault rifles."

"Living with his parents? And assault rifles?"

"I know. Tell me how they thought it was okay that this kid with a screw loose had a bunch of really powerful guns. Did they ever think that was, I don't know, *odd*? Because I'm not the best father on record, I'm sure, but I know who forgot to flush around here."

Right then, Cooper thought if there was anything suspicious to know about Ben's death, Mac was a good guy to have on the case. "I bet you're a good father," Cooper said, but he was still half laughing. "And this is a nice house, Mac."

"Eh, I'm getting used to it."

"How long have you been here?"

"A few years. Dee Dee was six — she's ten now. I bought it because it could hold this crew, was solidly built and on the school bus route, not that anyone around here would even consider the bus. They all want to be driven. They consider the bus a punishment."

"That can cut into your schedule."

"I have Lou. She's a teacher — she doesn't mind dropping them off. But we have major scheduling issues for picking up because

70

they have all kinds of after-school activities, from football practice to piano lessons. We manage, though."

"Your aunt Lou is a kick. And the spaghetti really was good. Very good."

"It is, you're right. I'm lucky there's someone who will make spaghetti for me. It's just that we've been eating the same ten things since I was ten years old."

Aunt Lou had been cooking his meals since he was ten and was now cooking for his family? Mac must have seen his surprise, because he continued.

"My parents were killed in a car accident when I was a kid and Lou raised me the rest of the way. My wife left me with three kids when Dee Dee was nine months old. Lou has saved my life more than once."

Cooper was speechless. His biggest worry had been the fact that he'd never been able to settle down, make a relationship with a woman go the distance. He was so far from fatherhood he couldn't even fathom being dumped with three kids to raise.

"The house is big enough, with a generous yard, near a town small enough to know everyone. If I were a rich man, I'd have a house with a view of the ocean, but up high. Not something ridiculous, just a roomy, airy house with a lot of windows. You probably haven't been around long enough to wonder why this place is called Thunder Point but the way the storm clouds come into the bay, the way the lightning flashes over the water . . ." He shook his head. "This is a really beautiful place. Sometimes I take the squad car out to the spot where the Cheap Drinks sign is and sit on the hill and watch the weather over the bay. Or watch the sunset. Or the fog lift and the sunbeams streak through."

Coop thought about everything Mac had told him for a minute. This man had had mega challenges that Cooper had never faced. Being orphaned? Being left a single father with not one but three children? And looking so regular? Acting so normal, like it was just one foot in front of the other.

But all Cooper said was, "This seems to be a good house."

Mac replied, "It's good enough for us."

While a couple of representatives from a cleanup company wandered through the bait shop, Cooper went to the dock and called the lawyer whose name appeared on the letterhead of Ben's will. He explained what he'd found on Ben's property. "Before I write a check for the cleanup, I should know whether this will that I've been in possession of for less than twenty-four hours is legitimate."

"Absolutely ironclad. If you read it carefully, you'll find that everything is held in the Bailey Oceanfront Trust. There is a thirty-thousand-dollar lien you'll have to assume, however. He borrowed against the land to pay for the tow truck. Borrowed, rather than selling off any land. It's a considerable parcel, Mr. Cooper. Mr. Bailey didn't have any investments and very little in the way of savings, but he didn't like having bills. There's some cash set aside for property tax."

"Why do you suppose he bought a tow truck?" Cooper asked.

"I couldn't tell you. He said he needed it. You have over two hundred acres that includes beachfront, Mr. Cooper."

"Over two hundred?" he asked in shock.

"That's what county records show. I recommend you have the land surveyed."

"Holy Jesus!"

"As I said, considerable."

"You don't understand," Cooper said. "Ben Bailey acted like a poor boy with a bait shop!"

"As far as I know, he didn't have much money. Ben, and his father before him, were land poor."

Just land? Just a couple hundred acres, *including beautiful beachfront property*? From where Cooper stood on the dock, he could look west to the ocean and the vast promontory; south to the rocky, hilly landscape dotted with Douglas fir; east to more hills with some bad roads leading to the highway; and north across the beautiful beach to the small town and marina. He'd have to see a map, but from where he stood he couldn't understand why Ben hadn't done anything more ambitious than keep the lights on. Why hadn't he cashed in at least a piece of it and built himself a decent house! Why hadn't he found himself a good woman and settled down? Ben was a couple of years older than Cooper, right around forty. And what had he done with himself?

Cooper looked out at the land mass south of the bay. That would be the bird sanctuary. Cooper hadn't even walked out there. Would the birds give the land up for a big house with a drop-dead view? But maybe Ben, like Cooper, didn't want to be tied to a big house that just had to be kept in repair. And cleaned. And would echo.

But the stretch of beach from the town all the way to the tip of Ben's land would accommodate a resort with at least a thousand rooms or a few hundred villas or condos . . .

74

maybe even a golf course. How would that look, right up against an ordinary town with a bunch of fishing boats in the marina?

It would look, he thought, like a major payday.

"Mr. Cooper." A man holding a clipboard signaled him. He was all suited up, a face mask hanging around his neck, wearing heavy-duty rubber gloves. These guys looked like escapees from a hazmat team, Cooper thought, but then they must run into a lot of real bad stuff like floods and fires. Homicide? Cooper went up the stairs and met him on the deck, wrinkling his nose. "You got problems," the man said. "You got rot, mold, septic backup, plumbing is going bad, and then there's the smell."

"Sounds terrible."

"No termites," he said with a lame smile.

"What do you recommend?"

"We can't turn over a good property to you unless we pretty much gut it. It needs a new septic system, plumbing repairs, and we can't get at that mold without tearing out some walls and flooring. The good news is, you have some water-damaged, rotting wood that would have to go anyway, so you kill two birds with one stone. You let us tear out the old wood to get to the mold and we'll only charge you once."

75

"I don't plan to keep it. So now what do you recommend?" he asked.

"You could raze it," he said. "Sell the lot it's on. But if you're thinking about selling the structure, you'd have to do some serious work. Massive remodel. And I can't guarantee you'd get your money's worth. See how it sits right in the middle of this land? The people who own the rest of this beach and land, they'd be the ones to ask. Maybe they'd buy your lot just to get you out of here so they can put up a hotel and strip mall. You should ask." He looked around, stretching his neck. "Not exactly a prime location for that, though. This place is kind of out-of-the-way."

Cooper was silent a moment. "You got an estimate to gut it?"

The man ripped off the top sheet and passed it to him — $5,890.00. "That doesn't include plumbing, septic system or removal of damaged, rotting wood. That would be another several thousand. Then you're left with a frame, pretty much."

"Roughly six thousand? Just to tear it apart?"

"That's a real nice estimate. And that bar? As bars go, it's terrible. It's a good fifty years old. And it's not an antique. It's just old and cheap. And rotting."

"Is anything on this place all right?" Cooper asked.

The guy gave a nod. "Good deck. It's newer than the structure. And as far as we can tell, the foundation is solid — but I wouldn't guarantee it. You have a really bad roof. If you get it in your head to renovate, I'd recommend a new roof. We don't do renovation, but I'd bet you're looking at over a hundred grand there. But hey, do you know what people would pay for your view?"

Cooper ran a hand around the back of his neck which, despite the cold, was sweating. "If I decide to just knock it down, can you do it?"

"Nope," he said, shaking his head. "But I can recommend a good demolition team. I can also recommend plumbers, septic repair or replacement, interior work, roofers. These are the people we work with on a regular basis — contractors of every stripe. We specialize in fire-and-flood damage — after our work is done, the rebuilding starts."

"Don't you ever go in and just clean up the mess?" Cooper asked.

"Pretty often. But this one is bad."

"Just because the electricity was off for a few weeks and the bait died?"

"It was in serious decline, filling up with

mold, before that happened. You might want to check with your insurance company — they might help. But this place has been neglected for a long time. Looks like someone tried to get that septic system up and running for a while, when it should've been replaced." He lifted bushy eyebrows. "You?"

"No, not me. I have to think about what I'm going to do."

"Fair enough," the man said, sticking out his hand.

"If I decide to do something with this, how much notice do you need?"

"It's turning winter. The schedule isn't too bad. But if you don't act soon, we're going to be weathered out."

"I'll try to think fast," Cooper said. "Got any more of those face masks?"

The man reached into his pocket and pulled out several. "Just so you know — they're not that effective against the smell in there."

"I'm sure."

"Just out of curiosity, why didn't you fix the place up before it got so bad?"

"It wasn't mine until recently. The man who owned it died."

"Really? Well, hell, man! Cash it in! The land it's on is probably worth something."

He knew that, Cooper did. But something

about the whole thing just gnawed at him. He wasn't going to be able to make a decision until he understood why Ben Bailey lived with mold and rotting wood. The fact that he was pretty unmotivated didn't explain it. Ben could've made one phone call and traded some land for enough money to build himself something nice. "So," he said to the man with the cleanup crew, "how much to make that fish tank and any rotting food go away?"

"Twenty-five hundred. But that won't solve your septic problems. We can deal with that, too, short of replacing it. But that won't leave you a sound building and the plumbing won't be serviceable."

"I just want time to look around the inside. And think. And brother, I can't think when it smells like that."

"Twenty-five hundred makes it unpleasant rather than deadly."

"Done. How fast?"

"Tomorrow. We'll bring in a crew, a Dumpster and some fans to air the place out."

"Let's do it. I have to look around in there before I can figure out what to do next. Right now I'm leaning toward a bulldozer."

"Can't say I blame you, Mr. Cooper."

# FOUR

Rawley lived in a little inland town called Elmore. Mac gave Cooper directions to his place. Besides a gas station, post office, elementary school and Dairy Queen, Elmore wasn't much of a town. The larger town of Bandon wasn't far away and possibly served the small population's needs.

The house was a small, old, brick structure with a porch. That classic pickup was parked on the side, identifying the place as belonging to Rawley. The yard was well kept and the grass still green, though the trees and shrubs were showing signs of fall with either color or brown. When Cooper knocked on the door and Rawley answered, the last thing he expected was the homey, clean, orderly house he saw inside.

"Hey. Got a minute?" Cooper asked.

Rawley gave his version of a nod, which was a smirk and a tilt of his head, stepping back so Cooper could enter. Inside was a living room and dining room that looked like a woman had left it behind — lace covers on the worn arms of chairs and sofa, pictures of farm scenes on the walls, a buffet with a couple of good glass bowls on top of a fabric runner, candlesticks on the table. All old, all maintained. In front of the fire sat an elderly man in a wheelchair. He was dressed in overalls and a long-sleeved shirt — clean — and on his feet were socks only. No point in shoes if you never walked.

"Very nice, Rawley," Cooper said, taking it in. "That your dad?"

Rawley nodded.

Cooper had never been a patient man, but this was really stretching what patience he had very thin. "I wish you'd talk," he said. "Unless you're mute."

"I'll talk when I got something to say," he said.

"Well, there," Cooper said. "You doing okay since Ben's death?"

"Not hardly," Rawley said.

*Well, there you go again,* Cooper thought. Honest, if not informative. "Anything you need that I can get for you, now that he's gone?"

"Can't think what," Rawley said.

At that statement, the old man turned his chair around to face Cooper. He didn't exactly hold his head up, and Cooper could see that he was very likely a stroke victim. He turned the chair with his left arm, the right kinked in protectively at his side, and the right side of his face — mouth and eye — sagged.

"You looking for work?" Cooper asked.

"Hadn't been. Why? You gonna open up Ben's place?"

"No, but I'm cleaning it up and clearing it out. It's got troubles — rot and mold and dead fish. Tomorrow a crew is coming out to clean out and remove the fish tanks, rotten food, trash . . ."

"Police locked it up and wouldn't let me in," Rawley said by way of explanation.

"I know. And the electric company turned off the power," Cooper said. "The result is a stink and mess. But once they get the place so I can breathe in there, I have to go through his things. You know — pitch, give away, sell, whatever. There might be some things in there you want. If you help out, I can pay you what Ben paid you."

Rawley grinned and showed off a stunning set of dentures. "He paid me a ton."

"Gimme a break, Ben didn't have shit. And he couldn't tolerate a lie, either."

"Eight dollars an hour," Rawley said. "When?"

"In three days, I guess. Your dad okay alone if you work?"

The old man inhaled sharply and briefly lifted his head. It looked like he scowled, but with the uneven features, it was hard to tell. His good eye narrowed.

"He's okay. If I work, the neighbor checks on him twice a day. I leave him fixed up for what he needs."

"Okay, then. If you're interested."

Rawley gave a nod. No questions, no suggestions, no commentary.

"Rawley, I don't know what I'm going to do with the place. Fair warning. This could be a week of work and that's all. I might just tear the place down and sell the land."

"You'll figure it out," Rawley said, apparently unconcerned.

"Yeah, I guess." Cooper scratched his neck. "See you then." He turned to leave.

"Hold on," Rawley said. He went into the kitchen, which was just through the dining room arch, then came back with a package. Cookies, wrapped in Saran, no plate, no ziplock bag. "Can't be much around that toy hauler for snacks. They're sugar-free, on account of Dad."

"Right," Cooper said, accepting them. "Thanks. That's real nice."

Rawley just shrugged.

Cooper left with yet another mystery about Ben. Rawley lived in a house that was well cared for, yet Ben's place was mostly a wreck. How did that add up? Did Rawley take care of himself, but do a sad job for Ben?

Once in his truck, Cooper tried a cookie. Not bad, for sugar-free. Soft and tasty. He just shook his head.

Three days later, the smell wasn't too bad and Cooper could get inside Ben's place without choking. He had the electricity turned on; it not only offered functional lighting in the shop, but he ran an extension to the trailer to save on his generator. Just having a crew there to take out garbage and install fans brought attention to the place, and when the weather was decent, people who were out on the beach felt a need to wander closer, to find Cooper on the deck or the dock. Usually they would stop to say hello or hang out for a while, to ask what was going on. A kayaker rowed up to the dock, got out and asked what was going to happen to the place now.

"I don't exactly know," he said honestly. "I guess I'm responsible for it, but I'm not interested in running a business."

"Neither was Ben," the guy said, laughing. "But people around Thunder Point liked the place, even if we didn't want to go inside too much."

"What did you like it for?" Cooper asked.

"Gossip and drinks, mainly. And Ben used to pick up his deli food every couple of days from Carrie — when he couldn't talk her into delivering. She'd do that if her daughter was free to mind the deli. That's good stuff, Carrie's stuff, and Ben never even marked it up. He had egg sandwich kind of things for the morning, sandwiches and pizza for later, desserts and stuff. It was good. It was all wrapped — he didn't cook it. Know what I mean?"

"All I saw in there was a microwave and a stove and oven that looked . . ." He didn't want to say *ancient,* but although the kitchen was spotless, the appliances didn't look very reliable. The bar, though small, was neat and well stocked. The glasses, though dusty, looked as if they'd been washed, not that he'd trust them.

A man and woman with a dog saw him on the dock and said, "You're the new guy, right?"

"I guess I am."

"I'm Charlie and this here's Donna, the wife. So, when you gonna open up?"

"Don't know that I will," Cooper said.

"For now I'm just cleaning the place up. I'm not much of a cook . . ."

"Ben didn't really cook. He *warmed.*"

"Did Ben live on egg sandwiches and deli stuff?" Cooper asked.

"I don't know," Charlie said. "He was good with drinks. All drinks. Coffee, cappuccino, wine, beer and liquor. If the day was nice, I'd end up here with a bunch of guys from town for a drink or two. Sport fishermen came here for a few before taking their boats over to the marina."

"What about Cliffhanger's? Or Waylan's?"

"Cliffhanger's is expensive and Waylan's is a shit hole. But they have HD TV. The owner is trying to make it a sports bar. If you open up, get a TV."

"Gotcha," Cooper said.

Cooper and Rawley went through Ben's living quarters, which were, to his surprise, tidy. He suspected Rawley had taken care of that, too. Ben had been in possession of a minimal wardrobe. "You want the clothes?" he asked Rawley.

"Too big for me," he said. "I could use some old shirts and sweats for Dad. The rest could go to the VA."

"Sure," Cooper said.

"I'll take 'em home and wash 'em up first. Then drop 'em off at the VA."

"That's above and beyond . . ." Cooper said.

"They deserve that. At least."

Cooper was impressed. He was beginning to suspect that Rawley was a good and generous man, under his grump and grumble.

Ben had an old TV and stereo, a boom box — apparently he hadn't graduated to the iPod yet — and bookcase that held many books about Oregon wildlife, mostly birds. He found Ben's laptop, their primary means of communication the past ten years, and therein he found out a few things about Ben that he might've known if he'd been paying attention. Ben was an involved ornithologist. He might not hold any kind of degree, but the history on his computer showed almost daily visits to websites and blogs about birds, further explaining the preserve on his land.

Cooper had walked through the preserve all the way to the high cliff edge towering over the Pacific a few days earlier. The growth was thick but he'd found what appeared to be a seldom-traveled path through the spruce, Douglas fir and shrubs. The bright colors of fall battled with the dark green of fir trees; among the ground cover he saw withered plants he was willing to bet sprang into bloom with the spring and summer warmth. He'd spotted the remnants of many old nests, perhaps abandoned for the winter. There were some shells and some dead eggs, not to mention a few low-flying seabirds threatened by his presence. One lone eagle circled overhead for a little while. There was one tree in which perched a few birds that looked like small cranes.

Ben had saved a lot of online documents about bird preserves, about rare and endangered birds. There were pictures on his computer, pictures he'd taken himself — he was an avid bird-watcher. And there were large, high-powered binoculars hanging from nails all over the place.

He also found that Ben had saved many emails from Cooper and from Luke Riordan but very few from other people. It spurred a memory of an email Cooper had gotten from Ben, in which he casually said, "Since my father passed a couple of years ago . . ." Cooper had thought, a couple of *years* ago? He hadn't notified his friends of his father's death?

And then Cooper asked himself, who would he write about something like that? While Cooper liked a lot of people, he could count his good friends on one hand.

But Cooper had sisters, brothers-in-law,

nieces and nephews who were always in touch. At least he was connected.

It was going to take him a long time to get through all of Ben's saved emails, but over time he'd manage. There could be information in there about his intention for the property. There could even be some stray clue about what led to his death, if he had some issue with an enemy no one really knew about. He doubted it, but it was worth checking.

The weather was good that afternoon. Rawley had gone home with a lot of laundry to do and Cooper relaxed on the deck with the laptop. He counted nine kids on the beach — two wearing wet suits with paddleboards and oars out on the still bay, four batting a volleyball around, though they didn't have a net set up, three girls parked on the sand, talking. There were three ATVs lined up behind them, although he hadn't seen them arrive.

Cooper was just enjoying his view and the kids seemed to be having good, clean fun. There was a little monkey business — a guy grabbed a girl, stole a kiss, got punched, which made him laugh hysterically and then chase her, catch her, get a more receptive welcome the second time. The two guys with the boards went almost to the mouth of the bay, where the Pacific waves were high and challenging. Inside the bay was smooth as silk, dark as ink. Wet suits, very intelligent — the air was cold and the ocean much colder. But they were obviously pros; they barely got their feet wet. In the summer, Cooper bet there was a lot of snorkeling, maybe diving, maybe running surf boards out beyond the bay.

He shot a note off to his sister Rochelle and told her this was a pretty cool place, in fact. He had no idea what to do with it, though. Dry camping in the fifth wheel was not exactly convenient — he had to find a trailer park, dump the lav and reload potable water every few days. But he could at least run off the bar's power and not his battery. He hadn't told anyone in his family the extent to which he was tied to all this — he didn't want any advice. His family, especially his sisters, was very good at telling him what he should do.

He saw the dog again, but not with the girl this time. A young man or boy was with him, throwing a ball for the dog as he walked. Husband? he wondered.

Then he saw the guy trying to give the kids on the beach a wide berth, walking all the way down to the surf to get by them without contact. The guys, six of them, two in wet suits, made a line across his path. The dog walker went the other way, headed inland for the hill, calling the dog to follow. The teenage boys reversed their position, blocking him again. The dog, half as big as a human, cowered behind his master.

Cooper, who had been in way too much trouble for fighting when he was younger, could see the fight brewing. He knew what was coming, and it was six on one. Then the guy who must be the ringleader shoved the loner. The loner stood taller; his shoulders widened a little, ready. The ringleader was seriously talking him down, leaning into him, verbally assaulting him. Then he shoved him again and the loner put his fists up.

"Not gonna happen, assholes," Cooper said aloud to no one. He put down the laptop. Then he stood, put two fingers in his mouth and rent the air with a deafening whistle.

They all turned to see him standing on the deck of the now-defunct bait shop. His legs were braced apart, hands on his hips, and he watched. He hated bullies. He was ready to leap over the deck rail and barrel down to the beach to stand up for this guy, even though the guy, the loner, might be the problem. It didn't matter if the loner had done something terrible, you don't do that — you don't attack someone in a fight that isn't fair and balanced.

The teens watched him; he watched the teens.

Then the barricade wisely separated and the loner passed, headed for Cooper's dock.

He wasn't headed for Cooper. He went to the bottom of the steps that led up to the bar and sat. From there he threw the ball for the dog. Cooper let this go for about five minutes, then he descended to meet the guy. A very cranky-looking teenager looked up at him and said, "Thanks for that. I guess."

"You *guess*? Would you rather I just watch them beat you up?"

"They probably wouldn't have." He looked back down to accept the Great Dane's ball and throw it again.

"*Probably* wouldn't have?" Cooper asked.

The kid shrugged.

"Have a little disagreement with your friends?"

The kid looked up and laughed. "Dude, they are *not* my friends!"

"Who are they, then?"

"Teammates. And that's all."

Cooper took another two steps down and sat on a step even with the kid. "You throw the last game or something?"

The kid gave him a very impatient look. He held on to the ball, all slimy with dog spit. The dog sat and panted happily, full of expectation. "You wouldn't understand," the kid said, finally throwing the ball.

"Wanna try me?"

The kid shot him an angry look. All defensive, hurt, full of impotent rage, and Cooper thought, *Holy shit — that's me!* About twenty years ago or so . . .

"I'm the new kid," he said. "Just moved here. Just in time for football, which was my fatal mistake. I wasn't supposed to get on the team, much less make touchdowns. The asshole on the beach, he's a senior. Team captain. He was counting on three things this year — being all-conference, being homecoming king and getting laid by every cheerleader in Coos County."

Cooper had a strange reaction to that. First of all, being the new kid felt all too familiar to him. Getting in fights, though long ago, was fiercely memorable. Homecoming king — not Cooper! And cheerleaders? When he was in high school, he hadn't been lucky enough to even date one, let alone anything more. He thought about Mac's daughter, whom he'd met when he'd had dinner with the McCains a few nights ago. Eve was a lovely, virginal, delightful sixteen-year-old cheerleader who *no one* should be allowed to touch. Just to be ornery, he asked, "How many of those things are you going to rack up?"

The kid looked at him incredulously. "Seriously? Like I could ever get all-conference or get a date. Come on."

"The kid who shoved you — who is he?"

A bitter laugh. "Jag Morrison. Crown prince of Thunder Point. And yes, that's short for Jaguar, if you can believe anyone would name their kid that."

"Shew," Cooper said, shaking his head.

"Yeah."

Cooper let that settle a little bit. Obviously there was some very bad blood there. It could be about anything — about this kid being a better ball player, about a girl, about anything. Finally Cooper asked, "Your dog have a name, kid?"

He laughed without humor. "Are you ready for it? Hamlet. It's Danish."

"You could use a tougher dog."

"Tell me about it," he said.

"How about you? Name?"

"How about *you*?" he shot back.

"Sorry," he said, putting out his hand. "Hank Cooper. People just call me Cooper."

The kid relaxed a little. "Landon Dupre."

He shot a glance at the teenagers on the beach, who were not going anywhere. It occurred to Cooper that they were looking for a second chance at bullying and intimidating Landon.

"Nice to meet you, Landon. So, what do your parents have to say about this new-kid issue you've got going on?"

"I don't have parents."

"Ah. So who do you report to?"

"Report to?" he mimicked with a mean laugh. "Gimme a break."

"Look, I'm trying to figure out, in the nicest possible way, if your parents back you up, if you're a street urchin, in foster care or just plain contrary."

"I live with my sister," he said. His voice dropped, as did his chin. It was either a measure of respect or misery.

"Ah, the girl in the red slicker."

Landon looked up at him. "You know her?"

"I know the dog — she's had him out on the beach a couple of times. He's hard to miss, big as a horse."

"And dumb as a stump."

"Now, you shouldn't put him down like that," Cooper said. "You might damage his self-esteem." Then grinned at the kid. "Why'd you get him?"

"My sister got him for me. He was a rescue — his owner had to deploy. It was her idea of some kind of consolation prize because she moved me right before my best season ever."

The dog was back, dropping the ball, sitting expectantly, saliva running out of his jowls. "Hamlet, here, he has a drooling issue."

"It's horrible. I don't know what was wrong with a good old German shepherd."

Cooper laughed in spite of himself, happy he was not this kid's guardian. "Why'd you move here?"

"Divorce."

"You're divorced?" Cooper asked facetiously.

Landon's head snapped around at Cooper and, seeing his smile, melted a little bit. "*She* got divorced, couldn't afford so much house, wanted a smaller town so she could keep track of me better — which I *so* appreciate, if you can understand. And she didn't enjoy running into the ex. Now I get that, but really, do we have to move to Podunk, Oregon, where the natives just want to kick the shit out of me every day? Seriously?"

"Have you told her?" Cooper asked. He almost looked over his shoulder to see who was talking. This was the weirdest interaction he'd ever had. He sounded like his father.

The kid's chin dropped again. "I'm not hiding behind my sister, dude. Besides, she's got her own troubles."

Cooper, who had big sisters, absolutely got that. But all he said was, "Is this 'dude' thing almost over? Calling everyone dude? I never caught on to that. . . ."

"Well, *dude,* you might wanna catch up."

"Or you might," he said. "So, anyone back you up? I mean, anyone? Teachers? Ministers? Corrections officers?"

"Funny. You're a real comedian."

"I am, huh. But I'm serious, everyone needs a wingman. I got in fights when I was your age. I don't know what it was about me. . . ."

"Want a second opinion?" he said.

Cooper laughed at his sarcasm. "Okay, never mind. I think I'm catching on."

"Ben," Landon said. "Ben was my friend."

Stunned, Cooper was silent. Then he put a hand on Landon's shoulder. "He was my friend, too. I'm sorry, man."

"Yeah. Well. Whatever happened? It shouldn't have."

He gathered strays, Cooper thought. He gave Rawley work, protected Landon and made sure Gina's Jeep was running. Who knew how many others he helped? He protected the birds and fish. He had a lot of friends and no real friends. He took care of the town in his way, keeping this little piece of beach safe.

# FIVE

The weather turned stormy not long after Landon finally made his escape across the beach to the town. The bait shop could get pretty lonely during a storm. Cooper guessed that with the wet Oregon weather, there were plenty of nights like this. So he showered in the trailer, then took the truck the short way into town, across the beach, and decided it was time to hit Cliffhanger's for a meal.

It wasn't crowded, which came as no surprise. He had watched the fishing boats come in before the rain clouds and the last of the sunlight left the bay, and he supposed those guys were happy to be home, eating a hot meal in front of a warm fire. There was a large hearth in the restaurant that could be seen in the bar and it made him think of Jack's place in Virgin River. A lot could be done to that old bait shop of Ben's to make it a cozier hangout — like a fireplace, for starters, he thought. Then he told himself to stop it — no matter what some piece of paper said, he really had no stake in it. He was only going through the motions for Ben's sake. For some reason, his old friend trusted him.

He hadn't expected to see a familiar face in the restaurant, so he was pleasantly surprised when he realized Mac was sitting at the bar, nursing a beer and talking to the bartender. He wasn't dressed for duty tonight. Cooper approached and said, "Hey, Deputy."

"Cooper," he said, putting out his hand. "What brings you out on such a wet night?"

"Food," he said, sitting up at the bar.

"Cliff, bring my friend Cooper a beer."

"Cliff?" Cooper repeated with a short laugh. "That's convenient."

"Yeah, right," the guy said. "What's your pleasure?"

"Draft," Cooper said. "This must be your place, Cliff."

"Must be. Menu?"

"Thanks."

"Just get the grouper," Mac said.

Cooper peered at him. "And how do I want that done?"

"He'll have the grouper. Just trust me. So,

what's happening on the other side of the beach?"

"Got most of the smell out, went through most of Ben's things, donated, threw away stuff, you know. It's not functional. Ben was working on that septic system way back when I was waiting for him to meet me in California. I guess he never quite got it fixed," Cooper said.

"So, what next?"

Cooper drank some beer. "I don't know. I'm thinking. I pulled down part of a wall — I don't know if there's mold or rot. Maybe it needs to be leveled. I don't know."

"You're still here," Mac observed.

He took another swallow of beer and shook his head. "Feels like unfinished business around here. I find out something new every day, but half the time it leaves me with more questions."

"About his death?"

"About his life," Cooper said. "How'd he make ends meet? He bought deli food from the deli, but he didn't mark it up. . . ."

"I think Carrie gave him a break," Mac said. "He bought all his supplies, including liquor, from big-box stores and I bet he made a decent profit on that. I mean, there was no rent, right?"

"He took care of things. Of people. I have

Rawley working again, for now."

Mac grew serious for a moment, then put a firm hand on his back, as if to say thanks.

"I ran into a kid on the beach today who was Ben's friend, so he says," Cooper went on. "Ben's created a habitat for those birds on the point. I feel like I should find out what Rawley needs before I leave. Like I owe it to Ben. I wonder, though . . . he took care of people but everything is broken down to the point of falling apart. How'd he live?"

"I don't think making money was ever a priority of Ben's, but don't quote me. You probably know more about his business than I do. Than any of us do."

"Well, he didn't have much money, for one thing. And didn't worry about it, from what I can figure out. Why didn't he give that place to someone else? Why didn't he give it to the town?"

Mac laughed. He took a pull on his beer. "The town would've sold it. Like I said, there are people in town who like things the way they are — simple. Then there are people who think a big business on the bay would be good for the town."

"What do you think?" Cooper asked.

He gave a lame shrug. "I think a big business, like a golf resort or something, would turn us into a town full of busboys, waiters, maids and valets. I think it would put Carrie's deli, the Pizza Hut and the diner out of business. But it could help the chamber of commerce and commercial fishermen, especially if we ended up with a five-star restaurant at that resort. You want to know what I'm talking about? Drive up to Bandon Dunes. People come from all over the world to stay there, play golf there, hold events from business conferences to weddings there. It's really something. Very high-class. There's a lot good about it. And the help comes from Bandon."

"It's work. . . ."

"And not to be taken lightly," Mac admitted.

"It could help the local economy," Cooper said. "Increase the value of your property."

"It could," Mac said. "You've been here about a week. Have you told anyone about Ben's will?"

"I might've mentioned I was responsible for the bait shop, but you're the only one with the details. You and Rawley."

"Well, Rawley doesn't talk. People are already assuming things that are probably true — like that you own it. And you could sell it."

"There's still a little legal wrangling to be

done," Cooper said. "I don't have to hang around for that, though."

"Why are you still here?"

"As near as I can explain, I want to understand Ben's intentions, if I can. That doesn't mean I'm planning to meet his expectations — maybe I just can't. But I owe it to the guy to see if I can figure them out before I make a plan."

Mac glanced over his shoulder, glanced back and said, "Well, get ready to make a plan, Cooper. Incoming . . ."

Almost before he finished his sentence, a woman appeared. She was at least fifty-five, but trying to look thirty-five. Her suit was some kind of satiny red material, low cut to reveal her cleavage. The miniskirt exposed legs that were short, and her pumps were high, very high. Hair bleached blond, of course. Nails, long and red. She wasn't dressed for church; in fact, she'd look pretty at home with a pole to swing around.

"Well, Mac, how are you?" she said, leaning toward the deputy for a cheek press and kiss-kiss. "And who is your friend?"

"Ray Anne, meet Cooper. Cooper, this is Ray Anne. Cooper was a friend of Ben's."

Her face crumpled on cue. "Oh, Cooper, I'm so sorry for your loss. Ben will be greatly missed."

"Thank you. Pleased to meet you," he said. But he knew beyond a doubt that Ben didn't have a relationship with this woman. In contrast, he had understood Ben's relationship with Rawley almost immediately.

There were a few minutes of chat, Ray Anne asking after Lou and the kids, wondering if any progress had been made on that traffic light in town. Did Mac hear anything about a "domestic situation" involving Charlie and Donna? To which Mac replied, "No, was there a situation?"

Without answering, she turned to Cooper. "I heard a friend of Ben's was in town. How is everything out at his place?"

"A wreck," Cooper said. "I'm exploring ways to deal with it."

"Well, if you need any help, feel free to call."

A business card appeared; she was a Realtor. Apparently, the woman knew sleight of hand. That card must have been in her hand the whole time, yet had remained invisible until her strike. Cooper looked at it briefly, looked back at Ray Anne, smiled and said, "Thank you."

"I know every good contractor in the area, no matter what you need — paint, flooring, structure damage, anything . . ."

She knew everything. "Mold removal?" he asked.

"Yes!" she said, beaming. She tapped the hand that held the card. "Just give me a call. That's my cell. Anytime!"

"Appreciated," he said. The grouper arrived.

"There's your dinner," she said. "I'm sure I'll be seeing you around town. Take care. And let me know if there's anything you need, Hank. Always more than happy to help a friend."

Mac and Cooper turned to their identical dinners. Cooper took a bite. "This is good," he said.

"Told ya," Mac returned.

"So, she knows everything. She probably knows my social security number. You introduced me as Cooper, but she called me Hank. I'd bet she knows the acreage on Ben's place."

"That would be my guess," Mac said.

Cooper ate a little more grouper. "And I bet I could get laid for a couple hundred acres."

Mac turned toward him and, with the slightest smile, said, "You can get laid for just talking about it."

Cooper tried not to laugh, as Ray Anne was still working the room, taking a run on

106

the bar, then stopping off at tables. "This common with her?"

"I think so," Mac said, eating more of his dinner. "You're the first newcomer we've had around here in a while, however."

"You ever, um, experienced that?"

"The attention? Or the payoff?" Mac asked.

"Well, since we're sharing confidences . . ."

"Cooper, I work in this town. My kids go to school here, my aunt's a teacher here. Lou's known Ray Anne a long time. In a word, no. I have truly dense areas in my brain, but not that dense. Really, she's not my style. I never did have a mother fixation."

"I never had a mother who looked like that," Cooper said.

They ate in silence and by the time Cooper pushed away his plate, Ray Anne had left the restaurant. "So, Mac, did the family desert you tonight?" he asked.

Mac sat back. "Not exactly. It's Lou's bunco night with some good friends from Coquille and she'll be out late. I picked up a pizza for the kids and ran for my life." He wiped his mouth with his napkin. "I stood at the door, threw it in and said I'd be home in two hours. They jumped on it like starving hounds."

"Two *whole* hours?" Cooper asked with a laugh.

"I have to check homework. If I don't check homework, Lou's on me like a cheap suit."

"Checking homework. That can't be so bad."

"You checked homework lately, pal?"

"Whose homework do you think I'd check?"

"Well, that's not the point, Cooper. The point is, it's torture. If I were in school now, I wouldn't have graduated sixth grade. In short, I'd rather give up a nut. But that's the price of fatherhood."

Lou stood in front of the bathroom mirror in only her panties, gently lifting her breasts. Then she took a side view and sighed. Although they were small, she felt they drooped to an unflattering degree; they used to be perky. She let them go. Then with her fingers gently pulling at her cheeks, back toward her ears, she wondered for the millionth time if she could look ten years younger with a face-lift.

"Lou, come back," Joe called from the bedroom.

*I'm not greedy,* she thought. *Just ten years.* She sighed again and went back to the bedroom. Joe Metcalf was fifty and, besides being handsome, he was in terrific shape. George Clooney shape. He was strong as an ox, wide-shouldered, flat-bellied, with long legs, big wonderful hands and beautiful teeth. As she approached the bed, he turned off the TV and opened his arms. "What were you doing in there?" he asked, his lips going immediately to her neck.

"We call it freshening up," she said, tilting her head back to give him more of her neck.

"I bet you were brooding."

"Now why would you say that?" she asked, pulling back.

"Because it's something you tend to do. I think all our problems would be solved if you brought me out of the closet. Why are you keeping me a secret, Lou? Why am I still 'bunco night'?"

She hesitated. It was so complicated. Mostly it was his age — ten years younger. Even though his hair would be gray if he grew it out, with that shaved head, he could pass for forty-five. "I don't want the kids to feel vulnerable, to feel like my attention could be sliding away from them."

"It won't, Lou. We'll spend whatever time together is reasonable for you. I have kids, too."

"Yours are on their own."

"Thank God," he said with a sigh. He rolled onto his back but he kept an arm around her. Joe was the divorced father of a son and daughter, twenty-five and twenty-three, respectively. "They still have way too many needs, however. A wallet drain."

"They'll be married with children before you know it," Lou said. "And so will mine. And I'll feel like a great-grandmother. Oh, my God." She dropped her head onto his naked shoulder.

He laughed at her and his hand found her ass. "Best-looking great-grandmother in the state, maybe the country."

She lifted her head, messy red-gold curls flopping around. "When you're seventy I'll be eighty. Eighty."

"Christ, like you're screwing a nineteen-year-old. I hope I live to seventy. I can't wait to see what you bring to eighty!"

Lou and Joe had met through an online dating service. They made a date for coffee and he looked, well, mature. When she asked, "How old are you?", he answered, "How old do you want me to be?" She had answered, "Fifty-nine," and he said, "Consider it done."

It was weeks before she learned the truth. She thought he just looked damn good for his age, which men had an annoying ten-

110

dency to do. It had been programmed that way by the world — men became distinguished while women faded and aged.

He'd been divorced for ten years, had tried dating from time to time but nothing really clicked and he wanted to meet someone he had things in common with who would join him for movies, dinner, social things. Oh, he liked to eat, went to movies seldom, but . . . "Okay, the truth? I wanted to have sex again before I died. With someone I liked."

What a coincidence. So did she.

He was a retired air force colonel who now worked for the Oregon State Police as a trooper. It was his mission to retire, for the second time, at sixty. And now that he'd recovered from his divorce — his ex was remarried and his kids had completed college — he could count on a comfortable old age. Part of his job in Coos County was to assist the Sheriff's Department. That was a little close for comfort for Lou.

"I don't see why," he argued. "Police people are like a family. They intermarry all the time."

"Marry!"

"Well, we have to be going somewhere!" he said. "Besides, Mac and I get along fine. He likes me. We work well together when we have to."

"Let me think, let me think!" she had pleaded. She'd been pleading that for a year.

But Lou's little secret was that this was all she'd ever wanted. If she'd met him when she was twenty-one, she'd have married him in a heartbeat — provided he hadn't been eleven. She'd have been a good wife to him. In fact, what she'd always wanted was a home, a spouse, kids. Crazy as it seemed now, she'd never even come close. She had been twenty-five when her brother and sister-in-law had Mac, thirty-five when their deaths left him orphaned and she became his parent. She'd been only forty-four when Mac came to her and confessed his girl-friend was pregnant, and fifty when Cee Jay left him and the three kids. While raising Mac's kids was hard work — cutting into her social life and sleep, costing time and money — if she could, she would kiss Cee Jay for giving her these precious children.

Once or twice a week, she met Joe. Some-times they went out for dinner, sometimes they stayed in, sometimes they even went somewhere other than his house for the night. She stole a long weekend from her family to go to Victoria with him — that was fabulous. He brought out her best self and she adored him. She just didn't want to saddle him with an old woman, which she felt she would be before long. And she didn't want anyone to laugh at the idea that she thought she was young enough for this, for him. Not the way they laughed at Ray Anne. Even Lou found Ray Anne ridiculous.

He slid down her panties. "It's up to you, babe — I don't want to push you too much and I'm not giving you up. But I sure like the way you play bunco."

There were two situations that always tempted Cooper to cut and run. Being at complete odds with his environment, as with the Army or certain jobs. Or feeling a little too comfortable and secure. That had happened to him a few times, a couple of which were very difficult. There were a couple of times he'd been with a woman with whom he thought he could go the distance. He'd had visions of the kind of happy home his parents had. When it didn't work out, he was dealt a double blow — he was not only informed he'd let the women down, a painful enough thing for a man who'd been doing his best, but he had suffered the pain of loss and isolation. Naturally he tried to avoid both — work unsuited to him and women he couldn't hold on to. For the past several years, he'd avoided romantic relationships that could gut him in the end. That whole not-sleeping, feeling the deep ache that came from failure, enduring the sudden loneliness of being rejected . . . it was bad for his disposition. He only got involved with women he didn't care about too much. He just didn't like the risks he associated with settling down.

Cooper thought it might be in his best interest to put up a for-sale sign on this beach property and take off. It might be the safest thing to do. But the train wreck of a bar/bait shop tugged at him. He wasn't sure what that was about. He had no real stake in it. It was a gift, a piece of luck.

It was nice to be back on the water, even though the bait shop was a pimple on the otherwise beautiful landscape. It was a disaster; fixing it looked about as easy as scaling Everest. He didn't know where to start — or whether to start.

Cooper couldn't remember ever having such difficulty making a decision. He generally made his decisions too fast, without really thinking things through. Enlisting in the Army, taking a job or quitting a job. Then there had been two engagements, five years apart, that were probably doomed from the start even if he hadn't seen it. He surprised himself this time. The Cooper he thought he was would have either sold or leveled that dying old shack by now.

He felt an odd sense of peace. And it scared him to death.

A couple days later, Cooper found himself watching a quiet sunset with an empty beach. The fishing boats had docked. Cooper headed for town, the long way. He thought he'd like either a burger at the diner or pizza. But as he approached the high school, he saw the football field was all lit up, the parking lot overflowing. He could hear cheers and the thumping of high school band music even with the windows up. He turned in to the school, drove around to the back and then hunted for a space but ended up on the back overflow dirt lot. There were buses representing the Carver High Badgers and as he walked toward the field, he could see that both the home and visiting bleachers were full.

By God, the whole town was there.

He paid his five bucks, but the bleachers were so crammed, he just hung around the end, standing. There was an announcer on the loudspeaker. He saw Eve on the sidelines and wondered which of the cheerleaders belonged to Gina. He watched a few plays. The score was 10–7 in favor of the Badgers nearing the half. He picked up from people that Thunder Point never beat Carver High, at least not in too many years to remember. And then, with the clock ticking down to the half, there was a fumble, a recovery and — "Dupre has the ball and runs it! Going, going, and we . . . have . . . *touchdown!* Sixty yards and touchdown for the Cougars!"

The team, the cheerleaders and the fans were all roaring. A few of the Cougars rushed the quarterback and high-fived, hugged and slapped him on the back. The score went to 10–13, Cougars. They kicked and got the point just before the half, when both teams jogged off the field and were replaced by the band.

There was a rush on the concession stand and even though by now Cooper was starving, he saw the line was long and dense. He'd be better off taking his chances on Cliff's or the Pizza Hut.

"Kid's a natural athlete," said a passerby on his way to the concession stand.

"We haven't seen anything like him since I've lived here," said another.

Maybe things weren't as terrible for the kid as he believed — the team and the crowd seemed to approve of his game. Despite the growls of hunger Cooper was suffering, he wasn't going anywhere.

After standing there for about ten minutes, with a steady stream of people moving in and out of the bleachers, someone said his name.

"Cooper? Cooper, what are you doing here?"

He turned to see Gina, blond hair down tonight, wearing a Cougars sweatshirt under her jacket. "I was on my way into town and saw the game, so I just stopped off here. So, which one is yours?" he asked, tipping his head toward the cheerleaders.

"The redhead on the end — that's Ashley. Right next to her is Mac's daughter, Eve."

"I spotted Eve. I had dinner at Mac's one night and met the kids," he said.

"You want to sit with us? We're right up there," she said, pointing. "We can cram you in. We try to get here early and hold seats on the fifty yard line."

When he turned to look, Mac was standing, waving his arms. For the first time he thought, maybe there's something going on there. Mac and Gina. It would make perfect sense. A couple of single parents, a lot in common . . .

He liked Gina — she was pretty and sassy. "Are you sure?" he asked. "I've never seen so many people at a high school game."

"The town gets into the local sports," she

said. "And I don't know if you've noticed, there isn't a big entertainment industry here. We're the real *Friday Night Lights.*"

"Sure, I'll come up. Thanks."

"I'm on my way to the bathroom. See you for the second half."

Cooper went to the bleachers to sit with Mac and Lou. Mac pulled a cola out of a small cooler and offered it. The kids were off running around the bleachers, looking for anyone to sit with but their family.

The dancers joined the marching band on the field, about a dozen of them. Cooper told them what Gina had said about the town being the real *Friday Night Lights.*

"Have you counted the kids on the field tonight? Between football players, cheerleaders, pom-pom girls and band, you have any idea the number of hours the parents of this town have invested in just this activity?" Lou asked him. "Plus the fact, after all this, we can't afford anything else."

"They're pretty good for a town this size," Cooper added.

"They are," Mac said. "We work 'em hard to keep 'em out of trouble."

The second half was an even better ball game, but not easier for the Cougars. The Badgers caught up and passed them, the Cougars got behind by 10, then they got within reach and the people from Thunder Point were going crazy. There were a couple of fights on the field, a couple of really bad tackles and penalties. A Cougar was taken out of the game and it got down to the wire.

And then he did it again — Dupre recovered the ball and ran ninety yards for a touchdown, putting them two points ahead. The clock ran down and in a fever of excitement, the Cougars pulled off a win.

Even Cooper was on his feet, yelling till he was hoarse. He found himself hugged by Gina and Lou, slapped on the back by Mac.

"That's the first time they've been able to beat the Badgers since we moved here."

"Why is that?"

"Carver High," he said. "Big old farm boys from inland. They breed 'em hard and tough. It's been said they come out of the womb in shoulder pads."

"But you don't believe that," Cooper said with a laugh.

"The important thing is, *they* believe it," Mac said. "I have to gather up kids. See you around?"

"Yeah, probably. I won't head out without giving you a call, how's that."

"Good enough. I can at least give you directions out of here."

Cooper let the majority of the crowd

disperse; the line of cars and buses leaving the parking lot was moving real slow and he was parked at the back of the overflow lot. He had a bad feeling he was going to be left to forage for food back in his trailer. The crowd was likely headed for the few eateries in town. The kids might be headed for the beach, but that didn't worry him. After a game like that, he was happy for them to have a place to celebrate.

There was a lot of horn honking, yelling, cheering and general enthusiastic mania going on. Cooper stood right where he'd been sitting, watching it all for fifteen or twenty minutes. He was at the fifty yard line, about ten rows up. The Badgers were headed for their buses; the lights in the stadium were cracking off one by one, leaving him in the shadows. He was surprised to find that attending a high school football game in a little town, not even his town, was the most fun he'd had in a while. He'd been sweating under his sweater and jacket, that's how much the tension of the game got to him. Other than joining his family at nieces' and nephews' events on rare occasions, this was a first for him. At least since his own high school experience, which had been a little like Landon's. Except he hadn't been a quarterback.

120

He sat down for a minute, elbows on knees, looking out at the dark field. He thought for a moment what it must be like to be Mac — the law of the town, at the heart of the town, surrounded by all this excitement and connection, friends, family and something pulling at him every second. For a second he was envious, even though Cooper could go skiing in the Alps next week if he felt like it and Mac definitely could not. Mac was probably saving for college.

Cooper was happy to see that things might not be as bad for Landon Dupre as he thought. The kid played a good game and there was no question he had the town's support. They thought they had themselves a football hero.

There weren't many people left. The concession stand was closed up. There were a few groups standing around in the parking lot, probably making after-game plans. The field was dark, the bleachers deserted, the Badger buses gone. Cooper felt a little silly. Before he could think about why he was sitting there getting all nostalgic, he told himself that by now the lines for a pizza or a Big Mac wouldn't be so long. He headed toward the parking lot.

He was out of the stadium before he heard

voices. He couldn't hear the words but he could tell by the tone that these voices weren't celebrating or having fun. There was some kind of trouble — an argument of some kind. He told himself to keep going. It could be a drug deal gone bad; it could be a parent/teenager situation. But he stopped walking and listened. A hard, demanding, abusive voice; an answer that he understood — *no!* Just one word. *No.* That was all it took and he walked toward the voice.

They were under the visiting team bleachers. In the dark he couldn't be sure of the number, but he thought it was four or five. Boys. Big boys. At least equal to him in size. He walked softly, wishing he had a gun, then relieved he didn't — that's how people get killed, misinterpreting some situation in the dark of night.

"I told you *exactly* what to do!" a guy said.

"And I told you that *wasn't* going to happen! I don't trip! I don't fumble."

*Landon!*

Cooper walked a little faster. Ten long strides under the bleachers brought them into clear view. Two guys holding Landon's arms, two guys facing him, one doing the talking. "You don't want to push this. I'm the team captain! You do what I tell you to do."

"Lose the game," Landon said. "You don't see that as wrong?"

"We wouldn't have lost! I had to get in that game, asshole, and with you showing off all the time —"

"Hello, boys," Cooper said. He leaned against a strut, crossing his arms over his chest. "Just congratulating Dupre on his game?"

The boys holding his arms immediately let go. That's when Cooper noticed a trickle of blood running down the corner of Landon's mouth. He didn't get that in the game. It was fresh.

"What are you doing here?" their ringleader, who Cooper now knew to be Jag, demanded. "You some kind of pervert, hanging around the high school after dark, under the bleachers?"

Cooper laughed. He rubbed a hand over his head, giving a lazy scratch. "Okay, let me see if I have this right. You're about to kick the shit out of your quarterback for winning a game instead of fumbling, tripping and throwing it so you could get in the game in his place, and you wonder if *I'm* a pervert? Son, I'm going to save you a lot of trouble. Dupre, let's go. I'm hungry."

"Who *is* this dickhead?" the kid asked.

Cooper had to be a little impressed. He did ask it with a great deal of authority.

One of the boys who'd been holding Landon leaned toward Jag and said, "He owns the beach now."

Jag was shocked for a minute, but then he laughed. "Well then, excuse me, your eminence. You actually own that shit hole on the beach. Well, hell, I guess you must be pretty important."

Cooper frowned. "Dupre," he said. "Let's go."

"We have business," Jag said.

"Not anymore. You're all done here."

Jag stepped forward and got right up in Cooper's grill. He jabbed a finger into Cooper's chest and said, "We're talking to Dupre. And you. Are. Excused," he said, giving a singular jab with each of his last three words.

Cooper looked down at the finger, then up at Jag's face. Then he leisurely grabbed that offensive finger in one hand and bent it back until the kid yelped and went down on one knee. Jag tried to wiggle out, but it was useless. With the other hand Cooper grabbed a handful of the kneeling kid's hair. He looked over his head at Jag's posse. "You're going to want to get him out of here," he said. "You really don't want to get into it with me. I hate bullies. Hate fighting. But if I have to fight, I know every dirty trick."

He released Jag with enough of a shove that he fell backward. Then he met Landon's eyes.

"Let's go," he said again, in a controlled voice. "Now."

# SIX

Cooper and Landon walked briskly to the parking lot. There was no question Landon was jittery. "Stop looking over your shoulder," Cooper said. "I'll hear them if they're coming."

"What if you don't?"

"I will. Where's your car?"

"Behind the school, in the student lot."

"And I suppose they have cars there, too?"

"Yeah."

"There's my truck," he said, pointing. "I'm going to drive you to your car, then I'll follow you out of here. I'll follow you home, if you want me to, but I'd rather go somewhere we can get food. I'm not kidding, I'm starving."

"And if I don't feel like doing that?" Landon asked.

Cooper didn't say anything. He waited until they got to the truck and said, "Get in." Once they were both in the cab, Cooper

turned toward Landon. "Here's the deal. I know what happened tonight. I get it. The kid's an ass, a bully without a conscience, and he seems to have a posse. I've been there, believe me. We're gonna have a talk about your options — either over food or in your living room."

"My sister is there!" he said. "I don't need her all into this. She will seriously make it worse. Even worse than you have!"

He lifted eyebrows. "Did she go to the game?"

"She was there. But she takes her own car in case I have someplace to go. I never do, but in case."

Cooper started the truck. "Call her. Tell her you're going out for a burger and you won't be late."

"Can't we do this some other time?" he said. "Like when the whole town isn't packed into the joints? Just let me out at my truck and I'll —"

"Call her. Drive to Cliffhanger's and I'll follow you. I doubt the whole booster club will be hanging out there. And we both know where most of the team will be. On the beach."

Landon sighed, giving in. "Turn left into the parking lot. That's my truck, the green Mazda. I'll call my sister from the

truck. . . ."

"Make it a quick call, will you? I'm sure those boys are pissed off and trying to decide what to do to you next."

He started to get out of the truck, then looked back at Cooper. "What if you *are* some kind of pervert?"

"I just saved your life. Now I'm going to feed you and give you a few pointers. Don't make me regret it."

"That's what perverts do," Landon said.

Cooper leaned toward him. "Perverts don't let you drive yourself. You're making me tired. After we talk about assholes like Jag, we'll talk about perverts. Now go!"

Mac drove his aunt Lou and the younger kids home after the game. Once he got them all inside, he said, "I'm going to take a run through town, make sure all is quiet. . . ."

"It won't be quiet after a win like that," Lou said as she reached into the refrigerator for a diet cola. "Don't go sitting out on the hill, spying on the beach."

"I don't do that," he said to her back.

"Yes, you do," she said, leaving the kitchen.

He stood there in indecision for a moment. Then he reached into the refrigerator, grabbed two beers and left the house. The

night was clear and cold and there were a million stars. He only drove about ten blocks, to a neighborhood perched on the hill right above the main street. He parked and walked up the steps to the porch and knocked, hanging on to the beers in one hand.

Gina answered in her plaid winter jammies and heavy socks. "What are you doing here?"

He gave a shrug. "I'm in search of adult company and I've had enough of Lou. I'm sick of her bossing me around."

"What did she say?"

"She said, 'Don't go sit on the hill and spy on the beach.' " He held a beer toward her. "Come on out."

She grabbed her jacket off the hook inside the door and slipped into it, turned off the porch light and then accepted the beer. "What were you going to do?" she asked.

"Sit on the hill and spy on the beach," he said.

She laughed at him. "I guess you think no one notices you there." She sat on the top step and twisted the cap off the beer. "Just what do you think is going to happen out there?"

He sat beside her. He twisted off his own cap. "I'll know it when I see it," he said,

taking a pull on the beer. "My relationship with Lou . . . it's getting to me. We're like an old married couple."

"Well, at least you recruited her," Gina said. "And why wouldn't you be like that? You've been together longer than most people our age have been married. Don't be stupid. Don't complain. You'd be lost without her."

"I'd be lost without her," he agreed. "Maybe that's what annoys me. It's unnatural."

"Don't cry to me. I live with my mother."

"Here's something I've been wanting to ask you," he said. "Are you going to work at the diner for the rest of your life?"

"Probably. Why?"

"Aren't you almost done with your degree?"

"Almost. I even have some credits toward a master's. I'm a real speed demon. A short seventeen years to my high school diploma and almost a degree."

"Shouldn't you be looking for something better? Where you don't have to wipe up after people?"

"Seriously?" she asked. "Are you seriously asking me that?"

"Hey, I have no degree at all. No almost about it."

"Okay, first of all, Stu takes very good care of me. I make more money at the diner than I'd make a lot of other places. I've become indispensable to him, so he has to keep me happy. And I can do everything I need to do — go to school part-time, take care of Ashley and keep up with all her activities, help my mom in the deli, get the days off I need as long as everything else is covered. Second, my degree will be in social work. I'd have to work for the county. The pay is miserable."

"But there's benefits," he said.

"I have benefits. Maybe not the best benefits, but . . ."

"Retirement?" he asked.

"A little," she said. "Not that I expect to retire. What are you getting at?"

"I don't know," he said, slumping a little bit. "None of my business, really, but sometimes I think you work too hard."

"You're right about that," she said. "But I have a good gig going, Mac. One kid with a granny backup, a decent if not extraordinary education, some benefits, a boss who lets me take any time I need." She took a drink of her beer. "This was a good idea, a beer. Thanks. I could use better advice, though," she added.

He chuckled. "I'll remember that."

131

"See that you do. It's really beautiful tonight. You don't notice things like that when you're in the middle of a wild and crazy football game."

"Have you met the new doctor yet?"

She shook her head. "Have you?"

"Briefly. He stopped in to say hello before he started ripping the boards off the windows next door. His wife is dead, he's got a couple of little kids and he brought a babysitter with him. Very pretty."

She sighed. "That's an au pair, Mac. She's from Mexico. In exchange for room and board, an education and, with luck, citizenship, she's a full-time nanny. And she's about twelve."

"No . . ."

"Okay, she's nineteen. And I hear the doctor is a hottie."

"Where'd you hear that?" he asked.

She peered at him in the dark and lifted one brow. "Where do you think?"

"Ray Anne?" he asked.

"She's keeping pretty close tabs on him."

Mac grinned. "I think you stay at the diner because you have access to all the gossip there."

She grinned back. "Just like at the cop shop."

"True," he said. He was quiet for a long

moment. "Another year and our girls will graduate. Go to college."

"Are you mourning that already?" she asked him.

"Ha! I'm counting the days! Think they'll go to the same school?"

"No telling," she said. "That depends on whether Eve wants to follow Ashley, who will definitely follow Downy."

As Mac knew, Ashley had been dating her boyfriend, Downy, since he was a senior at Thunder Point High. Downy was now in his first year at State. In fact, Mac had been in his first year at State when he got his high school girlfriend knocked up. He shuddered. "Doesn't that worry you?" he asked.

"No," Gina said. "Downy is a good boy, and Ash is an ambitious girl. So far they seem to make a good team. They don't want to get tripped up now."

"I hope you're right," he said. He took a breath. "And I hope Eve doesn't have a serious boyfriend until she's thirty."

"Why?" Gina asked. "Because that's the way she'll be most happy?"

Mac just looked at her. Gina was so pretty, so smart. If it weren't for all the complications in their lives, all the responsibilities, now would be a logical time to pull her closer, kiss her in a way that left her trembling. But he wouldn't. "That's the thing," he said. "You and I both know that the thing that makes us most happy at sixteen doesn't work out to be so smart at thirty."

"Or thirty-five?" she asked.

"Or thirty-five," he confirmed.

After a long silence she said, very softly, "One of these days, Mac, you're going to discover you have no regrets."

"Huh?" he questioned.

"Nothing. I have to get to bed. I work early and I'm freezing. Done with that beer? Want me to pitch it for you?"

"Uh, yeah." He handed it over. "Thanks. And thanks for keeping me company for a while."

"Anytime. Buddy."

Cooper called another one right — the town was packed with vehicles and people spilling out onto the sidewalks around fast-food restaurants and the diner, but Cliffhanger's wasn't busy. In fact, though it was barely after nine, Cooper wondered if they were thinking of closing. He went straight to the bar, "Looks kind of quiet," he said to Cliff. "There's time for a couple of burgers, right?"

Landon, wearing his letter jacket, walked in behind him. Now that they were in a well-lit restaurant, Cooper noticed the bruise on Landon's cheek and wondered where that had come from.

"Come on, man," Cliff said good-naturedly. "I want to find out about the game. Word is those Badgers finally got what was coming to 'em."

"I can help with that," Cooper said. He dropped an arm casually around Landon's shoulders. "I promised the quarterback a burger."

Cliff broke into a grin. "You got it."

"And give me a draft — I've had a hard night."

Landon shot him a look. "*You've* had a hard night?"

"My pleasure. Dupre? For you?"

"Draft," he said.

Cliff smiled. "Nice try. Second choice?"

"All right. Coke."

"Grab a table, boys. I'll put in your order and get your drinks."

Cooper pointed to a table, knowing a minor couldn't sit up at the bar. When they were seated, Landon said, "That could've been a mistake. We might draw a crowd."

"That's okay. We just have to get a couple of things straight. It won't take long. That kid, Jag, asked you to throw a game to get him back to first string, right? And when you said no, he threatened you. If I hadn't come along, he was going to beat you up. You can't let it go, Landon. Trust me."

"I'll handle it. . . ."

"Maybe you would — eventually. Listen, this kind of bullying isn't a first. It also isn't rare, which ought to disgust the whole human race. In every junior high and high school, and sometimes even elementary school, there's some idiot who anoints himself king. He gathers up some plebes who are either as mean as he is or stupid enough to think if they stick with the self-proclaimed leader, they won't get hurt. Then they search out their victims and make a lifestyle out of working 'em over. Terrible things come out of it. At least you were important enough to be threatened, because *you're* actually a threat, but that doesn't make it easier. I have one question. Did you ever think about it? Just doing what he wanted you to do?"

Landon looked shocked. He shook his head. "You say you get it, but you don't. I wasn't the only one they wanted to cheat, I was just the only one they promised to beat up. That fumble? Right before the end of the first half? You think that guy lost control of the ball? He'd be one of the *plebes*. He dropped that ball for Morrison."

Cooper couldn't help it, he grinned. Jag Morrison had himself a gang that worked hard for him, even at their own expense. But instead of letting the fumble go — maybe letting the game go — Landon stepped up, recovered the ball and ran it. He brought his A-game.

"This isn't just about me," Landon continued. "You spend ten minutes in the halls at school and you get how much it means to them, beating those Badgers."

"Even though you could get hurt," Cooper said. It was not a question.

"You think the only way I might get hurt is being jumped in the parking lot or dragged under the bleachers? I have to play against my own team *and* the other team — they are not about protecting their quarterback."

"Are you saying all of them are in it?"

"Nah, just a few. But sometimes the right few. At least I know which ones they are."

Cooper nodded at Landon's face. "And the bruise?"

Landon ducked briefly. "I walked into a door."

Cooper was quiet for a moment. Then he said, "Right."

The drinks came and Cooper was thinking, damn kid has no idea what kind of athletic skill that takes — trying to score with a good defense and with your own team working against you. Where the hell was the coach?

Cliff put down the drinks and pulled up a chair. "Your burgers are coming, so while we wait, why don't you tell me about the game?"

Cooper watched as Landon gave Cliff a play-by-play. His own nieces and nephews were not yet teenagers, though they were certainly getting there too quickly. Besides his friends' kids, whom he knew very casually, this might be his first experience with a young man of sixteen. And it was most definitely his first experience with a kid like Landon.

Landon played it straight, excusing the fumbles, lack of defense and missed passes and dismissing his own plays, which were nothing short of heroic. He was fast as lightning and could jump over fallen opponents. He said things like, "That was a lucky break," and "I bet that doesn't happen twice." He never suggested members of his own team worked against him or even that what he'd managed had taken talent.

Their food arrived and Cliff stuck around. They lingered over burgers and football talk for more than an hour and Cooper was glad to see Landon getting the attention he deserved, praise he didn't get much of from his team.

When they were in the parking lot, Landon said, "You had tips?"

Cooper just laughed. "Not on playing football, that's for sure. You've got that down. It's getting late . . ."

"Late? How old are you?" Landon asked with a hint of humor.

"Right now I feel real old. You'll probably have that dog out for a walk this weekend. And I'll probably be around that old shack on the beach."

Gina and Mac had been good friends since the time their daughters had hooked up as best friends when they were twelve. The first time he showed up at Gina's house to check out her surroundings before letting Eve spend the night with her new best friend, Gina had fallen for him. She never let on, of course. They had a couple of teenage girls to watch over. But they always ended up sitting together at town events, school functions, that sort of thing. There was the occasional beer on her front porch or even at Cliff's, but the best was morning coffee at the diner when it wasn't busy. She could set her watch by him. At around ten o'clock, barring pressing police work, he'd come into the diner. Six days a week. Fishermen were out at dawn or before; the lunch crowd didn't show until eleven-thirty. Between breakfast and lunch was when they'd catch up on gossip, scheduling and kids' activities. Mac and Gina, Aunt Lou and Carrie backed each other up when it came to carpooling and chaperoning. Between all of them, plus teachers and coaches, they ran herd on these girls and Mac's other two younger kids. They were not going to let Eve and Ashley fall victim to the kind of mistakes their mothers had made.

Their rapport was good. Gina could feel the sexual tension building in the light touch of hands, the smile or laugh, the conversation about things in their lives that had nothing to do with their daughters.

After about a year of relying on each other, trading news and confidences, there had been a kiss; a breathless embrace. They pushed apart desperately but reluctantly. And yet there was a second time, lasting a bit longer, that felt even more passionate to Gina. She had been in the ecstasy of expectation. She had felt for some time that they were more than buddies.

But at their morning coffee after that second embrace and kiss, Mac had con-fronted it. He seemed remorseful. "We can't let this happen," he had told her. "We have daughters who are best friends, a lot of responsibilities, people depending on us. Carrie and Lou . . . and I have a whole town, not to mention two more children . . ."

She remembered clearly — and with embarrassment — that her mouth had hung open. After a year of sharing details of their lives, some of which she considered deeply personal, and after two hot and meaningful kisses, he was running for his life?

"Relationships are fragile," he said. "We've both been through it. We can't experiment with this . . . this getting closer. If it didn't work, look how many people would be affected. Mostly, there's you and I. We've already had our guts ripped out, right?"

She was stunned silent for a moment. She was so offended. Hurt. "Right," she finally said. "Dr. Phil."

"Gina, you're special. Damn, I just want to do the right thing."

He didn't seem to realize he'd just drawn blood with his gentlemanly comment. She sensed that her instinctive response — *Then throw me down and have your amazing way with me* — might scare him even more.

So, apparently the one thing they did not

141

have in common was readiness. After becoming an unmarried teenage mother, Gina hadn't actually dated again until Ashley was in school. In the ten years since then there hadn't been very many dates and only one guy had been semiserious. Emphasis on the *semi.*

"Your friendship is important to me," he told her. "I need it."

"Sure. Your friendship is important to me, too," she had said. "But I didn't kiss you. I kissed you *back.* And I wanted to. So understand something, Mac. If you ever do anything like that again, you better mean it. And you better not turn and run."

After a long silence, he said, "Understood."

She pulled back then, gathered in her emotions and desires like poker chips she'd just won, so he wouldn't know. Because she didn't want him if he didn't want her. She hadn't needed Dr. Phil to tell her relationships were risks. That was the point, wasn't it? She wasn't fifteen anymore. She no longer risked her heart without weighing all the facts. She knew him well enough and knew enough about him to realize he'd be worth it.

But she wouldn't have him unless he also thought that of her.

So for years they'd continued as friends, had midmorning coffee together, sat together at games and watched their daughters cheer, worked as a team at too many pancake breakfasts and school carnivals to count, and remained best friends and confidants without any pesky kissing. Or fondling. Or *anything.*

But she still felt that lilt in her chest when he walked in the door. She tried to tamp it down, but her blue eyes glowed. He sat down at the counter, diner empty, and she filled his cup with a smile. "I don't think this town is going to get over last night's game anytime soon," he said.

"I know I won't. I'm hoarse. I could hardly sleep. I'm still vibrating under the skin. Thanks for bringing over a beer last night — that was nice of you."

"Eve didn't get in until twelve forty-five."

"After the biggest game of the year? Of *five* years? What an impossible child. I think you should ground her for life. Or just execute her."

Mac smiled that lazy one-sided smile. "I didn't say a word."

"But you were waiting up," she said with a lift of her light brown eyebrows over twinkling eyes.

"Well, that's a given."

She knew that he'd want to be sure Eve came home in shape — not traumatized, compromised, inebriated, using, holding, et cetera. The cop in him gave him the experience to make very good judgments, but it was the father in him who cared about the child. A couple of times he'd asked Gina for advice, because teenage girls don't have to be in crisis to come home a mess. A failed date, a falling-out with a girlfriend, a disappointment — any number of dramas could look like trouble. Sometimes it took a woman, a mother, to be able to separate the real trouble from its look-alike. She found herself honored that he'd talk to her about those things even though he had Aunt Lou at home.

When Gina was a pregnant teenager and, later, as the single mother of a little one, she'd have traded so much for any father figure for her baby. Now, with Ashley a teenager, she was proud of the parent she'd become. But she'd still give the moon for her daughter to have a father like Mac.

"Ashley was in by midnight, but that's because she brought her boyfriend with her. I tried to stay awake and listen to what was going on in the living room, but I didn't last long."

"That's getting really serious, isn't it?"

Mac asked. "Ashley and Downy?"

"Uh-huh."

"You talk to her about that?" he asked.

"I talked to both of them," she said. "I can't control their emotions but I can damn sure give them the facts and have a discussion about the consequences."

"I hope we don't end up doing some damage in the other direction," he said, lifting his cup. "We could end up with two lonely old maids on our hands. I want our girls to have full lives, I just don't want them too full, too soon."

Gina poured herself a cup of coffee. "You mean end up as two lonely old maids like us?"

"I'd pay any amount of money for a few hours of loneliness," he said.

"We'll get a break soon," she said. "A day or two between football, hockey and basketball."

"We should go see a movie," he said. "We haven't done that in a while."

This was not an overture — they'd gone to a few movies over the past few years. Despite the fact that neither of them ever saw other people, nothing romantic happened between them.

"Maybe," she said. "Not a bloody one."

"What's the point, then," he joked. "We

145

have to see something we can't experience in real life. Maybe a sci-fi, then. Or horror movie. Not some chick thing all about true love. . . ."

"Trust me, Mac. I don't experience that in real life."

Silence hung out there and she thought, *Don't you dare do this again! Unless you mean it!*

"Fine," he said. "Once we get through football, you can pick the movie."

# SEVEN

Cooper found himself disappointed that he hadn't seen Landon all weekend. He did see the dog and the girl with the red slicker; she apparently walked that dog rain or shine. That would be Sarah, Landon's sister. She didn't come near the bait shop or dock, but the dog did. At the base of the steps that led to the beach, Ham ran right up to Cooper and dropped the ball at his feet. He gave it a mighty throw in the direction of the girl and that was the end of it. From that point on, the dog and girl headed back toward the town.

He still hadn't had a good look at her face, her hood pulled up and all. He had to wonder how this whole thing came to be. Here they were, Sarah and Landon, so far on the fringes of the community, both always alone. He'd catch up with Landon eventually. After what he'd seen, what he knew, Cooper wouldn't be missing a ball game from now on.

On Monday, the sun came out. The day was unseasonably warm on the beach and Cooper was sitting on the deck with his phone and laptop, trying to learn more about his friend. Ben, and perhaps his father before him, had an odd way of running their business. If they discovered a need, they tried to fill it. If someone needed a place to wash their clothes, *voila!* A Laundromat appeared, even if it served only a few people. A few breakdowns on the freeway? Buy a ninety-thousand-dollar tow truck.

Ben wasn't the only one with a patchwork business. Cooper had seen the same thing in many of the small towns he'd passed through lately. Tires/Lube/Laundromat/Chinese Food/Dry Cleaning. It was a survival instinct.

He looked up as Mac came around the corner, his boots hitting the wood deck hard.

"You're still here," Mac said by way of greeting.

"Still here," Cooper answered. "You ready for me to move on?"

Mac shrugged. "No matter to me. This is your place. What you have going there?" Mac asked, indicating two closed laptops

148

on the table beside Cooper. "Dueling computers?"

"I found Ben's laptop. It's got a bunch of websites and message boards bookmarked on it, plus a lot of emails he saved, dating back about five years. I don't really expect to find anything, but I'll read through 'em."

"For?" Mac asked.

"I don't know. It's not like Ben kept a journal, but there might be something important in there. Maybe I'll figure out what he expected from me. Maybe he wrote an email to someone about trouble he had around here or something."

"You don't have to limit yourself to saved emails, you know," Mac said. "You can look through old and deleted emails and websites."

"I'll get to that eventually," Cooper said.

"You'll let me know if you find anything, right?" Mac said.

"Absolutely. Rawley and I went through his things. Found Ben's old truck and a Razor, his off-road all-terrain vehicle, in that shed. I gave Rawley the truck. He didn't say thank you, just took the keys. But the truck's still sitting there. I guess he doesn't have a way to move it without asking someone to help and God forbid he ask me. That Rawley — he didn't say ten words while we worked, but he's an interesting guy. Clothes he couldn't use that he wanted to give to the Vets, he washed them before he bagged them up to give away. I think he's the only reason that place didn't fall down years ago. Now the shack is empty, kind of clean, but full of mold we can't see. Uninhabitable."

"You comfortable in that thing?" Mac asked, indicating the toy hauler.

Cooper laughed. "I'll tell you what's a pain — dry camping. I can't go a whole week before I have to muster that camper up the hill and down the freeway to an RV park where I can dump and fill the tank with water. I'm cooking and cleaning dishes with bottled water, and I only shower with water from the tank, although I'm sure it's safe. But at least the electricity is turned on so I can run an extension to the shack."

Mac laughed. "Is that all you got for your time? Electricity?"

"I'm sure as hell not trusting the plumbing. But I have a plan. I have a bunch of contractors coming out this week to give me estimates on repairs and reconstruction. I think maybe I'll get the shack in shape and sell it. I'll just sell the structure and the parcel it's on, though. I'm going to hang on to the beach and the point until I have a better idea of what to do."

Mac was clearly surprised. "But you're not going to open for business?"

"Nah, that's just not me. Look at me, man. I'm a nomad. Thirty-seven years old and all I have to show for it is a toy hauler and some toys. I've never stayed long in one place. I wouldn't be here at all except for Ben. I can't stay here. Still . . . I don't have any objection to getting rich but I just can't sell off a beach and a promontory he obviously wanted to keep."

"But you're going to fix it?"

"Just to sell it," Cooper clarified. "Then I'm gone. I'll put someone in charge of the beach and the bird sanctuary. How about you? Pay you twenty-five bucks a month."

Mac laughed. "Wow, that's a hard offer to pass up. This project is going to set you back some, isn't it?"

"Yeah, it's going to seriously cut into my nest egg, but I'm going to sell Ben's tow truck. I finally saw it. He kept it at the Shell station in town and I think they've been using it since he died. The look on the guy's face when I said I owned it and wanted to sell it was nothing short of grievous. Poor guy. He thought it was found property."

"I didn't know you were looking for it, Cooper. I could've told you exactly where it was. Sorry about that."

"Don't worry about it — that was one of Rawley's ten words."

"That tow truck, that was up his alley — he liked to work on cars and trucks. He always kept Gina's old Jeep running for her. He wouldn't take money but I swear to God, when she told him something was wrong with it, his whole face lit up."

"I guess he wasn't as interested in working on this place. You know how old it is?" Cooper asked. "Some parts of it, more than fifty years. The deck is relatively new, but I don't see how it can survive a renovation."

"You're a strange guy, Cooper."

"Is that right?" he asked, laughing.

"What are you going to do with yourself while this place gets worked on?"

"I guess I'll help here and there. I'm not a builder, but I'm a competent helper. And I'll take in another football game or two — haven't done that in years."

"What are you going to eat?" Mac asked.

"I've been feeding myself for a long time, Mac. No Auntie Lou in my kitchen. The food around here isn't bad at all. And I bought myself a little grill."

"You're kind of high-class homeless."

"I beg your pardon. I have a master bedroom and a kitchen. And HDTV on satellite. And a great view. Speaking of views . . . I see just about everything that goes on down on the beach. I've been wondering, if I saw something that disturbed me but that I didn't really want to get involved in, are you a guy I could mention it to?"

Mac got a slightly troubled look on his face, then he pulled up a chair and sat down. He rubbed a big hand down his face. His expression was serious when he said, "I'm not exactly your priest, Cooper. If you saw something I should know about, then yeah, I might want to look into it."

"Like . . . ?"

"You see anything illegal? Underage drinking? Drugs?"

Cooper couldn't suppress a laugh. "Nah, haven't seen that, but I'm sure there's plenty of that going on. The kids, they're not stupid — they don't haul up a keg in the back of one of those Rhinos, but I'd bet my right arm there's beer down there, tucked in a sleeve or small cooler. Might be pot, might be something else going on. But what if I saw someone getting . . . I don't know . . . intimidated."

"Assault?" Mac asked.

Cooper gave a shrug. "I don't think I could call it that. Not quite. Teenage boys, they're gonna fight sometimes, right? If I

153

saw some intimidating, shoving, that sort of thing, that's not something you can do anything about, right?"

"Why don't you let me be the judge of that, Cooper," Mac said, leaning toward him a little with that icy blue gaze looking right through him.

Cooper almost laughed. "So that's how you do it. Get the bad guys to talk. You look at 'em like you already know what they're going to say. So just on a hypothetical — what could you do? About a little bullying?"

"Sometimes all I have to do is talk to a few people. I am the law, after all."

"You are the law," Cooper agreed. "Tell you what, I'll pay attention. Right now the kid who's having a little trouble, he's real self-conscious about being a snitch. I've been there — *you've* probably been there. I'll keep an eye on that, since I'm here. I'll let you know if there's anything to tell. Deputy." Then he grinned.

Mac leaned back. "You do that. I'd like you to remember, Eve spends some time with her friends on that beach. I don't want her getting shoved around. . . ."

"Nah, I haven't seen anything like that."

"You wouldn't keep anything like that to yourself, would you?" Mac asked. "Because girls are just as bad as boys, trust me."

"I'll take your word for that. Don't worry, if I saw Eve having issues down there, I'd let you know right away."

Mac relaxed a little bit. "I hate bullies," he said.

Cooper was back to his old self — making decisions fast, full speed ahead. It took a total of five contractors in even fewer days to get a bid he could live with, both in time and money. It was a huge job, but it was going to be done as fast as possible during a wet and cold time of year. They'd gut the bait shop, disposing of most of the interior. They could save the freezer, cooler, microwave and refrigerated cases where Ben had kept deli items. Rawley wanted to give the washers and dryers to some religious group he knew about — they lived kind of isolated along a river south of Coquille and didn't have much. Cooper told him to take he pots, pans and dishes, too. He stored the unopened liquor in the shed alongside the quad and truck. As soon as Rawley got that truck out of there, Cooper would put his own toys in there. All the racks of cheap souvenirs were tossed. He wasn't keeping the bait tanks — there was plenty of bait at the marina.

The bait tanks had been kept in the

unfinished basement. The floor in the cellar was dirt and the walls cinder block. There was a door to the outside located under the deck, so fishermen could get their bait without walking through the bar. The room was large and deep and, remarkably, there was no mold or rot in the struts and beams, though they could use reinforcing.

Ben had fallen down the staircase that led to the cellar. Cooper kept looking at those stairs, wondering. How could this thing have happened to his friend? Ben was so freaking big . . . how could he have died from a fall? He should have left a big hole in the dirt floor instead. But wondering got him nowhere, and there was work to do.

Before all the junk had been carted off or the first nail driven in, Cooper started getting visitors from 101 on sunny days, mostly on the weekend. Bikers, cyclists, the occasional motorist — folks who'd been stopping off at Ben's for years and wondered when the place would be open again. They ranged from the young, fit athletes who pedaled across the countryside to those graybeards on Harleys that Mac had been talking about. It became evident Ben hadn't relied solely on beach traffic.

Coop ended up spending a lot of time at the diner, showing Gina some of the plans.

What he wanted to do was retain the things Ben and the town seemed to value most: the beach, the untouched promontory, the deli/bar, space for gathering.

"I don't know why you're going to all this trouble," she said. "You can sell the place as-is and just that small parcel it sits on, plus the dock and road, and let the next owner worry about renovation."

"I could," he said. "But I want to sell a bar. A café. The same bar and deli that was there before, just in better shape, because I think the town relies on it, needs it. It's the only thing on the beach. And Ben wanted the beach open, for whatever reason. If I tear it down and sell that piece of land, who knows what you'll end up with in that spot. Could be a car wash or drive-in theater."

"But why do you care, Cooper?"

"I'm not sure," he said. "Because my friend seemed to want it that way? Because people use Ben's place all the time, even when it's cold? Let's face it, if I let the whole thing go, it'll change everything about this place."

"Some people would consider that a good thing," she said. "Not me, though. The fact is, even though we aren't a rich town, we have a very low unemployment rate. A lot of people work away from Thunder Point, some as far as North Bend, but they work. This place doesn't have tearooms and souvenir shops, and the closest malls are in Bandon and Coquille. And we're out here on the ocean by ourselves. I like it that way.

"But there are lots of people who think we could do with more revenue for things like schools, libraries, parks, that sort of thing. And of course there's the real estate — it would be worth so much more. There are people around here who are more than ready to make their killing, and they need a resort to do it."

"Why?"

"There's no incentive to build fancy houses or condos in a dumpy little town."

"What about the north promontory?" he asked. "The point opposite Ben's refuge on the other side of the bay. There must be land still available out there."

"There is. But the waterfront is owned by Cliff. He knows a big resort would put Cliff-hanger's out of business. And his whole family has been in fishing for years. He wouldn't do as well if the marina was full of pleasure boats and all Ben's land was full of resort, the land surrounding the beach all condos and villas."

"Wow," Cooper said. "There's a lot more to this town than I thought."

"And you think the kids could go build a bonfire on that beach after a ball game when Hyatt or Marriott owns it? There will be a security gate to get in!" Then she grinned. "Since you're still here, you going to the game?"

"I wouldn't miss it," he said.

"Well, this one's in Coquille — an away game."

"You going?" he asked.

"Yeah, we have to go — our girls are cheering. And it's kind of what we do."

*We.* He didn't miss that. "You and Mac?"

"And Lou. The younger kids. Sometimes my mother."

He just smiled. "Sounds romantic," he said.

"Cooper, it's not romantic. We do stuff with the kids. We have since Eve and Ashley became friends. It works out."

"What if your kids weren't friends?" he found himself asking.

She leaned on the counter. "Well, gee. Then I might ask him to the Sadie Hawkins dance, I guess. But that hasn't come up." She refilled his cup. "Homecoming is in less than two weeks. There's a dance. I'll sign you up to chaperone."

"Very funny."

"Oh, you thought I was being funny? It's

the Saturday night after the Friday-night game. Dress nice."

"Get real, Gina."

"I'm as real as it gets. Need directions to tomorrow night's game?"

"Yes. Thanks."

Landon decided he was going to have to have a man-to-man talk with Cooper. He'd been avoiding him, which wasn't too hard to do — his sister had been around a lot and when she wasn't, he'd had football practice and then a shit pot full of homework. But at Friday night's game in Coquille, Cooper had been there, spending most of his time hanging around the sidelines. One time, when Landon looked up, he'd been talking to Eve's dad, the local law. He'd been pointing at Landon and a couple of the other players; the deputy had been grim faced and nodding.

And that dog wouldn't hunt.

"Landon?"

He pulled one more book out of his locker and turned to find himself eye to eye with the most beautiful girl at Thunder High, Eve McCain. She was smiling at him and he returned the smile so fast, so lame, he felt like an instant loser. He felt like some idiot who'd just won the lottery. He

160

crumpled in the face of the sexiest girl on the planet.

He recovered his cool. "Hey," he said.

"Good game, Friday night."

"Thanks. Not a real tough game." And thankfully they'd let Jag Morrison, the future homecoming king, play a lot. Therefore Jag left him alone.

"Still. So, I was going to wait till after Chemistry, but I was wondering who you're taking to the dance?"

He gave a shrug. "I probably won't go," he said.

She stiffened in shock. "But you have to go! Everyone on the team has to go!"

He felt a laugh come to his lips. Jag Morrison was destined to be a real king, the homecoming king, a position only open to seniors. He'd get that crown even if he had to buy it. Therefore that dance didn't feel like the ideal place to be, even if he wanted to go. "I'll probably show up for a little while. . . ."

"Well . . . would you like to show up for a little while with me?" she asked. And the usually bold and vivacious Eve blushed shyly. "I mean, I can't believe you don't have a date."

"No. Wait. *You* don't have a date? You?" He was thunderstruck, to borrow a phrase

161

from one of their most famous cheers.

She laughed lightly and shook her head, clutching books tight against her chest. "It's pretty hard to ask, too, so try not to hurt my feelings too bad."

"I can't believe you'd even . . . Jeez," he said, scratching his head. "Me?"

"Why not?" she shot back. "I thought we were friends."

"Absolutely. Of course. Yes, we're friends, of course we are."

"So?"

He thought for a moment before he said. "You're sure?"

"Oh, I'm sure. Can you drive or should I?"

"I can drive, sure. Maybe I can borrow my sister's ride. I just have that little truck. It's okay, but . . ."

"Landon, the truck is fine for me. Whatever you want."

"Wow," he said. "Just wow. I really can't believe no one asked you."

"Oh, I was asked, just not by the right person. . . ." She started to back away. "Bell's gonna ring . . ."

He snagged a piece of her sleeve. "Yeah? Who asked?"

She grinned. "Wanna know your competition, huh? Well, he's not — I can't stand him. I'd never go out with him."

"Yeah?" Landon asked, grinning hugely. "Who's that?"

"Morrison. Jag Morrison. He's just a stupid ass. I gotta go. See you later, like after practice or something." And she whirled around and was gone.

Landon turned back to his locker, closed it and let his head fall against the cold steel. *Oh, man,* he thought. *I can't believe this is happening. My life is definitely over.*

Landon's sister worked two nights in a row in North Bend so she could be off the weekend of the high school homecoming game. That gave Landon just the right amount of freedom to check in with Cooper. It was a misty, moonless night, but he jogged Ham across the beach, confident there wouldn't be people out there. He saw the lights on in Ben's place and heard music, so he ran up the stairs to the deck and pounded on the door.

Cooper answered. He was wearing a dirty old sweatshirt covered with sawdust, a tool belt around his hips, a surgical-type mask over his mouth and nose and a crowbar in his hand. The music came from an old paint-splattered radio. Cooper pulled down the mask. "Well, I thought you were avoid-

163

ing me," he said with a grin. He looked down at the Great Dane, who sat patiently beside Landon. "Hello, Hamlet. Kind of calm tonight, aren't you?"

"I ran him across the beach." Landon almost forgot his mission. Cooper was surrounded by debris — piles of wood, dismantled bar and shelves, boxes of what looked like Ben's things. "What are you doing?"

"I'm going to clean the place up, renovate. So I can sell it."

"Sell it? You're going to just sell it?" Landon asked.

"Well, it needs a lot of work first. But in a few months I'll sell this and the piece of land it sits on."

"We have to talk," Landon said.

Cooper thought about this for a second, then put down the crowbar and removed the tool belt. "Let's go in the house and get a drink. I don't suppose he knows how to wipe his feet?" he said, shooting a look at Ham.

Landon pulled a rag out of his back pocket. "I got it," he said.

The house was, of course, Cooper's fifth wheel, the toy hauler. Cooper went first, brushing off his shirt and pants. Landon did as he was asked, wiping the sand off

Ham's feet and, for good measure, the drool off his mouth. When he stepped inside, he said, "Nice." Then, hanging on to the dog's collar, he picked a chair by the door and kept the dog sitting politely at his side.

Cooper went to the kitchen and washed up. He opened the refrigerator and helped himself to a beer. "I have bottled water, tea, cola and Gatorade."

Landon shook his head. "I'm not going to be here long."

Cooper gave an impatient sigh and reached for a cola. He handed the can to Landon. "Your sidekick there need a drink?"

Knowing they were talking about him, Ham sat up a little straighter.

"He wouldn't turn it down, thanks."

Cooper filled a saucepan with water, grabbed a towel to put under it and delivered the water.

"Remind me never to have dinner here," Landon said.

"I'm planning to wash it."

"This place is nicer than I thought," Landon said. "You wouldn't expect this."

"The toys are under the tarp behind the trailer. I have to keep it nice — I live in it. I lived in it for two years in Corpus Christi. I couldn't see renting or buying anything when I had this. It's plenty for one person."

"You don't settle down, do you?"

He shook his head. "Nope."

"Well, we have that in common," Landon said.

"How's that?" Cooper said, sitting on the couch across from Landon.

Instead of an answer, Landon said, "Listen, I saw you at the game. In Coquille."

"I was pretty obvious," Cooper said. "I intended to be obvious. You didn't have any trouble, did you?"

"No, but listen, you can't be telling the deputy what's going on. You can't. You'll just make it worse, I'm telling you."

"I didn't tell Mac you were getting shoved around."

"It looked like it."

"I know what it looked like. We were talking football, talking plays. I pointed to a few players I knew, made sure they saw me pointing them out to the deputy, but we were talking football." He took a drink from his bottle of beer. "They can't beat you up if I tell on them, Landon. I was there, remember? I can talk about what I heard and saw and that doesn't make you a snitch."

Landon scooted forward on his chair. "You think they're going to see it that way?"

"They may be stupid, Landon, but I do

166

believe they know that if they beat you up, they're going to answer to me. And one of my only friends here is Mac, who seems to know what he's doing. You should tell him, but if you won't, I'll just look like the bad guy for a while. How's that?"

"You shouldn't get into this, Cooper. You don't have to do this."

Cooper gave a shrug. "Listen, I was the new guy a lot when I was your age. I wasn't the star football player, but I always had trouble fitting in. And there was always some asshole who thought pushing me around and making my life miserable would be fun. By the way, I've been meaning to ask you . . . what makes Morrison so special?"

"Money, I think. His family is about the richest family around and he has two older brothers who have big football fame at Thunder High — big athletic scholarships. Not pro ball kind of stuff, but they're a lot older and finished with college and everyone around here thinks the Morrisons are awesome. I only know Jag and he is not awesome. He's not even that much of a football player."

"Huh," Cooper said. "They live in that big house out on the point, right? Where do they get the money?"

"Hell if I know," Landon said. "The brothers have trophies in the trophy case and people talk about them like they're legend. That's all I know. The coach and Mr. Morrison are old friends."

"How convenient . . ."

"And my situation is just going to get more interesting because Jag asked Eve McCain to the homecoming dance and she said no." Cooper's eyebrows shot up. "So then she asked me. And I should've said no, but I couldn't. I said yes."

"You *couldn't* . . . ?"

"Man, I should've said no, just to keep her as far from this Morrison thing as possible, but I didn't know till after that he'd asked her first. And my God, she's so hot. And nice, so nice. And funny, too. Plus, she said it was hard to ask me and also said to please not hurt her feelings too much." He shook his head. "I couldn't tell her no, man. It would've killed us both."

"Whoa."

"Yeah, Morrison might just have more to be pissed about . . ."

"Okay, now we *do* have an issue, because I gave Mac my word that if I saw anything going on that put his daughter in a bad place, I would definitely tell him. . . ."

Landon sat tall. "And have you? Seen that?"

"Come on, Landon, let's be straight here — you're worried about it. You as much as said so. . . ."

He shook his head. "I don't think Morrison would ever do anything to Eve. But he'd get even with me if he could."

Cooper relaxed, propping an ankle over his knee. He took a long, leisurely drink of his beer. Then he said, "Good thing I go to games. And even though I was mad at her for it, it's a good thing Gina conned me into helping her and Mac chaperone the dance."

Landon hit his head with the heel of his hand. "Aw, man!"

"My feeling exactly," Cooper said. "So, if you have any trouble, speak up."

"You can't say anything, Cooper," he said pleadingly.

"I probably won't have to, but you should. You should at least tell the coach and, if necessary, tell Mac. You're going out with Eve. It's your job to keep her safe."

"Right. Tell Mr. Morrison's good friend, the coach. . . ."

"Look, you know what I think. Just think about what's the right thing to do, for Eve if not for yourself, okay? Now, let's change the subject. I haven't seen you in over a week, except at the game. Where've you been?"

"My sister has been around a lot. She's working tonight so me and Ham, we're on our own."

"I know you moved here because she got a divorce, but you said you're like me — you don't settle down. Why's that?"

"My sister's job. She's reassigned every couple of years. Sometimes even more often. Our folks died right after she started with the Coast Guard. At first she was going to leave me with our aunt Frances, who is the aunt from hell, by the way. I begged and pleaded and finally just started running away a lot until not only did Sarah take me, Aunt Frances gave her a door prize for getting me off her hands."

"Not so close to Aunt Frances, huh?"

"I hate her. She hates me. If she ever goes missing or her body turns up somewhere, I should be a suspect."

"I see. Jesus, you're a lot of work," Cooper said.

"Oh, but I'm not. I'm easy. I never get in trouble, I get good grades, I take care of things at home and you know why? Because all Sarah has to do to straighten me right out is say *Aunt Frances.*"

"What the hell did Aunt Frances do to you?"

"General bitching, 24/7. She screamed, she slapped. She locked me in my room, took away dinner, hated me and punished me every second."

"Gotcha," Cooper said. "I guess a big kid like you couldn't deal with that."

The look that came into Landon's eyes was almost scary. "I was five," he said seriously. "A five-year-old kid whose parents had just been killed in an accident."

Cooper just connected with that stare for a long time and said nothing. "What about your uncle?" he finally asked.

"No uncle," Landon said. "One of the many things that probably made her such a bitch."

"Aunt Frances doesn't sound like a nice person."

"Not a nice person."

Cooper leaned back. He drank a little of his beer. Then he said, "I'm sorry, man. So. What does Sarah do for the Coast Guard?"

"Search and rescue. She's a helicopter pilot."

Cooper choked. Then he coughed. Finally, he said, "That right?"

"You need me to pound on your back?" Landon asked.

171

"Nah, I'm okay," he rasped. "Helicopter pilot?"

"Yep. She works out of the North Bend station. She's pretty senior but she has to sit alert sometimes. Overnight. She finally trusts me enough to leave me without a keeper. I think Ham here was a trick to hedge her bets — he has to be fed and let out, so I have to be home to do that. She has the old neighbors next door monitoring my truck — they don't have anything better to do but look out the window and watch when I come home from school, leave for school, that kind of thing. And she calls me. A lot."

On cue, Landon's cell phone rang. He answered, "Yes, my queen?"

Cooper laughed and shook his head.

"I took Ham out for a run and stopped at Ben's place. The guy who owns it now was working on it, so we checked it out, had a Coke. Nah, he's okay. Well, he might be a perv, but I won't let him touch my special places . . ."

Cooper almost fell off the couch.

"I'm leaving here and running home in a minute. If I run Ham hard maybe he won't run in his sleep or snore all night. Yeah, everything is fine. Yeah, I locked the door. Yeah, I ate . . . that leftover Hamburger Kill

Me shit you made the other night. Yeah, I got my homework done. Yeah, I — Jesus, Sarah! Let me talk to you at home, all right? I'll call and check in when I get there."

Landon stood up. "I have to go. Sarah and her husband used to keep separate schedules so I always had one of them around, but since the divorce she's been a little neurotic."

"I completely understand," Cooper said.

Landon laughed. "No, you don't, but that's okay. I'm doing the best I can with her. She'll lighten up eventually."

"You want me to call you? Make sure you got home okay?" Cooper asked.

Landon shot him a look. "Bite me," he said, opening the door.

"Hold on," Cooper said, calling him back. He went to the kitchen counter and grabbed his cell phone. "Program my number into your phone."

"Why?"

"So you can call me if you need me," Cooper said. When Landon just stared at him and made no move to get his phone out of his pocket, Cooper went on. "Look, I'm going to be here awhile and I don't have any ties. I don't even have a dog. I'm usually around — no job and only a couple of friends. I'm the best person for you to call if you have some kind of, I don't know, problem."

"Like if I'm getting beat up under the bleachers?"

"Or if you run out of gas. Or the dog eats a bunch of fishing hooks and lures and wants to die and needs the vet and your sister is out rescuing other people. Or the old couple next door get in the cross fire when the mob is trying to take you out. Or —"

"Yeah, yeah, okay," he said, bringing out the phone. "What is it?"

Cooper fed him the numbers. Landon plugged them in and put the phone away. "I want yours," Cooper said.

"Why?"

Cooper took a breath. "In case I need help. In case I'm gagging on the mold in that shack of Ben's. In case —"

"All right! Jesus!" Landon reeled off the numbers. "There. We're all hooked up. But don't be calling me. I have enough people watching me!"

Cooper chuckled as he watched Landon and Hamlet jog down the steps to the beach. Then he sat down to drink his beer and grew more serious. A picture came to mind unbidden — a little five-year-old kid, the family he knew snatched away from him, being *slapped.* A kid that age and size being starved as punishment? He should've been allowed *anything;* he should've been allowed to eat marshmallows for dinner if that got him through. And a five-year-old runaway? He was damn lucky to be alive.

Aunt Frances was going to have to work very hard to stay out of hell.

And yet this kid . . . look at him now. Just the kind of kid the deputy should want to take his daughter to the dance — athletic, humble, intelligent, humorous. Responsible. Who got the credit for that? Was Landon just an old soul? Or did the sister do something special?

Cooper had been hanging around because he was curious about Ben's life, Ben's town. Now he realized he had another reason. Landon shouldn't be let down again.

# EIGHT

When Landon got home from Cooper's, he waited until about nine, then dug out the school roster he had for chem lab and dialed Eve's cell phone. He'd never called her before. He never would've had the stones to call her for anything but chemistry if Cooper hadn't said something about how his job was to keep her safe. He dreaded this, but fair was fair.

She answered sleepily. "Hullo?"

"Oh, hi. It's Landon. Damn, did I wake you up?"

"Hmm, no, but I was reading history, which to me is as good as taking a nap. What's up, Landon?"

"Well . . . I have to talk to you about something. About the dance. We might have a problem . . ."

"Oh, no!" she said, suddenly alert. "You're going to hurt my feelings now, aren't you? You changed your mind?"

"No! No way. But listen . . ." He paused and scratched his head. "Eve, I don't want to make a big deal out of this, but I should tell you something. Something about Jag."

"What? That he's an ass?"

Landon couldn't help it, he laughed. "Yeah, there's that. And also, he's not exactly happy with me these days."

To his surprise, now she laughed. "Landon, he's not going to be happy with anyone who can play football."

"Huh?"

"He really thought, being a senior, this was supposed to automatically be his year to rule. He'd be mad at anyone who did better than him. Ignore him, he's a loser."

"Huh," he said again, but this time it wasn't a question. "Thing is, he's a lot worse than not friendly. It's like he's gunning for me, y'know? It's pretty hard to ignore someone who slams you into the lockers whenever he gets a chance."

"Seriously? Landon, you can't let him do that!"

"He doesn't usually travel alone, Eve. He's got a pack."

She made a growling sound. "And I know exactly who they are, too. Sinclair, Wormitz and Pickering. All losers. You should tell someone. Like the coach, maybe."

He rubbed a hand through his hair. "I think it's different with girls, Eve. You know what it makes a guy look like if he can't handle it? I don't want to tell anyone, I want to handle it. He flies under the radar. He always manages to catch me at least semi-alone."

"Because he's a sneak and a liar. Want *me* to tell someone?"

"No! No. Listen, I only wanted to tell you because you and me, at the dance, it's going to look to Jag like he lost one more thing to me. And I don't want anything bad to happen to you. I don't want him to even call you a name. You might want to rethink this idea of us going together."

"Oh, I will. In fact, I just gave it a big rethink. Ashley asked me to double with her and her boyfriend and I thought no. I didn't want to throw you into the deep end with people you barely know. But now maybe yes is a better idea. You haven't been here long enough to get to know Ash's boyfriend — he graduated last year. Crawford Downy. He just goes by Downy."

He was silent for a moment. Thunder Point was proud of its football stars. Their pictures and trophies were displayed in the school's hallways. "Isn't he at State?"

"Yep. But he's crazy about Ash and

doesn't like her to miss all the important high school things, and he sure doesn't want her going with anyone else. Anyway, he's all-conference alumni — he'll be back for the game. He's a very nice guy. And he's also a big guy, very big."

"Whoa."

"So if it's not a problem for you, we'll double. Not for me," she said. "Jag wouldn't dare give me trouble. I'm not new here anymore, I have plenty of friends, plus there's my dad . . . He's not going to bother me. And he better not give you any more trouble. He's such a creep."

"Whoa," Landon said again. "But listen, if you could somehow manage not to spread around that I was crying about getting picked on . . ."

"Landon, I wouldn't do that."

"It's just that it's kind of humiliating to have your girlfriend running interference . . ." When the words were out of his mouth, he cringed and hit himself in the forehead with the heel of his hand. He ground his teeth and listened to the long silence.

"Am I your girlfriend?" she asked softly.

"Well, that position is definitely still open. . . ."

She laughed at him. "Where do I apply?"

"You can apply right now if you're any good at chemistry. It's really kicking my ass."

"You're better than I am. Didn't you get an A on the last test?"

"I have to get A's or my sister will finish the ass-kicking job."

"We should hook up your sister and my dad. He needs a woman in his life to get him out of mine and Aunt Lou's. We're getting kind of tired of his hyper-vigilance."

Landon kicked off his shoes and lay down on the couch with his phone to his ear. Ham settled in on the floor beside him. "Is that a fact?" he asked. "Be patient. Sarah got a divorce less than a year ago. She wants all men killed. All except me — I still get a pass."

They talked like that for an hour, about their families, about school, about moving to a new town and settling in. Landon hadn't done much of this kind of late-night, long talking on the phone to a girl. He'd never been shy, but he'd always been a little uncertain around girls. He just couldn't believe they liked him. Athletically, he was confident; academically, not so much, but he was willing to put all his muscle into schoolwork. He had to. The only way he was going to go to college was on scholarship.

But girls? There, his confidence failed him.

Eve McCain was easily the prettiest, smartest, best girl in school. They were in three classes together and he'd been watching her since school started, admiring everything about her. But even though they'd talked, he hadn't approached her. He was friendly, he was helpful, but he'd been through too much lately and couldn't handle rejection. He hadn't had a date yet in his life, unless you counted gang dates for pizza or parties after games, and that was at his old school in North Bend, where he'd also been the new kid. He'd been invited to join "the crowd" at the Thunder Point beach, but given Morrison would be there, he'd made excuses and never went.

So after a rocky few months, this felt brand-new. And very sexy.

School let out early on Friday for the homecoming festivities, but not before a student assembly for the coronation. Since attendance wasn't required, the kids who didn't want to be involved in school activities skipped out. Landon considered leaving, but in the end, he was curious. He tucked himself into the back of the auditorium and watched.

There was a lot of pomp; the cheerleaders

181

performed — minus the one cheerleader who was a homecoming queen candidate — the principal spoke, the football coach revved them up. Then the band played while the candidates walked down the auditorium aisles to the stage. They were all dressed up in formal gowns and nice suits. On the stage, they met, touched hands, gave a brief bow to the assemblage, separated and stood in a line of four girls and four boys. They would all ride in the parade later. After that, the football players would race into the locker room and dress for the game tonight.

Finally the results of the vote were announced. Stacy Kraemer and Justin Moore were crowned by last year's royalty. *Justin Moore? Not Jag?* There was a part of him that thought, *Karma's a bitch, man.* But another part of him knew that Jag Morrison would be in an even worse mood tonight. He'd been pretty cocky about this whole king business. It was customary to crown the football captain — unless he was an ass who not too many people liked. Justin was a tight end and good at his job; he didn't hang with Jag.

Straight after the coronation was the parade setup. Each class had made a float. It wasn't the Rose Bowl parade, but as floats went they weren't too bad. Since only seniors could be nominated for homecoming king and queen, their class always got the float that bore the thrones. Justin and Stacy took their places, ready for the parade to begin. The juniors had a papier-mâché cougar on their float; the sophomores celebrated the harvest with a football player in its midst; and the freshmen paid tribute to the fishing industry with the bow of a boat and a papier-mâché marlin, even though you'd never catch a marlin this far north off the Pacific coast.

The band led the floats down Thunder Point's main street and they made two loops on the track around the football field. When the parade reached the track, Justin Moore jumped off the seniors' float to go dress out for the game. There was a lot of noise, laughter and trash talk in the locker room and Landon acknowledged that maybe, just maybe, Jag Morrison wasn't king of the school, just the prince of a very small clique. That was somehow a little less intimidating. Finally, as the band played the school song, the team burst through a paper sign stretched across the goalpost to the cheers of the crowd.

Landon didn't have high expectations for the homecoming game. They'd beat Stafford High before and they weren't a strong team.

Good for homecoming and good for Jag. As Landon had expected, Coach Rayborough started Jag in the game. Landon didn't mind staying on the sidelines, watching the game and other things. He caught sight of Cooper standing at the end of the bleachers for a while in the beginning, then he disappeared. He recognized Crawford Downy from his picture in the school's trophy case. Downy was knocking fists with old friends, talking with the coach as if he was assisting.

But the game went downhill. Jag fumbled. He threw two incomplete passes and then he threw an interception and Stafford scored. The coach brought him in, talked to him, knocked him on the helmet, sent him back. Fumble, fumble, Stafford recovered the ball and ran it. Not too far, but they were clearly headed for another touchdown. Thunder's defense rallied, got the ball and Jag threw another incomplete pass. The score was 7–0 Stafford. Coach wouldn't want to get to halftime behind.

"Dupre!"

He was being brought in. Landon jogged over to the coach, got his instructions and went onto the field. He recovered the ball from Stafford. He went into the huddle, called the play, received the ball. He backed away from Stafford's offense and made a

184

perfect pass that landed them within running distance of a touchdown. When he next got the ball, he passed to a wide receiver and Thunder scored. The crowd went wild. Even though he hadn't run the ball, they chanted his name, along with the wide receiver's. But the attention wasn't as much fun as executing the play — making it happen, getting a win. Landon just plain loved the game. He could feel the pressure and excitement of that down to his toes. By the half, they had Stafford by three points.

Landon figured the coach would pull him now and let Jag have another shot, but he didn't. In fact, he didn't let Jag play again until the end of the game, when they had Stafford by fourteen points and there wasn't much time left. Jag tried valiantly to score and failed, but at least he didn't give the ball to Stafford.

During a time-out, Eve crept over to where he stood on the sidelines with the team and whispered that they were still decorating the gym for tomorrow night's dance, if he wanted to help. He told her he'd be there after the game.

When the game ended, Thunder High had a big win and was rewarded by screaming, thumping, yelling noises from the stands. Landon got a lot of fist bumps and slaps on the back, and he congratulated his teammates, too. He noticed that Jag was morose, lagging behind the team, but he ordered himself to ignore him as they jogged off the field and into the locker room.

He'd barely gotten his shoes off when the coach called him to his office. He stepped into the small room with a glass window to the lockers to find Downy leaning one hip against Coach's desk.

"Here he is, Downy. Meet Landon Dupre. Landon, this is Crawford Downy. He took us all the way to the state play-offs last year."

Downy put out his hand. "We had a good team. Nice to meet you, Dupre. Good job out there."

"Hey, thanks," Landon said, taking his hand. "I'm sorry I never got to see you play."

"Maybe you'll end up at State and we'll play together."

"How did you end up at State?" Landon asked.

"Scholarship. State wasn't the only option, though," Downy said.

They talked a little bit about Oregon State's record, about the fact that Landon was hoping for some help with college tuition, about double-dating for the dance. Downy continued, "Anyway, we have lots of time to talk about college life this weekend. I got sucked into decorating tonight, because that's where Ashley's going to be."

"Then I'll see you there. I was recruited by Eve."

They shook hands again. By the time Landon got back to the locker room, most of the team was either dressing or exiting the showers. In the coach's office, he could see Downy. He looked completely at home, still leaning on the desk, laughing with his old coach while Coach Rayborough leaned back in his chair.

Landon stripped down, wrapped a towel around his waist and headed for the showers. From his office, the coach could see the locker area; the coach's office was a no-female zone while guys were dressing. The shower area and the latrines were out of sight. The last three guys, toweling off and laughing, exited the shower just as Landon was going in.

"Great game, Dupre!"

"Show us the Thunder, Dupre!"

He just smiled and went about his business. He was planning to make it fast. Eve was in his very near future. He was lathered up, his hair loaded with suds, when he heard his name. "Dupre."

He pried open one eye and peered at Jag

Morrison, leaning in the doorway to the showers. He was fully dressed in pleated pants, thin-soled brown shoes and a navy sweater. The sleeves were shoved up on his forearms to show off his gold watch. His hands were in his pants pockets, one leg crossed over the other. He was a damn *GQ* ad.

"What?" Landon asked. "Little busy here." He let the spray hit him, rinsing off much of the dripping soap.

"No one likes a wise guy, Dupre. Don't think you can come here and just take over. I told you, this is my turf."

Landon wiped a hand down his face. "Where's your posse, Morrison? You don't usually come at me alone. I figure you're afraid I'll wipe up the floor with you."

Jag took a step into the shower room. "In your dreams. I just stopped by to tell you your party is about over here."

Landon laughed at him. "Is that so? Kind of looks more like your party already ended. Now get out of here, unless you're only here to view some naked male." Then he turned, presented his back and leaned into the shower. After a few seconds he looked over his shoulder and sighed in relief. Morrison was gone.

Both palms braced against the wall, Landon let the hot water wash over his head and down his face. He'd never spoken a word to Morrison before the trouble began. A couple of practices before school started had revealed Landon to be the stronger quarterback and that was all it took. *Don't think you're going to start the game, Dupre. This is my team.* That first threat had worked out pretty well for Jag — Landon hadn't started. The coach gave Jag every opportunity and only put Landon in when Jag couldn't carry or pass the ball. But he couldn't keep him out all the time, and it wasn't long before Jag told Landon to trip and drop the ball. When that didn't work, Jag and his gang of three started delivering their physical threats — a slug, a shove, an attempted trip. That night under the bleachers had been the worst episode. Cooper had saved his ass, but he'd got the message: they'd hold him down to beat him up.

"*Dupre.*"

He turned suddenly and just as suddenly an elbow or a bat or whatever it was slammed the side of his head into the hard tiles. The shower handle hit him in the ribs. On the way down, as he scrambled for something to grip, the lever hit him in the face.

Then it was lights-out.

"He's a damn fine ball player," Coach Rayborough was telling Downy. "But he's having a little trouble fitting in."

"That'll pass, if he's a good guy," Downy said.

"That's what I think. He works hard, never misses a practice, plays his heart out, supports his teammates . . ."

"How about grades?"

"Never had a problem with his grades," Coach said. "Not like some of the seniors on the team, who are hanging on by the hair on their teeth." He looked through the window into the quiet locker room. Everyone was gone, even the trainers. "Let's shut 'er down."

"Good idea," Downy said. "I've gotta go string lights and blow up balloons tonight. If I play my cards right, it could all end in a *date.*"

They were laughing as they exited the office. Before turning off the lights, the coach looked into the locker room. There were a few wet towels strewn over benches. "Someone forgot to close his locker," he muttered, walking toward the open locker.

The dawning came slowly — the locker

was not only open, the player's clothes were inside, the duffel holding his football uniform and gear sitting on the floor, shoes under the bench, shower running . . .

"Hey!" he yelled. "Somebody in there?"

No answer. Coach Rayborough walked toward the showers. It wouldn't be the first time some idiot left the water running. They get a little hyper after a —

"Downy! Call nine-one-one!"

The coach shut off the shower and knelt beside Landon. The second he lifted the kid's head, Landon started to groan. His head lolled.

"Jesus, Dupre, what the hell? You pass out?"

"He didn't pass out," Downy said from the door. "EMTs are on the way."

Landon tried to sit up, moaning.

"Stay down, Dupre," the coach said. "What the hell happened?"

But Landon kept struggling to get up, his arm flailing.

"Coach." Downy grabbed the towel off the hook by the shower and tossed it at him. "Cover him up. He didn't pass out. He got jumped in the showers. Who did it, Landon?"

Landon just groaned and reached a wet

hand toward his face. His jaw was already starting to swell and his lip was bleeding. He could feel the goose egg rising on his forehead.

Downy crouched. "Tell me before the EMTs and cops get here."

"Cops?"

"Landon, this asshole is not getting away with this," Downy said. "Was it Morrison?"

"Morrison?" the coach asked, clearly astonished.

"He's a prick, Coach," Downy said. "I've been watching him knock kids around since the fourth grade. He gave my little brother some trouble until I stepped in."

"Morrison?" the coach asked again. "I never saw that in him!"

Downy looked at him. "Of course you didn't," Downy said. "Trust me. Was it Morrison?" he asked Landon again.

And Landon nodded weakly. His vision had cleared and he was thinking straight, though he had one hell of a headache. He could pretend that a powerful whack on the head caused him to weaken in front of the coach and Downy, spilling Morrison's name. But that wasn't it at all. He'd had enough. So, the guy had been doing this to anyone he perceived weaker since he was a little kid? Big surprise. Time for him to be stopped.

"It was Morrison," Landon said. "This wasn't the first time. He had his boys hold me so he could punch me out once. And he ordered me to throw a game so I'd look bad and he could play. Said it was *his* team. *His* school."

The coach's eyes grew narrow and steely. News about a less-than-loyal player got to him the worst. Downy stood slowly, went into the locker room and grabbed a stack of towels. He propped one under Landon's head and used a few more to cover his shivering body. "Stay calm. They'll be here pretty quick and they have blankets. Who do we call for you?"

"My sister. Sarah. She's in my phone. My locker."

"Got it."

"You're going to be okay, Dupre," the coach said. "You seeing double or anything?" Landon shook his head. "That's a good sign. You have to stay down. In case there's something wrong with your back."

"There's nothing wrong with my back, but I bit the hell out of my tongue. Do I have all my teeth? Because my words don't sound right."

"Looks like it. Salsa-free diet for a week or so, though. I'm going to get an ice pack for that lump on your head."

"Aw, God," Landon said with a shiver. "Ice."

"I'll make this right, Dupre," the coach said. "You should've just told me."

"What for?" Landon asked. "You still can't believe it. You only believe it because Downy told you."

He was quiet for a minute before he said, "All that just changed, son."

# NINE

When the call came that a deputy was needed at the school, Mac was already there — not working, waiting for Lou and his kids. Lou was helping a couple of teachers chaperone the students decorating in the gym, and his two younger kids refused to go home until they saw what Eve and her friends were doing. So there he was, standing around in the gym, talking to a couple of the parents, when he caught the call on his phone.

The deputy on duty was needed to respond to an assault in the men's locker room.

In the locker room? Assault?

By the time Mac handed the kids over to Lou and walked across the gym floor to the locker room, the EMTs were headed through the locker room's back door from the parking lot with their bags. Steve Pritkus — the deputy on duty — was right behind them. He met them right outside the showers.

It didn't take the medical techs long to ensure Landon was stable and get him on a gurney. Even though he'd already moved his spine, they insisted on a backboard, which they promised would go away as soon as X-rays were taken and a doctor had a look. While they trussed him up and covered him, the deputies had a chat with Coach Rayborough and Crawford Downy. Their stories matched up. By the time Landon was ready to transport, Mac and Deputy Pritkus had a chance to ask him a few questions. Then the EMTs took him out through the locker room's back door, which led to the parking lot. It was through that door that the team ran to the field.

Just as the ambulance was ready to get under way, Sarah Dupre showed up. After the EMTs reassured her that her brother would be all right, she followed the ambulance to the hospital in Bandon. There were no lights or sirens, just a nice, safe transport.

But Mac had a picture of the kid's swollen, bleeding face on his cell phone. And Landon Dupre's assurance that he'd be pressing charges.

"I think we start in the gym where a lot of the kids are," Mac said. "Morrison's car is still in the lot. Everyone in town knows that white BMW."

"You got it, boss," Pritkus said. They'd already asked the coach and Downy not to discuss the situation with parents or students. They went back into the gym through the school. A small crowd had gathered around the door to the locker room, surrounding Downy and the coach. Jag Morrison kept his distance, and appeared to be putting the moves on a girl. She was sitting on the bleachers while he stood in front of her, one long leg lifted up, foot on the bleacher next to her. He had a hand in a pocket while another one was gesturing as he talked, smiled, laughed, apparently not interested in the hubbub around the locker room.

It twisted in Mac's gut. He'd never warmed to this kid but it always surprised him when he ran into a suspect so confident, so nonchalant. Could he have really just smashed in a guy's face, left him lying naked on the shower-room floor, and gone about the business of trying to get himself a date?

"Dad? Dad?" Eve said, tugging at his sleeve. "Is Landon okay? Did he get hurt in the game? Did he fall in the shower? Dad?"

He looked down at her, his brow wrinkled. "He's going to be fine, honey. I have things to do right now."

"What happened? Where is he? I want to go see him."

"They took him to Bandon, but he's fine. His sister went with him. They don't need a lot of kids swarming the hospital. I'm sure he'll be checked over and released."

"Dad, Landon's my date for the dance. I want to see him! If Aunt Lou takes me, can I go? Please?"

"Tell Lou I'm passing the baton to her. And tell her I need her to keep an eye on Ryan and Dee Dee a bit longer, too. I have some work to do now."

Her eyes shot down the bleachers to Jag, then up to her father's face. She gasped. "Oh, God, Jag hurt him, didn't he. Landon said Jag was always on him, shoving him, slamming him up against the lockers!"

Mac held her attention with his gaze. "Eve, I want you to go back to Lou and the kids. I'm going to take Mr. Morrison for a ride. And I don't want you to talk about this with anyone yet. There's a legal process that has to happen."

She bit her lip, then nodded gravely. "Can I go see Landon?"

"You tell Lou it's all up to her. I'm going to be tied up for a while."

■ ■ ■ ■

"Jag Morrison," Mac said. "I'd like you to come with Deputy Pritkus and me, please."

"What?" he said, pulling his foot off the bleachers and straightening.

"We're going to walk outside to the patrol car," Mac said.

He laughed. "I don't think so," he said, shaking his head. "What do you want?"

"We're going to walk outside, where Deputy Pritkus is going to read you your rights and charge you with a crime. You can come along or we can put on the cuffs and escort you that way. If I were you, I'd vote for nice and polite."

"Crime? What the fuck? *Crime?*"

"Assault," Pritkus said. He pulled his cuffs off the back of his belt.

"Whoa, whoa," Morrison said. "Hold on — I wouldn't assault anyone! You're crazy! I'm not going anywhere!"

"That's good, because I kind of like the idea of you in handcuffs," Mac said. "There's a young man on his way to the hospital in an ambulance, thanks to you. He lost consciousness for a while, but not his memory."

"No way," he said, holding up his palms,

backing away. "This is someone just trying to get me into trouble. Are there *witnesses*?"

"Cuffs it is," Mac said.

With one deputy on each side, they wrestled his arms behind his back and into the cuffs. By the time it was accomplished, he was on his knees. The focus of the students had shifted away from the locker-room door to Jag's arrest. Mac and Pritkus hoisted him up, dragged him outside. Right before putting him into the back of the deputy's cruiser, he was read his rights.

"I want my parents! I want my mother!" Morrison yelled as they shoved him in the backseat.

They let him sit there, yelling and rocking the car, while Mac used his cell to call another deputy. He didn't want to leave the town uncovered while Pritkus drove Morrison over to the jail in Coquille. And Mac wanted to make sure he was processed.

"We could probably get away with taking him to the Thunder Point office," Mac said. "He's going to be released to his parents' custody anyway. But I just watched a kid get put in an ambulance. I want Morrison to at least see the inside of a jail. With any luck, there are some scary sons of bitches in the jail tonight."

"I vote for Coquille," Pritkus said. "Try

Charlie Adams. He's probably looking for a little call-out overtime. He never says no."

"You read my mind, Pritkus. Meanwhile, I'm going to go visit the Morrisons."

When Coach Rayborough called Sarah Dupre, she jumped in her car, racing to the high school to find EMTs pulling a gurney toward an ambulance that was parked behind the school. For a search-and-rescue pilot who'd seen more than her fair share of injuries, sometimes the worst kind, her cool was long gone, even before she laid eyes on Landon. This was her little brother, her only family!

She rushed to him, asking the EMTs if he was going to be all right. They said they thought so, but the verdict rested with the doctor. He had briefly lost consciousness. But he was now alert and his pupils were equal.

"Landon, who did this to you?"

"The deputy's on it, Sarah. I told him. Some punk ball player who's probably just jealous."

"Should I ride in the ambulance with you?" She directed her gaze at one of the EMTs.

"If you follow us to Bandon, you'll have your car to take him home after he's treated and released," the young man said.

She drove behind the ambulance, taking small comfort in the fact that they weren't running lights and siren. Then, once they cleared town, the ambulance lit up. They didn't drive real fast, but they rolled code. Sarah knew what was happening — they were lit up so other motorists would be aware that they were loaded. She knew Landon hadn't had a heart attack or brain seizure. All the same, her chest constricted and she gripped her steering wheel with all her might. She followed closer than was allowed by law and she didn't care. She was just plain scared to death.

Feelings of helplessness weren't alien to Sarah. Her parents died when she was twenty-three and in helicopter flight school; Landon had been five. Aunt Frances had taken him in and Sarah visited him on the weekends she was able to get away from training. But it was torture; Frances pronounced him bad and undisciplined, while the tales of cruelty Landon reported chilled her to the bone. Then he started running away. He didn't get far, but still . . .

She had to ask for a leave from training, hire a lawyer, get custody of her brother, even though she had no idea how she'd take care of him and serve in the Coast Guard.

Her commander worked with her, put her in the next training class after she'd had time to figure out how to be a single mother. It could have been compassionate; it could have been the USCG worried about some discrimination complaint. She preferred to go with compassionate.

But damn! Life was crazy in those days. She was trying to get through helicopter training, which was so much harder than fixed wing, grieve her parents, try to get her little brother through his grief and fear — all at the same time. She grew thin and tired. So tired.

But she made it through that obstacle. Then on to Kodiak, Alaska, flying rescues out of the Bering Sea — which turned her into a damn fine pilot, because the challenge was steep. Luckily, her fellow pilots were dedicated to helping her learn and grow professionally. Then Michigan, then Florida — where she fell in love with Derek Stiles.

Suddenly, she thought she had a family again. Derek was so loving and so devoted to Landon. There was someone to share responsibility for a change. For the first time since becoming Landon's guardian, she dreamed of a softer, better life for them both . . . even though a little voice inside her warned her to be cautious. They married a year later. Then on to North Bend, Oregon — first Sarah and then Derek.

That's where the marriage ended. A marriage that should never have begun. He'd been unfaithful from the beginning. And at a place deep inside her, she'd known it.

*I'm sorry, Sarah, I really love you. I guess I'm not cut out to be monogamous.*

*But my friend?*

*I'm sorry. I had a thing with Susan. It didn't make sense, but it was there.*

She'd known. There had been red flags everywhere, but she'd forced them from her mind because she loved him, depended on him. Landon had become like a stepson to Derek. She relied on Derek to look after him, to go to his games when she couldn't. And Landon relied on Derek to be the man in his life. But she had to end it, because Derek was never going to belong to her, to them. Just like any mother, she had to try to deal with the fact that Derek had let Landon down, as well. But ironically, it was Landon who said, "You don't have to stay with him, Sarah. Not for me, that's for sure."

Her career and her brother were all she had, and for their sake Sarah pulled herself together. She and Derek decided they could be civilized. They'd try to work separate schedules in North Bend when possible, but if they were thrown together, they'd be grown-ups about it. Sarah refused to let it show on the job that her heart had been ripped out.

But she was helpless and alone again and the pain of it was horrible. So she looked into finding the best community, the friendliest, with the most proactive football coach for Landon, and they moved to Thunder Point.

She thought she'd brought them both to a kinder, safer, more manageable place. But now she felt that helplessness *again.* Here he was, in the ambulance ahead of her. If she understood the coach, he'd been jumped in the shower, left naked and unconscious on the cold, tile floor.

She was intercepted in the E.R. by an admissions nurse. "A physician's assistant is examining your son —"

"Brother," she corrected. "But I have custody. Our parents are deceased." She dug around in her purse. "Here are my insurance cards."

"I'm going to have you get to work on admission paperwork," the nurse said. "Since he came in on a backboard, I think he'll be lined up for X-rays right away so spinal injury can be ruled out. That takes a while. Then you can see him."

"Sure," she said. Her hand shook as she accepted the clipboard and pen. She sat down, rather than standing there at the counter, so the nurse wouldn't see her tremble.

They kept Landon in X-ray a long time. She longed to step outside and call someone, but there *was* no one. In moving to Thunder Point in early August, she'd isolated herself. Oh, there was Gina, but they were just casual friends and she didn't have her number. There were football and PTA parents, but none of them were people she'd call with tears in her voice. For that matter, she wasn't sure who Landon's friends were. She saw his teammates high-five and fist bump him, but there hadn't been any friends at the house and he didn't go out much.

Finally she was allowed in the E.R. exam room. There she found Landon sitting up, free of the backboard, talking on the phone while holding the ice pack to the other side of his face. "Yeah, I told the deputy and I said I'd press charges, so that's done." Then he laughed and said, "Oh, I don't know if that's good or not. It might've just bought me more trouble. Hey, my sister's here to take me home, so I gotta go. Just wanted you to know . . . it's all good. I'm fine."

He clicked off and looked at Sarah.

"Who was that?" she asked. *Who do you check in with after you've been beat up?*

"That guy I told you about — Cooper. The one who has Ben's place now."

"Oh? And how old is this Cooper person?"

"I don't know," he said with a shrug. "Old." Then he grinned and winced. "A little older than you, I think. He's friends with the deputy. He took me out for a hamburger after the Carver game."

"You didn't tell me that," she said. She had gone to that game. She'd been available if he'd wanted a hamburger. "Just where did you meet this Cooper?"

"On the beach, Sarah. I was running Ham and he was at the bait shop. I stopped to ask him what was going on there."

"And now you're calling him?"

"He's friends with the deputy!" Landon stressed. "I didn't want him to hear about this and go looking for me to see if I'm all right! Jesus."

"It just sounds very suspicious," she said.

"Yeah? Well, Cooper didn't jump me in the shower and bash my face in." He pulled the ice pack away from his purple cheek and black eye and she closed her eyes and just shuddered. "A senior by the name of Jag Morrison did this. And he's been threatening me since school started. He was the star quarterback — you should use the term loosely. He can't throw a pass to save his life, but he was the best they had. He does not like having a junior from out of town slip into his position."

"How long has this been going on?" she asked, scowling. "I've met the Morrisons. I sat with them at a game once."

"Since about the third or fourth practice. I've been holding him off."

"Why didn't you *tell* me?"

"Aw, jeez, Sarah, twenty reasons. How about we start with I don't want my sister talking to the principal or the guy's parents. I don't want to hide behind your skirt. And . . . you've been going through your own shit lately. Since we got rid of Derek, you haven't been exactly . . . strong. You haven't been strong — there, it's been said. I didn't want to put one more thing on you — especially if I could handle it."

She pulled the ice pack away from his face. "How about next time you tell me and save your face," she said quietly.

"Yeah, right. It's too late to save my face now. And I even have a date for the dance. I guess she won't want to go now."

"A date? Who?"

"Eve McCain. The deputy's daughter. She asked me." Then he grinned and said, "Ow." He pressed the ice back against the right side of his face.

She shook her head and tried not to laugh. "We have communication issues," she pointed out.

"You have communication issues," he said. "You're going through the divorce blues and, hey, I get that. I'm kind of going through them, too. Not only did I have to change schools, but that prick didn't even ask for joint custody or visitation! How do you think that makes me feel?"

A soft smile came across her face. "I let you swear too much," she said, secretly admitting it gave her enormous pleasure to hear him call Derek a prick. Most of the time she felt just inches from losing it. Landon's anger sat very well with her. Maybe they should take one evening a week to sit around cursing him, saying every mean and evil thing they could think of. The bastard — breaking their hearts like that.

"Don't look now, Sarah, but I think it's too late. At least I know when not to say those things."

"We have to talk more, Landon," she said.

"Sarah, you're the one who hasn't been talking. When you get more over Derek, we'll talk more. Look, it's okay. You'll get over him. Only a real mean fucker would start dating before the marriage even gets started, so cut yourself some slack."

Her eyes welled with tears she wouldn't let fall. She had been forced to be strong on so many levels — her family history, her job, taking custody of a young boy. And all with so few tools at her disposal. When something hit her — like Derek's cheating — she withdrew into herself. Not good. Not good at all.

"Well," the doctor said, pulling aside the drape and coming into the exam area. "We're not seeing any reason to admit you, but I want you and your sister to be on the lookout for symptoms of concussion. The nurse will give you a list of instructions. I know the P.A. asked, but I'd like to hear the answer. Did you get hit in the game?"

He shook his head. "I'm too fast for 'em. I guess I need to get a little faster in the shower." Then he tried his handsome grin again, and again he said, "Ow."

The doctor chuckled.

"I can sit up with him tonight, if that's necessary."

"I don't know if that's required, Mrs. . . .

ah," he looked down. "Dupre."

"Meet Lt. Commander Sarah Dupre, my big sister," Landon said. "My keeper. My ball and chain. Coast Guard Search and Rescue. And she's single."

He laughed again. "Pleasure," he said, sticking out his hand toward her. "I'm married, but it's still a pleasure. And we thank you for all the help you give us here, on the coast and wherever you're needed."

"That's a shame, you being married," Landon said. "My sister hasn't been out in a while and you can't imagine how that impacts my social life."

The emotional strain of having Landon hurt left Sarah exhausted. She was afraid she might sleep too soundly to check on him during the night and considered setting the alarm on her cell phone, just to be sure she woke up at least every hour. That turned out to be completely unnecessary — she spent the night on the couch, where she barely dozed.

It brought to mind those days right after she had rescued him from Aunt Frances. He didn't talk about his experience, but he was so shaken she slept with him every night, holding him close and safe. He never complained, but sometimes he cried in his sleep, his little body trembling in her arms.

Now he was almost a man and she was running out of ways to keep him safe.

She crept into his room at regular intervals, nearly tripping over Ham, although she couldn't imagine what good it did. How do you hold off a concussion? But his face, beautiful even with bruises and swelling from having taken a beating, fed her soul. He was so childlike in sleep, a little boy in a man's body, at peace and trusting.

Her. Trusting her.

He had been her priority for ten years. She'd always found a way to put him first and had been fortunate enough to get support from other Coast Guard families and her commanders. But lately? It wasn't so much the divorce as it was Derek who had kept her completely off-balance. She had failed Landon. He'd been thrown into a new school, put on a new team, bullied and picked on without her being even slightly aware, struck up a friendship with some middle-aged man she knew nothing about . . .

She was going to have to talk to him about that. But first, she had to get some sleep.

Morning came with the crunching sounds of Ham and Landon having breakfast. She pried open one eye. Landon sat at the kitchen table, shoveling cornflakes into his mouth while Ham was nose into the big bowl by the back door devouring dog food. She sat up, rubbed her eyes and looked at her brother.

"I'll make you a couple of eggs," she said.

Landon let the spoon rest in the bowl. "Sarah, you slept on the couch in your clothes. You don't have to make me an egg. If I'd wanted an egg, I would've made one. I have a black eye, not a broken arm. I did make you some coffee, however."

She moved to the table. "Thank God. I'm exhausted."

"Me, too. I woke up about once an hour. Someone was prowling around my bedroom."

She leaned on her hand. "You could've said something. . . ."

"And ruin your fun?" He got up and poured her a cup of coffee. "I'm going back to bed, though. And I'm locking my door."

She accepted the cup, blowing on it and taking a sip. "The purple is coming out," she said, gesturing with her cup to his face. "I mean coming out even more. I think you got a bruise on your bruise."

"Yeah."

"I'm sorry, Landon. This is my fault. I

wasn't paying attention. I had no idea you were fighting this problem. I was so caught up in my own. . . ."

Again the spoon rested in the bowl. "Sarah, I didn't want you to know. I didn't want *anyone* to know. I wanted to be able to take care of it myself. It wasn't until I heard Crawford Downy telling the coach that Morrison has been kicking kids around since fourth grade that I decided the best way to take care of it was to out him. I don't know if you'll get this, but there's a big difference between tattling to the coach or the teacher and just taking him on, publicly. It's the difference between a billboard and a whisper. Morrison snuck up on me in the shower. He was handcuffed and taken away. I can't see how he's going to get out of this one." He shook his head. "Up until he did that, he was nothing but sneaky shoves and bragging and badgering."

"But you talked to that guy, that Cooper . . ."

"Not exactly," Landon said. "I was out on the beach with Ham, throwing the ball for him, and Morrison and some of his leeches were there, paddleboarding and stuff. They were giving me a little trouble. Not letting me pass. Ham the fearless was hiding behind me. Cooper was out on the deck at

Ben's. He gave a whistle. That's all. Just to say he was watching. And of course that chickenshit Morrison pulled off the posse. I walked down the beach, ended up at the dock. I just talked to him for a while, that's all. It was like he knew what was going on before I had to explain anything. He said he'd moved around a lot — he'd been the new guy a lot."

"Oh," she said.

"He's all right, Sarah. Stop worrying about Cooper."

How would Landon know that? Cooper could be a very manipulative con artist or pedophile. But she knew better than to pretend to be the all-wise big sister. That was usually the kiss of death. So she said, "Sure. Right."

When Landon went back to bed, she pulled on her rubber boots and red jacket. Ham started wiggling around and snuffling. "Shh," she said. "Just get your ball!" She hurried to get him out of the house before he woke Landon.

It was a cold, sunny morning but Sarah's mood was stormy. She wasn't really processing all the events of the past few months — the divorce, the tension she'd felt working with Derek, the move, the attack on Landon. Crisis was somehow easier to manage than that old impotence of not being in control, not being able to resolve things.

She jogged across the beach, throwing the ball for Hamlet. She didn't really have a plan until she'd run all the way up the beach stairs to the bait shop, Ham on her heels, and went around the building to the trailer. She knew she might be acting a little irrationally, but she banged on the door. Then she banged on the door again, harder. She could hear him inside, walking. Finally he jerked the door open, wearing only a towel, with shaving cream on half his face, an impressive tattoo covering his right shoulder and running down his biceps. She demanded, "What the hell is going on with you and my brother?"

He frowned at her. "And this must be Sarah," he said calmly. "Would you like to come inside?"

She stepped back. "Why don't you just come outside?" she asked, knowing it was a ridiculous request.

"I'm much better at conversation with my pants on," he said. "Stand by." He let the door drift closed and was back a moment later with a small towel. "Wipe Ham's mouth and feet and come inside. I'll put on some clothes, we'll talk about whatever has you upset and then maybe I'll get back to my shower. That work for you?"

Inexplicably, she hated him for being calm. She felt more out of control than ever, yet more determined to be the stronger one. She snatched the towel out of his hand and said, "Get your pants."

Cooper gave Sarah Dupre a brief salute. He walked past his galley kitchen and up three steps to his bathroom and bedroom. He closed the door. He leaned on the bathroom counter, looked in the mirror at his half-shaved face and whispered, "Holy crap." Hot damn! He checked — his tongue was not hanging out but his eyes were a little hot. She was a freaking knockout.

Her hair was short, thick and dark and framed her face in a sexy, provocative way. Her eyes were so big, so chocolate, surrounded by thick, black lashes. Her lips — oh, my God, those lips. Ruby, full, heart-shaped lips that just begged to be . . . *Stop,* he told himself. She hid her small body under that thigh-length red jacket with a hood and a loose white shirt beneath that, but he could see a shapely form inside. He blinked his eyes closed hard, then checked to see if he was drooling.

Landon hadn't told him how stunning she was. But then again, how many teenage boys brag about how pretty their sisters are?

It didn't take a genius to figure out that she had her wind up about his friendship with Landon. Now, this was a first. He'd faced off with protective fathers over daughters and even had a very uncomfortable run-in with an ex-husband. There had been an occasion or two when a woman couldn't decide between Cooper and another guy . . . But this? A beautiful woman who almost brought him to his knees, angry and upset over his friendship with her little brother? Whoa. He had an urge to call his older sister, Rochelle, and ask her what was happening here. She was no expert, but she was never short on advice.

He pulled on jeans and a white undershirt. He found her sitting in the same chair Landon had last occupied. She sprang to her feet. "Sit down," he said gently. Then he went to the kitchen, filled the saucepan for Ham, grabbed another towel to put under it because the dog was a sloppy and ferocious drinker, and set him up. "We have our routine," he said casually.

"How many times have you had this routine?" she wanted to know.

"Once."

While Ham was lapping, Cooper took the

couch. "Now, what has you so angry?" he asked.

"I'm not angry. I just want to know what this relationship with my brother is about. I have questions."

"All right," he said, leaning forward on the couch, elbows on his knees, hands clasped together. "I saw Landon get into a little altercation on the beach. Nothing big or scary. Some kid was giving him crap and shoved him. I talked to him after that, found out he was getting bullied. Ostracized by some of his teammates. You know why, right?"

She just shook her head.

"He's a better ball player than the senior, the team captain. I went to a game a week or so ago, just by accident — I was looking for food but the whole town was at the high school, at the game, so I went. I ran into a few people I knew — the McCains and their friends. It was amazing. Landon's damn good. When I was leaving, I overheard a scuffle and found that same kid from the beach and some of his friends ganging up on Landon. He didn't get hurt or anything, but I did have a talk with him and suggested he tell you or the coach or the deputy. That bully thing, that's just all wrong. You never know where that's going to stop."

"In the locker-room shower?" she asked, lifting one brow.

He ran a hand over his head. "Yeah, I should've done something. It's a hard call. Sixteen-year-old boys, they have their pride. It's not like Landon's getting knocked around because he's the little guy or the nerdy guy. He said he could handle it and I thought he probably could. He's a big guy, Landon. Tough. But I apologize. I should've gone over his head."

She looked around the trailer. "But why are you here?" she asked. "What are you doing here, interceding for my brother? Do you work? What do you *do*?"

He gave her a second to catch her breath. What did she think? That he was some perv trolling for young men out of a trailer? "I'm between jobs."

"Is that so?" she asked with an accusatory tone.

"It is so," he said. "Ben and I were friends. We were going to meet in the mountains, go hunting. He died suddenly. Instead of looking for work, I came up here to find out what happened to him."

"He fell down the stairs, mysterious circumstances," she informed him. "And the idea of Landon hanging around here after that? I don't love that idea."

"I guess I don't blame you. If it's any comfort, Deputy McCain and I have a pretty tight watch on the place. But nothing more mysterious than my friend tripping has materialized. I think, Sarah, it was probably just a sad accident."

"Yet you're still here. Living in a trailer."

He laughed at her suddenly. She was ferocious, and amazingly beautiful as she played the lioness. "Listen, Sarah, wanna lighten up? I live in the trailer because I can't live in Ben's place. It's a disaster. I'm trying to clean it up."

"And then?"

"Leave," he said. "But you're a little insulting. I lived in this trailer for two years in Corpus Christi."

"Doing what?"

He leaned toward her. "Flying helicopter transport to offshore oil rigs in the Gulf for an oil company. Not rescue, transport. I've been flying helicopters since the Army. Fifteen years. I'll probably fly again, but not offshore. Something else." He loved the shocked look on her face. "After Ben's death, plans changed. Right now, what I have to do is put this place right and settle Ben's business. He had no family left. It's going to take a few months. So I have a legitimate reason for being here. I'm not parked here to sell teenagers drugs or do any other disreputable or unlawful business. I asked Landon for his cell phone number and gave him mine in case . . . I don't know, in case he needed someone's help. He told me you were sitting alert for the Coast Guard and sometimes he was on his own." He looked at her. "I was just being a good neighbor. Your brother, he's a decent kid. And he's proud of you. He cares about you. He said you've been through a lot lately."

She stood. "Hmm. Yes. Well, that's none of your concern."

Cooper also stood. "I'm not concerned, Sarah. I'm what used to be called supportive. And you're a really tough broad."

"Don't call me a broad."

"Give me a reason."

"Look, Mr. . . ."

"Cooper. Hank Cooper, but hardly anyone calls me Hank. Just Cooper."

But she was apparently bent on some formality, probably as a way to keep a distance between them. "Mr. Cooper, I'm responsible for Landon. Just me. It can be a challenge, given my job. But I just want to protect him."

Cooper shook his head. "You're going to have a problem with that."

"Oh? And why is that?"

"Because I think he wants to protect you."

"He's sixteen!"

Cooper gave a nod. "A very smart, strong and brave sixteen with some real high standards. He must have had a good role model."

"He's had *no* role model. Our father died when Landon was five, and my ex-husband is a jackass who abandoned him!"

Cooper put his hands in the back pockets of his jeans and rocked on his heels. He gave her a small smile. "It didn't have to be a male role model, Sarah."

Her mouth actually dropped open slightly. It appeared to take her a moment to absorb this. He could almost see the wheels turning. A compliment from the bad man in the trailer?

She closed her mouth. She stood a little taller. "Listen, Mr. Cooper, I'm going to be watching you and if you do anything to hurt my brother, you're going to pay."

"Understood," he said, but he couldn't wipe the smile off his face.

"Ham!" she ordered, going for the door. But the dog was way ahead of her and she almost fell over him. She jumped out of the trailer, stumbled over the dog and headed for the beach.

Cooper watched her go. He whistled. "Whew. Tough broad."

# TEN

Cooper dusted off his suit. Well, it was his suit *now.* Rochelle's husband, Dave, wore suits to work every day, but a year or so ago, he'd been bitten by the chips-and-beer fairy, growing out of a few of his expensive suits. Of course Rochelle tried to put him on a diet, which was semi-successful, but the tight suits went away. So did the tight and oh-so-expensive Italian dress shirts. Up to that point, Cooper had one fairly late model sports coat and some nice slacks. He did have occasional dates and a wedding or funeral every couple of years.

He wasn't big on suits. Yet, he looked in the mirror and couldn't help but be impressed. He wondered if he'd survive in a desk job.

No. He wouldn't.

The school gymnasium had been transformed for the dance and was full of kids, at least a couple hundred. It was also pretty flush with adults. Cooper was about the best-dressed one there, thanks to his beefy brother-in-law. Since Mac was tall, he was the first one Cooper picked out of the crowd. He got around to Mac's side by skirting a wall decorated in crepe paper. Mac was close to the refreshment table and, after shaking Cooper's hand, he passed a plastic cup toward him. "Punch?"

Cooper looked into the cup. "It's pink," he said.

"I know. Wait till you taste it."

"How much of that crap do you have to drink before you can go home?"

Mac chuckled. "My job is to make sure nothing adult gets poured into the punch bowl."

"You're an amateur," Cooper said. "With all these chaperones around the punch bowl, they'll pour it right into their cups."

"Right, but I've got Gina and Lou in the crowd. They both have eyes in the back of their heads. How'd you get talked into this?"

Cooper gave a snort and shook his head. He spread his jacket and put his hands in his pockets. "By now you've probably figured out, Landon's the kid I was keeping an eye on. When Gina asked me — no, make that *ordered* me — to join the chaperone crew, I thought maybe it wasn't a bad idea. It's not like I have a lot of social commitments around here and I'm getting a little tired of mold."

"You should've told me about Landon," Mac said.

"You're right. I guess I should've. So, by now there's probably no real reason for me to be here. Is he here? Landon?"

Mac gave a nod. "Dancing with my daughter. As I watch."

"Try to go easy, Mac. You were sixteen once."

"That's why I'm watching."

Cooper laughed. "So, I know Landon went to the hospital to be checked out, but he's okay except for a black eye. What about the other kid?"

"He went to jail."

"Seriously?" Cooper asked, shocked.

"You act surprised. Landon was jumped from behind, but he saw his assailant and named him. He's filing charges, thank God. You know, I don't usually get a big kick out of arresting people. Hooking 'em up and taking them to jail. But that one," he said. "I kind of enjoyed that. Little bastard. Fighting is bad enough, dirty fighting is just cheap and nasty."

"Morrison isn't here tonight, is he?" Cooper asked.

"He's been suspended from school. There will be some straightening out to do before he shows up again. And it isn't official, but I think he's all done playing football. There are only three games left, but if I know the coach, he's finished, even when he gets back into school."

"Well, before you write this one off, be sure to ask Landon about Morrison's friends. He has a posse, don't ask me why. Right after the Carver game, I just happened upon a little scuffle. Two big boys were holding Landon so Morrison could hit him."

Mac scrubbed a hand down his face. "Aw, man . . ."

"I don't know their names, but I could pick them out. It would be better, though, if Landon just told you. Is there likely to be any trouble from them tonight?"

"Doubtful," Mac said. "That Eve, she's her father's daughter, all right. Once she found out Morrison was giving Landon a hard time, she fixed them up with a double date. Ashley's boyfriend is an alumnus, very large, very well liked around here. I'll give Landon a call tomorrow, see if we can wrap this up. Any other little gems you were saving?"

Cooper missed some of the question. Out

of the corner of his eye he caught sight of a woman he recognized. Sarah was here. She seemed to be staying close to the gym doors, half-hidden by a fake pillar with crepe paper and balloons attached to it.

"Huh?" he said to Mac.

"I said, is there anything else I should know?"

"Can't think of a thing, Mac. Hey, I think I've learned my lesson here. If I'd told you what was going on, maybe Landon would be a little pissed, but he probably wouldn't have gotten hurt."

"And there you go," Mac said.

"Um, I see someone I should say hello to," Cooper said. "Landon's sister is here. Guard that punch."

"You know it."

Cooper swung by the refreshment table, got a little plastic cup of that pink shit, a small napkin and walked toward Sarah. She was peering around the fake pillar and had her back to him as he approached on her other side — and what a back it was. She was wearing a long-sleeved, formfitting black sweater-type dress with some kind of animal skin belt and black, high-heeled boots. Although Cooper would have no way of knowing, he suspected she didn't buy those boots in Thunder Point.

"Are you hiding?" he asked.

She jumped and whirled around, her hand pressed to her throat. She let her eyes close briefly. "You scared me to death!"

"Sorry," he said. "You seemed to be peeking out from around the decorations. Are you incognito tonight?"

"I'm a little on the low-profile side." She took a breath. "It's been a very long day."

He offered her the cup. "Punch?"

She looked at it and made a face. "It's pink."

"And no little umbrella, either. We have more in common than you'd think."

"Listen, about this morning . . ."

"Forget it," he said. "He's your brother. He got hurt. You were worried."

"Well, thanks, but I wasn't exactly asking for forgiveness."

His eyebrows shot up. Figured.

"It's just that, I had no right to be so hostile. That came out of nowhere. It wasn't worry. When I don't have control of the situation . . . ack," she said, rubbing her temples with her fingers. "Okay, I apologize for being so mean, but not for being suspicious of you. Any mother or older sister or guardian would be. Anyway, let's start fresh. Look at you — you do not look like an ordinary helicopter pilot who's fixing up a run-down bait shop. That's a four-thousand-dollar suit. None of the helicopter pilots I know wear four-thousand-dollar suits. They don't even *want* to."

Cooper grinned. "And this is a hundred-and-fifty-dollar shirt. It's Italian."

"Clotheshorse, eh? Or drug lord?"

He shook his head and laughed. "My brother-in-law is an executive who got fat. My sister sent me three suits, a bunch of shirts and some bad ties that cost a fortune. Gina told me to dress up."

A short laugh escaped her and her face was briefly transformed. She was beautiful to start with, her skin flawless, her cheeks flushed pink and those dark-coffee eyes so hot. "Well, you clean up all right."

"Why, thank you, Sarah. So, Mac tells me Landon is here, dancing with his daughter."

The smile vanished and she groaned, dropping her chin.

"I take it he's recovered?" Cooper asked.

"He looks like hell. Black eye, split lip, bruised cheek and a big old lump on his head. He shouldn't be out tonight. We did not have an amicable day."

"But does he feel okay?" Cooper asked.

"He feels like the luckiest kid in the world because the ravishing Eve McCain wanted to go to the dance with him even though

231

his face looks like hamburger. But I wouldn't let him drive. I offered to drive him and he said he'd throw himself in front of a train first."

"She is ravishing," Cooper said with humor. "And she's nice. But most important, her daddy is the law around here. He put the guy who hit Landon in jail."

That got her attention. "Jail? Does Landon know that?"

"I don't know. I'm sure the kid's parents got him out pretty quick, but he did go to jail. That makes me feel better. He's a snotty little dick."

Again with the smile, larger this time. Sarah had been hanging out with Coast Guard pilots for probably ten years. Cooper was speaking her language. Salty. But dear God, she was beautiful when she smiled like that.

"Does Landon know you're here?"

She nodded. "And he's not very happy about it. I wasn't going to come tonight, but then . . . He likes that I go to the games, but this? He wants to be alone with his girl."

"His girl's daddy's watching. And her daddy is —"

"I know, the law." She laughed again. "Did you know the young girls call him Deputy Yummy Pants?"

Cooper barked out a laugh so loud people turned toward him. She put a hand on his arm to shush him.

"Shh. I hear he doesn't warm to it," she said. "And he's a big boy with a gun."

"I'll be careful with that information." Cooper looked around. "I think these people have things under control. I could buy you something to drink that's not pink."

"Oh . . . I don't think so. . . ."

"Dinner," he said. "I'll throw in dinner. Or if you've had dinner, I'll buy you a drink and dessert."

"Listen, you're taking this good-neighbor thing kind of far. It wouldn't be such a good idea. I mean, you're Landon's friend and I'm watching you to see if I have to beat you up for any reason."

His lips twitched with a smile; getting beat up by her could be erotic. As hell. "Take a chance. We can talk about the town. Or your brother. Or helicopters, if you don't get enough of that at work. I don't know about you, but this isn't what I feel like doing tonight."

"Yeah, but there's Landon . . . I hate to get too far away."

"Text him. Tell him we're going to dinner and we'll be nearby if he needs anything." He smiled at her. "Let's get out of here."

Cooper suggested they stay in town, for her peace of mind, even though there were some great restaurants within thirty minutes of Thunder Point. She appreciated that. And he wanted to go in one car. "I'd be more than happy to take my truck, but I think given that narrow skirt of yours, we should go in your car. If you don't mind bringing me back for my truck, that is."

"We could just go in separate cars," she said.

"Nah. Come on, let's ride together. But first, shoot a text to Landon."

She took out her phone in the high school parking lot and her thumbs got busy on the letters. "I hope he's not all cranky about me going out after all the arguing we did today about him going out."

Cooper laughed. "He's going to think I'm doing him a favor." Then his voice lowered slightly. "But I'm not."

"Wow," she said. "He texted right back. Have fun?"

"Good," Cooper said. "Let's go. I've only figured out a couple of things in this town, but one is that when the town is occupied with school events like games, Cliffhanger's is quiet." He grabbed her elbow and started to walk her around to the passenger side of a compact SUV. "Want me to drive?" he asked.

"My car? I don't think so."

"All right then," he said, backtracking and holding the driver's door for her. When you spent a lot of your life in a flight suit and combat boots, doors didn't get opened for you a lot, so she slid in. He got in the passenger seat, moving it back as far as it would go.

When she was behind the wheel and they were under way, he said, "Good old Landon. I went to exactly one high school dance. I mean, *real* high school dance, like with a girl. The nonformal kind I'd hit with a couple of buddies, if I had a couple of buddies, and we'd prowl around the outskirts, ogle the girls so we'd have something to talk about later."

"And how was the one you actually went to? With a girl?"

"Didn't work out the way I thought it would," he said with a laugh. "It took so much courage to ask her that my expectations might've been a little high. She had a terrible time. Somehow I couldn't do anything right. She was miserable. Now I can't even remember her name, which makes me hope she can't remember mine."

"She remembers," Sarah said. "Do you remember anything about her?"

"Blond hair and boobs," he answered.

"I give you some credit for being honest, but not a lot. Of credit, that is. Did it ever occur to you that women don't really like being remembered for their hair color or their boobs?"

"Of course it does, now. And I'm very sorry, Commander Dupre, but even though I don't read *Psychology Today*, I do know that humans are visual creatures. There has to be an initial visual attraction and then, once you get to know a person better, you can fully appreciate all their other fine qualities. If you never get to know their traits and talents, you remember hair and boobs."

"Very shallow," she said. But what sprang instantly to mind was his torso in a towel. The amazing tattoo, his broad shoulders, fantastic biceps, terrific pecs, perfect chest hair — not too much, not too little — and that narrow waist. Her reaction pissed her off. "It's *Lieutenant* Commander," she said.

"If it's any comfort, I've come a long way since high school."

"So you no longer think about hair and boobs?"

She pulled into Cliffhanger's parking lot,

which was not full. As she found a space and parked he said, "I didn't say that." He went around to the driver's side to open her door, but she was already getting out, treating him to a beautiful shot of thigh as she did so.

Holding her elbow, he steered her into the restaurant. Right inside the door was the bar, where he'd eaten last time he was there. Beyond the bar was a fancier dining room, tablecloths and everything. He lifted a hand to the bartender. "Hey, Cliff."

"Hey, Cooper. Funeral?"

Cooper just laughed and kept steering her.

"Let's get a corner table like that one over there, near the fireplace. Damn, it's cold," he said. "I've been in the Gulf too long, I think. What's winter like around here?"

"Colder," she said with a laugh. "We just moved here this summer from North Bend, right up the road. But I did three years in Kodiak, three in Michigan. This is nothing. You have no fireplace in that trailer of yours."

He maneuvered her toward a table in the corner, not far from the restaurant's hearth. Only a few tables in the whole place were occupied, all of them far enough away so that no conversations would be overheard. He helped her out of her long, black coat and folded it over a vacant chair. "No fireplace *and* it rocks in the wind. Even though there's been sun almost every day, the wind off the bay can get chilly. I've been cold since the day I got here. I'm going to have to buy some sealskin or something."

The second she sat down, the bartender was standing beside their table with menus. Cooper was shrugging out of his jacket, draping it over the back of the chair. "Bring me a beer, Cliff. This is Miss Dupre — Sarah." Cliff gave a nod. "Sarah, what would you like to drink?"

"A Chardonnay will do the trick."

"Draft and Chardonnay," Cooper said. Then he sat down, his back to the room, and loosened his tie. He removed his cuff links, slid them into his shirt pocket and rolled up his sleeves to just under his elbows. He leaned those elbows on the table, looked at her with a half smile and said, "I'm sorry that it was some difficult business for your brother that introduced me to him, but I'm glad it led to meeting you."

It was that comment — combined with the fact that the small tuft of hair peeking out of his opened collar and his muscled forearms were achingly sexy — that caused her to say, "I've been divorced for nine

238

months."

He lifted one brow. "Wanna talk about it?"

"Not particularly."

"And you brought it up because . . . ?"

"If you have an idea that this chance meeting is going to lead to something, you'd be mistaken."

He shook his head. "Sarah, we're both over thirty. Hopefully, we've overcome the idea that dinner means sex. Unless it's an exceptional dinner."

"We'll split the check," she said.

"Don't be ridiculous. You pay for dinner. Believe me, you'll feel more in control that way."

"You know, I can tell you think you're funny, not taking me seriously."

"Oh, you're wrong!" he said. "I think it would be a catastrophe to not take you too seriously. A disaster of unparalleled proportion."

"Hilarious," she said.

Cliff put her wine in front of her first, then put the draft down.

"Ah," Cooper said. "Liquor. Thank God."

"Have you decided yet?" Cliff asked.

"We'll have the grouper," Cooper said. "Salad starters, please. Ranch for me."

"Oil and vinegar, on the side," she said.

"And make sure Lieutenant Commander

Dupre gets the check." He winked at her, and Cliff ran for his life.

She took a sip of her wine. "How do you know I won't expect sex if I pay."

"Well, cheers," he said, lifting his draft. "Although I'd feel cheap and dirty the whole time, I can live with that."

Much as it galled her, she laughed at him. "Ever married?" she asked. "Children?"

"No and no. I think I probably saved some poor woman a world of misery," he said.

"No doubt. So, how much did Landon tell you about me? About us?"

"Not a lot. He said he's moved around with you and the Coast Guard. And I know about Aunt Frances."

She looked down. Then met his eyes and saw warmth and sympathy there. "Our darkest year," she admitted. "Our parents died, I had to take a compassionate leave to settle things, which put me back to the next class. I put Landon with the bitch who has no name, then had to take leave a second time to get him out of there. That poor kid. He should be so screwed up, all he's been through, and he's incredible."

"And Aunt Frances?" he asked.

She shook her head. "Our parting was ugly. We don't keep in touch. Well, we were in touch through lawyers briefly — she was my father's only sibling and she actually fought Landon and I for some of the insurance money left, since she had been named in the will to take Landon. That will was written when Landon was a baby and I was barely eighteen, not ready to take on a child. But that she would abuse him and then expect a payoff . . . ! We settled, but we will not stay in touch."

He sat back and let out a breath. "I was right. That woman is going to have a hard time staying out of hell. Maybe she's dead?"

"I think she's too mean to die. You said you were the new kid a lot? Military roots?"

He shook his head. "Very boring roots, really. Corporate moves. My dad is an accountant. He rose to CFO of a big company based in Tampa, and the company folded when I was thirteen. I have three sisters — they were nine, fifteen and seventeen at the time. While he was looking for something permanent, something with growth potential, he worked as a consultant on some long-term contract jobs. We moved three times and landed in Albuquerque right at the start of my junior year. The folks rented a house and bought one in a different school district a year later. That gave me four schools in as many years."

"And it was hard," she said.

"It was terrible. I can look back and say I learned a few things, but here I am, almost forty, and I haven't stayed in one place for long since. Because it's just me, I pull up stakes the second I don't like the way the wind is blowing."

"And how's the wind blowing in this place?" she asked.

"It's a very strange wind," he said. "Not because of Thunder Point — it's not a bad place at all. For mysterious reasons known only to my deceased friend, Ben, I am responsible for his property. It's a disaster. It's been kind of hard to decide how to handle it. While the cleanup is getting done, the contractor's architect is measuring, drawing up final plans, and there you have it. A few months from now, it'll be a new bait shop, without the bait."

She made a confused face.

"That place really needs to be a bar and deli — drinks and prepackaged food that doesn't have to be made on site. Low-maintenance, so it can be managed by one person. We'll reinforce, finish off the cellar, remodel and rebuild the dock. Hopefully someone will be able to see the potential. . . ."

He talked about lumber and studs and beams, but Sarah didn't hear.

Across the room a couple and their teen-age son stood from a table, grabbed their coats and were about to leave. It was Mr. and Mrs. Morrison, with Jag. When they saw her, they stopped midway across the dining room. Sarah hadn't noticed them before, but she knew them from the games. Mrs. Morrison was a beautiful, painfully thin woman of about forty-five or so, with hair so blond it was almost white. Mr. Morrison was shorter and older than his wife and he wore a most miserable rug.

There was a staring contest going on. Sarah slowly stood and was vaguely aware of Cooper looking over his shoulder. Then he, too, fell silent.

Sarah and the Morrisons' gazes were locked on one another. Then Mrs. Morrison lifted her nose and began to walk away.

"Have you nothing to say to me?" Sarah said because she couldn't help herself. "Nothing at all?"

Mrs. Morrison's head snapped around and she wore a sneer so angry that Sarah actually flinched.

"And what would you have me say? That I'm very unhappy about the way you contrived this entire event with the sole purpose of some kind of revenge on my son?"

"Huh?" she said, completely confused.

"Revenge?"

"Landon fell in a slippery shower but saw a perfect opportunity to make Jag seem responsible. Obviously a jealous move, one that's caused a world of trouble!"

Jag, who stood a few feet behind his parents, actually smiled.

"Effie, just let it go. Our lawyer can handle this."

"Lawyer?" Cooper asked. Then a huff of unamused laughter escaped him. "I don't think you want to slide down this slope any further. A couple of weeks ago I found Jag and his friends holding Landon against his will while Jag punched him."

"Mom, that's the guy who broke my finger."

Cooper put one hand in his pants pocket and glared. "Is that so? Where's the cast?"

"He wore a splint," Mr. Morrison said. "The sore finger, that's what held him back in the game."

"Right," Cooper said. "And by the way, that would be the second time I witnessed your son bullying and intimidating Landon. The first time was on the beach, from the deck of the bait shop."

Sarah noticed Cliff standing in the doorway to the dining room, nervously twisting his hands in a dish towel. There were three other tables of patrons looking at this confrontation in what appeared to be fascination. They were all sitting behind Jag and his parents and couldn't see the Morrisons' faces. There was not a clink of a fork or murmur.

Jag's mother looked Sarah up and down coldly, meanly. Then she spoke to Cooper. "Well, I see your incentive in making up these stories now. . . ."

"Mrs. Morrison, it isn't a good idea to insult Commander Dupre. It only suggests where Jag learned his bad manners."

"Effie, we'll go now," Mr. Morrison said. "We're not going to participate in some cheap public display. This will be handled legally." Mr. Morrison moved to his wife's side, slipped his arm through hers and led the way out of the dining room.

And Jag, unbelievably, stood still. He silently laughed, tipping his head back. Then he stared at Sarah and made little kissing motions with his lips. And then he closed his eyes into mere slits and ran his tongue around his lips, all the while his hands in his pockets, his expression aggressive and sexual.

Sarah lost it. She suddenly took a couple of steps as if she'd charge him. Cooper grabbed her around the waist and held on to her, lifting her off the floor. She was reaching toward Jag, kicking her feet.

Jag jumped back into a table, crashing into it and sending glassware tumbling. He yelled, "Hey!" as if he were under attack, though Sarah hadn't gotten near him. His parents turned back toward the dining room, ready to rescue their poor, victimized son.

Cliff ran forward, grabbed the boy by the arm to right him, then murmured something like, "We'll take care of this," and hustled him out of the dining room.

Cooper slowly put Sarah on her feet. He turned her around. He looked calm. She looked furious. "Sit down," he said softly.

Sarah went back to her chair, but she was seething. Trembling. She could feel eyes on her; she could feel the hot flush on her cheeks. She took a sip of her wine. Then she whispered, "Did you see?"

"I saw," Cooper said with a black frown. "He set you up. He's a punk."

She shook her head, still stunned. "Listen, Cooper, I've been in one or two seedy waterfront bars where you have to be careful and I've never been treated like that."

"I believe it. Even in ugly grunt bars, only the lowest, drunkest men pull that stuff. And he's seventeen?"

"I think I'd like to leave," she said.

"No, Sarah. We're going to stay. We're going to sit here awhile and talk quietly. I want you to have your wine, try to eat your dinner."

Cliff came to their table. "You folks okay?" he asked softly.

"We're fine," Cooper said. "We're very excited about that grouper."

"Good!" he said, grinning.

But Sarah's hand went to her stomach. When Cliff left she said, "I'm not all that excited."

He smiled at her. "Time to get a grip. If you're going to live in a little town, you have to know who you can trust. You can trust the grouper."

"You broke his finger?" she asked.

"Nah. He got in my face, poked me in the chest and told me to take off and leave Landon. I didn't feel like it. I made a point, that's all. His finger is fine. I wanted to mess up his face, lying little prick. He's lucky we walked away."

She smiled at him. "Are you all right?"

"You *are* buying dinner," he said. "My shins hurt."

And her flush deepened.

# ELEVEN

Cooper wanted to keep Sarah at the restaurant for a reasonable length of time. For one thing, he wanted to be sure she was completely calmed down and thinking straight. He also intended to be sure they discussed some very important things. While they ate salads, he opened the conversation. Mr. and Mrs. Morrison clearly considered themselves privileged and above the rules. Jag took it even a step further. He was vindictive, cruel and obviously spoiled, with a powerful family who would back him up even when all the facts pointed to his dishonesty and immorality.

"Listen, Sarah, that kid? He's fearless and dark, dangerous. Obviously, he comes by it honestly — his mother is just as creepy. First of all, if you ever see any of them, the Morrisons, I want you to cross the street to avoid them. Second, we're going to take this even more seriously and make sure Landon is safe. And third . . ." He shook his head. "I don't know how I'm going to describe it, but I'm going to tell Mac about what just happened. It was very sick and twisted."

"They mentioned a lawyer."

"People say *lawyer* a lot more than they use lawyers. But they do need one. Their kid went to jail, will have to appear before a judge and has been suspended from school. Landon doesn't need a lawyer."

"Are you sure?" she asked. "Because it sounds like they really believe Landon would lie about this."

"I think they do believe it, but that doesn't make it true," he said.

"Where does a kid like that end up in life?" Sarah asked him.

"Probably cell block five," Cooper said. "And if so, he'll find out what it's like to be jumped from behind. Listen, the real important issue here is Landon. He wants to be a big manly guy, all sixteen-year-old boys do. He doesn't want to appear afraid. You're going to have to find a way to convince him to take Morrison very seriously."

She huffed. "I can try. You might have better luck with that than me."

"If there's an opportunity, I will. And I'll talk to Mac, but I think you should do that, too. Ask Mac what steps you and Landon should take to be safe. Hopefully, the kid's just an ass."

She shook her head. "I'm trying to figure out how to explain that I could interpret him throwing me kisses and licking his lips as dangerous. . . ."

"It wasn't that, Sarah. It was the gleam in his eyes. If he'd done that to my girl in front of me ten years ago, I might've taken him out. As for Mac, I don't think he'll even question you when it comes to your feelings about Morrison. After all, his daughter is involved, if only on the edge of this situation."

She was looking at him steadily. Earnestly. "I never thought I'd be relying on a complete stranger for help with this."

Cooper was considering many possible responses when Cliff brought the grouper.

"Here we go," Cliff said. "Most popular dish in the house. And listen, folks, I'm sorry about what happened earlier. I didn't see what he did to get a rise out of you, but I didn't have to. I've dealt with that kid and his mother before. His dad, Puck Morrison, is not such a bad guy, unless you're doing business with him. Then he can get a little fierce, but I never knew him to turn on anyone . . ."

"Puck?" Cooper asked.

"From old hockey days." Then he laughed. "Real old. Puck's got about thirty years on his wife. I knew her way back. She used to be a tiny little thing with a bad temper. Came from nothin' — she's a town girl — but you'd think she came from Buckingham Palace. Puck came from Eugene. Effie's the second wife. He wasn't quite done with the first one when Effie stepped in. That's mostly just gossip, but I been around a long time and knew Effie before she had boobs. Seriously, I think Puck bought her boobs, then married her. Or maybe then his wife left him, along with their two older sons. I don't know what they were doing here tonight. Morrisons don't usually darken my door. Puck drops in by himself sometimes, just for a beer or some gossip, but the wife likes the country club. She doesn't waste a lot of time in this old town. . . ."

He just talked on and on while Cooper and Sarah listened. When he slowed down just a little, Cooper said, "Pull up a chair, Cliff. Have a cup of coffee with us."

"Nah, but thanks," he said, not catching the sarcasm. "Enjoy that grouper. Most popular dish in the house."

Cooper and Sarah just smiled at each other across the table. Cooper lifted his fork and said, "Try it. It really is good."

As she took a small bite, Cooper was aware of the shift in mood at their table, thanks to Cliff. At least for the moment, it seemed as if Sarah wasn't thinking about that snotty punk or her brother or her troubles. She chewed slowly, lifted her brows and said, "Wow. Excellent! You must come here a lot."

He shook his head. "Just a couple of times. It was recommended and I liked it." He took his own bite. "So, I told you I was in four schools in four years. I had no idea I'd end up in the Army, in helicopters. I enlisted because I figured everyone in the Army was from somewhere else and it was probably the only place I wouldn't be the new guy. But what about you? You move around a lot as a kid?"

She shook her head. Born and raised in Boca Raton, Florida, she grew up surfing, sailing, swimming, diving, playing volleyball, softball and soccer. The conversation was slow and easy, punctuated by his questions and their bites of grouper, rice and asparagus. She loved the sea, thus the Coast Guard. She'd thought she'd like flying, then learned she *loved* flying helicopters. Until the death of her parents, she'd led a charmed life.

She married another Coast Guard helicopter pilot, a man her age but junior in rank by a few years. And she described it as a foolish mistake.

"There were red flags. I questioned his fidelity before the wedding but he somehow convinced me I was imagining things, that he could never be interested in another woman. It turned out I married a man who thought being faithful was optional. Once caught, he calmly explained he wasn't cut out for marriage. For monogamy."

Cooper was stunned. Of all the stupid and insensitive things he'd done, that hadn't been one of them. If he became attracted to another woman, enough to want to take her to bed, he saw that as a signal whatever relationship he was in wasn't working. Duh. He wasn't naive; men cheated all the time and some rationalized that any woman who wiggled past them was fair game.

"Why do you look so dumbfounded?" Sarah asked him.

He closed his mouth. "Sorry. I'm not fifteen. I know it happens all the time. But before the marriage? Why'd he want to get married?"

"I have a better question. It wasn't the first time. The Coast Guard is like a small town, especially after about six years. So why didn't anybody tell me? Why didn't someone say, *Hey, Sarah, this guy's really been around and he's broken a few hearts?*"

Cooper couldn't stop the stain that darkened his cheeks, though he fought it. He'd been accused of breaking hearts, but not by cheating. His crimes were slightly different. He'd been called shiftless and unable to put down roots or plan a real future. He couldn't seem to get attached. He'd been twice engaged — once because he'd been with a good woman and thought it was time and once because his girlfriend of the moment, also a good woman, asked and he couldn't think of a reason to say no. Both times he'd been informed he had commitment issues. He was told he was emotionally unavailable, whatever that meant. One said he had problems with intimacy, but he thought his only problem was not enough intimacy — and then he was informed that sex was not intimacy. Really? He was too much of a loner, couldn't connect, didn't understand women. Probably true, as far as he knew. And although the breaking up had hurt him enough to try avoiding women, he realized he was probably better off than with either of them.

And there'd been a whole lot of short-term women. Some very short-term. Right now as he looked across the table at Sarah, who was so *hot,* he asked himself why. Shouldn't he have found a long-term mate by now? Did he have a missing chromosome?

"You look completely embarrassed," she pointed out to him.

He cleared his throat. "I've been told I'm a bad bet. That I'm afraid of commitment, intimacy, et cetera. I never thought I was afraid. You don't have to believe this — I probably wouldn't if I were you — but I didn't cheat. I'm no Prince Charming, but I didn't do that."

Unbelievably, she laughed.

Cliff chose that minute to bring them coffee and pick up the plates. For someone who had wanted to leave and didn't think she could eat, Sarah had killed that grouper. Cliff asked if they'd like drinks or dessert and they both shook their heads.

"So, why is that funny?" Cooper asked.

"First of all, it doesn't matter whether I believe you. I have no stake in your past affairs. And second, I'm laughing at myself for depending on help from a guy who has a long history of fear of intimacy and commitment."

"Yeah, that's been said about me, but I think I'm completely dependable." He lifted his coffee. Sipped. "I asked how that could be the case, since I had no resistance to getting married."

"Oh, so you were engaged," she said.

"Twice."

"And they broke it off?" she asked.

"One of each — I was asked to leave the first time. It was about that something I didn't seem to have and that I still don't understand. And the second time, I had to end it because of all the arguing. But it seemed to be about that mysterious missing factor again."

"Easy come, easy go," she said.

He looked at her over the rim of his coffee cup for a long moment. Then he said, "No, Sarah. There wasn't anything easy about it."

She cleared her throat. "And yet you find yourself completely dependable?" she asked.

"I do. Hey, I'm here trying to sort out the wishes of some dead guy because he was my friend. I could load up the camper and go, right? It's not like Ben would put a curse on me. And I didn't even agree to this job."

"They why are you doing it?"

"Because no one else will. And it's the right thing to do — he was a decent guy. Besides," he said, "it's not like I can't spare a few months."

"Well, I can't take a few months off," she

said. "Are you rich?"

"Far from it. But there's just the fifth wheel, paid for, and no kids. I have three sisters who make sure our parents are fine. I can afford to do this for Ben."

"You must have been real close," she said. "Best friends."

Cooper put his elbows on the table and laced his fingers together, looking down for a moment. Then he met her eyes. "I guess. Guys are different, you know. . . ."

"Oh, yes, I know."

"I liked Ben. He was my lead mechanic. He made me laugh. I got a kick out of him and tossing back a few with him was always a good time. We stayed in touch. He visited a few times in ten years, but I'd never come up here before. Our whole friendship was mostly emails and phone calls. We had things in common — I had the Gulf of Mexico and he had the Pacific. When I was flying for oil companies, there were a couple of spills, and he called to ask if there was a local wildlife rescue organization I'd like him to make a donation to. He's always cared about the wildlife, although I didn't realize how much until I got here. I trusted him. But the truth is, besides my family, I don't have a lot of friends. Just a few. Good ones, but not that many."

After a long moment of silence she said, "Me, either."

"I see you as having lots of girlfriends to drink wine with, shop with."

She shook her head. "I work in a man's world. There's one other female pilot at the station, married. We get along fine, but . . . our lives are different. And sometimes the wives of the guys I work with don't . . ." They were wary of her, like they didn't trust her. It wasn't easy being one of the few women in a unit and being single besides. The last time she had a close girlfriend, she found out she'd been sharing her with her fiancé. "No, I don't have a lot of girlfriends. Just a few women I'm friendly with, that's all."

"Sometimes that's all you need," he said.

And then Cooper told her about his buddy, Luke, and Luke's brothers. Sarah had a couple of guys at the station she'd bonded with, and she was getting to know Gina, whom she liked.

Cliff was standing beside their table and they both looked up at him. The leather folder containing the check sat on the table and their coffees had been refilled but neither of them seemed to be aware of it.

"Tell you what, folks," Cliff said. "How about I leave the keys here and you lock up when you're ready?"

It took a second to sink in, then they laughed. The restaurant was empty and Cooper had no memory of seeing people leave. He reached for his wallet.

"No, you don't," Sarah said, grabbing the check. She held it in her custody until she could wrangle her credit card out of her purse. "This one is mine. You kept me from being convicted of murder."

"Two seconds," Cliff said, running off with the check.

Cooper stood and pulled on his jacket. He picked up her long, black coat and held it for her. "Thank you, Commander. I'll get the next one."

"You do that, Cooper. Just keep an eye on my brother for me, that's thanks enough." Then Cliff was back with a receipt for her to sign. "Sorry we kept you up, Cliff," she said.

"Have a nice night, folks," he said, following them to the door and locking it.

"Is it late?" she asked Cooper.

"Apparently it's late for Cliff. My watch says ten-twenty."

They drove back to the high school for his truck, talking and laughing. There were still cars in the well-lit lot, still music coming from the gymnasium, but not a soul around the parking lot. Undoubtedly, some kids had managed to escape from under the chaperones' gazes, but there was still action in there. They got out of the car and gravitated to the front, leaning against the hood and gazing at the school. Sarah sighed. "Another thing to say thank you for. Even though things got a little whacko at Cliff's, I could have been trapped behind a decorated pillar in there until midnight."

Cooper crossed his arms over his chest. "That was a nasty business at Cliff's, but worth seeing. Now there's no question about what you're dealing with." Then he shifted toward her. "In spite of that, I have to say, Sarah, I enjoyed dinner."

She turned so they faced each other and smiled. "Maybe I'll take you out again sometime."

He pulled on her arm and brought her closer, against him. "You're a good date," he said.

"You thought of it as a date?"

He nodded. "From the beginning."

"Well, I have some bad news, Cooper. I've given up dating."

He couldn't help but grin. "Going to go old maid?"

She smirked. "I could change my mind in

ten or twenty years. For now, no dating. No men."

"Probably a very smart decision." Then he leaned toward her and got his face close enough so he could feel her breath on his face. "Kind of a waste, though." And then he touched her lips with his.

"Mmm," she said, closing those large eyes.

He pulled her closer, tilting his head to kiss her. He cradled her head in one hand and held her firmly but gently against his mouth. After the briefest moment, she parted her lips slightly so that their tongues could touch. When that happened he inhaled sharply, damned pleased at the response. One arm around her waist pulled her tight against him, and he moved over her opened mouth hungrily. He kissed her long and hard, even though he thought he shouldn't. When he finally pulled back just an inch, he said, "News flash. I'm a man."

"Friend," she said. "Just a friend with some common interests."

"And one of them is kissing."

She laughed. "I'm human, after all."

"Give me five minutes. I could wear you down."

"In your dreams."

"What are you doing tomorrow?" he asked.

"Laundry," she said. "Sunday catch up. Monday is work."

"Hmm. Want me to help with laundry? I've been doing my own for years. I'm probably really good with the dainties."

She chuckled a little. "No, thanks."

He kissed her again, a little harder. Deeper. He let his tongue loose to play. Her arms slid up to his shoulders and she held on, joining a little tongue dancing. Everything he tasted said yes. He pulled back. "Probably smart not to get involved with someone like me," he said.

"Not to worry, champ. I'm not going to get involved with anyone."

"Good. I tend to piss women off."

And then she pulled him back to her mouth and went after him with steam and power of her own and almost brought him to his knees. How'd she manage to taste like honey and smell like flowers after dinner at Cliff's? He pulled her hard against him and devoured her, unsure whether he was relieved or disappointed that she wouldn't feel his erection through that long, heavy coat she wore. And then her hands were against his chest, gently pushing him away. Not shoving, just a little push so he'd back off. She smiled into his eyes.

"So far, the way you don't get involved is

made to order," he told her.

"I'm going home now, Cooper. Thanks for helping out. And everything."

"Sure," he said, taking a step back. "Want me to follow you home?"

She shook her head. "I'm good." She gently slugged his chest. "Drive careful."

"Yeah," he said, breathless.

When she turned to get back into her car, he followed. He held the door and then closed it for her. He waved her off. And then he stood by his truck for a little while as she drove off.

"Holy shit," he whispered. "Damn."

Landon and Eve left the homecoming dance with Downy and Ashley at about nine-thirty. They got a pizza in town and took it to Landon's house because no one was home, thanks to Cooper. What a pal.

They snarfed down pizza and Cokes, laughing over stories everyone had to share. The second the pizza was gone, Downy grabbed his girl, lifted her up and said, "Come here, my girlfriend, and drive me out of my mind some more." He carried her to the living room, where he chose the sofa for some rock-star-quality making out. After five minutes, he pulled her down the hall of the little house.

Landon was stunned, his mouth hanging open. "Is he doing what it looks like he's doing?"

Eve smiled. "I prefer not to think about that too much. And of course, anything my best friend said to me is confidential."

"Of course, yeah," he said.

She grinned at him. "You have to wonder, though, right?"

"But he wouldn't do the nasty here, in my bedroom, when my sister could be walking in anytime?"

"Probably not," she said.

He smiled at her, knowing it was crooked. "Eve, I'm sorry you got stuck going to a big dance with a guy whose face is mashed in."

She pushed back her kitchen chair and went to him, sitting on his lap. "You're still handsome, even with your face mashed in. You got altogether too much attention from the girls, too."

"That's because of you," he said. "They couldn't believe I was with you."

"Does your mouth hurt?" she asked.

He tilted his head and then slowly touched the place where his lip was split. "Just a little, right here."

"Hmm," she said, leaning forward and kissing him gently right beside it. Then she pressed her lips against his cheek. Then the goose egg on his forehead. Then his lips again. Then she smiled.

"I could heal up and be less interesting," he said. "Think you'd go out with me again?"

"I could. But you're going to have to ask me next time."

"It's kinda cool having the prettiest girl at school ask me for a date," he said. "I'd really like to take you out tomorrow, but maybe by next Saturday night my face won't look like I've been in a wreck." He put his arms around her waist. "I want my lip healed, that's for sure."

"Oh?" she teased. "And why is that?"

"You're not the only one who's a good kisser, you know. I'm not bad — when it doesn't make me bleed."

She laughed at him. "When's your birthday? Maybe for your birthday."

"What a coincidence," Landon said. "Next Saturday night is my birthday!"

She pulled away a bit, but put her arms around his neck. "I think you're lying. You wouldn't lie to me, would you, Landon?"

"And the Saturday night after that is my birthday, too," he said, leaning toward her, his lips ready. "Go easy now," he whispered.

And she gave him a light kiss on the side of his mouth.

"More," he whispered, and she was happy to comply, treating him to sweet, soft kisses for a few minutes.

"When you first moved here," Landon asked, "was it easy? Did you fit right in?"

"I fit right in with Ash, but we had some issues — like the girlfriends she already had had for a long time were jealous of me because Ash liked me. It took a while before that passed. When my dad took this job and bought the house, I didn't want to come. I was in seventh grade and I gave him a hard time. He was more patient than he should've been, but Lou just about lost it. You don't want to mess with Aunt Lou. You moved a lot, right?"

"Coast Guard. You're gonna move, that's how it is. But I loved Alaska. Even though I was just a little kid when we were in Kodiak, I hated to leave. I'd go back there in a second. I'll go wherever a football team will cover my tuition for college, but if I had my choice, I'd head back to Kodiak."

"I haven't been very many places," Eve said. "We've been on some cool camping trips, but if we can't drive there, we can't go."

He smiled his lopsided smile and touched her cheek. "Nothing wrong with that, Eve. I like camping. So does Sarah."

"In summer, sometimes a bunch of us camp on the beach," she said.

"Really? All night?"

She nodded. "And we try not to notice the deputy's SUV parked at the edge of the beach."

He tightened his arms around her. "Guess there's no zipping sleeping bags together. . . ."

"Don't worry, Landon. He probably nods off. At least that's what he does in his chair every night."

"So. There is a God."

Gina looked around the colorful gymnasium, now almost empty of people. The teens who had driven their dates started to leave by nine or so; the chaperones followed suit as the number of kids on the dance floor thinned out. Lou McCain was among the first to leave; she wanted to check on Ryan and Dee Dee. Quite a few kids, maybe fifty, hung around the dance until the last dog died and they were herded out the door. Aside from the refreshments, there was very little cleanup. The kids who put up the decorations would be back to strip them down on Sunday afternoon.

Mac stood near the back door of the gym talking with one of the deputies, Charlie

Adams. He rocked back on his heels and laughed — a good sign. Charlie must have stopped by to say the town was quiet with nothing much going on.

God, but he was perfect. Perfect-*looking*. As men go, Deputy Yummy Pants was an amazing specimen, but he was apparently a eunuch. Or gay. But either was impossible to grasp. In the four years they'd been good friends, there'd been those couple of times he'd kissed her with awesome, sincere passion . . . then backed right off on the excuse of parenthood.

She often wondered if he had some chickie buried somewhere out of sight, some woman he saw regularly who scratched his itch so that around town he could appear completely unattached. Maybe she was a terrible kisser and he came to his senses?

Men flirted with her regularly. She was behind the counter at the diner, after all. Nearly every man in town passed her way at one time or another, as did the occasional out-of-towner — the UPS guy, the beverage guy, the guy who delivered the meat. She'd grown up in this town. She'd known a lot of the people forever. After having a baby in high school and keeping her, living with her mother as she did, it had taken quite a lot to retrench her reputation and emerge as one of Thunder Point's best-liked and most-respected residents. Back in high school, she imagined people whispered that she was a slut. Now they thought of her as upstanding, thanks to years of church, PTA and town meetings. Oh, and very little traffic with the opposite sex, though she had dated a bit here and there.

Not in the past few years, however. It seemed pointless.

Before she could brood any longer, Mac was walking toward her with her coat slung over one arm. She wanted to be angry with him for tying up her heart the way he had, but she couldn't. He might not be her boyfriend or lover, but he was always there for her. Always. The best friend she'd ever had.

"Thanks," she said, taking her coat and shrugging into it.

"I'll walk you out," he said, taking her elbow.

"Thank God the diner doesn't open at five on Sunday mornings," she grumbled. "I'm exhausted."

"You need more days off."

"I need bigger tips," she said as she laughed.

"Yeah, me, too." He opened the back door for her. "And a good time was had by all," he said. "No fights, no accidents and, as far as I know, no illegal drugs or drinking."

"Or they're getting better at hiding it," she added.

"Never saw a hint of trouble."

"Oh, there was little stuff. Predictable stuff. A couple of girls crying in the bathroom. One over her date, who was acting like an idiot, raving about some other girl's cleavage. There was one notable clothing malfunction that had to be pinned back into place — an entire breast escaped and every high school boy in the room claimed to have seen it. And then you have the mean girls — Patrice, Stellie and Harmony." She sighed. "I think Harmony is the worst one. She just can't live up to her name."

"What did the mean girls do?" he wanted to know.

"Being a guy, you probably wouldn't catch on. They stick together in a little clot, whisper, shift their eyes toward their victim *du jour* — some younger, simpler, more vulnerable creature — and then they giggle. That sort of thing. Lean toward each other on the dance floor, whisper and stare, laugh. Spread rumors, like saying Lindsay got her dress at the Goodwill until Lindsay — who did get her dress at the Goodwill — ends up in the bathroom crying, begging to just go home."

He looked a little shell-shocked. "That's *horrible!*"

"With all the things you see on the job, I'm surprised you're surprised. People can behave very badly. Especially teenagers." It didn't even bear mentioning what her generation of mean girls had to say about her when she turned up pregnant at fifteen.

"I can't stand to think of some nice girl like Lindsay crying over her secondhand dress! My kids have all worn secondhand clothes. Lou gets pretty excited about good hand-me-downs and, God knows, a sheriff's deputy with three kids isn't shopping at the high-end stores. How'd you know that was happening?"

She gave a shrug. "I've done my share of bathroom crying. Not for a very long time, however."

"Eve and Ash aren't putting up with crap like that, are they?" he asked. "If you knew, you'd tell me, right?"

She stopped walking and turned to look up at him. "Listen, Mac, the girls are pretty secure. They present a strong front. Ash has got Downy on alert and not only is he a big strong boy, but there's still a little hero worship at the school. In spite of that, they occasionally have their dramas. But if I knew either of them were being persecuted by mean girls, I'd tell Lou."

"Not me?"

"Lou would probably tell you, if she thought it was serious. But men tend to say things like, *Aw, don't let 'em get to you.* Girls need sympathy. Vindication. A soft shoulder to cry on, encouragement. Men just want their girls to rise above it."

"Is that true?" he asked.

She nodded.

He thought for a minute. "I think you might be right. I might say something like that. And I might think it was the right thing to say."

"Yeah. It's not about how much you love your daughters, Mac. It's more what you're programmed to say."

He walked with her again and opened the door to her Jeep. "How do you know these things? You haven't had a man around in forever. No dad, no husband, no steady boyfriend unless you keep him hidden. Yet you know how men work."

She slipped into her Jeep and smiled at him. "Pure genius," she said. "See you later."

# TWELVE

The diner on Sunday mornings was a different kind of place than the rest of the week. It was a good place for families to stop on the way home from church or on the way to some outing. There were also weekend athletes and pleasure seekers — cyclists or, in warmer weather, sports fishermen, paddleboard enthusiasts, people taking their boats out for a nice day on the bay.

Gina didn't work at the diner every Sunday, but she didn't mind when she did. She liked the mornings and only worked the dinner hour if she was filling in for someone. From her place behind the counter, she saw the new town doctor pull his van up to his storefront clinic across the street. He got out, this time with two children — a little girl and little boy. He had one on each hand, but rather than going inside the clinic, he walked across the street to the diner. Gina had only seen him from a distance, going in or out of that space. And she had never seen the children.

They were so little, so young. She'd heard from Mac that he was a single father, but it was hard to imagine how he could put in doctor hours and parent full-time, even with a babysitter. He held the door for them, first the little girl, then the little boy. She could tell from across the street that he was a nice-looking man, but up close he was better than that — he was gorgeous. And the children? Delicious.

"Morning," she said from behind the counter. "Sit anywhere you like."

"How about right here? At the counter?"

"Be my guest."

He lifted his daughter onto a stool first, then his son. The little girl had shiny hair pulled back with barrettes and wore a little green jumper over a long-sleeved T-shirt and white tights. The little boy, his hair cut in a short, adult style and neatly combed, had a couple of cowlicks. He wore jeans and little boots and a denim jacket. Both the kids had mahogany-colored hair and huge brown eyes, while the doctor had dark blond hair with blue eyes. Very kind blue eyes.

When the kids were settled on their stools, he put out his hand. "Scott Grant," he said.

She took the hand. "Gina James. So nice

274

to meet you. And who are your friends?"

"This is Jenny and this is Will. Age three and four."

"They're beautiful," she said. "So? Coffee? Juice? Breakfast? Parenting advice for when they're teenagers?"

"I appreciate it," he said with a laugh. "I'd love a cup of coffee and the kids would like juice — maybe apple? And if you have it, cereal for them."

"And for you?" she asked, filling his cup.

"Just coffee," he said. "I woke up early and already had breakfast."

She quickly set up the juice and cereal for the kids. Then she said, "It's very exciting to have a clinic opening up. We haven't had a doctor's office in town for about five years now. We had a couple of doctors here when I was growing up, but one retired and one moved, joining a busy practice in Eugene. The nearest hospital or urgent care is Bandon. If you need a few stitches or some blood work, it's a major time investment."

"I know. I hope that will change, but we're a long way from opening. I'm working in Bandon now, helping out a family practitioner and taking call at the hospital E.R. while I get this set up. Just buying and installing the equipment is a major undertaking — and the office still needs cleaning up and decorating. And I haven't even thought about staff. I don't suppose you know any R.N.s around here who are looking for a change?"

"I don't. I'm sorry. But if you give me a list of what you're looking for, this isn't a bad place to spread the word."

"Thanks, that's a good idea."

"And I understand you have an au pair for the kids? Small town, you know," she added with a smile and shrug.

"Gabriella. I knew her parents in Vancouver. She's a brilliant girl, if a little old-fashioned. She's also beautiful. Smart and hardworking and dependable . . ." He stopped, looking a little startled by what he'd said. He leaned toward her as if he needed to say something very personal. "Hey," he said. "Small town here. Are people around here going to be put off or suspicious of my relationship with a nineteen-year-old au pair? I'm a thirty-six-year-old man, a widower, and have absolutely no —"

She held up a hand and smiled at him. "Don't borrow trouble," she said. "We're kind of a bunch of hicks on the water around here, but I know of a couple of girls from town who took au pair jobs to get to Europe. You'll probably find that she's referred to more often as your babysitter."

"There aren't many options," he said. "I can't afford a full-time housekeeper and nanny."

"It'll be okay, Scott. If I might ask, why Thunder Point?"

"Well, slower pace, so I don't miss too much of the kids' growing up. But it's really an experiment. I've never lived in a small town. This town has a good reputation, you know. A lot of community involvement, good schools, low crime . . ."

"I know," she said. "We're not very cosmopolitan, but it's a good place."

"The cost of living is low," he added.

"And speaking of living, where are you living?"

"Bandon, for the time being, keeping an eye open for something in town. I've looked at a couple of rentals, but they were in pretty bad shape."

"One problem with a small town, property doesn't turn over too often." Gina smiled. "I'll keep an eye open for that, too."

Thirty minutes later Gina had introduced Dr. Grant to a few folks from town who had come in for breakfast, made a short list of what he was looking for in housing and staff, and shook his hand as they said goodbye. A few people came and went, leaving

Gina plenty of time to refill napkin holders, salt-and-pepper shakers, sugar caddies. The little bell on the diner door tinkled just as Gina was filling her last ketchup bottle. She smiled to see Sarah come in. "Hey," she said.

"Hey, yourself." She sat up on a stool.

"You're early today and no Hamlet," Gina said, peering out the diner's glass door. "Breakfast?" There was a family of five in a big booth in the corner, the youngest in a high chair, and an elderly couple in another booth. Both parties were finishing their meals. It was late for breakfast, early for lunch. Stu could be seen through the cook's slat in the wall, moving around with his iPod earbuds in his ears.

"Not today, thanks. But I won't turn down a cup of coffee. I'll take Ham out later, or Landon will. How are you recuperating from all the hard work you and the others did for the dance last night?"

"Not much work on my part," Gina said, filling a cup. "The kids and teachers did most of the work. I just showed up to keep an eye on things. And things seemed to go fairly smoothly."

"I got home last night to find my brother, Eve McCain, your daughter and Downy at my house. I went out to dinner."

"I noticed you were gone," she said with a smile. "The kids usually pick my house to hang after a dance, if they're not on the beach. My mother has no problem turning the volume up on the TV in her bedroom and falling asleep. They could be building bombs for all she knows."

"They seemed to be sitting around the kitchen table at my house after devouring a pizza and a bunch of Cokes, laughing at whatever. I was home by ten-thirty," Sarah told her. "It was such a relief to see Landon hanging out with friends."

"I noticed a certain newcomer was also gone."

"Cooper and I went to dinner at Cliff-hanger's."

"I like him. Cooper. He seems like a good guy."

"He does, doesn't he? Landon likes him and I'll admit, I'm getting kind of used to the idea of Cooper looking out for Landon. He's probably doing that because there's no man around the house. As long as Cooper doesn't sell him to the circus, that could be helpful."

"Have you raised him entirely alone?" Gina asked.

"Almost. I took custody when he was six, ten years ago, after our parents died. I lived with a guy for a year when Landon was thirteen, then was married to him for almost a year when we were separated. He was devoted to Landon . . . until we broke up." She gave a shrug. "For a couple of years there, I had someone to pitch in. And I was married for almost a year. Derek, my ex, liked to watch Landon play ball. I've been divorced nine months now. Derek was the only guy I let in, and he was a big mistake. Apparently I'm not real good at picking 'em."

Gina smiled and poured herself a cup of coffee. "Want help? I can spot a loser a mile away. Now, that is. I wasn't so good at it when I was a teenager. I had a doozy then. I was fortunate enough not to marry him. Through no brilliance of my own, I might add. I sobbed every miserable night, hoping he'd come back and beg me to marry him. But I was a kid. Left with a kid."

"And now you have Mac," Sarah said.

The family of five were leaving. Dad stopped at the counter to give Gina the check and some money, telling her to keep the change.

"No," Gina told Sarah with a laugh, shaking her head. "Mac and I are friends. We have been since our daughters hooked up as best friends. As friends go, he's the best.

I don't think he's dating anyone — he hasn't ever brought a woman around to games or town things, but there might be someone somewhere. Why? Are you interested?"

"You get teased about him," Sarah said. "People put you two together."

"People must have very vivid imaginations. If I had a guy, hopefully you'd at least see some hand-holding. Mac and I have gone to a movie or two, but usually he's dragging a kid or Lou along. We sit together at the games, but other than that . . ."

"I thought you were a couple. Maybe discreet, but a couple . . ."

Gina shook her head. "No. I guess a lot of people think that. I think they can't imagine a friend of the opposite sex. Nah, I love Mac, but he's a free agent. If you like him, go for it."

"You're not making this easy," Sarah said.

Gina tilted her head and shot Sarah a nonplussed expression. "I could gift wrap him for you, I guess."

"I don't trust men," Sarah said. "I don't even trust many women and I don't trust myself, either. I thought my ex was a prince, the catch of a lifetime. He was Mr. Romance, so it never occurred to me he could be that attentive and affectionate with me if he . . ." She cleared her throat. "It turned out he had a lot of romantic energy. And a very short attention span."

"Ew. Hate those."

"It would take a lot to tempt me now. I have zero interest in being dumped by a man again."

"Now some people would say you should get back on that horse," Gina said with a laugh.

"And did you? After you had Ashley?"

The elderly couple slowly made their way to the counter. Gina took their ticket, their money, rang them up with a smile, told them to have a nice Sunday.

Then she returned to Sarah. "It took me a while. Ashley was my life and I was all about protecting her from my potential mistakes."

"I have a lot of that going on," Sarah admitted. "When Derek left, he left Landon, too. And he left Landon with a sister who was an emotional cripple. I have to be careful. He's a big kid, very mature for his age, but he's still just a kid."

"I know. They think they know everything, but they're just kids. And they're right at that age when the biggest mistakes seem to hit them. I'm living proof of that. I didn't go out on a date till Ashley was five years old. And then I was cautious. So careful my few dates lost interest in me, not the other way around. I think I always felt safest if I wasn't involved with a guy."

"Me, too," Sarah said. "Except . . . I kissed Cooper."

Surprise registered on Gina's face for a moment, then she said, "I take it that didn't fit into your plans?"

Sarah took a sip of coffee. "I've been asked out a couple of times since the divorce. I even had one guy from a Coast Guard station not too far away get all excited that I was divorced and ask me out a number of times before he finally got the message, I am not dating. Not. Period. And I have not been tempted to even rethink it. I figured when I was about forty and Landon was all grown-up and on his own, I might consider it, but not anytime soon."

"I guess kissing isn't exactly dating," Gina said carefully.

"It terrifies me to even think about a relationship with a man. It was like this with Derek — he was so attentive, and it took him two seconds to get close to Landon," Sarah said. "Even though Landon might not realize it, he's vulnerable. Besides, our lives work pretty well, the two of us. He's such a great kid. We take good care of each other. I'm not risking Landon's feelings by getting mixed up with some guy, especially some

283

guy he likes." She shook her head. "Red flags everywhere. Everywhere. You have no idea what Derek put us through."

Gina gulped. "I don't want to ask, but . . ."

"But I brought it up. Derek cheated."

"I assumed that's what you meant by a lot of romantic energy."

Sarah sipped her coffee again. "A good friend of mine," she said, and her cheeks brightened.

"What a dog!"

Sarah laughed suddenly. "It was a dog, as a matter of fact, that showed me his true colors. I called his cell and I heard a dog barking in the background. It sounded just like the dog next door to my ex-friend Susan's house. That dog never shut up. He was there and he lied — and I let him convince me I was insane, that he could never do such a thing."

Gina took a moment to refill her coffee cup. "No wonder you don't trust women. How did you find out?"

"She decided to unburden her guilty conscience," Sarah said. "I think she was angry with Derek. I think she was losing him, but not to me. He admitted they'd had a thing. A purely physical thing. And he was sorry, but he said he wasn't good at monogamy and hoped we could —" she cleared her throat "— work with that."

"My God," Gina said in a breath. She leaned toward Sarah. "This doesn't even happen on *General Hospital.* How did Landon take it?"

"I tried to keep him from knowing, but he figured it out. I think he hates Derek. No, I know he hates Derek. And now I've gone and kissed Cooper, his friend."

"Maybe it was an accident," Gina said. "He's pretty sweet and sexy, after all."

"So, there you have it. Cooper is all wrong. All wrong." She shook her head. "Not only is he male, which makes him dangerous, he is a rover. A nomad. He's planning to leave the minute that bait shop is fixed up. No, sir, I'm not going to fall for him. No way."

"Understandable . . ."

"I have never wanted to be kissed more in my life. I wanted to rip his clothes off. I wanted to climb all over him. I didn't just let him kiss me, I nearly ate him alive. Right after I told him there was no way I was dating or getting involved with a man. He probably thinks I'm a lunatic."

They stared at each other for a long, silent moment. Then Gina said, "Wow."

"I think I have to move," Sarah said, dropping her head into her hand and running her fingers through her short hair.

Gina felt a warm flush rise up her neck to her face. Sarah would have no way of knowing that Gina also had one of those ferocious big-girl crushes, and no solution in sight. Gina had not confided in anyone, not even her mother — and she was very close to Carrie. She didn't dare. One slip would find Ashley talking to Eve about it and then Lou would soon know and Lou . . . Lou couldn't be trusted to keep from saying something to Mac. And then? Who knew? Mac might quit coming by for coffee or stop sitting with her at games if he thought she was some maniac about to debauch him.

"Oh, God, I've embarrassed you," Sarah said. "Oh, Gina, I'm sorry! It's just that it's been so long since I've had a woman to talk to about stuff like this. Oh, hell, it's been so long since I *had* stuff like this."

Gina shook her head. "No, it's not that. Not at all. It's just that I've been in your shoes. Quite a while ago, really, but I do remember. That powerful crush, that feeling of complete helplessness."

"Helplessness. The thing I really can't deal with at all. You can't do what I do if you feel out of control and helpless. Man . . . if we hadn't been standing in a parking lot . . ."

"Parking lot?" Gina asked.

"At the high school. But there was no one around."

"That you know of," Gina said. "There could've been teenagers in parked cars, making out. Or whatever."

Sarah groaned. She rubbed the bridge of her nose with a finger and thumb. "Thank God Landon was already home."

"It's probably fine. There was probably no one to see. But maybe you should be prepared, in case, you know . . ."

"What am I going to do? Say?"

"Smile. Like this," Gina said, demonstrating a mysterious smile. "You're over twenty-one. He's over twenty-one. Kissing isn't illegal and it doesn't necessarily lead to marriage. Sometimes it doesn't even lead to more kissing. It's not poor form to have a kiss good-night after a dinner out. You really don't have to explain to anyone. You certainly don't have to apologize."

"Right," she said, giving a nod. "Except, this would be such a mistake."

"Remember, people aren't in your head, Sarah. They don't know the idea of a man scares you to death or that you're determined not to set yourself up for disappointment again. No one knows but me, and I'm not telling." Then she grinned. "We should

287

go out sometime. I mean, really out — not just to Cliffhanger's. We should go to Bandon or Coquille or something. Someplace where we're not sharing secrets in front of the neighbors." Then she threw a look over her shoulder. "Or the cook."

"Oh, my God! Do you think Stu . . . ?"

"One thing about Stu, if he hears something interesting, he can't stay out of it. He'd be right out here giving you advice. This is his downtime before lunch. He's probably done cleaning his kitchen and in his office, pretending to do paperwork while he watches sports on his little TV. Paperwork that he'll just ask me to do later."

"I hope so."

"Don't be so embarrassed. If it had been Ray Anne in the parking lot, she'd have been bent over the hood of the car with her skirt around her waist in just seconds."

"No way!"

"Way. Some people think the high school football team was named in her honor. The Cougars."

They both laughed and Gina refilled their coffees.

"What am I going to do about him? I really can't afford to move."

"You'll figure it out," Gina said, lifting her cup. "One thing I do know, though. A couple of girls like us, we shouldn't have such pathetic love lives. It just isn't healthy."

"I've only tried having a love life a couple of times since college — and it hasn't gone well."

After a moment of silence, Gina said, "A good friend of yours?"

"Yeah. I know. Does it get any worse than that?"

"Holy Jesus, girlfriend. That's almost as bad as getting knocked up at fifteen."

Cooper was sitting on a chair he'd dragged down to the dock because the building noise in the bar was too loud to think. The renovation had started and was in full swing, the progress already measurable. He was impressed they were working on Saturday. The contractor said, "Every day off is a day without pay."

This was right up Rawley's alley. He came over every morning, never said a thing, worked as support staff. If he was asked to do something, like hold a board or tool or drag some debris to the industrial-size Dumpster, he gave a nod and did so. He left when he was ready. Or maybe when he figured his father needed him at home. Cooper was doing his best to log his hours so he could pay him.

Cooper's laptop was open and he was surfing the net when he saw her. Sarah, with Ham, racing through the surf at water's edge. It had been way too long; a week had passed like a year. Even now, her trek across the beach was too slow.

He stopped looking at the laptop. A smile tugged at his lips. She had a way of walking that just knocked him out, a gentle sway, a purposeful yet unhurried stride. It wasn't erotic or flirtatious, it was all woman — a woman who knew what she wanted. And as she got near, she smiled at him. Ham made it to him first and he took the soggy ball out of his drooling mouth and threw it. He wiped his hand on his pants. Within seconds, Hamlet was back for another throw.

"Hey," she said.

He closed the laptop. "Where have you been?"

She put a foot up on the dock. "Mostly working."

"24/7?" he asked.

"Did you need something, Cooper?"

He *needed* another one of those crazy, deep, incredible kisses that made him go all flat-footed. "I wanted to call you, ask you to dinner. My treat. I don't have your phone number."

Instead of answering with an excited acceptance to both the date and her number, she asked, "Whatcha doing there? Emails?"

"Looking at job postings."

"Ah, you're ready to go back to work?"

"Just looking. I'm curious about what's out there. I'll have to get a job eventually."

"So, what's out there?"

"Lots of instructor positions, mostly civilian jobs with the Army. Some civilian rescue, one corporate chopper, and then there's firefighting — primarily California, Arizona and Colorado."

"Interesting. Obviously, I've never looked. Anything around here?"

"The closest is California."

"Are you sending in résumés?" she asked.

He shook his head. "I'm just curious. I'm not ready yet."

She laughed at that. "I have to admit, I'm envious. Aside from leave, I haven't taken much time off. Never more than two weeks, and I usually eat most of that up moving. You don't like to make plans, do you, Cooper?"

He shrugged. "I make some. I need to see my family pretty soon — they're getting cranky. It's been almost a year. I'm teasing them with a possible Christmas showing, but it's still a maybe. You *do* like plans, don't you, Sarah?"

She nodded and smiled. "Down to the second, months in advance, if possible. I'm very well organized."

"Or controlling," he suggested.

"Possibly, but that's irrelevant, as I only control my own activities. I try to stay flexible where my brother is concerned."

"Landon's looking better," Cooper said.

"I figured you'd seen him this week — he had to take a week off from football practice. He's a little irritable. He goes to practice to watch — although I'm not sure what he's watching more closely, the plays or the cheerleaders."

"Did you talk to him about Morrison?" Cooper asked.

"I did. I told him about the restaurant scene. Did he say anything to you?"

"Not until I told him myself. It seemed to make him angry and more worried about you than himself. Have you talked to Mac?"

"I called him early last week. And Mac also talked to Landon. He has an edge, you know. Landon and Mac's daughter are an item — the romance of the homecoming dance hasn't worn off. Landon is now convinced to tell Mac if there's any trouble." She smiled at him. "I'm surprised you didn't ask Landon for my cell number if you wanted it."

"I wasn't sure if that was a good idea," he said. "Unless you confide in your brother, he doesn't know we . . ." He cleared his throat. "What we did after dinner."

"It was just a kiss, Cooper."

"Nah. I've been kissed. It wasn't *just* a kiss. I've been thinking —"

He was cut off by the sound of a horn. He turned to see a late-model BMW inching its way down the road toward the building. The driver honked again.

"Who's that?" Sarah asked.

"I have no idea," he said, not making a move.

"Should you go see?"

"No," he said. "I should get your phone number. And we should plan a date or something."

But the BMW parked and who should get out but Ray Anne. She stood next to her car and waved at them.

"Shit," Cooper said. He waved back, but he didn't move.

"Cooper, I think she wants you to go up there, talk to her or something."

"I'm busy," he said. "Now come on, don't make me beg."

Sarah laughed at him. "I think that idea has merit. Beg for me, Cooper."

*"Hank! Hank Cooper!"* came Ray Anne's

293

distant cry. Ah, there she was, standing on the deck with a briefcase in one hand and a purse strap over her shoulder. It was a beautiful, sunny day, but it was still chilly on the bay. Ray Anne was dressed in a short black skirt with a slit up one side that was apparent even from this great distance. She also wore a short black jacket with something red under it, her cleavage straining to be free, and high-heeled boots. Her teased blond hair didn't move in the wind.

Cooper just waved again, not getting up.

"Cooper," Sarah said disapprovingly, but with humor in her voice. "You are incredibly rude."

"I'm rude? Did I go to her house, stand up on her hill and shout at her? I didn't invite her, she didn't call ahead. She's rude. I'm busy!"

"Does she have your number?" Sarah asked.

"Oh, you can count on it, although I didn't give it to her. I also never told her my given name, but she called me Hank the first time we met, even though Mac introduced me as Cooper. She wants something."

"Undoubtedly," Sarah said.

And here she came, picking her way down the wooden stairs that led to the beach, not exactly the best path for high heels and a tight, short skirt.

"If she falls, you're going to have to marry her to keep from getting sued," Sarah said.

"I'm going to put a rail on those stairs. Two rails, one on each side." Cooper groaned. "Come on, Sarah. Make her go away."

"Actually, I think I'm going to go away. You're on your own."

"Great," he grumbled. "This started out so well, too. I was just about to score."

"Don't look now, hotshot — with very little effort, you can still score." And then she laughed again. "I just love it."

"You're going to pay for this," he said.

"Well, Hank! Sarah!" Ray Anne was a little breathless. "What are you two up to?"

"Well, I'm walking the dog on the beach," Sarah said. "How are you, Ray Anne?"

"Wonderful! Fantastic! Bleech," she added as Hamlet nudged her with his drooling mouth and left a gob on her short black skirt.

"Oh, sorry," Sarah said, pulling a rag out of her pocket and wiping at the skirt. "He doesn't mean to be disgusting, he's just a sweet dog with a saliva issue. There, I think I got it. Does that look all right to you?"

"Fine," Ray Anne said impatiently. "Shouldn't he be on a leash?"

"Probably, but it would have very little impact on the saliva problem or his ability to spread it. He's just about as big as you are, Ray Anne." Then she turned to Cooper. "Nice seeing you, Cooper. Good luck on the job search." And she turned abruptly and fled.

"Job search?" Ray Anne asked. "What kind of job?"

"Just poking around the internet to see if there's anything interesting out there. What brings you to the beach, Ray Anne?"

"Oh. I wanted to talk to you about something. About your property."

# THIRTEEN

So, Ray Anne wanted to talk about his property? He didn't even stand up. "What's on your mind?" he asked, half his attention focused on Sarah jogging across the beach with her dog. He fully realized he wasn't being polite. His mother would twist his ear for this kind of behavior. Cooper wasn't typically like this around a lady, but first of all, Ray Anne was no lady. Second, she wanted something and at his expense. Third, she had foiled what he considered to be an important move with Sarah.

"Why don't we go inside," she suggested. "It's a little cold on the water."

"I think it feels good out here. And there's too much construction going on in the shop for us to have a conversation there." He wasn't about to get behind closed doors with her. He was quite sure she wouldn't attack him, but he was in no mood for innuendo. "Why don't you just tell me what brings you to my humble dock."

With a heavy sigh, Ray Anne continued. "The rumor is you're planning to sell this beautiful property. I'm hoping for two things. Number one, that you'll give me a chance to represent you and, two, that you'll let me bring you an interested party."

He lifted both eyebrows. "You already have an interested buyer?"

"Hank, there's been serious interest in this property for twenty years," she said. "This is primo beachfront with a lot of attached land."

"But it's all uphill!" he exclaimed. "What can anyone do with a beach at the bottom of a hill?"

"I guess you've never seen Newport Coast, California. Look it up on Google later — it's gorgeous, one of the best resort properties in the U.S. Ben and his father wouldn't consider selling even a portion of this land and it could've made them wealthy."

"I see," he said. "Who is the interested party?"

She laughed. "Hank, this is business. I can't disclose that information without a contract to represent the sale."

"Ah. Of course," he said. "And why would I want to be represented in the sale by the agent for the buyer?"

She smiled very broadly. "Because, darling, there could be a substantial discount in fees. No matter who represents you, no one can make you sell at any price, so you're always in the driver's seat. And I always represent the seller, even when I can find a buyer."

"Interesting."

"Have you never sold property before?" she asked.

"Not personally. But I bet I'm a pretty quick study." He finally stood, towering over her five-foot-two frame.

"The thing is, Ray Anne, I'm really not there yet. Right now I just want to get Ben's personal effects taken care of and fix up that shop. I haven't decided what I'm going to do yet."

"What are some of the options you're considering?" she asked.

"I'm considering just renting it," he said, and watched her face fall. For just a moment, he felt kind of bad — that hadn't been one of his considerations at all. Obviously, there was no big commission if he did that. "Or I might sell the structure and the land it sits on. Or —" he shrugged "— who knows? I have plenty of time to think things over."

"But you're not interested in staying here,

operating the business?"

He shook his head. "Not that it's not a beautiful place. It's just not the work I want to do."

"And just what work do you want to do?"

He found it hard to believe she didn't know. He suspected Ray Anne of superior investigative skills. "By trade, I'm a helicopter pilot. For the last fifteen years, since the Army."

"Really?" she asked. "No kidding? I guess you know Sarah Dupre is a helicopter pilot."

"It seems we have that in common."

"Fantastic! Okay, listen, Hank —"

"Cooper," he said. "People call me Cooper."

She ignored him. "It doesn't matter to me how long you think this over, but can I just show you some numbers? You should be fully aware of your options. And can we please get out of this *wind*?" She patted her hair, as if to keep it from blowing.

He grinned at her. Her short blond hair wasn't even moving in the wind. She wanted to be inside with him. She wanted to corner him. "Sure," he said. "We can sit on the deck."

"The deck? If it's too noisy inside the shop, maybe we could go in your trailer?"

"Nah, it's not a good idea. The maid

hasn't been in today yet. But if you'd like me to come to your office someday . . ."

"The deck it is," she said, heading for the beach stairs.

He smiled as he watched her head up the stairs. She wasn't going to let him get away if she had his attention. He knew too well that she fully intended to impress and excite him with some appraised values and comparisons. So they would sit on the porch with the sound of saws and hammers drowning out their conversation. But he would not make any kind of commitment.

He held a chair beside one of the deck tables for Ray Anne and sat opposite. She pulled a stack of papers out of her leather briefcase and began explaining some of the appraised values of beachfront property in the area. Cooper tried to keep his expression flat, as if he already knew the staggering amount this inheritance could be worth, as if he was not at all surprised. In fact, he was blown away. It could be worth millions to a big hotel or resort chain.

It briefly crossed his mind that any fool would stop the building inside the shop and just hammer up a for-sale sign.

"Impressive, wouldn't you say?" Ray Anne asked.

"Very nice," he said. "And who is this

interested party?"

"Again, Hank, I'm not willing to disclose that without a contract to represent the sale of the property."

"And I'm not ready to make that decision yet," he said.

"Well, here's what we can do. We can make an agreement that when and if you do make the decision to sell — which of course you must, if you're not planning to stay here and operate a business on this site — that I will be your agent."

"There is no must about anything, Ray Anne," he said. "I haven't decided what I'm going to do, when I'm going to do it, if I'm going to do anything at all."

"But you're not planning to take up residence here?"

He shrugged, tilting his head. "There are so many possibilities. I might just hold the title for forty years, let my heirs make that decision."

"Heirs?" she asked with piqued interest.

"I have a large family," he said.

"Children?" she asked.

His phone tweeted in his pocket. He pulled it out and looked at the caller ID. "Excuse me, Ray Anne. I have to take this."

When Sarah walked into her small house,

Ham went straight for the water bowl. Sarah could hear the shower running. Two seconds later, she heard the blow-dryer. Landon's pocket paraphernalia sat on the table — wallet, truck keys, loose change, iPhone.

She scrolled through his contacts, found Cooper's name and number and jotted it down on her grocery list, stuffing it in her pocket. Within five minutes, Landon was in the kitchen, scooping his gear off the table-top.

"Where are you off to?" she asked.

"Homework at Eve's," he said.

Complete waste of a Saturday unless you were helplessly in love, she thought. "Will you be home for dinner?"

"I hope not," he said. "You'll be okay, right?"

"I think I can manage," she said with a smile. "Maybe I'll go out. Or get a pizza. Or hit the leftovers."

"Don't cook for me, okay?"

"Okay." She laughed. "Can you let me know your plans?"

"Don't I always?" Landon asked.

When he was gone, she pulled her list and her phone out of her pocket. She put in the numbers. When Cooper answered, she said, "Now you have my number. And obviously, I have yours."

He chuckled. "How'd you manage that?"

"I peeked in Landon's phone directory. He's gone to do homework with Eve, looking more like he was going for a job interview."

Again with the laugh, which was altogether too sexy and low. "I'm in the middle of something, but almost finished. Can I call you back? Five minutes or so?"

"I hope I didn't interrupt anything . . . *important.*"

"Nah. Perfect timing. Talk to you soon."

She disconnected, but held the phone in a tight grip. *It's okay,* she thought. *I'm a big girl. A grown-up. I can handle this.* And then she shivered, right before she felt a warm flush spread through her.

She'd had a week to think about it. It scared her to death, but she wanted to check it out. She would just have to guard her heart with every fiber of strength she had.

Shaking Ray Anne hadn't been too hard. He merely stood and said he should get back to work. She concealed her disappointment well, hiding behind her agent's smile. "I'll just leave you these papers, because I know you're going to think about this and change your mind."

"Anything is possible."

When she was gone, he tore up the agreement and made a dinner date with Sarah.

Cooper took Sarah to a small, family-owned Italian restaurant in Bandon, not too far from Thunder Point but definitely out of the way. There was a pizza counter in the front and twelve booths and four tables in the back. It was kind of dark and strung with plastic grapes and fake greenery. Even though it was a Saturday night, it wasn't crowded but the pizza counter was busy. Pop was the chef, with a son helping.

"Nice," Sarah said as she slid into a booth across from Cooper. "Very nice. Just the thing."

"Not real fancy," he pointed out.

"I'm telling you, this is what I like. Small, quaint, friendly and hopefully delicious."

Of the hundred things Cooper had discovered about this Thunder Point adventure so far, Sarah Dupre was the one that really got his blood pressure up. She looked good enough to eat. "Did you call Landon? Tell him where you'd be?"

"Sort of. I texted him that we were going out for Italian. He texted back to have fun and he wouldn't wait up."

"Smart-ass," Cooper said. "Wonder where he gets that."

She ordered a cabernet, he ordered a beer

and they pored over old, plastic-covered menus. "God, I want one of everything," she said.

He ordered a calamari appetizer first, then she settled on linguine alla vongole — clams in white sauce — while he ordered cioppino. When the waitress, presumably one of the daughters or daughters-in-law, left, he raised his glass. "To small, dark, Italian restaurants."

She clinked his glass, took a sip and then said, "Just to be clear, I'm not getting involved with a man."

"I believe you've made that clear several times now."

"I'm serious. I like you, Cooper, but I'm essentially a single mother and just post-divorce. You understand."

"I told you I understood," he said.

"I just don't want you to have any expectations," she said.

"Did I put you through all these protests when you bought me dinner?"

"I'm not just talking about sex, I mean I'm not in a position to get emotionally involved. I'm not girlfriend material."

"Sarah, I'm going to say this once — that's up to you. I'm not worried about whether you get emotionally involved. As long as I get the sex." At that exact moment, the waitress stood beside their table with the calamari. She hesitated slightly before putting it down. Then she withdrew quickly.

He smiled slyly. Winked. He had done that on purpose.

Sarah started laughing and her entire face lit up, her dark eyes twinkled, her cheeks turned pink. He had known he wanted her from the first second he saw her, when she came to the trailer and tried to pin his ears back for being Landon's friend. The truth was, fierce or silly, she turned him on. He really *didn't* care whether she got emotionally involved. It might be better for her if she managed to avoid that. But he definitely hoped they could get physically involved.

"Well, you're not getting that, either," she said.

"Mmm, wait till you taste this," he said, chewing a piece of calamari. "This is so excellent, you might change your mind!"

"How'd you find this place?" she asked.

"Mac. The man is like a walking Yellow Pages. Anything you need, from mold removal to good restaurant, he's your man." He plucked another piece off the plate, but before he put it in his mouth, he asked, "How in the world did you end up flying for the Coast Guard?"

"I didn't expect to fly, to tell you the truth.

I just wanted to be on the water. I had fantasies about rescue swimming, but then I thought, instead of jumping out of the chopper, how about commanding it, flying it. I had no idea whether I'd like it. I did a lot of swimming, diving and sailing growing up, but the highest I'd ever gotten off the ground was a zip-line."

"When did you change your mind?"

"In college. I joined a USCG scholarship program when I was nineteen. When I looked at the different places I could go as an officer, I got dazzled by the helicopter."

"Was it the right choice?" he asked.

"It was. We've had some real adrenaline-pumping missions. Especially out of the Bering Sea." She shook her head. "I didn't think I was ready for that."

"And?"

"Kodiak was the best experience of my life." She glowed a little bit when she said that. "It was my first permanent move with the Coast Guard after flight school. I had lost my parents a year before, had a little six-year-old along for the ride, it was one of the most challenging rescue locations in the U.S., and it was awesome. Sometimes a rescue station is as good as its commander, and ours was incredible. That's where Landon started playing ball with the com-

308

mander's youngest son. Commander Titchke took us under his wing. He not only helped us settle in, and his family helped me with Landon, but he trained me in the Bering Sea. I did things — the team did things — I never imagined we'd do. Once we had two ships taking on water on opposite sides of the island in a storm so violent we couldn't even drop a line. Seven souls on one, four on another, plus injuries. And we brought them in. It took four crews, it took pulling crew members off vacations or days off, but we saved eleven people that day. Risk management for that operation was tight as I've ever seen. There was no room for error or we'd not only lose the vessels and injured, we'd lose the rescue crews. I think my heart pounded for a month." She took a bite. "I have a lot of stories like that from Kodiak. I could bore you for hours."

He couldn't help but grin at her. "It sounds scary fun."

"It gets in your blood, I think. That rush."

"You like the edge. You're a wild woman."

"Nah. I never take unnecessary chances, never. It's precise and sometimes I can be a perfectionist and . . ."

"Sometimes?" he asked with a laugh as their salads arrived.

"I let you eat calamari while I bored you with Coast Guard stories. It's your turn — tell me about your flying. About Iraq and your civilian gigs."

Even though Cooper had gone to Iraq in a Black Hawk right at the beginning of the war, somehow it just didn't seem as wildly exciting as what Sarah had done, was doing. But he told her about it. He was six years in the Army, then got out to pursue civilian flying. Since work was hard to find, he worked for civilian contractors hired by the U.S. in foreign countries — an expatriate, a mercenary. Eventually, he ended up working for oil companies.

"Was it good work?" she asked just as their main courses were delivered.

"I'd say so. And the money was good. It was easy work most of the time, good people. And then there was a big oil spill. Major. National news for months, billions of dollars of damage. It made the *Valdez* look like a dress rehearsal. A couple of the platforms I was flying to shut down — we pulled all the people off. I've never seen anything like it. Of course I'd watched news reports of spills before, but there's nothing like actually seeing it. The company had to downsize and I was more than willing to walk.

"I worked for two more companies after that, flying to offshore wells, but I couldn't stop seeing what might happen. It wasn't my business — I was flying — I didn't compromise safety. My boss, the chief pilot, didn't compromise safety. But . . ." He shook his head. "Once you see what a major spill can do to a few towns on the coast and a big piece of ocean, it just gets to you. You know?"

She smiled patiently. "The Coast Guard is the environment's friend, Cooper. You know that."

"I know. So I quit that last job and planned to take a few months off, meet Ben and another friend to hunt in the mountains. I was looking for a break long enough to decide where to go and what to do next. Then everything changed with Ben's death. I'll get another flying job," he said. "But I think it'll have to be a different kind of flying job."

"When?"

"I don't know. After Christmas, maybe. After the bar's looking good and I can sell it. I have to figure out how to deal with that."

She grinned. "Ray Anne will help you unload it, I'm sure."

"How did you know?" he asked, because

he hadn't said anything about Ray Anne's real estate ambitions.

She gave him a slow smile. "I'm just brilliant, that's all."

"What about you?" he asked. "How long will you be here?"

"In about a year, I'll be looking at assignments. Landon will be a senior. If it goes the way we've planned, Landon will know where he wants to go to college by then. With any luck, he'll have an early acceptance. I can manage to sit tight until he graduates. And I'll try my best not to be too far away." She looked down at her pasta. "He'll need family close enough to visit while he's in college. It's different when it's just two of us."

He could only smile at her, give her a nod. She was a remarkable woman. She did a difficult and demanding job, but it didn't change her first priority — her brother.

He admired her. That hadn't happened to him in a long while.

On her second glass of wine, Sarah forgot to be afraid of her feelings toward Cooper. She experienced a lift in her spirits that she hadn't felt in too long. She'd been so hurt and angry she'd forgotten how wonderful it was to laugh, to have something in common with a date, to feel friendship growing. To lust, because she was feeling that, too. Her evening with Cooper was perfect. They listened to each other's work and flying stories intensely, they laughed over foibles and family issues — Cooper had a fairly large extended family and while she had no one to speak of, raising Landon had been worth a laugh or two. They growled in unison when the conversation turned to Jag Morrison and his family. She enjoyed him. He was intelligent, funny and, oh, mama, was he handsome. Although he was mostly flirtatiousness and wit, there was a warmth about him that embraced her.

And he'd be moving away soon. Perfect.

The food was delicious, the small restaurant perfect. Sarah realized this was the thing she'd been missing. A companion.

As they walked out to his truck, she said, "Thank you, Cooper. I enjoyed that."

"Good. We'll do it again."

She laughed softly. "My first date since . . . well, since my ex moved out. Over a year ago."

He threaded his fingers through hers. "My first date in a while, too."

"Who was your last date?" she asked.

He stopped walking. "I have to think. It was probably Judy, a woman I met in

Corpus Christi. About a year ago. Interesting woman. But it was one date. I don't know how to explain why. It just didn't click."

"Well," she said with a laugh, "I was pretty pissed at our first meeting. And I take this to mean you think we clicked. Or maybe you like angry women? Either that or there aren't any other women in this town you'll take a chance on."

"There are plenty of women around," he said. He touched her cheek with a gentle finger. "It's early."

"What did you have in mind?"

"Come back to my place for a while. It's not much, but it's comfortable. Your house is vulnerable — could be teenagers there, taking advantage of the fact that you're out for the evening. I could make you a cup of coffee. Or a drink." He shrugged. He grinned. "I'm flexible."

Sarah thought, *We both know what we want.*

He leaned down to put a soft kiss on her mouth. "Take a chance on me, Sarah. I can play by your rules."

It had been so long since a man seemed to know her, know what she needed, wanted. She nodded. "I think a cup of coffee at your place would be all right."

# FOURTEEN

Cooper opened the door to his RV and let Sarah step inside first. He'd left a dim light on over the stove. It cast a gentle glow on the room and when he closed the door, he slipped an arm around her and pulled her close. He placed a soft kiss on her lips. "Just let me get my arms around you for a second and then I'll make some —"

She put her hands on his cheeks and pulled his mouth down to hers, cutting him off. Lips touched lips for a mere second before his arms tightened around her and he took her mouth by storm, opening his mouth over hers. A growl came from deep inside him as he went after her. She purred and he groaned. Then he turned with her in his arms and pressed her against the wall just inside the door. Her arms were locked around his neck and he ran a hand over her butt, down the back of her thigh and lifted her leg from behind the knee to his hip, pushing himself against her.

He was hard that fast. No big surprise. He'd been having hard thoughts all the way home, even though they'd talked and laughed like old friends. This was still completely unplanned, but he thrust his pelvis against hers. And she pushed back.

"Jesus, Sarah . . ." he murmured against her mouth.

Her fingers threaded into the short hair over his ears and she clung to him, kissing him deeply, welcoming his tongue. And she whispered, "Uh-huh . . ."

His hand found a breast, then slipped under her sweater and found more of a breast, though still covered by a lacy bra. He ran a finger around the lace, found her neck with his mouth and kissed, sucked, ran a thumb over her erect nipple. "God," he whispered. "Jesus. God."

She chuckled softly. "Are you praying?"

"Oh, God, yes," he whispered, grinding against her. "Or begging . . . maybe that's just begging. . . ."

He made a study of her neck, ear, temple and chin with his lips, with his tongue, going back to her mouth again and again, growing breathless and crazy. He pushed up her sweater and found that nipple with his lips. And then she slid her arms from

316

around his neck to his waist, from his waist to his butt, pulling him against her. And she hummed.

He ran that hand over her bottom and down her thigh to that raised knee again, but this time he went all the way to her heel and slid off her boot. Those delicious tight jeans wouldn't come off over the boot.

"Yes," she whispered. "Yes."

His fingers found the waist of her jeans, the snap, the zipper. He slid a hand inside, lower and lower, until he was feeling a soft tuft of hair and then the damp softness of her. God, she was at least as turned-on as he. Ready, so ready. That's all it took to have him praying again. But he said, "This is crazy. Good crazy. So good . . ."

"Crazy," she agreed, just as her hands found the snap of his jeans. "Good."

Cooper kept telling himself to slow down, to slow *way* down, to let go and find a place to lay her down, but he couldn't seem to get past the lust barrier and neither could she. When she lowered his zipper, it got even more desperate and complicated. As she took him in her hand, his head almost exploded and he muttered, "Condom. Condom. Condom."

He had to let go of her briefly to get into his back pocket. He fumbled to find the condom, but once it was in his hand, she took it away from him. "Let me," she said. But she took her time with him, enjoying him for a while, stroking him, kissing him all the while.

"Sarah," he begged. "Get on with it. Please."

She suited him up, then slid her leg down from his hip. He gently but a little desperately lowered her jeans, pulling off one leg, then the other. He probed her with his fingers then lifted her off the ground, her back against the wall. A million possible endearments ran through his head. But he said, "Help."

She threaded her hand between their bodies, found him, helped him find his way inside. He was half out of his mind and long past thinking logically; he slid in and gave a deep groan. She, on the other hand, gave a rather loud "Ahh!" He held her still and fast for a long moment. Then, holding her up under her thighs, he began to move, every thrust bringing him closer to an insane, brainless ecstasy. He thought about saying he was sorry, that he'd make it up to her later, but then she cried out. Her legs tightened around him, her internal muscles clenched and pulled the most amazing orgasm out of him as she came. And came.

Her arms locked around his neck; she moaned in pleasure; she held him so tight as he plunged into her again and again and again. It was a long time before all that pelvic action slowed then stopped. Cooper was completely out of breath; his knees went weak. She was panting and holding on for dear life.

"Baby," he said in a desperate whisper. "Please don't move."

"I can't." She sighed.

"Just don't move," he said again. "You could break off meaningful parts. . . ."

She sighed again, nuzzling, kissing his cheek.

"Honey . . . Sarah . . . I'm sorry, baby. . . ."

"Sorry?" she asked weakly.

"Jesus, I took you. Against the wall. In three minutes. And you still have your jacket on."

She was quiet a moment. "That's a relief. I thought I took you."

"That, too. My God. Don't move. That was . . . I can't even describe that. It was . . . Jeez."

"I'm getting a little uncomfortable."

"Soon," he said. He kissed her neck, then her lips. "Soon." He kissed her again, with passion. "Ah, Sarah. I'm surprised I have legs. I've never . . ."

"Never? You certainly acted like you knew what you were doing. Come on, Cooper. I have to get down now. Please?"

He pulled his head back just slightly to look down at them. Her jacket hung off one shoulder, her sweater pushed up over her breasts, and she was naked from the waist down. His sweater was askew, his shirttails hanging out, and his pants drooped. He laughed. "We look like we just survived a hurricane." He lifted her up a bit, let her drop her legs to the ground. But he kept his hands on her bare butt. "No coffee tonight, baby. Bed. We have to go to bed."

She couldn't help but laugh at him. "What if I don't want to go to bed?"

"Then you'll be getting real familiar with this wall." He hoisted up his pants but didn't bother zipping. Then he bent down, grabbed her jeans in one hand and scooped her up in his arms. He carried her up the three steps to his bedroom, putting her down on the bed. He helped her out of her jacket, removed his and said, "Don't go anywhere. I'll be right back." And he left the room.

The bathroom was very close to the bedroom, of course. Everything was close to everything — it was a trailer. While he was in the bathroom, she yelled, "I'm feeling a little . . . *exposed* here."

"Get under the covers," he yelled back.

"I'm not sure I'm in the mood for that. What if I want coffee?"

He walked back into the room. Hands on his hips, jeans still unzipped, he loomed over her. He smiled at her. "You know what I realized about thirty seconds after opening the door tonight? You didn't want coffee." Then he pulled his sweater over his head.

"Now what?" she asked.

He reached for the hem of her sweater and pulled it off. "I want to hold you. And maybe try regular sex, if the spirit moves us."

"What's that?" she asked, automatically unhooking her bra and tossing it.

"You know," he said, getting rid of his boots and pants. "The plain old regular but excellent kind, complete with foreplay, which we didn't get to before. No danger of back injury or broken bones, but very good just the same." He pulled the covers back and she twisted into them. He crawled in beside her and pulled her into his arms. "Although, what we just did . . . I think that was one of the best things I've ever done. Or one of the best things that's ever been done to me. I don't think there's any way to top it." He pulled her closer, kissed her

321

cheek, running his big callused hand over her soft skin.

"I'm feeling a little unsure of myself," she said, snuggling closer to him. "I've never done this before."

"What? Vanilla sex?"

"Sex without any commitment at all. I mean, I've had plenty of sex, don't get me wrong. Okay, not plenty . . . not that much, actually. But I always thought it was going somewhere. That there was love. Or something."

"Well, don't write me off so fast," Cooper said. "Maybe in about an hour and a half, you'll think you love me."

"But I'm afraid of that — I don't ever want to be in love again. I can't get involved, you know that. For a hundred reasons. I'm vulnerable. I just got divorced. I have major responsibilities. But I've never even considered something like this before — sex with someone I like, but without any emotional investment."

And, Cooper thought, that was the only kind he'd ever had. He was usually the one to say *I can't get involved*. He'd had a lot of logical reasons, some like hers. He was being deployed or transferred, moving, just broke up with someone, you name it. There were a couple of times he had forgotten to

322

say he couldn't get involved and he'd ended up engaged, wondering what the hell had happened. But he'd never really been in love. Not even close. And here he was, suddenly wondering what that would feel like. Wondering what he'd been missing.

"I'm not sure I know what to do," she said.

He ran his fingers through the short hair over her temple. "You don't have to know anything, honey. You just have to be yourself, be honest, tell me what you need and let it happen naturally. I'm not going to try to trip you up."

"You won't have . . . expectations?"

He shook his head.

"You won't use me for sex and then just turn your back on me? Suddenly?"

"Hey, I'm not a bad guy. We wouldn't be together right now if we didn't like each other. I never turn my back on a friend. No matter what."

"I can trust you, then?"

"You can trust me."

"You won't be with other women while you're with me? Because I'd have to kill you."

"I wouldn't do that. I might not be a settling-down kind of guy, but I'm definitely a one-woman-at-a-time kind of guy."

"That's all I want right now — to be the

323

only woman with a guy who I like and who I trust. A friend. Oh, man, don't ever let me have two glasses of wine again," she said.

"You can't blame the wine," he said.

She tilted her head and smiled into his eyes. "You're right. I'm just so tired of not having a friend. And because . . . well, that up-against-the-wall thing is one of the best things that ever happened to me."

He smiled back, the corners of his eyes crinkling. "I'll have to start lifting weights, so I'm sure to keep you happy." Then his smile vanished and he kissed her. "Right now, I think we should try the old-fashioned kind — no trapeze, no props, no 6.8 difficulty."

She slid her hand down his belly and found out what he was talking about. She closed her hand around him and his eyes rolled back in his head. He wanted her again. Bad.

Sarah wasn't the first woman Cooper had been involved with who had kids. There hadn't been many — and there'd never been one with a sixteen-year-old at home — but he didn't have to be told how important it was that she set an example for Landon.

He pulled up in front of her house at eleven-thirty. Landon's truck was already in the carport beside her SUV.

"Do I look like I just had a fattening dinner and a couple of hours of wonderful sex?" she asked him.

Cooper lifted her chin and turned her face to and fro. "If he doesn't look into your eyes, you're safe."

"Swell."

"If he recognizes that flush and glow, it's time to have another one of those sex talks with him," Cooper suggested.

"He says if I bring up safe and responsible sex one more time, he's running away from home."

Cooper laughed at her. "You'll be fine." He gave her a brief kiss. "Sweet dreams."

He watched her go into the house before he drove away across the beach. The sand was hard packed close to the hill. There were a few people on the beach, sitting close to a campfire. He wasn't sure if they were kids or adults — he didn't see any all-terrain vehicles or motorcycles. But he wasn't worried. In fact, it gave him a good feeling to have someone using the beach.

When he went inside the trailer, the first thing he noticed was her scent. He wasn't sure if she'd left it behind or if it was still on his breath, his tongue. The place seemed oddly empty without her there.

He cracked open a beer and went to his bedroom, sitting on the rumpled sheets, flicking on the TV. But he didn't watch. He thought about Sarah and the way her body felt beneath his hands, the way he felt inside her. Her laugh. Her sarcasm. *That's a relief. I thought I took you.* Her sincerity and honesty. She wanted to have a relationship without strings, but didn't really know how. Ha. He was so glad he hadn't confessed that seemed to be the only kind he knew how to have.

He wanted her with him tonight, through the night. He'd wanted plenty of women, but there was something fresh about this time. It was new. It was deep. There wasn't anything confusing about it — it was honest. He could already feel her hooks in him. He was an expert at not caring deeply, yet this time it wasn't working for him. He wanted her in every way — physically, intellectually, emotionally. And she didn't want him back in that way. In fact, she needed his help in remaining unattached.

"Shit," he said aloud to no one. "I'm screwed."

The last football game for Thunder Point High School was a home game and the night was mild and clear. The McCain contingent occupied their fifty yard line seats, but this time Sarah was included with Cooper and Gina had convinced her mom to come. Carrie was a huge supporter of the team, and good friends with Lou, but running a deli and catering service required that she be up by four in the morning for baking and cooking and it was rare that she stayed up past eight in the evening.

There was lots of laughter, chatter and cheering, but Gina was aware almost instantly that the relationship between Sarah and Cooper had grown more serious. At first it was just in the way he looked at her. It was as if the very sight of her made Cooper happy. While Sarah stared out at the field, watching her brother play, Cooper would throw a long glance her way and his lips would curve in a secret smile while his eyes got a little dreamy. And before long, Gina saw him reach for her hand, hold it, give it a squeeze.

It was with that simple action that Gina felt her throat close and her eyes cloud.

They'd known each other for what? A few weeks? A couple of months? Of course they were bonded over Landon's problems, but they weren't attracted to each other because of Sarah's brother. Gina wondered how deep, how intense the relationship was now, but of course she couldn't ask. In fact, learning this way, at a raucous football game, was a blessing; no one would notice that she was so envious she could have wept. By halftime, when Cooper and Mac wandered off to stretch their legs, leaving the women, she was composed again.

Gina turned to Sarah and said, "When did *that* happen? You and Cooper?"

Sarah shrugged. "A week, maybe ten days ago."

"I like him," Carrie said.

"Good man, Cooper," Lou said.

Gina leaned close to Sarah's ear and asked, "Next level?"

Before Sarah could even think about answering, Carrie said, "Gina!"

"Damn, she's got the ears of a bloodhound," Gina said.

"Well, it's none of your business," Carrie said. "Besides, it's obvious."

"It is?" Sarah and Gina said in unison.

With a wave of her hand, Carrie said, "It's in the touch, the look, just the energy. Go ahead and deny it, Sarah."

To Gina's surprise, Sarah only laughed. "We're just friends," she said. "It's very comfortable but not serious."

"Ah, friends with benefits," Carrie said. "The *modern* way."

"Not exactly," Sarah said. "We're dating, that's all. Cooper completely understands that a serious or even potentially serious relationship is out of the question for me. I've been divorced less than a year. My first priorities are Landon and my job and, believe me, I'm in no way ready to get involved in anything long-term. Too risky for me. My wounds are still a little fresh. And Cooper . . . ? Well, he makes no secret about the fact that he has a few things to do here and then he'll be leaving. He's been doing the internet-job-search thing."

"What about the beach?" Gina asked.

"He hasn't decided. But he's a helicopter pilot, military first and then civilian. There aren't any helicopter jobs around here outside of the Coast Guard. He's leaving, girls. And you know what? That makes him kind of safe for me."

"Unless you accidentally fall in love with him," Gina said.

"I already love him, but not in that typical romantic way. Not the way I fell for my ex before I knew he was a cruel, selfish bastard. I love the way Cooper keeps an eye out for my brother, love the way he makes me laugh, love that I can trust his friendship. And in two or three months, we're not going to live in the same town, but if we're still good friends, maybe we'll stay in touch. Right now, all I want is a nice guy to go to dinner with sometimes and who will hold my hand in public. That's all I want. All I have room for in my life."

"Fling?" Lou asked.

"I'm not going to put a label on it. We could decide this is not the best idea in two weeks. Or we could stumble along for a while. We did make a promise to each other — that if it wasn't the right thing for one of us and we had to step away, there would be no drama. I'm not going to hold a man hostage. No way."

It hit Gina hard and suddenly. She would take any part of that, any little part. A date, a little hand-holding, some late-night chats on the phone, whatever. She'd go along with that whole "not serious" thing if that's all there was.

But it was Lou who asked, "Think you can stick to that?"

"Yeah," she said. "Right now if I went out with a man who was looking for a wife or even a live-in partner, I'd run for my life. We'll go out some night, a girl's night, and I'll tell you about the ex, the cheating bastard who dumped me and my brother after less than a year." She shook her head. "Not easy for me to trust men now. Just the fact that I trust Cooper's friendship is a big step."

"Yeah," Lou said. "She can stick to it."

It was only a few moments before the men were back with snacks and everything in the conversation changed as they waited for the second half to start. Except for one thing. Gina thought she had a better grasp of Mac's fear of relationships. It must be a little like Sarah's, but with a lot more tenacity — his wife had left him ten years ago. She knew all about his ex-wife's betrayal. Not from Mac, though he'd mentioned a few details, but from Lou, whose anger over what Cee Jay had done to her family was enormous and frightening.

The game was won by a landslide, Landon once again the star. The parents had all been warned that there would be celebrating tonight, closing off football for the season. Everyone grabbed their bleacher cushions, lap blankets, coolers and trash and headed out. But Gina stayed for a moment. She remembered being a high school sophomore, sitting right here on these bleachers. The games were thrilling, the crowds of kids even more so. The forbidden parties afterward were electrifying. Gina had a boyfriend who hung out with a lot of Thunder Point High kids, but he wasn't a student. He'd dropped out the year before and was an auto mechanic in Bandon, which made him dangerous and arousing. He liked the games and after-parties; he liked the girls, fast driving and late nights. And Gina — he liked Gina. She held him off for their first five secret dates and then gave in and got pregnant.

When she told her boyfriend, he split. Moved. Bolted. She heard he went to Idaho to work. A few years later his parents moved away from Thunder Point, into a seniors' community near their married daughter and grandchildren. All ties were broken. Hell, there hadn't been any ties! No one had even acknowledged that Ashley was his child.

She hadn't gone to another high school football game until Ashley began cheering.

"Hey," Mac called from several seats below. "Coming?"

*Not in years,* she wanted to say. Instead, she said, "Coming."

It's not as though Gina hadn't realized before tonight that she had no romantic partner in her life. Never had. She'd had a few meaningless dates that had never shown potential and one big heartthrob who kept her at arm's length.

Mac put out his hand as she stepped down the bleachers and she let him help her. They walked together toward the parking lot.

"Good game," he said.

She nodded.

"I can't wait to see what that kid does next year," Mac said. "Dupre. He's some ball player."

*Her buddy, Mac,* she thought. *Her pal.*

"Hey, what's up with you? You're quiet."

She stopped walking and looked up at him. She thought, *This has gone on long enough. I have to get on with my life. He's never going to be mine.* "Headache," she said.

"Too much noise?" he asked.

"Maybe."

"The kids are all going out. Lou can take Dee Dee and Ryan home. How bad is that headache? We could grab a beer and still be home by curfew."

*And then I can go home and fall asleep to that old fantasy that we might be more than pals? When it's never going to happen?* "Maybe another time, Mac. I'm working in the morning."

"You sure?" he asked. "We could get you an aspirin or something."

"I think I need my bed." They got to the parking lot and she veered off toward her car. Carrie stood there, talking with Lou, waiting for her.

"See you later, then," he said.

"Later," she answered. *And later and later and later and later . . .*

The next morning, Gina cursed the door-bell. It was eleven o'clock. Carrie was at the deli, Ashley had gone shopping with Eve, Gina was finally alone and desperately needed to be. She had held her wrecked emotions inside until she could have some space, some privacy. She ignored the door-bell, but it rang again and again. With her red nose and watering eyes, she finally threw her ratty old robe over her pajamas and opened the door to meanly tell the stupid SOB who was leaning on the bell to get off her porch.

"Hi. You okay?" Mac asked.

"What are you doing here?" she shot back.

"You called in sick to the diner. You never call in sick." He peered at her closely. "God, you look awful."

She glared at him. "Thanks so much."

"Do you want me to take you to the doctor? Do you have a fever?"

"No! It's a cold, it'll pass! But I'm not feeling like company."

He pushed his way inside. "I'll make you some tea or soup or something. You go lay on the couch. Did your headache turn into a cold? Must've been sinus or something. Maybe I should get some soup from Carrie."

She rolled her eyes. *Oh, God,* she internally wailed. Just what she needed — Mac. And Mac at the deli, looking for chicken soup? Carrie, who left for work before dawn, had no idea Gina was staying home, claiming a cold. She was supposed to be having a richly deserved self-pity party! This was her only chance. She sank down onto the couch and pressed a tissue up to her face. "Mac, all I really need is to sleep."

He stepped back into the living room, holding a can of chicken soup — Chicken & Stars, not something the owner of a deli would brag about. "I could warm this up for you."

"No, thank you," she said. "Please go. Before you breathe my air and get sick."

He sat down in the chair across the small room from her, transferring the can from hand to hand. He just looked at her for a moment. She blew her nose. She tried a little cough.

"You're not sick," he said. "You're crying. Why are you crying? What happened? Who did this to you?"

She shook her head and in spite of her determination, her eyes welled with unshed tears. She was not going to talk to him about this! "Mac, it's very personal. Please. Don't push."

"But what is it?" he asked again, leaning toward her, his elbows on his knees, gripping the soup can. "Is Ashley in trouble? Is Carrie all right? Did someone hurt you? Do you need money?"

"Oh, for God's sake! No! No! No! Will you leave this alone?"

"I can't," he said. "I've never seen you cry. Tell me, Gina."

"You're pissing me off!"

"Tell me!"

"Cooper and Sarah were holding hands at the game!" she blurted. Then she dropped her head into her hands. "Damn it. Damn it. Damn it!"

Mac was silent. She lifted her head, wiped off her eyes and nose with the tissue and saw by his expression that he was stunned. "You have a thing for Cooper?" he asked quietly.

She just looked at him in wonder. She shook her head. "No, Mac, I don't have a thing for Cooper. I haven't had a date in five years. I saw Sarah and Cooper holding hands and it hit me — they've only known each other a few weeks. And I'm alone. Way too alone."

"You're not alone, Gina. You have your mom, your daughter, friends . . ."

"You're an idiot." She stood up. "And now you have to go because at this moment I *want* to be alone!" She went to the front door and opened it.

Mac slowly stood. "I don't think I understand what's —"

"I know you don't. Gimme that soup," she said, snatching it from his hand.

"I thought, if you're not sick, maybe you want to go out tonight. It's Lou's bunco night, but Eve can watch the kids and —"

"I'm busy," she said, cutting him off. "Maybe another time. Now if you don't mind . . ."

"Jesus, Gina," he said.

"See you later," she said. "Nice of you to check on me. Bye."

"Gina . . ."

"No, really, Mac. Goodbye."

"Are you mad at *me*?" he asked.

"I'm mad at the world! Now get out of here before I call the cops!"

"I *am* the cops. I think you're losing it, Gina. Get a grip," he said. But he left.

And she threw herself on her bed and cried.

# FIFTEEN

When the door from the garage opened, Lou was standing in the kitchen, ready to leave for the evening. "I thought you'd never get home. Where have you been all day?"

"I checked in," he reminded her.

"Yes, but I didn't realize ordering a cord of firewood, checking your messages at the office and taking a look at the progress on Cooper's bar was going to eat up six hours."

"Am I making you late?" he asked.

"No, not yet."

He sat down at the kitchen table. "Eve staying home tonight?"

"That's her plan, but I think the boyfriend is coming over. You're okay with that, right? I'm going out to dinner with my bunco partner. If I have more than a glass and a half of wine, I might stay over. I'll text you so I don't wake you with a ringing phone. And if I do spend the night, I'll be home in the morning, first thing."

"Just enjoy yourself," he said. "Listen, you got a minute?"

"Sure. I might even have ten."

"Can this be between us? I think it's personal. Don't talk to Carrie about it, all right?"

It was the look on his face more than his request that had her sitting down at the table with him. "What's the matter?"

"I'm not sure. Gina wasn't at the diner this morning. Stu said she called in sick, so I went to her house to check on her. She said she had a cold, but she didn't have a cold. She was crying. And she was angry. Mad as hell. When I asked her what was wrong, she said Cooper and Sarah were holding hands. So I asked her if she had a crush on Cooper and she called me an idiot and asked me to leave."

"Oh, Mac," Lou said. "You're such an idiot."

"Now see, this is obviously some female language I don't get. How does that make me an idiot?"

Lou leaned her chin on her hand. "Mac, do you think she's going to wait for you forever?"

"Huh?" he asked stupidly.

"This town is amazing, isn't it? The way we talk about everything and nothing? Some gossip takes about thirty seconds to spread worldwide and some things are kept almost religiously secret. You and Gina, Mac. Best friends for years. Closer than brother and sister. More fond than lovers. And yet, it goes nowhere? No two people more right for each other, but —"

"We're parents, Lou. We're friends because the kids are friends. It would be a mistake to complicate that."

She just shook her head. "We should've talked about this years ago. It wouldn't be very complicated, given the fact that you know each other better than a lot of married couples. What's taking you so long? You're crazy about her. And there's absolutely no doubt she's crazy about you. Neither of you has been even tempted by anyone else."

He squirmed in his chair. That in itself was telling — this great, big, muscled, fearless guy, fidgeting awkwardly. "History, that's what's keeping us from dating. You should understand that better than anyone."

"Excuse me, I'm a little confused. What history?"

He gave a short, humorless laugh. "How about she was dumped by the father of her baby and I was dumped by the mother of my children? That good enough? We might be a couple of people with good reason to be careful!"

Lou just looked at him for a long moment. "She was fifteen," she said. "And you? You were only nineteen when you married your pregnant girlfriend and she was . . . Oh, don't even make me go there. I have a good idea she knew exactly what she was doing. I know it's an optimistic stretch, but you and Gina have probably grown up a lot since then. You're obviously attracted to each other."

"What if we dated and didn't like each other?" he said.

"You'll always like each other. What if you dated and realized you weren't meant to be a couple? Grown-ups deal with that without rancor. But right now what you've got is a woman who has waited for you to make a move for years. Her frustration must be beyond words. And we all know you don't have another woman anywhere."

"We? Who, we?"

"The whole stupid town," she said. "Seriously, Mac. There are hardly any secrets around here — no one should know that better than you."

"Okay, now wait a minute. If everyone thinks we're meant for each other and this close to getting together, why is she crying after years of friendship? Which, by the way, we agreed was the best thing."

"Really? You both decided? Somehow I doubt that was Gina's idea. But I'll give you the benefit of the doubt and assume it was. Then the reason for her tears would be this — Sarah and Cooper hit town, meet in an extremely complicated way, are attracted to each other and, without overthinking it, form some kind of relationship. One that puts a shine in both their eyes. Gina must have wondered what she's done wrong. She might be thinking you don't find her attractive or appealing."

"Don't be ridiculous," he said. "It's just —" He didn't finish.

"It's just that you screwed up at the age of nineteen, no pun intended, and you still can't let yourself off the hook for it?"

"It left me with quite a load — three kids and an opinionated aunt," he said, lifting an eyebrow.

"Well, we've done pretty damn well with the spoils," she said. "We've kept it all under control for years. *Our* kids are doing very well. Here's what I think you should do, Deputy Yummy Pants. I think you should weigh how damn lucky you are that a woman as solid and beautiful and wonderful as Gina would even consider you. Most men don't get a chance like that in a life-time. And it sounds like she's had just about enough."

He just stared at her. "I might need a beer," he finally said. He pushed back his chair but she got up, got him a bottle of beer from the refrigerator and sat back down. He twisted off the cap and took a drink. "What if I let her down?"

"You've never let anyone down in your life. *You've* been let down. In spades. But you've always lived up to your commit-ments."

"Lou, I wasn't happy." He nearly whis-pered it, as if it was the deepest secret of all. "I wanted to marry Cee Jay, and I was miserable. I don't want to risk that again."

"I know. By now you should know what makes you happy." She shook her head and laughed. "Talk about the pink elephant in the living room! Has no one ever asked you why you're not hooked up with Gina?"

"No one," he said. "Never."

She *tsked* and shook her head. "Amazing. Well, you should think about all this before she gets away from you. If I were Gina, I'd be asking myself why I'm wasting my time. I'd sign on to a dating service."

"Again?" he asked, and smiled.

"You don't know anything. And I have to

343

get going," she said, standing. "We'll talk about this again after you've had time to think. And listen, don't let Eve go over to Landon's house tonight. Sarah is working all weekend — sitting on call for emergencies or something in North Bend."

"I know," he said. "Cooper mentioned that. So. You always look so nice for bunco."

She sat down. She hated this. But Lou was, if anything, fair. It was time to be honest with Mac. "I'm not going to play bunco. I'm going to meet my secret boyfriend who is ten years younger than I am, a different race than me, and happens to work with you on occasion."

Mac smiled at her. "I know. Joe. Nice guy."

"He *told* you?" she asked, horrified.

"I followed you."

"You *what*?"

He gave a shrug. "I couldn't remember ever hearing of these women you were playing bunco with in Coquille, so I followed you. I wanted to be sure you were safe."

"Oh, for Jesus' sake," she said. "Why didn't you just ask me?"

"Because you didn't want to talk about it and, unlike you, I was letting you hold on to your privacy. And I'm willing to bet you've never seen *Dancing with the Stars* or the reruns you lock yourself in your room to watch. I can hear you talking on your phone. And *giggling.*"

She leaned toward him and leveled him with her mean-aunt look. "If you're such a damn smart detective, how is it you don't know you're in love with Gina?"

"Let me tell you something you probably already know. When Cee Jay got pregnant, even though we were kids with hardly an income between us, I was the happiest kid alive. Wanna know why? Because I was going to get to have sex without hiding in the backseat of a car every night for the rest of my life. That's what I thought love was, and it was a disaster. My life went to hell. I'm a tough guy — I can take it. But I can't stand the idea of putting Gina or the kids through something like that."

"Mac . . ."

"What about you, Lou? You've dated before. Plenty. Why are you hiding this one? Is it because Joe's black?"

"Of course not. I like him so much, but I want you and the kids to have no doubt that I'm planning to stick this out, see everyone grown-up and on their own. And by the time I do that, I'll be seventy. Seventy, Mac. Joe might change his mind."

Mac smiled at her. "I bet most of this town thinks two of the most self-assured people here are you and I. I'm afraid of going after a girl and you're afraid some guy will dump you for getting older. Which, by the way, is going to happen to him, too — getting older, I mean."

"Not as fast," she said grimly. "I've been thinking about a face-lift."

"You're the best-looking fifty-year-old in town."

She smiled broadly. "Thanks, Mac. Really, thanks. Since I'm sixty."

"I know."

Lou let herself into Joe's house and found him in the kitchen, chopping vegetables for a salad. She leaned in the doorway and just took him in — so tall and broad, his bald head shiny and latte-colored. He had the most wonderful eyebrows — black, arched, expressive.

He looked up and smiled. "Hello, beautiful."

"Good, we're staying in," she said. "You cooked?"

"I bought a roasted chicken from the grocery, and I'm making a salad. Glass of wine?"

"A double, please. He knows, Joe. Mac knows."

"Well, I didn't tell him, although I wanted

to." He grabbed the chilled white out of the refrigerator and a glass from the cupboard. "Did you tell him?"

She shook her head. "Apparently he's known for months. He followed me to one of my bunco games."

Joe laughed. "That dog."

"He asked me if I'm hiding you because you're black."

"Seriously? People hardly give a biracial couple a second glance. Did you tell him you're hiding me because I sometimes work with him?"

She shook her head. "I told him the truth." She took a sip of her wine. "I told him it's because I love you and I'm afraid by the time I'm done raising my kids, his kids, I'll be almost seventy. And you'll finally come to your senses. When it's too late for me to get over you."

His lips curled in a smile and he came around the work island to face her. He put his hands on her slender waist. "I should be annoyed by that, you know. That you keep expecting me to bail out on you because of something as trivial as age. But I'm not. Know why?"

"Why?"

"Because I don't mind convincing you

347

that's idiotic. Bring that glass of wine to bed."

They walked together toward the bedroom, holding hands. Lou said, "I'm sixty, been single all my life. I've had a few serious crushes that I thought might turn into something, but here I am, in love for the first time. At my age."

"Good. Stop complaining."

"Older people can get sick, you know. You could end up caring for some old woman."

"I pulled a speeding car over last night. A man was rushing his wife to the hospital. She'd been diagnosed with cancer, had been sick on and off for a few years and was getting worse. She was having trouble breathing, had chest pains and he thought it might be an embolism. He thought he was losing her. She was thirty-two."

"Oh, the poor things . . ."

"I lit it up and escorted them to the hospital. Let's let that age thing you're always worrying about go, Lou. Let's just have us some fun, now that Mac knows. All right?"

"Fun. Right." She slid her hand up his chest to his shoulder. "What are you doing for Thanksgiving in two weeks? Will you be with your kids this year?"

"One is going skiing with friends and the

other is spending the holiday with her mother and stepfather."

"How'd you like to make your debut?"

He grinned at her. "Sounds like a plan."

Thanksgiving Day, the weather was clear, wind moderate, temperature in the low forties on the Pacific, lower in the mountains where it was snowing. Sarah was at work until four o'clock, at which time she would head out of North Bend for Thunder Point and her boss would take over command. On holidays they tried to divide the watch. Crews of pilots, maintenance and EMTs would work the day shift, and the folks that had the day shift off would have their holiday meal early and come in later.

The station was quiet. This was a busy place Monday through Friday, when so much support staff, from clerical to maintenance, populated the place. But on nights, weekends and holidays, they operated with a slightly smaller workforce for emergencies. There were no training flights or inspections; Sarah wouldn't fly unless there was a rescue mission. She used her time catching up on officer efficiency reports, schedules for training flights and inventory of her helicopters. The helicopters had been put through the preflight checklists, gassed and were ready to go.

She was at her desk but kept looking at her watch, more than ready to call this workday over.

"Sarah."

She looked up and saw her ex-husband standing in the doorway. "You're early," she said, looking at her watch again. He wasn't due for an hour.

"I thought I'd offer you an early out for the holiday. Do you have plans?"

"I do," she said, putting down her pen and leaning back in her chair. "I'm having dinner with friends."

"And Landon?"

She lifted her brows. "The same friends," she answered.

"I guess Thunder Point is working out?" Derek asked. "You seem happier."

She just gave a nod, but she couldn't help thinking about how much happier than she'd been in so long. There were a couple of very dark years until now, from the time she had been forced to acknowledge Derek's cheating, through the extended, black process of freeing herself when all she'd really wanted was for him to love her more than anything, more than anyone. When she looked at him now, she could summon that pain and disappointment. Of course, if she tried, she could find that rage and humiliation again. But it was hard now. Landon was happy with Eve, hanging out with friends and the McCain family. And she had Cooper, who was safe.

"I've been thinking, Sarah," Derek said. "Maybe over the holidays, we could get together. You and me and Landon. Last year wasn't good. It was —"

She laughed at him before he could finish. "Our divorce was final three days before Christmas. No, Derek, we're not going to spend holidays together." She didn't bother to tell him it had been the worst Christmas of her life, rivaled only by the Christmas right after her parents died.

He stepped into the room. He straightened. "I'd like to see Landon."

"He has the same cell phone number he's had for the past two years, but I'm going to go out on a limb here and say that he won't be interested."

"I thought maybe you'd tell him I might be calling."

"Might? Might? You seriously want me to tell Landon his long-lost brother-in-law *might* be calling him?"

"I didn't want to be long and lost," he said. "It just seemed kinder to Landon not to put him in the middle of our problems."

"Derek, no one put him there and he was in the middle of it. You know that. When you were unfaithful to the marriage, you were unfaithful to him, too."

"We really need to have a conversation about —"

"No," she said. "Just no."

"Look, I think enough time has passed for us to have a conversation, maybe mend some fences."

"We're not going to talk about this here. This is work."

"Will you have dinner with me? Meet me for a drink?" he asked. "Sometime between now and Christmas?"

"Absolutely not," she said, standing. She briefly remembered how attractive and sexy she'd once found him. He had been irresistible. If she'd known about his little problem with monogamy, she not only wouldn't have married him, she would never have gone on a date with him. "We weren't right for each other, we ended it as well as we could, it's over. Landon is getting his confidence back and seems happy. Let's just try to be professional."

"Sarah, I heard through the grapevine that I'm getting orders. Is that your doing?"

"*My* doing?" she asked, stunned. Then she laughed. "Derek, if I could work a deal like that, I'd have done it a year and a half ago! Where are you going?"

"Kodiak," he said, completely glum.

"Son of a bitch," she muttered. He didn't want to go. She knew he didn't like to be cold, to sleep in daylight, to be challenged too much. She'd give just about anything to be reassigned to Kodiak, to the Bering Sea.

"I think I'll be out of here in a few months or less. I want to be friends, to see Landon, to —"

She came around her desk. She was shaking her head. "You're way too late, Derek. You'd have to unscrew a whole bunch of women, to start with. And you never said goodbye to Landon — he's not feeling real brotherly toward you. In fact, he's pretty pissed, and not just because of what you did to me. You left him, too."

"Come on, you didn't exactly make me feel welcome."

"Oh, sorry," she said sarcastically. "I'm not going to discuss this with you, especially not here. No dinner, no drink, and I don't give a shit about your fences. You made your choice. Your fences are all beyond repair."

"Sarah," he said. "You have influence. People like you, respect you. Can you get me out of Kodiak?"

"I'd take it off your hands in a second if I

353

could. But I have commitments. I'm determined that Landon will graduate from his current high school."

He stared at her for a long moment. "Oh, man, I missed all the signals!" he said suddenly. Then he laughed. "You've been smiling lately — you've been less mean. You're in a relationship!"

She didn't flinch. "Last count, you're in twenty relationships. Derek, I am so done with you. If you're ready to take over, I'll leave for the day. My brother is waiting for me."

But he wasn't done laughing. "Holy crap, I didn't think it would ever happen — I know that look! Someone's got you all softened up. Sarah's getting laid!"

She got right in his face, put her palm against his chest and said, "I just thought of a way to keep you out of Kodiak. Sexual harassment charges and court martial. That sound better than the Bering Sea?"

"Come on, Sarah. What's a little teasing between friends?" he asked.

She walked away from him, leaving everything on her desk. She went to the locker room to change out of her flight suit. Using her cell phone from there, she called the rescue diver on her team. "Paul, do me a favor. Keep me out of prison. Occupy Stiles.

He's giving me shit and I want to make a clean getaway before I kill him."

"You bet, boss."

She could count on Paul. She'd have to get his family some kind of nice Christmas basket.

She changed into her jeans, blouse, sweater, boots. She put on some makeup, something she never did before leaving the station. Suddenly she wondered, could Cooper be as insensitive and cruel as Derek? Because she felt about Cooper right now just as she had once felt about Derek and it scared her to death. She had laughed with Derek as much, as often. She had relied on him in almost the same way she relied on Cooper — as someone not just for her, but for Landon. And sex with Derek had been good.

But if she was honest, she had never really trusted Derek. She knew firsthand that he didn't always keep his word, that he could lie easily, but she had dismissed these as minor flaws because they were never about issues that really mattered. He would tell a friend he'd completely forgotten he was going to help him move when, really, he had decided he'd rather watch the ball game. He would promise to be home right after work and be two hours late, but he had excuses that at least sounded believable. *Sorry, babe, we got arguing about a few completely miscalled plays, the game was in overtime, we added a beer to the discussion — in which I was totally right, by the way — and before I knew it . . .*

But it had been tough to ignore what happened the day they got married.

*Are you at Susan's house?*

*Susan's? Why would I be at Susan's?*

*I hear that dog — the one next door to her. The one that never shuts up.*

*What dog?*

*I heard it in the background.*

*I don't hear anything. Sure it's not somewhere you are?*

*I'm at the spa! And Susan isn't!*

*Well, call her, Sarah. I'm about to walk out the door. I'll see you at four. Stop going crazy. You're just having nerves.*

*Aren't* you? *Having nerves?*

*No, Sarah. I'm ready.*

The one question Derek had never been able to answer — why in the world did he marry Sarah if he still acted like a single guy? Screwing around? "It's not like I planned it. It just happened. And I don't love her — I love you."

So maybe she should thank Derek for showing her the light? Because without

356

some of his most disastrous lies, betrayals and infidelities, she would have fallen in love with Cooper in just a few weeks. But she had learned. Boy, had she learned.

She slid into the blazer she was wearing to Thanksgiving dinner at the McCains'. And then the bell went off, followed by the intercom calling for a rescue team.

She had been leaving early, thanks to Derek, but at the sound, she was out of her clothes and back into her flight suit faster than lightning. She ran to the chopper.

"Suspected heart attack, fifty-seven-year-old male, on *The Misty Morning.* Sixty-foot sailing vessel, luxury Oyster, about twenty miles northwest. Here are your coordinates," the crew chief said. "Ready?"

"Ready," she said. "We did the preflight checklist and gassed her up earlier. Paul finished the inventory. Is our guy conscious?"

"So far. Want to wait for a doctor?"

"We stand a better chance of bringing him in than waiting for the doc. Tell them to lower the sails. Paul? You have everything?" she yelled.

He was pulling on the bottom half of a wet suit. With all the rigging on a sailboat, she might have to put him in the water. "Got it," he yelled back. Then, carrying his gear, he jogged to the helicopter.

Derek was pacing. She could tell he wanted on this flight, even though she would be pilot in command. Thankfully her copilot, sharp young Lieutenant JG, was on board, ready for their takeoff preflight. She was plugging in the coordinates. "We can eat up twenty miles in ten minutes."

Copilot, maintenance crew chief, EMT all buckled in; takeoff preflight done. It was showtime.

"And we are airborne," she said into the radio. "Schuman, remind me that if I'm ever going to have a heart attack, I want to have it on a sixty-foot yacht."

"Yes, ma'am," he said.

Air traffic control gave her altitude and heading, and in two minutes, it was all water underneath them. Nine and a half minutes later, they had the vessel in sight. "We have a lot of rigging, but I can get you down on the deck, Paul. Harness up. Ready to go."

"Aye, ma'am."

"We can deploy the rescue basket after you assess."

"Roger," he said, sitting in the open door of the chopper.

With the crew chief managing the reel, Paul descended to the deck. He dropped the emergency bag before he released the

358

harness. The passengers seemed to be gathered around the patient. It was maybe four minutes before Paul said into his radio, "We have a possible coronary, patient's breathing on his own, severe chest pain. Let's take him aboard, Commander. Have medical and transport standing by."

The crew chief deployed the basket. Sarah maneuvered around the rigging and in just a few minutes the patient was aboard and they were headed in. Her mind was on nothing but flying until she was landing. It was then that she saw Derek again, through the open hangar doors, loitering around the debrief area. She wondered why he took so much pleasure in screwing with her head? Was it because she outranked him? Because she had caught him in his lies and thrown him out? Why didn't he take the high road, realize he'd tortured her enough and make himself invisible? Or at least a little less obvious?

The ambulance crew rushed forward with a stretcher and she shut down the helicopter. "Debrief in five," she said. "Then if we're lucky, we're headed out for the rest of the day."

There was paperwork to file after a rescue, a crew debrief, but Sarah took a moment to text Landon. Had to fly; rescue mission. Don't wait for me. Tell everyone to eat.

He texted back: Everyone okay?

So far, she responded.

# SIXTEEN

Lou McCain wasn't that much of a cook — other than her trademark spaghetti — and she knew it. But Thanksgiving at her house had been a tradition since they'd moved to Thunder Point. They always invited Gina and her gang, too. On every other day of the year, Carrie — her closest friend — cooked and baked for the deli. Gina helped with that, plus served in the diner. Lou thought it was the mark of a good friend to feed them on this particular day.

But this year was special: she was springing Joe on them.

While Eve helped her stuff the turkey, Lou broke the news. "I've invited a gentleman your dad knows to dinner. Joe Metcalf. He's a state trooper."

"Why? Is he all alone for the holiday?"

"Well, as it happens, he is, but that's not why I invited him." She took a deep breath. "I've been dating him a little."

"Really?" Eve asked, stunned. "And you never said anything?"

"I wanted to make sure I liked him before bringing him home for dinner."

"Highway Patrol? How old is this guy?"

"You had to ask. . . . He might be a little younger than me, but not all that much. It's not like I'm some cougar . . ."

Eve giggled and covered her mouth.

"Oh, I'm sure you think this is funny. I've been a little nervous about this, so you might lend some support. After all, I've been squarely on your team when you want the car, when you're out on dates. Without me, you'd be wearing a chastity belt."

"True," Eve said. "Okay, tell me more about this guy."

"Well, he's African-American. Mostly."

"Mostly? Does that mean he's black?"

"Latte," she said. "He's also Native American, lots of different European and Caribbean." And then she smiled. "He's very beautiful."

When Joe arrived at one in the afternoon, Mac met him with a hearty handshake and invited him to grab a beer and come into the living room by the fire. But Joe said, "Give me a little while." He took off his jacket, draped it on a kitchen chair and said, "Let me help Lou in the kitchen first. She's not that much of a cook. Today I can guarantee pretty canapés, no lumps in the potatoes, very smooth gravy and sweet potato pie like you've never had. I'd do pies, but my understanding is your friend Carrie is bringing them."

"You cook?" Mac asked. "And bake?"

"My mother made sure I knew all her recipes so I wouldn't starve. I can make fried chicken so good you'll cry."

"Damn," Mac said. "Lou, you have a nerve keeping Joe all to yourself for so long! The last time I had fried chicken, it came from the Colonel."

"I was a colonel," Joe reminded him.

It all worked. Ryan and Dee Dee hardly noticed that Joe was new to the gathering; Carrie was delighted to finally meet him; Gina was shocked and pleased. Even Cooper, whom Mac had invited, seemed comfortable around Joe, even though they'd just met.

There was only one pall on the celebration — Sarah didn't make it. There were two more rescue flights, far more than was typical in a single day. She stayed for the debriefs, made sure everything was stable before she even attempted to leave. It was seven-thirty when she texted Landon that she was exhausted and just needed to go home. Holidays could be like that for first responders — accidents, crimes, severe illness, sometimes brought on by overindulgence. Lou was sorry Sarah couldn't celebrate with Landon and Cooper, because she felt a surge of satisfaction when she saw her family all together around the table — and Joe there, too.

Cooper found Thanksgiving at the McCains to be as close to a family gathering as he'd been to in years. He hung out with the men in Mac's living room while the women stayed mostly in the kitchen. The kids were downstairs in the basement-turned-rumpus-room until Ryan and Dee Dee came up because, "They're *kissing!*"

Then it was on Joe and Cooper to keep Mac upstairs. "Take it easy, Mac," Joe said. "Kissing is good. If they still have their clothes on."

He wished Sarah had been there, even if she was in the kitchen with the women, but he understood about work. He liked that everyone trusted Sarah enough that no one was worried about her. Landon was used to this and had a lot of respect for his sister's ability. Cooper had been a pilot himself and since the weather was good, he wasn't concerned. It was a house full of first responders — people were used to call-outs.

After dinner, Ashley and her boyfriend, Downy, showed up for dessert; they had been with his family for part of the day. Then there was a round of charades. If someone had told Cooper a year ago he'd play charades with three generations of people and laugh his ass off, he'd have called them crazy. After charades, they broke out the Wii and had a bowling and rock star competition.

Cooper hung around the McCains until the text came to Landon, then he pulled the kid aside and, in a quiet voice, said, "I'm going to take off. I think I'll beg a covered dish from Aunt Lou for your sister and wait for her at your house."

"You don't, like, have a key, do you?" Landon asked.

"No. She's on her way, right? I'll sit out front."

Landon looked a little troubled. "Okay."

Lou was more than happy to fix up some leftovers for Sarah, something she could put in the microwave, plus some pie. She even forced a bottle of wine on him, in case there wasn't any at Sarah's house. And then Landon walked Cooper to his truck.

"Listen, maybe we should talk about this," Landon said.

"This?"

"I want Sarah to go out, to have fun. In fact, I need her to. When all she's got is me, it just . . . I don't know . . . just gets very heavy. But her ex — he hurt her. It was a terrible thing to watch."

"What did he do to her, Landon?" Cooper asked. "Anything I should know about that, anything above and beyond the usual rigors of divorce?"

"I could tell you, but I don't know how she'd take it. Ask her yourself, Coop. Let her tell you. And then, go out, have fun, whatever. But if you hurt her, if you do anything that makes her cry every day for six months, I swear to God . . ."

"Landon, I don't want Sarah to be hurt. I like her. It might be easier to avoid that if I knew what I'm not supposed to do."

"Well, for starters, don't cheat on her. That's all I'm saying."

Cooper shrugged. "That's easy. I'm kind of simple — one woman is about all I can handle. More than one at a time? Bigger than I am, that's for sure."

"Okay," Landon said. "Good to know. Because Sarah hasn't had many boyfriends. Derek, he was a surprise. I'm sure she went out with guys because I had babysitters sometimes, but Derek was the first one she got serious about and I was thirteen. So what I'm saying here is, Sarah doesn't have a lot of experience with guys. If you screw her up . . ."

He felt a smile come to his lips. Sarah wasn't inexperienced. Or maybe she was a natural. But one thing was clear — she hadn't paraded an army of beaux past her little brother, yet another thing for which he admired her.

Cooper put a hand on his shoulder. "I promise," he said. "But, Landon, I'm leaving after Christmas. January, maybe February at the latest. I told Sarah, and you knew from the start, I'm going to have to find work. This place? I like it — it's a good place. But I'm just passing through."

"I know. I get that. That's not the same thing as using someone. Hurting someone. I said all I have to say." He pulled his keys out of his pocket.

"Wait a minute," Cooper said. "Maybe you should tell me what the ex did to you."

"If you'd asked me that a few months ago, I would have had a load of crap to lay on you. First, he practically killed my sister, she was so sad. And I haven't heard a word from him since he left us over a year ago. We had to move because Sarah couldn't make the mortgage by herself. And she moved me to Nowhereville. But now? I don't want to hear from him and I like No-whereville. And there's Eve . . ."

Cooper chuckled. "I might be just a cockeyed optimist, but things seem to work out the way they're supposed to."

Landon gave him a key off his key ring. "Let yourself in. Warm up her dinner. She comes off a bunch of rescues just shot to hell."

"When are you going to be home?" Cooper asked. "So I can pass that on to your sister."

"When Deputy Yummy Pants throws me out," he said.

A loud bark of laughter escaped Cooper.

"That's what the women call him behind his back. Believe me, from where I'm sitting, he's not all that sexy. I'll leave when he says I'm leaving. Let Ham out, will you? And leave my key on the kitchen table, okay?"

"Sure, kid. Behave yourself." And he left for Sarah's house.

She wasn't home yet. This was only the second time Cooper had been to Sarah's house and his first time inside. It was very small, he knew from their conversations — two whole bedrooms. But she had a fenced backyard, absolutely necessary for Ham. And there was a small fireplace in the living room. Probably the best part about the house was the front porch. It was covered and stretched the length of the front of the house. If she owned the property or if she were staying here permanently, she could enclose it or screen it. From that front porch, there was a view of the bay and, in the distance, a small light across the beach. The light he'd left on over the door of his fifth wheel. She could also see the town, the main street, the marina.

He took off his boots inside the front door. He let Ham out the back door and, using the wood and pinecone starters, he built a fire. Then he put the covered dish holding the turkey dinner beside the microwave on the counter and the wine in the refrigerator.

When she walked in the back door, she looked stunned. "What are you doing here?"

He stood from the sofa. "I brought you some leftovers and made you a fire. Landon gave me a key — I left it on the table. Listen, I don't have to stay. You must be worn-out. Long day?"

She shrugged out of her coat and tossed it over the back of a kitchen chair. "Fourteen hours, the last two just mopping up the paperwork. Three rescues in one day — unprecedented. I was going to stop off for a bottle of wine, but since it's Thanksgiving evening, not much is open."

"Got you covered, Commander," he said. "Aunt Lou wouldn't let me leave without one. I'll open it for you."

"You're a good man to have around," she said, going to the sofa. She pulled off her boots. He must have found the corkscrew right away; she heard only one drawer slide open. When he started opening kitchen cupboards, she said, "Over the toaster oven, next to the refrigerator." A minute later he brought her a glass of wine.

"Maybe I should get going."

"Only if you want to," she said. "I'm up to a little quiet company. I'm sorry I missed the dinner."

"We played charades," he said, then surprised himself with a laugh. He sat beside her. "Landon had a father-son talk with me. This time I was the son. He's pretty worried, Sarah. Afraid that getting mixed up with me is going to leave you brokenhearted and broken-down."

"Ah, poor Landon. You can't blame him. It was so hard on him, seeing me fall apart the way I did over the divorce. This doesn't have anything to do with you, Cooper. In fact, it's very nice to have a friend like you. And I've gotten closer to Gina and let me tell you, it's been a while since I had a

370

girlfriend. I needed that, too."

With a finger, he ran her short hair around her ear. He smiled. "Will you think I'm a complete pig if I tell you that sleeping with you really winds my watch?"

She grinned. "We've never slept."

"Because you drive me out of my mind. I've needed a friend like you, too."

She chuckled. "Needed to get laid, huh?"

"That, too. Listen, I made a slight change in plans. While the bait shop is being worked on, while Rawley is around to keep an eye on the reconstruction, I'm going to head to Albuquerque to visit my family."

"Now?" she asked.

"In a week."

"I thought you planned to go for Christmas?" she asked, sipping her wine.

"I was considering it. But I decided I wanted to be around here. Do you have plans?"

"I only work Christmas Eve until four, unless it turns into another day like today. And I have Landon, when he's not with Eve." She curled up against Cooper's side. "This is his first girlfriend, unless you count Cindy Freeman when he was seven."

"He's a goner," Cooper said, putting his arms around her. "Have you talked to him about, you know . . ."

"Talked to him and armed him. But God, I hope he doesn't have sex." She lifted her head. "Is there any way we can keep them from having sex?"

Cooper just shook his head. "Has he talked about you having sex with a nomad who lives in a tin can?"

She shook her head. "He must be leaving that up to me."

"Good. You turned out to have very good judgment about that."

"You mean the way I jumped your bones on the second date?"

"My favorite part. Want me to warm your dinner?"

"No. Can you put it in the refrigerator when you're up getting me another glass of wine?"

"Yes, ma'am," he said, reluctantly pulling away from her. And then he was back, handing her the wine and pulling her against him. In lieu of hot, crazy sex, just holding her was very satisfying. He told her what he'd heard at the McCains' about Christmas, about the decorating of the town, about parties, about a legendary open house at Gina and Carrie's house, catered by the only caterer in town. "And we're included, if interested."

"Lovely," she said, sipping. She tilted her

head to look up at him. "But I don't want you to worry — if your plans change and you have to be with family, it's not going to be a problem."

Ah, she was holding him at arm's length. Even though he didn't have the details, it was enough to know she'd had a real bad experience. It was hard for her to trust. A year ago, five years ago, even ten years ago — this was him. He was always afraid to get too close. "Barring some family emergency, I'll be here," he said. "Tell me about the rescues."

So while she cuddled up to him and sipped her wine, she told him about one possible coronary, a boat taking on water forty miles offshore, a hiker who'd spent Thanksgiving day in the woods at about five thousand feet, lost and with hypothermia. And then her glass was nearly empty. "Will you put this on the coffee table, please?"

He laughed at her. "Is it good having your very own valet?"

"It is good," she said, resting her head against his chest. "And you double as a pillow very nicely, too."

He pulled a throw off the end of the sofa and covered her and some of himself, as well. "Wanna make out?" he asked her.

"Hmm. Can't. Landon could be coming

in anytime now. Plus I don't know how to make out with you without taking my clothes off and making crazy, insane, insatiable love to you."

He laughed and it ended in a low growl and a kiss on her forehead. "Don't seek help for that, all right?"

"All right," she said. "If I walk Ham tomorrow, maybe you can get a nooner."

"I'll take it," he whispered. And then he let his eyes close while he held her before he thought about it much longer — that she was the best thing he'd ever come across. And she was afraid to let him in.

Her soft snore put him to sleep. He had no idea what time it was when he heard the back door and Ham's excitement. His feet were propped on the coffee table, and she was curled in a small ball against him with one leg thrown over his. He had both arms around her. He opened one eye to see Landon standing in front of them, his hands on his hips, a smile on his face.

"Oh, you kids," Landon said with a smile. "I'm going to bed."

Cooper gave a small nod and just pulled Sarah closer. His contentment was too rich for him to get up and leave.

The diner had been closed on Thanksgiving

Day. It opened bright and early the next morning, though the crowd was sparse. Quite a few people took a long weekend and many left town to be with family in other towns or states. Gina had the diner's laptop open on the counter, paying a few bills for Stu, when Scott Grant came in. This time, no small children — he was alone.

"Good morning," she said, closing her laptop.

He sat up at the counter right in front of her in Mac's seat. "Do you live here, Gina?" he asked with a smile.

"You'd think so, right? I work a lot when I'm not in school. When I have classes, Stu adjusts my schedule as much as possible. I work the day shift, from early morning to midafternoon. I have three busy periods in here — early-early morning, early-late morning and lunch. I only work nights if someone's sick or needs time off. I hate nights. I'm a morning person."

He smiled. "I must be, too. I've never seen anyone but you behind the counter."

"It's a small diner. Usually only one person at a time is needed, except on Friday and Saturday nights. Then Stu's wife, Belinda, and one of our teenagers work together, and it's like open warfare. I stay as far away as possible. How was your Thanks-

375

giving?"

"Surprisingly bearable. My mother and mother-in-law are in town. Which is why I'm here."

"Oh, really?" she asked, lifting a brow.

"Gabriella is in Vancouver with her family for a few days, and the grandmothers are here with me. The house is small and getting a little close. If you get my drift."

"If you don't mind me asking, why don't you live closer to your family?" she asked, while automatically pouring him a cup of coffee.

"I could lie and say it was all about work, but that wouldn't be entirely true. I did medical school and residency in California — Serena and I were happy there. Our mothers are widows, overbearing, controlling and in competition with each other. I've been fantasizing a way back to California ever since. When the Vancouver hospital where I'd been working since before I lost Serena started downsizing, I started looking. I really need a fresh start. And space from the grandmothers. It's hard to get on with your life with your mother and mother-in-law breathing down your neck."

"I see," she said. "So, that's your only family?"

"Oh, no," he said with a laugh. "I have a

sister, two years older, who said, 'Thanks a whole hell of a lot,' when I told her we were moving. I guess I left her with our mother, who needs a lot of attention. Unfortunately for me, my mother is pretty focused on her poor widowed son and motherless grandchildren. But when she's not focused on me, she's very busy trying to get my sister married." He sipped his coffee. "They're leaving Monday. Can I stay with you until then?"

She laughed at him.

"So, I don't know your schedule, but is there a good time to, you know, go out? Because I've been on one date since my wife died. That was in Vancouver and she saw two little kids — Jenny wasn't potty trained yet — and she ran for her life."

Gina was stunned. Her mouth fell open. "Me?" she asked.

"Something wrong with you? You in a relationship or something?"

"Um . . . no. Did you know I am the single, never-married mother of a sixteen-year-old and I live with my mother?"

"I didn't know that, as a matter of fact. Level with me, Gina — is she like my mother? Demanding, oversensitive and generally controlling? Because really . . . been there, done that."

"No," she said with a laugh. "My mother is awesome. She's Carrie of Carrie's Deli and Catering. She's an angel come to earth, with an edge. She's real good people, but she doesn't suffer fools gladly."

"Oh, that's a relief. So . . . that means what? I have to get you home early?"

"Oh, my gosh, do you have any idea how long it's been since I've been on a date?"

"Well, don't panic — I met my wife in high school. I know, ridiculous, right? So I've had one date, and I think I wasn't very good at it. And before you start to worry, I'm not looking for a mother for my poor motherless children or anything like that. I'd just like to go out with someone instead of with a bunch of hospital staff or two little kids or alone. I think I'm about due for some fun. And I want to learn more about your town and the people around here. I bet you can tell me a lot."

"Oh, yes, that I can do. I'm not working Sunday morning."

"Great. I have grandmothers to keep busy with babysitting and going crazy wondering who I might be going out with! It's childish, but it serves them right. Pick you up at six?"

"Fantastic. Now, you want some eggs or something?"

"Sounds good. Eggs, over easy —"

"No, don't go there," she said. "Omelet or scrambled or over hard. Stu is a sweet man, but not a gentle hand in the kitchen."

"Okay, omelet. Is bacon okay?"

"It's his specialty. Crispy. And wheat toast and some home fries?"

"Excellent. Then I'm going over to the shop to work a little bit. Want to write down your address for me? Is your house hard to find?"

"It's two blocks from here, Scott." She slapped his order ticket on the cook's counter. "You can see it from the front of the store. I'll write down the address."

When he was finishing up his breakfast, he asked, "So, what kind of classes?"

"Social work. I think, after I do an internship, I'd like to be a counselor. That's way down the road for me, though. Right now Ashley is my priority — getting her through college and on her own."

"Really? And could the citizens of Thunder Point use a counselor?"

"Every last person here," she said, grinning.

Mac went to the diner at around ten in the morning and caught Gina reading. "Hey, slow morning?"

She closed the book. "Day after Thanks-

379

giving is always a little quiet. People have tons of leftovers to plow through."

He sat at the counter and she poured him coffee. "I had a nice time yesterday, Gina."

"It was a good day, wasn't it? I think everyone enjoyed it."

"And you're not mad at me anymore," he said.

She took a steadying breath. "I apologize. You were in the line of fire. I'm not angry with you, Mac. I was angry with myself and took it out on you."

"And would you mind sharing? What are you angry with yourself about?"

"It's kind of hard to explain, but here goes. When I saw Sarah and Cooper holding hands and gazing at each other, I became so envious. I haven't been on a date in years! I haven't had anyone hold my hand or gaze into my eyes like I'm special in so long . . . maybe ever! I'm only thirty-two. I have nearly raised a daughter, almost have a degree, and I don't have a life. And I am bloody sick of not having a life. That's all it was — just a woman mourning her abandoned womanhood."

Mac thought, *My timing is perfect!* Outside of police work, his timing was seldom on, but for once . . . "Then I'm in the right place at the right time. Let's go out Saturday night. No kids, no aunt, no mother. Just you and me."

"Oh," she said uncomfortably. "Listen, it's not like I don't appreciate the gesture, but I'm not looking for another friendly little buddy hookup. I'll hang out with you anytime, Mac. Your friendship is very important to me. But I actually want a real date with the potential for a little hand-holding. Maybe even a kiss good-night."

"Well, I —"

"I have a date with Scott Grant for Saturday night. We're going out to dinner. Without kids."

"Scott Grant?" he asked, though he knew exactly who that was.

"Dr. Grant?" she returned.

"I know," he said, irritably. "You like him?"

"Of course I like him or I wouldn't go out with him," she said. "He's very nice. I don't have any expectations, but he wants to take me out and —"

"You might've warned me," Mac said.

Her brows knit. "Of what?"

"That you needed to have a date. After all, we've been —"

"Buddies," she said. "Pals. No offense, Mac, but I don't need another pal. I wouldn't trade you for anything, but I really think I'm now mature enough for a boy-

381

friend. It doesn't have to be happily ever after, I just want a shot at it. I'm not saying that will be Scott Grant, but what the hell. I'm going on a date!"

"I've taken you out!" he boomed.

"Not exactly," she corrected. "We've gone out together, but you made yourself very clear — you can't have a relationship. You have children to raise. And I am ready for a relationship."

"Aw, fuck," he said, which he almost never said in front of a woman.

"Yeah, and that," she said.

"Gina!" he barked, appalled.

"Well, forgive me for living!"

"I just swore because I was late in asking you out, behind Medical Man. Not because it was a game plan! Look, I'll take you out, hold your hand, look at you like you're special —"

"Whoa, thanks so much. But I have plans," she said, lifting her chin. "And I think three years was enough time to give you to get ready. I'm going to move on. But gee, really, thanks so much for the offer."

"Come on, Gina," he said with a bit of a whine. "You know what I mean."

"Breakfast, Mac? Or just coffee today?" she asked.

"You're still mad at me. Jesus, I had no

idea this was happening in your head. You should have *told* me!"

She leaned on the counter and looked into his eyes. "Mac, my dear friend, here is something you should probably know about women without being told. We don't want to have to tell a man we need to be wanted. We'd really like that to come naturally. We'd like a man to pursue us because he wants us, not because he's out of options."

"Okay."

"So — omelet or scrambled?"

"Are we done talking about this?"

"All done."

# Seventeen

As a matter of tradition, the chamber of commerce pulled out the Christmas decorations on the Saturday after Thanksgiving. In between serving and cooking, this was the day Stu and Gina worked on decorating the diner, with the help of Stu's wife, Belinda, and Ashley. Carrie put up a wreath on her door and garland on the deli showcase. Everyone managed to pass through town at a point, whether to help or watch. Cooper was hanging around and, since he was handy, he was up on a ladder adding streamers and garland to the old-fashioned light posts on the main street. Even Wayland Carmichael was decorating his bar, Wayland's. The good doctor showed up for a while and hung a decorated sign on his door that said Clinic Coming Soon.

Sarah showed up for a while with Ham, on her way to the beach, and Cooper climbed down his ladder to talk to her. He slipped an arm around her waist, kissed her cheek, laughed with her for a minute. When she went on her way to walk the dog, he gave her a pat on the rump.

Mac made his way to Cooper. "You barely hit town and you already found yourself a woman."

Cooper just smiled. He gave a nod, but his gaze was following Sarah. When she turned the corner, he looked at Mac. "Which begs the question, what's taking you so long? Didn't you say you've been divorced for years?"

"Sore subject," Mac said.

Cooper looked across the street and Mac followed with his eyes. Gina was holding a wreath for the front door, talking to Scott Grant, laughing. "What about Gina? You two seem to get along."

Mac frowned. "She's going out with the new doctor."

"Well, that sucks. Maybe it won't work out."

As they watched, Gina and Scott laughed at something. Then Scott tweaked her cheek, whispered something that made her smile and turned to leave. Before getting in his car, he lifted his hand to wave to Mac and Cooper.

"Right," Mac said glumly.

"I have to go," Cooper said. "I'm going to meet Sarah at my place."

"I don't need to know that."

"Sometimes she's tired from her jog and needs to lie down awhile."

"Really, you can keep it to yourself, asshole."

"Hamlet likes to watch."

"You're a sick fucker, you know that?"

"I'm kidding, all right? I have Gatorade."

Mac spent the rest of the afternoon either putting up decorations or giving his opinion about what looked right. He did a lot of observing at the same time, watching everyone who had come to help. Like Ray Anne, in jeans so tight it was a miracle she could stoop or squat, heels with the jeans, leather vest over red silk blouse, cleavage and mistletoe in her hair. Talk about obvious. His aunt was giving Ray Anne a wide berth. Everyone knew they didn't get along.

Puck Morrison was in town for a while, his family notably absent. Mac observed that Puck seemed to be stooping, having a little trouble moving around. Everyone aged differently, but he thought Puck was about seventy, maybe a hair over. He looked worn-out. Maybe it was arthritis, slowing him down. One thing for sure, he'd look a lot better without that damn hairpiece he wore.

At about four, Wayland started passing out beer to the people still working on the street. Lou took off with the younger kids. Eve and Landon followed in Landon's truck — those two appeared to be joined at the hip. Ashley, Gina and Carrie walked home, giving him a wave as they left.

*Right. Gotta get dressed for that date.*

Mac went home. There was a nice smell in the kitchen, but no one was around. Then Lou walked in, dressed all nice, fixing an earring. "There you are," she said. "Eve is going out with Landon tonight — I think to a movie or something. The kids are downstairs playing video games. Dee Dee wanted a sleepover but I said not tonight, not after all day in town decorating. I'm going out. I didn't check plans with you — are you home tonight?"

"I'm home," he said wearily.

"It wouldn't really have mattered. Dee Dee and Ryan are fine on their own. There's meat loaf and mashed potatoes staying warm in the oven on low. Green beans in there, too. It's ready whenever you are. I'll be on my way."

"Bunco?" he asked, lifting one sardonic brow.

"Here's a thrill for you, Mac. I don't even know how to play bunco."

"Figures," he said.

"I'll be home later," she said. "I'm not staying over or anything. We're going out to dinner in North Bend, going to walk along the pier, you know."

"How would I know?" he asked churlishly.

"If you want to go out for a beer or something, give the kids dinner and tell them to lock the door. You have your cell phone."

But he didn't feel like being friendly. He'd been as friendly as he could manage all day. He was sunk in a deep pit of self-pity at the moment and it was best to indulge that alone. Everyone had someone, it seemed. Everyone except him. He'd made such perfect sense to himself years ago, when he thought it through and decided dating Gina was a bad idea. He'd been attracted to her — at first because she was beautiful, then he quickly learned that her mind and heart were even more beautiful. Plus, she had courage and she never gave up, even when the hardest times hit her. And naturally, especially with what he'd been through in his short marriage and divorce, the fact that her daughter was her priority earned her every ounce of respect he could muster. So in the back of his head, he'd had a plan. When the girls were college-bound or at least *almost* college-bound, he'd court her. He'd tell her then that he'd *always* wanted her, but he worried about the possible conflicts.

*Way to go, Deputy Yummy Pants,* he thought. He'd waited too long. He had Cooper to thank for that — Cooper hitting town and hooking up practically overnight, illustrating to Gina that she'd put all her eggs in the wrong damn basket. He thought he was being brave and strong, holding off while they each had such complicated lives. How was he supposed to know that she was needing a little loving as much as he was?

He couldn't get more stupid if he made an effort.

He cleaned the dishes after dinner, giving the kids a night off. He brewed himself a cup of coffee. He sat in his living room with his Labs and sulked, imagining her holding hands across the tablecloth with the doctor in a candlelit restaurant. He hated that doctor. Really, a doctor? A high school graduate up against a doctor? It was hopeless.

At almost eight o'clock his cell phone chimed and he saw it was Pritkus.

"Yeah, boss, it's Christmastime in Mayberry. Got a pretty ugly domestic out at the Morrisons', ambulance en route. I wouldn't mind a little help from a supervisor."

He stood before Pritkus stopped talking. "Who are you taking in for it?"

"Looks like the kid for sure and probably the missus, too. Puck is going in the ambulance. He's going to be fine, but when you see this place, you're gonna shit."

"On my way," he said.

He shouted for the kids as he pulled his shirt off and headed to his bedroom. He took only two minutes to get into his uniform, simultaneously telling Ryan and Dee Dee to lock him out, call his cell if they had any problems, stay in and if he was going to be later than ten he'd give them a call on the house phone. When they asked what it was about he said, "I'm not sure yet. Some kind of fight that Pritkus wants a supervisor to help with. Probably all paperwork now."

"Then why are you going so fast and hurry?" Dee Dee asked.

"Because when an officer asks for a supervisor, you always go fast and hurry, but there's nothing to worry about." He kissed their heads and shot out the door, pausing long enough to listen to the locks slide into place. He waited until he was out of his own neighborhood to hit the lights and siren. It was very rare in Thunder Point to see a Sheriff's Department SUV racing through town, lights flashing.

There were already two patrol cars at the residence, lights flashing. Two was one more car than they usually had in town and Mac's made it three. That kind of turnout was usually reserved for major catastrophes. The ornate front doors of the Morrison residence were standing open. With his hand resting comfortably on the handle of his gun, Mac walked inside, glass crunching beneath his boots.

The place looked like a bomb had gone off. There was toppled furniture and broken glass everywhere. In the formal living room, Jag and his mother sat on the sofa, cuffed, while Puck held an ice pack to his bleeding head. There was blood splattered here and there, on the floor and furniture, on the suspects and the victim.

"Who called it in?"

"Mrs. Morrison made the nine-one-one call," Pritkus said. "She said her son was attacking her husband. When we got here, the story changed to her husband was attacking her and she was defending herself."

"How convenient." Mac bent at the waist to be eye level with Puck. "Who did this, Mr. Morrison?"

"I'll tell my attorney."

"Who broke up all the china and crystal?"

"I did," Mrs. Morrison said. "Is it against

the law? It's mine, right? If I want to throw around the glassware, that's my business, right?"

Mac turned and stepped toward her. She looked like bloody hell, her hair a rat's nest, her eye makeup running in black rivers down her cheeks, the sleeve of her blouse torn. Skinny as she was, with that sneer on her lips, she looked like a war victim.

Puck, on the other hand, though his face was battered and his head bleeding, looked better without the hairpiece. As expected, he was completely bald with some spikes of short white hair all over his shiny dome.

"And whatever possessed you to start throwing things?" he asked.

"I was angry!" she said, stiffening her skinny spine.

"He's such a loser," Jag muttered.

Mac merely glanced at him. Apparently he had an opinion here. He lifted his eyebrows and waited. But it was Mrs. Morrison who spoke up.

"He informed us we're moving. Letting the house go, selling most of our possessions and moving because he can't make a goddamn living! I've wasted most of my life on him and now this? So I threw a plate or two? Isn't that allowed when someone tells you your life is over?"

"Is that right? Wasted your life?"

"Maybe if you hadn't spent it all, Effie," Puck said.

"How could I spend it all? Didn't you give most of it to your ex?"

"I have sons!"

"And you have a son right here!" she shrieked. "A son who's getting *nothing!*"

"He gets plenty. You get plenty."

"My brothers drove Hummers in high school," Jag grumbled. "You put them up in classy town houses for college. What've I got? A used car and a quad." He laughed meanly.

"First, no more country club, then no more vacations, then no new cars. We have used!" Effie cried out. "Then the credit cards. Then the house? I can't take it! You promised me! You promised me *everything!*"

"I promised you what I had and you took it. It is now gone!"

"Why the hell didn't you buy that stupid Bailey land and spin it into a big sale? I told you to go get it, but what did you do? Sent that hussy real estate agent to try to convince him! Loser! Jag's right, you're a loser."

"He didn't want to sell!" Puck said.

"You should've found a way!" she said.

Without quite knowing why, Mac looked at Jag, narrowing his eyes. Jag just glared at his father. Finally Jag said, "There were ways. He just didn't have the balls."

*Whoa,* Mac thought. He paused, went over procedure in his mind, because he really didn't want to screw this up. He smelled grand jury investigation becoming an indictment, not just on the battery, but possibly murder. Investigations weren't fast and they were dicey and complex.

"Did you have the balls, son?" he asked Jag. "Could you have made it work? The sale of that property?"

"Hey!" he shot out angrily. "My job is to go to *high school,* all right? It's *his* job to run the business, support the family! And he's an old loser!"

Mac slowly turned toward Puck. "Who hit you in the head? Who injured you?"

"I'll talk to my lawyer."

"That's fine. The missus and young Jag here are going for a ride. We have a domestic with injuries and that's what happens. Anyone we can call for you?"

"My sons," he said. "My older sons."

And that was just about all Mac needed to hear.

Mac worked on Sunday, much of that time looking at public records on his computer at his office, even though people who were finishing up the Christmas decorating kept coming into his office. What he wanted to know was what had brought Puck Morrison to this point in his life. What he learned was a lot of it was lust.

When Puck was a fresh young kid, he married Miranda Lessing, both of them from Eugene, Oregon. She gave him two sons, helped with his development and brokerage business and they became a successful team. When his sons were seven and nine he bought a nice piece of land on the point and built himself a showy house, surrounding it with an ornate wrought-iron fence. It looked, according to public record, like it was four years from the time he bought the land until the house was finished.

When he was in his fifties, he divorced his wife of thirty years and immediately married a twenty-two-year-old town girl, Effinesia Carter Sloan. She gave birth to her only son, Jaguar Morrison, three months later. They moved into the Morrison mansion at that time.

Wow, Mac thought. How cool the way public record matched up with the local lore. He'd heard this story. Carrie James had told Lou long ago about the scandal, about how Miranda — a kind, intelligent and giving woman by all accounts — left the big house, packed up her half of the furnishings and her half of the money, and went home to Eugene where she started a successful brokerage firm. Her sons worked for her, one in construction and one in sales.

There was no public record to support the gossip that Effie got her bosom before her marriage to Puck, but there was record of his financial difficulties and his ex-wife's financial success — enough to suggest maybe she'd been the brains behind their business partnership. Puck was a nice guy, though, funny and involved in the community and usually a good neighbor, if a little uppity sometimes. Guys around town didn't mind raising a glass with him from time to time, toasting this or that, telling a few off-color jokes.

No one from the Morrison debacle would admit to anything, but Mac put Puck in the hospital and Effie and Jag in jail, based on the 911 call and the interview at the scene. Their lawyer had them out before Mac completed his research of public records on Sunday.

On Monday he went to talk to the county district attorney and the coroner about whether there was sufficient cause to reopen the investigation into Ben Bailey's death. "I think this constitutes motive," he said. "I can't say I have evidence, but there were some very suspicious statements. And I'd like to know more."

"Who are you looking at?" the D.A. asked him.

"Well, Puck weighs about one-forty and is five foot four and seventy-three years old. His wife is five-five and a hundred and ten. But their boy, who doesn't seem to like the idea of settling for less than his older half brothers had, is a pretty big kid. And a lot of their angst seems to rest on that property of Ben's — something they seem to think could've rescued them. I just want to know if that's just talk . . . or if there's something more to discover."

Gina hadn't seen Mac, except from afar as he went in and out of his office across the street from the diner a few times. It appeared he wasn't working too much, and there was no explanation for it. Finally, on Thursday, he came in for his morning coffee at around ten. She put her hands on her hips. "Well. It's about time! Where have you been?"

"It's been a busy week." He sat on the stool in front of her.

"Busy with your disturbance out at the Morrisons'?" she asked.

"You know I can't talk about that," he said, but he smiled.

"You can talk to me! I'm the soul of discretion. All I want to know is, who hit who?"

"Depends on who you ask and when you ask them."

"Isn't a nine-one-one call a matter of public record?" she asked.

"When the case is no longer under investigation," he reminded her.

"Details! I heard it was Jag beating up his little old father."

"Jag and his mother were both arrested on battery charges. They were released on bail almost immediately, even though we have a twenty-four-hour hold on battery suspects. Time enough for the victim or possible victim to get away if he or she wants to get away. But with Puck in the hospital overnight —"

"Puck moved out of the house, I heard."

Mac lifted both brows. "Really? Now *that's* news. Where'd he go?"

"I don't know. Maybe to his older son's — someone said they saw his oldest son's truck pass through town. I have to tell you, Mac, the diner has been a real hotbed of gossip this week — and you were nowhere to be found!"

"I had serious paperwork and there were a couple of things in Coquille I had to do, so Steve Pritkus has been minding the town."

"Yeah, what did you do to him?" she demanded. "He used to be one of the best gossips around. Did you threaten him or something?"

Mac laughed at her. "I did. I told him he could tell anyone but you."

She slapped his arm. "You wouldn't dare!"

"Would so. Changing subjects, I want to know about the date. You threw me over for the doctor, so tell me about it."

"It was lovely," she said. "And I didn't throw you over. He asked, I accepted, we had a very nice dinner out in Coquille."

"Did he kiss you good-night?" he asked.

She leaned toward him, hands pressed on the counter. "Who hit little old Puck?"

He reached for her hand. "Was it really nice? The date?"

She stared down at their entwined fingers and thought, *Wow, I'm a little slow.* It took her going out with someone else to bring him to life, to get him to touch her. "He's a very nice guy. We're about the same age. And yes, I had a good time." *If you consider listening to someone talk about his peerless deceased wife for three hours fun,* she thought.

But she'd realized Scott really needed to do that. She was his first date in years, after all. And the first step was unloading all that stuff. At first she enjoyed their conversation — he wasn't grieving so much as remembering the perfect woman. And then he hooked her — it was therapy, and she was the therapist. She asked him all the right questions, he poured out his answers, and at the end of the evening she was tired and he acted like a man who'd just put down a fifty-pound weight.

"Think you might go out with him again?" Mac asked.

She gave a nod. "We're going to try sushi next Saturday night. I've never had sushi, never eaten with chopsticks. Could be interesting."

"You surprise me — sushi. I can't even think about eating raw fish."

"I'm going to try it. He says it's fun. Now really, what's up with you? I can't believe you've just been busy."

"Believe it. But there has been some local stuff to take care of. Cooper, for example. He's leaving tomorrow to go visit his family in New Mexico and I'm going to help Rawley babysit the construction crew working on that old bait shop. You should see it,

Gina — it already looks like a new place. The new septic system is in, plumbing is repaired and old Coop has his fifth wheel all hooked up to sewage, water and electric. Now he doesn't have to wrestle that big old toy hauler up the hill to go dump and reload water. And he's looking for work."

"What does that mean?"

"He's said all along that he'll settle up Ben's business, but then he has to get back to work. I imagine it means leaving Thunder Point."

"Gee," she said, feeling a little sad. "What about Sarah?" she asked.

"I don't know, Gina. I don't know what their arrangement is. You'd probably know more about that than me. Don't you girls talk?"

"Maybe not enough," she said quietly.

# EIGHTEEN

Mac was not in charge of the investigation surrounding the battery domestic at the Morrisons' or the possible homicide of Ben Bailey, but he knew what was happening. He was allowed to observe interviews and look at evidence in the closed case. At the time Ben Bailey died, neither the Morrison family nor Jag Morrison and his teenage friends were even on the radar. And Ben's injuries were consistent with a fall. There was even a mark where he theoretically hit his head on the wooden stair rail.

The investigation was proving interesting, but nothing had led to a new conclusion yet. Since Cooper was leaving town to visit family, Mac borrowed Ben's old laptop.

"I didn't find anything or I would've told you."

"I know, but I want to take a look, if you don't mind. And if it's okay, I'd like to borrow that Rhino of yours."

Cooper lifted one brow in question.

"Just want to see how it handles on the beach, if you don't mind."

"Thinking of getting one?"

"It's possible," he said with a shrug, although that was the furthest thing from his mind. What really occupied him these days was Gina dating their newest resident, the doctor. Mac had no reason to dislike Scott Grant, except the thought of Gina spending time with him and kissing him really did a number on his head. He couldn't be mad, though. It was his own damn fault.

The one great thing about winter in Oregon was that sunset was early. After dinner on Sunday, he asked Lou if she'd be home for the rest of the evening.

"Yes," she said. "Where are you going?"

He struggled with what to say. In the end, he just said, "Bunco."

"Ah," she said. "Finally."

He drove out to Coop's, loaded a couple of things in the Rhino, revved it up and took it back across the deserted beach, straight to Gina's house. Ashley answered the door.

"Hey, Ash," he said. "Can your mother come out and play?"

"Mom!" she yelled. "It's Mac."

Gina came to the door with a look of

confusion on her face. Clearly he was the last person she expected. Maybe last night's sushi date was so successful she was expecting the doctor. "You busy?" he asked.

"Well, that's a matter of opinion. I was ironing."

"Can you take a break? Go for a ride?" He turned, throwing an arm toward the Rhino, which looked like a baby Jeep.

"Mac, did you buy an ATV?"

"Nah, it's Cooper's. I have to say, it's pretty slick. It's kind of cold, though. Grab a jacket and I'll give you a little demo ride." She didn't move right away. She just stared at him for a long moment. Behind her there was the noise of family — the TV, Carrie talking to Ashley, the clinking around of dishes being loaded into the dishwasher. He could smell some kind of good meal. Having a cook in the house must be nice, he thought. "Come on, Gina. The moon is huge."

She still looked a little confused, but she reached for a jacket and hollered into the house that she was going out for a while. Then she went with him, bundled up and fastened her seat belt for the ride. He took her down the street and across the beach. There was no one out there tonight, which Mac found odd. A moon like this tended to draw people, but it was Sunday night and work started early.

"Oh, God," she said as they traveled across the beach, looking at the moon. "It's as beautiful as I've ever seen it."

"Yeah, really lights up the place. As it rises, it's going to lose all its punch, but we have a little while to enjoy it." He stopped the Rhino in the middle of the beach, right beside the campfire he'd set up on his way to pick her up. She sat in the Rhino and watched as he lit the fire; having a Dura-flame made it easy.

Then he went to the back of the ATV and pulled out a couple of aluminum-and-mesh beach chairs and a blanket, setting them up so they could look at the bay and the moon over the fire. He put the chairs close, then motioned for her to get out of the Rhino. She went to one of the chairs.

"You really thought this through."

"Not the setting so much. When I saw the moon last night, you were having sushi with the doctor." He pulled two bottles of beer from the back and held them up.

"It's surprisingly good, sushi. Very chichi. But I'm not too adventurous. Scott will eat anything, even if it appears to wiggle." She took a beer. "Thanks."

He sat down in the beach chair next to

her, opened both their beers and took a bolstering slug of his. "About Scott," he began. "How much do you like him?"

"I like him very much," she said. "He seems to be a terrific guy."

"Hmm. Like him a lot, huh?"

"I said I did. Now what's this about?"

He spread the blanket over them. "I can admit it . . . that kind of threw me, you going on dates. We've been sitting next to each other at high school football games, basketball games, hockey games, baseball games for years. I never thought you were interested in anyone."

"Oh, didn't you?" she asked.

"We even kissed once."

"Twice," she said. "And the next day you pronounced it a very bad idea. And said that it shouldn't happen again."

"Yeah, well, I've never been accused of being smooth."

"How'd you get some high school cheerleader knocked up if you didn't have some moves?" she asked with laughter in her voice.

"Ah, hell, I think she had all the moves. I was just a horny dumb ox who couldn't think at all. Which is why I really wanted to think where you were concerned." He turned to look at her. "I had a plan, Gina. I thought once our girls got closer to college, we'd probably start seeing each other as more than just neighbors."

"Really?" she asked. She took a sip of her beer. "I didn't get the memo."

He laughed at her. "I don't want to get in the way of anything you feel serious about, but if I'm not too late . . ."

"What? If you're not too late, what?"

"I don't want you with another man, Gina." He pulled her a little closer. "You're not just a friend and neighbor to me. I've had really strong feelings for you for years. I was just afraid of acting. If I let you down, I'd never forgive myself."

"Let me down, how?"

"Wow," he said, running a hand over his head. "I think you're going to be good at this counseling shit. If we were in a real relationship, a man/woman relationship, while our girls are best friends and if I somehow screwed it up — if it didn't work out, if there was fighting and crying and a nasty, painful breakup, if the girls' friendship was hurt . . ." He lifted her chin to look into her pretty eyes. "I didn't want to start anything I couldn't control, couldn't see to the end. I couldn't stand the idea of you being unhappy with me."

"The way Cee Jay was unhappy with you?"

"Well . . . yes." He shook his head. "She was unhappy from day one. She thought marriage was going to be some fairy tale. She thought it would make everything in her life work out, finally. But I was a scared kid, working day and night to keep us in out of the rain. And she was pregnant half the time, sick as a dog. There wasn't anything fun about it, it was horrible. And it was misery for just over six years. Then she left. Gina, I can't watch another woman go through that, and all because of me."

She couldn't help it, she laughed at him, but softly, and she touched his cheek tenderly. "You're a very sweet man and I adore you, but you're not afraid of letting me down. You're afraid you'll let yourself love me and I'll leave you."

His eyes grew round for a second. "I am?"

She nodded. "If you stop and think for two seconds, you know how I feel about you and how you feel about me. We've been best friends for years. But, Mac, I am goddamn sick and tired of being just your friend. And I'm tired of being alone. If I have to move on —"

He let out a heavy breath and put both his arms around her. "Me, too, Gina. Me, too. Moving on isn't what I have in mind. It's more like moving forward."

"If you kiss me and hold me and tempt me and then tell me it's all a mistake one more time, I'm going to grab that little pistol you think no one knows you carry on your ankle and just put you out of your misery. Am I clear?"

He laughed. "I might be better off." He leaned toward her and carefully kissed her, hanging on to his beer. "It's going to be dicey, you know."

"What?"

"Having a relationship. When was the last time you were alone with a man? Really alone?"

"I don't know," she said, snuggling into him. "It might be fun. Like being teenagers again. Sneaking around. Looking for a place to get alone. Sex in scary places."

He leaned back and, with a facetious grin, said, "Sex?"

She whacked him on the arm. "Seriously, tell me right now if there's no sex involved in this proposition, because I'll be the one backing out. I can't remember when I last had sex. It's been a long time. I might not remember how."

"Ooh," he said, shifting in his seat a little. "I'd suggest a reentry program right here, right now, but people have all these cell phones taking pictures. That's all I need."

She giggled.

"What about Scott? Is this going to create a problem?"

"Mac, all Scott wants is someone to talk to. He'd like to date again, get to know some women, explore whether the love of his life is really the last love of his life and he's done now. He spent our two dates talking about his late wife. He lost her less than twenty-four hours after his three-year-old daughter's birth. He's still grieving. But he's ready to move on and I'm sure he asked me out because I'm safe. Because he had some sense that I would listen to him."

"Gina, honey, I think you have this counseling thing pegged."

"And I think Scott's a good man who's going to be a friend. He's kind. He's generous. He has a mother and mother-in-law who are driving him batshit crazy and that's one of the reasons he moved here."

Mac chuckled. "Does he need one old-maid aunt to add to that cast?"

She nuzzled into the crook of his neck. "You smell good."

"I used that girlie shower gel Lou bought me for Christmas. I figured I had one shot at this."

"You waited so long," she told him.

"Not on purpose. I wish to hell I had

410

more to offer. I'm a cop on a low salary with three kids and an aunt. I'm looking at braces on two more mouths and three college educations. Gina, I'd really like to take you places, be alone with you, court you, but honestly, it's going to be hard."

"I guess we'll make out on the beach a lot," she said, not the least concerned. "Have you ever fantasized about doing it in the Sheriff's Department SUV?"

"No!" he barked, making her laugh. "You know I'm too straight and narrow for that."

She looked up. "That big moon just isn't going away."

"Are you warm enough?"

She put down her beer beside her chair, wrapped her arms around his neck and said, "I could be warmer."

He pulled her close and covered her mouth in a hot, deep kiss. She opened her lips for him and let him in and he felt like he'd gone straight to another planet. Everything inside him was on alert. He plunged long fingers into her blond hair and held her head in his hands, moving her a little this way, a little that way, deepening the kiss. She moaned beneath his lips and he let out a growl. He moved over her mouth for long seconds that stretched into minutes.

"God, you taste good," he whispered. "So

411

this is why I worried about kissing you. I'm hard."

"I'm that other thing," she said. And he knew exactly what she meant. Soft where he was hard.

"I could do you right now, under the blanket, take ten years of stress off your life," he offered.

She laughed at him. "Thanks for the self-less offer. I bet you don't even have protection."

"I do. I bought it in Coquille, too, so I wouldn't find myself standing next to Cliff in the drugstore, buying condoms. I have one in my pocket. It's the first time I've had a condom in my pocket in over ten years."

"Maybe we can sneak away sometime this week, while everyone we live with is at work or school."

"Tomorrow," he said, kissing her some more.

"Ah, tomorrow. You call the sheriff and tell him you need a little personal time. I'll tell Stu I need twenty minutes to run an errand."

"Twenty minutes?" he asked.

"It's been at least as long for me," she said. "Mac, are you sure this time?"

He pulled back a little so he could look into her eyes. "Gina, I've been in love with you for years. I'm sorry about three years ago. You should've whacked me over the head with a frying pan."

"I couldn't, you see," she said. "I thought it was possible you just wanted to be friends. As friends go, you've always been there for me. I couldn't give that up."

"I'll always be your friend," he said. "Your best friend, if you let me. But I want to be your lover, too." He groaned and shifted in his chair. "Soon. I want to be that soon." Then a look came over him. "Oh, Gina . . . I didn't even court you! God, I should date you first before I beg you to take off your clothes!"

She pulled his mouth back on hers, kissing him soundly. "It's okay, Mac. I'm ready. I've been ready for a long time." She kissed him again. "And promise to use that sexy bodywash again."

He leaned his forehead against hers. "Will you go steady with me?"

Less than twenty-four hours later, at two in the afternoon, a mere hour and a half before school let out, Gina was in Mac's bed. They went to Mac's house because his place wasn't at the center of town like Gina's. He was waiting for her when she pulled into his driveway and it took them roughly forty-five seconds to tear each other's clothes off and fall onto the bed, exploring each other with hungry fingers and devouring each other with starving kisses.

And then she laughed.

"Okay, I'm a tough guy, but is this funny?" he asked.

"Hilarious. A week ago, we were driving our girls to practices, sitting next to each other at games, never so much as holding hands, and here we are, naked. About sixteen hours after you make up your mind that you can handle having a girlfriend."

He ran a finger around the elastic of her panties. "Well, *I'm* naked, but you're not there yet. And it only took sixteen hours because you wouldn't do it under the blanket."

"Those days of doing it under a blanket or in a backseat are long gone. I hope. Listen, if Aunt Lou has to sew a couple of buttons back on your uniform, promise not to tell her I was ripping your clothes off."

He laughed then, too. "There are obviously things about Aunt Lou you don't know. She'd probably give me a prize if she knew this was happening."

"Just so we're clear . . ."

"We should go slower," he said.

She wiggled against him. "I think that ship

has sailed." She glanced over at his bedside clock. "We're down to an hour and fifteen minutes."

He must've taken that as invitation because he pulled off those panties and was poised above her, ready, stirring her up with the tip of his erection. Her response was to open her legs a little wider for him.

"Tell me what to do, honey," he said. "Tell me where to touch you. How to touch you. Because the most important thing in my life right now is making you come *hard*."

So she did as he asked, pulling him inside, directing his fingers to her clitoris. And he said, "Oh, God. Oh, my God."

He stroked her and thrust exactly twice and she exploded, gripping him so tightly she hoped she didn't actually hurt him. And what a blessing, because he followed her immediately, emitting a large groan and shuddering with his release. As he regained control he said, "We'll never get work making porn films."

She held him close, trying to breathe evenly.

"I love you," he said. "I love you, baby. I've loved you a long time."

And she cried. Laughing one minute, crying the next.

"Honey?" he asked, brushing her hair back.

She tried to cover her face because she was mortified. "I'm sorry," she whispered. "So emotional. I never thought I'd cry." But tears ran from her eyes into her hair.

"What's the matter, sweetheart? Was I too rough? Did I hurt you?"

"No, Mac, no. I . . ." She needed a few moments to compose herself. "I'm sorry, it was just that . . . I thought I might never have this in my life."

"Been a long time, huh, baby?"

"Ha." She sniffed. "This is the first time, Mac. There have only been two guys in my life — Ashley's father, who only said he loved me to get in my pants when I was all of fifteen and one other guy I dated for a little while, but we both knew immediately we weren't right for each other. I've never had a man I loved like this. God, I wondered if I ever would."

He wiped the tears from her cheeks, smiled and held her close. "You have one now."

"Everyone will know," she said.

"It's that kind of town. Will that bother you?" he asked.

She shook her head. "I got Deputy Yummy Pants."

"Oh, so you want to add spanking to this tryst," he said. "Who knew you were kinky . . ."

"All these girls and women want you, and you really want me?" she asked.

He nodded and brushed back her hair again. "Because you're the best."

Mac was resting in his quiet room, a Lab on each side of his chair, fire lit, his feet up and a book in his lap. A book he wasn't reading. He was feeling more at peace than he had in years and just prayed his cell phone wouldn't buzz or chime with some problem in town, because he just wanted to float on this cloud for a while. The afternoon was too short. He wanted more of Gina. He wanted to whisper to her, make love to her, feel her beautiful trim body close to his. . . .

"Dad? Got a minute?" Eve asked.

He opened his eyes. "Sure," he said, sitting up in the recliner and closing the book that was little more than a prop anyway. "What's up?"

She sat down on the sofa right across from him. "Ashley called. She said you and her mom . . ." She bit her lower lip.

"What, Eve?"

"She said you and Gina are now going together. Boyfriend and girlfriend."

"Ah," he said.

Well, one of the things they'd talked about before getting back into clothes was that their families shouldn't be the last to know. But also that they didn't need to know everything.

"I guess that's right," he said. "I think that's been coming a long time. Gina and I have been really close for years. We decided if we're honest, we're more than friends."

"What does that mean, exactly? More than friends?" she asked.

"It means we like each other more romantically than just neighbors. Kind of like Landon isn't just a friend, he's your boyfriend."

"Are you *sleeping* together? Having *sex*?"

He actually felt his cheeks get hot, but he'd be damned if he'd cave in to a sixteen-year-old girl. He valiantly held his ground. "Are you sleeping with Landon? Having sex?"

"Dad!"

"What?" he asked.

"Of course not! But I'm sixteen and we've only known each other since school started. You're thirty-six and —"

At least she didn't say she'd had sex years ago. "And?" he asked, lifting an eyebrow.

"And I don't think you've ever had a

girlfriend! Or even gone on dates."

He laughed a little. "You're right, Eve. But Gina and I have been friends for years, know each other very well, and I think she's a good woman. I hope to start taking her on dates. Is there a problem?"

"Well, how are Ash and I supposed to act with this new thing going on?"

He shot her a perplexed look. "Same as always?"

"But it's weird!"

He leaned back and put his feet up. He tried not to laugh. "You'll get used to it."

"And what if you get married and divorced?" she asked.

He sat up straight again. "Oh, for God's sake, Eve! Can we go out on two dates before you have us married and divorced?"

"Well? What if?"

"By the time all that can happen, you'll probably have already had your own marriage and divorce!" he blurted.

"That is *not* funny!"

"I thought it was kind of funny," he grumbled. "I'm just saying, aside from the fact that I hope to spend a little more time with Gina, there are no plans in the works to change the lives of everyone in our families." He snorted. "You'd think a person could get a little support around here."

"I just think it's weird," she said. "And I bet you're having sex!"

"I bet you're not going to find me willing to discuss my sex life with you in this lifetime," he snapped back.

"You mean you *have* a sex life?" she asked.

"For the love of Christ," he muttered. "Lou! Where's your aunt Lou?"

"She's watching *Designing Women* reruns in her bedroom," Eve said. "Does she know?"

"I'm sure she does," he said. "Listen, take it easy. I don't see how my life or your life is going to change much if I'm dating Gina. We'll still do all the school things together, I'll still have coffee with her at the diner when I'm free, we'll still have some holidays together, but I might get to hold her hand sometimes or put my arm around her or . . ."

"Or?" she asked, arching one judgmental brow at him.

"Or make out like rock stars, like you and Landon do! You know, if I'd given you this much static about dating someone, you would've gone ballistic! Why doesn't anyone tell single fathers about raising teenage girls? What's the matter with you? You love Gina!"

"I just don't want our family to go through another big, horrible thing — moving, starting over, all that. Don't you *remember?*"

*God,* he thought. *She remembers?*

"Of course I remember," he said. "Honey, you were only six when your mom left and what you probably don't remember is that she was very young and very unhappy. Gina's no kid. She's very stable and sensible. And she loves you. I'm sorry about your mom, but I did everything I could."

Big tears welled up in her eyes, but didn't fall. "I know," she said.

Mac cursed himself. He could be an idiot on so many levels. It had never occurred to him that a relationship might frighten Eve, that she still had some residual trauma from losing her mother the way she did.

He got up, went to the couch, sat next to her and put an arm around her. "Listen, honey, you have nothing to worry about. Everything is going to be fine. Gina's a good person, I'm a good person. Both of us put our kids first. Try to relax and enjoy seeing everyone happy. Maybe I finally found someone to sit in the truck with me while I spy on you kids on the beach, huh?"

She gave a little huff of laughter. "Kind of took me by surprise," she said.

"I don't know why. We've been best friends for years."

"Yeah, best friends going nowhere. I never

saw this coming."

"Then you're just about the only one. Word I got around town is that people were wondering what was taking me so long." He gave her a squeeze and laughed. "I know we tend to disagree sometimes . . . *wildly* disagree sometimes. But you should know I'd never do anything that would risk your sense of security. Your needs have always come first, Eve. You, Ryan and Dee Dee — always first." He shrugged. "But, angel, your old dad can use a little companionship, too."

She leaned against him and said, "I guess." He smiled to himself. She thought he was older than dirt. At thirty-six!

"Is Ash all worked up about this?"

"No. She thinks it's very cool. She said if we play our cards right, we can be sisters. Real sisters."

"Or, without playing any cards at all, you can be as close as sisters for as long as you want to."

"I know that," she said, snuggling closer.

He held his little girl for a while, remembering too well what she was like right after Cee Jay left, how she cried and wet the bed, how she rushed home from school every day to see if her mother had come home, how she stopped playing with the other kids on the playground but had an elaborate fantasy life in her bedroom with her dolls, playacting all kinds of complex scenarios about missing mothers. He took her to some counseling available through social services and she came around, adjusting to their strange life of a dad, three kids and aunt. He had to quit one of his jobs, move in with Lou, juggle a million things — but it worked. Finally there was no fighting, no angst, no crying.

And he got used to being lonely.

He didn't want to be lonely anymore.

An hour later Lou passed through the living room holding a cup of tea. "It's going to require a short period of adjustment. It'll be fine."

"Either you heard or she told you," he said.

"A little of both," she said with a shrug. "I'm glad you and Gina are being honest. I can say, from experience, keeping secrets really never works."

"Lou, do I need to talk to her about sex?"

"Oh, for the love of God! Really, Mac, whether you're having sex is none of her —"

"Not that, Lou, not that. She's sixteen. She's beautiful. She's got a boyfriend. We've had some talks but I don't want Eve at risk."

He rubbed his chin. "It's not my idea of a good time, but I can do it."

She smiled at him. "Gotcha covered, Yummy." He frowned darkly and she sat on the couch. "Eve and I have had many talks. She understands her parents were hot to trot and got started a little too young and even though the result was three beautiful children, too young can be too hard and can end badly. I told her if she ever wants to visit my gynecologist, a very kind and discreet woman, I will make an appointment, no questions asked. Eve's a very smart girl and she has high standards."

"I don't mean to just leave those kinds of things with you, Lou."

"I know. But I know how kids think, probably better than you do. And girls usually feel more comfortable talking to women. But by all means, if you want to have that discussion . . ."

"I might," he said. "I might. Not right away, though. Right now she's a little freaked-out to think of me dating her best friend's mother."

"Listen, Mac, this is a good problem. Eve will be fine. Just take a breather, huh? Try and enjoy life a little. Don't overthink this and mess up a good thing. You've put your life on hold for a lot of years and you have my admiration. But really, any longer and you'd become a stoic."

# NINETEEN

Cooper had a good visit with his family. He knew he had inconvenienced them by showing up two weeks before Christmas when everyone was very busy. But his three sisters, their husbands, two nieces and two nephews managed to coordinate a number of short visits here and there, and two big family meals at his parents' house. When it was just the adults gathered around the table after dinner, he told them about the bait shop and the renovation he was undertaking so he could sell. He didn't say how much land was attached.

Then he told them he'd been seeing someone.

It wasn't at that precise moment that he realized the reality of his situation with Sarah, but that nudged him ever closer to the truth. He privately acknowledged that, like a teenage boy, he had to talk to her every day. He texted her little snippets and phoned her at night. The only time she didn't answer his call was when she was flying, and then she called him back.

He needed her.

When he got back to Thunder Point he was already up to speed on the local gossip. The recent romantic development between Mac and Gina had Sarah's attention, but Cooper had been more interested in the ongoing situation with the Morrison family. From rumor, it sounded like that family had imploded, leaving behind an empty house surrounded by an ostentatious fence. Foreclosed, the rumor went.

Sarah was working when Cooper got back, so he checked in with the deputy. When he stopped in the small, storefront office, Mac was on the phone, so he waited patiently by the door. He noticed Ben's old laptop sitting on the desk. Then the deputy put down the phone and stood up.

"Welcome back," he said, smiling and sticking out his hand.

"So, I turn my back for five minutes and you decide to improve on your love life," Cooper said, extending his own hand.

"Well hell, they don't call me speedy for nothing."

Cooper let out a laugh. "They call you —"

Mac put up a hand. "Friends don't let friends say dangerous things."

Cooper grinned. "It's good to be back. Did you run off the Morrison clan?"

"I'd love to take credit for that, but I think they just came to the end of the line. It's been no secret that business hasn't been so good for brokers and developers around the state but I think the consensus was that Puck had more money than he knew what to do with and was untouched by the recession. Puck left first. He's back in Eugene. His sons by his first marriage might've taken him in. Then Mrs. Morrison and Jag moved on."

"So the town bully isn't in town anymore?" Cooper asked.

"The only thing I can really tell you about that is that he was instructed to make amends to Landon in order to get back into Thunder Point High and he refused, so his suspension turned into an expulsion. That doesn't mean he isn't around. Continued vigilance is recommended."

"Did he get into any trouble over that domestic? Hitting his dad?" Cooper asked.

"His court date is coming up. This will be his second offense and while he might not get the punishment he deserves, it's pretty damn clear he's a violent kid. And his badass self is almost eighteen. I don't think the court is going to pamper him. And the next time he pulls something, it's going to be bleak for him."

"Well, that's something, I guess," Cooper said. "Jesus, what's the matter with that imbecile? He must have grown up with ten times what most of the other kids around here have."

"Maybe that's what's the matter with him," Mac said. "I spend a lot of time feeling rotten that I can't give my kids more. Maybe I should rethink all that guilt. Maybe they're better off. At least they're not ungrateful little bastards." Then he laughed. "It takes so little to make them happy. I'm going to work on remembering that."

"You have good kids, Mac," Cooper said. He nodded toward the laptop. "Find anything on there?"

"I gave it to a forensic IT unit the department uses and they went through it and made a copy of the hard drive. I hope you gave permission for that because I said you did."

"Sure. But why didn't you do that in the first place?"

He shook his head. "Homicide and the coroner and the assistant D.A. went through the bait shop, and there was a postmortem.

There was no evidence of foul play." He shrugged. "And I have no idea if they found anything on the laptop, but their team can look at even the deleted and destroyed material. They're spooky." He lifted the laptop and opened it. "I did find something. I wondered if you noticed it, too."

He leaned a hip on the desk, balanced the laptop on his thigh and fired it up. He opened it and scrolled through email. It took a few minutes and he muttered, "Getting there . . ." Then he said, "Ah! Got it. He saved this. Do you remember this? It's four years old and might explain a few things about this arrangement you have with your friend's bait shop."

He turned the laptop around and handed it to Cooper.

I think I've had about enough of this place. Time to head out and find something new. I think I'd rather have an eagle's nest than a lot of corporate bullshit. Coop

Wandering yet again?

That seems to be my MO. I get restless real easy.

But don't they pay you a lot of money? Why

not just do the job for a few more years for the money? Find a place to settle down. They give you bonuses. Trust me, the eagles aren't real big on bonuses! Ben

I don't know. Chasing money for the sake of money . . . It's soulless. There's got to be more to life than that. Cooper

Cooper looked up at Mac. "He could've had tons of money if he'd sold some land. Even a little piece of it."

"I don't think that was the point of the email. We all knew Ben wasn't much for chasing money. Did you know there's at least one eagle's nest out there on the point?"

"I've seen the eagles, and I remember Ben telling me he had a nest — he was proud of that. They're built in those rocky precipices out there. But I went all the way out to the point and looked over the edge, and I couldn't see anything — it's all rocky all the way down to the water."

"And I don't think you can get a boat up close. Those waves against the rocks will take you out. But I think maybe Ben saved this email because of the thing about money. It's clear that money isn't the only thing that drives you."

"Well now, we don't know that for sure yet," Cooper said with a laugh. "That's easier to say when you have enough to live on forever. And I don't. Believe me." He closed the laptop. "So, you're done with this?"

"It's all yours. Want a cup of coffee?"

"That would be good. Across the street?"

"It doesn't look too busy over there," Mac said.

Cooper looked at his watch. "I have a little time. I want to run by the store. I'm cooking for Sarah and Landon tonight."

"Landon? Landon who?" Mac asked with a laugh. "You mean that quarterback who lives at my house now?"

Cooper rarely made any kind of a big deal over Christmas. Sometimes he went back to Albuquerque to spend time with the family, but he gave gift cards, not a lot of fussy presents. Those times he had girlfriends, he knew exactly what to give them — jewelry. The seriousness of the girlfriend determined the level of jewelry. For a girl you're dating but not deeply involved with, a spa package or gift certificate. In years past, he always skipped the company party. Occasionally coworkers had informal gatherings he sometimes attended. Hanging out with fellow pilots could be entertaining.

In Thunder Point it was a little different. First of all, people seemed to take turns entertaining, but nothing flashy. Lou and Mac had an open house and invited their local friends, who turned out to be half the town. Women wore Christmas sweaters with Santa or reindeer on them, men came in green-and-red sweaters and wool pants as opposed to jeans. For the first time in his life, Cooper asked a woman to dress him. He knew better than to show up in one of his hand-me-down suits or his jeans.

Sarah picked through his closet, pulled out some dark pants, a starched shirt, no tie, taupe V-neck sweater and the black shoes he almost never wore. "This will work," she said.

Carrie and Gina James had a gathering with the same theme. Their party featured meatballs, hot dips, cookies, fancy little cakes, and some *outstanding* bite-size crab and Parmesan hors d'oeuvres.

"If you eat any more of those, you're going to make yourself sick," Sarah said.

"I can't stop," he said.

Stu held his party at the diner one night, then Cliff had a free happy hour at Cliffhanger's with punch for the younger set. Again, there were a lot of Christmas sweaters and pressed black pants. Cooper made every event and, to his surprise, had a wonderful time. Well, except maybe for a while at Cliffhanger's when Ray Anne had a little too much to drink and Cooper drove her home. He had to lift her into his truck. She made a drunken suggestion that they "do it" just for the Christmas spirit and when he said that wouldn't work for him, she accepted that and said, "Well, then at least sign those agent papers for me, Hank!"

He hurried back to Cliff's so no one would assume . . .

The Coast Guard did not sleep on holidays, so Sarah couldn't make all the parties, but she hit a few. For Cooper, it was nice to have someone as classy and sweet as Sarah on his arm. But come Christmas Eve, she was scheduled to work. She'd have to be at the Coast Guard station, ready to fly if anyone needed rescue.

"It won't be the first time Landon and I had to adjust for holidays. Maybe the McCains will include him. I get off Christmas morning, so I'll be around for that."

"Let me," Cooper said.

"Let you what?"

"I'll stay at your house Christmas Eve. If he has somewhere to go, fine. I'll be there when he gets home. Then we'll have Christmas morning together."

"Oh, I don't know."

"Does it make you nervous to have me over on Christmas morning?" he asked her. "Because I can be useful. I know how to cook. I know how to clean up better."

"You know, it's that whole family thing. I worry about Landon thinking of himself as a part of a relationship, the way he did with Derek. He's only sixteen. He doesn't realize that we're close but not serious."

Cooper laughed at her. "Don't worry, Sarah. Landon hasn't thought about anyone but Eve in weeks."

"I guess that's right," she said, laughing with him.

So Cooper and Landon both went to the McCains for Christmas Eve where they ate seafood fresh from the marina and played poker until midnight. Eve pouted because she'd rather have had Landon's undivided attention, Mac roared his agony at drawing such bad cards, Cooper laughed his ass off and Lou took it all home.

And then came Christmas morning.

Bachelors like Cooper enjoyed holidays and were not overly sentimental about them. Sarah was somewhere between a spa package girlfriend and a jewelry girlfriend, mostly because she was so reluctant to let herself get involved. He understood a lot of this had to do with Landon. To that end, he had selected the perfect presents for both of them.

Early Christmas morning, after spending a night on Sarah's couch, he got up, fed the dog, wrote Landon a note and said he was running an errand and would be right back. He thought the kid would probably sleep late. In fact, Sarah might get home and read the note before Cooper got back.

He drove down the road to the beach, but he stopped at the marina. The boats were firing up. It was barely sunrise. It looked like a lot of the fishermen and a few crabbers were going out on Christmas morning. It hit him suddenly, these people had no choice. He'd known that, of course, but hadn't given it so much thought. He didn't know any of the men well and in fact the ones he'd met were the merest of acquaintances. He knew, however, that most of them worked their fathers' and grandfathers' and brothers' boats. Maybe they loved their work, but even if they didn't, it was their means of living.

But Cooper, always a loner, had had choices. He had never had to make long-term commitments or stay in jobs that weren't satisfying. All he had to do was take care of himself.

Watching those boats go out early Christmas morning, he felt a sense of envy. People depended on those men. They had families to take care of. He'd almost married twice and yet had never felt that sense of responsibility.

From where he sat in his truck, he could see the toy hauler. He'd lived in apartments, on a boat for two years, in his trailer — anything that he could uproot quickly and easily.

He put the truck in gear and headed across the beach. Inside the shed, along with Ben's old truck and RZR 800 — his Razor — were two top-of-the-line paddleboards, oars and two boxes. He'd cleaned up and gassed Ben's Razor, then he laid the boards across the back where a cooler might sit and fastened them in. The boxes went in the seat next to the driver. He laughed at himself — expert wrapper, he was not. There was a wide, red ribbon around each board and the plain white boxes had the identical ribbon. No paper, no froufrous, as his mom called them. He might be able to wear the hell out of a hand-me-down suit and buy some real top-notch toys, but he just was not good with wrapping presents.

He thought, however, that Landon was

going to go nuts for this one. And Sarah, being a beach girl at heart, would probably be happy, too. Nothing had ever felt better.

He drove the Razor across the beach and up to Sarah's house. Her SUV was parked in the driveway, so he pulled up behind it. In the kitchen was Sarah, still in her flight suit but in her stocking feet.

"Hey, thanks for making coffee," she said, stirring cream and sugar into a cup. "I'm going to need a nap today. We went out last night. Some folks on a Christmas Eve yacht ride got in a little trouble with some rocks. And booze, I'm thinking. What did you guys do?"

"Poker," he said, taking the coffee from her hands and pulling her against him for a delicious morning kiss. He went after her mouth like a starving man and realized that he wanted to wake up like that every morning.

When he let go of her, she laughed. "Poker? Are you corrupting my brother?"

"Shit, he had things to teach me. But Lou took the pot."

"Good for her. How about some breakfast? I'm all stocked up — eggs, sausage, bacon, sweet rolls. We can do omelets or take 'em straight."

"I bet you're starving," he said. "Can you

wait fifteen minutes if I cook?"

"Sure, but I don't want you stuck with cooking for the whole day. You already promised dinner."

"Dinner's easy. Hell, breakfast is easy. Go wake up Landon — I have something for him. For you, too."

"Now, we talked about this. We're not doing a big deal for presents. Just a little something, that's all. Nothing big. You agreed."

"Sarah, don't start complaining until you know if you have something to complain about. Get the kid. He's had enough sleep — he wiped me out last night."

She patted his cheek. "All right, but you better have kept your word."

Okay, he thought. So she'll lecture him a little bit later. He was a big boy, he could deal with that.

Landon stumbled out of his bedroom in a pair of sweats, no shirt, bare feet, his hair all wonky and sticking up all over the place. Like a little kid, he rubbed his eyes. Like a kid with stubble on his cheeks. "What, Cooper?"

"I got you and Sarah a Christmas present and it's in the driveway."

His eyes opened for that.

"Oh, if you've done anything crazy . . ."

Sarah warned.

He slipped an arm around her waist. "Take it easy, it's not what you think." And they followed Landon outside.

The cold didn't bother Landon at all, even in bare feet. The ribbons gave it away — he went straight to the boards. He yelped, "Woo-hoo! Sarah, look at this! Woo-hoo!"

She turned to look up at him. She smiled when she said, "Cooper, that's too much."

"I do what I want," he said.

"You don't follow directions very well."

He gave her a squeeze. "I thought that was your favorite part." To Landon he said, "By March, you'll be out there on the bay."

"Yeah!" he said, lifting one of the boards off the back of the Razor.

"There are two boxes in the front seat to put under the tree," Cooper added. "And this," he said, wrestling the keys from his pocket. "I'll need a ride home later."

"Huh?" Landon and Sarah said at the same time.

"It was Ben's. I think he'd like it if you had it. It's far from new, but it seems to be in good shape. I sure don't need it and I'm not going to sell it. And here's a tip — Rawley is good on engines and restoration if you need that. Let's get those boxes."

The boxes in the front seat of the Razor

440

didn't make it under the tree. Landon, a little beside himself, tore the ribbon off the top box, threw off the lid and held up a wet suit. "Holy crap!"

"Jesus," Cooper muttered. "He's completely out of control sometimes."

She looked up at him and said, "What have you done?"

He turned her toward him. "I did what I thought might make a good Christmas for you and Landon. And it made me happier than anything I've done in a long time."

Cooper had everything he wished for. He mixed up cheesy potatoes from the box, got his green bean casserole ready, rolls from Carrie's deli were on the counter and the ham was on the counter, coming to room temperature for later. And to make an afternoon near perfection, Landon took his new/old RZR to the McCain household where he planned to give rides all afternoon. And so Cooper was able to exercise his greatest desire by sneaking into Sarah's bedroom and curving around her small, sleeping form, pulling her close.

She turned in his arms and faced him, blinking open her eyes. "I bought you a sweater and you bought us a vehicle and a couple of paddleboards and wet suits worth

441

many hundreds of dollars."

"Best Christmas of my life," he said, kissing her forehead.

"Best Christmas of Landon's life, for sure."

"He's going to spend months praying for an early spring," Cooper said.

"You're getting too involved," she said.

"You're staying too afraid," he pointed out. "It's going to be okay, Sarah."

"I hope so."

"Trust me."

A few days after Christmas, Sarah and Cooper met Mac and Gina for a nice dinner at Cliffhanger's, their first official double date — no aunts, mothers, kids or dogs.

"I never thought I'd see the day," Gina said.

"There certainly aren't enough of them," Sarah agreed.

"Well, listen, I realize this is very last-minute," Gina said. "We're having a New Year's Eve thing at the house. It's for the kids, really. It's a way of keeping Eve and Ashley from doing something stupid with their stupid boyfriends, no offense, Sarah. They can invite a few friends, we'll lay in some food and the chaperones can play poker or something. You're invited, if you're interested."

Cooper grabbed Sarah's hand under the table. He pulled her toward him and whispered in her ear. "Say no, I beg of you."

She whispered back. "What's my excuse?"

"Plans," he said. "Just say no and I'll make you come three times on New Year's Eve. Three times."

Her face went red as a tomato. She looked at their friends and said, "Um, Cooper has plans for me."

As Cooper was taking her home, she said, "All right, Mr. Big Shot, what kind of plans do we have?"

"I don't care," he said. "Anything you want. I'll put on my expensive hand-me-down suit and take you out somewhere special. Or we can throw a couple of pizzas in the oven and eat them naked. I just want you, by yourself, not a bunch of teenagers. And it's not like I don't like teenagers, it's just that . . . you know . . . I want to make you scream my name a few times. That work for you?"

"I've never eaten pizza naked," she told him.

That was good enough for him and for the next couple of days he could barely contain himself. He had come to a few conclusions and it was time to level with

Sarah. That email Mac came across, that wasn't about money or eagles. That was about stability. About roots. He envied people with responsibility; he wanted a stronger connection and wasn't sure how that happened. Until now. Until Sarah.

She came to him for their private New Year's Eve party. It was still early in the evening and the first thing he did, right after locking the door, was to peel her clothes off as he walked her to the bedroom, leaving a trail of them along the way. He thought he was very accomplished, kissing her as he undressed her and himself, landing them on the bed, almost naked, where he made fast work of what was left of her clothing. And his.

He kissed her whole body until she begged him to get inside her. He was feeling so sure of himself and so powerful he said, "I meant it. I can make you come three times if you want me to."

"Once, for right now, should do the trick," she told him.

He grabbed for the little foil package on his bedside table and said, "Anything you want, honey. Anything. Just tell me."

"How about less talking and more doing."

He took instruction well, covering her mouth in a powerful kiss that curled her

444

toes and made her moan. It hadn't taken any time at all to know her body, to respond to her needs and desires, to find out exactly how to satisfy her. He could tell whether she wanted it fast and hard or slow and drawn out . . . and he delivered. Once he was inside her body, he knew the way and he knew the sounds that signaled she was ready. And that she was *there.*

He held himself back until he felt her clench and spasm around him, then he waited her out and wouldn't let himself go until she was complete. Sometimes when he emptied himself into her, it started a whole new orgasm for her. Like tonight. He held her tight, one arm under her shoulders, one large hand pressing her bottom against him, getting him deeper, his mouth on her mouth, claiming her.

"Aw, God," he groaned. "God, Sarah," he whispered.

And she ran fingers along the hair at his temples. "Cooper, one of these days I think you're going to kill me."

It took him a moment to catch his breath, but once he was in control again he said, "Sarah. Listen, Sarah. I love you."

And she turned her face away.

Cooper couldn't move. He was frozen in place, and he was still joined to her. He slowly touched the hair at her brow and gave them both a moment. Then with care, he rolled away from her, but he gathered her into his arms and pulled her close to him.

"Okay, Sarah, it's time. Talk to me."

She didn't move except to slowly stroke his hand for a moment.

With a thumb and forefinger to her chin, he turned her back to look at him. "I think you better tell me what he did to you."

"You know. He cheated."

"Oh-ho," he said on a humorless laugh, "I think there was more to it than that."

"Okay, he cheated with the maid of honor on the day of the wedding." His expression registered flat, in total disbelief. "Just when you think you've heard it all, right?"

He was speechless. The only thing that came to mind was *What kind of man?* And yet . . . "Sarah, you married him."

"I did," she said, giving a nod. "I suspected that day. I knew in my gut that very day, but he convinced me something that egregious couldn't be true. I didn't hear the truth until my ex-friend, my bridesmaid, decided to unburden herself a year later. And he came clean. He said he probably wasn't cut out to be monogamous."

"Aw, baby," he said, pulling her closer.

"I'm sorry."

"You don't have to be sorry. You're guilt-less."

He realized she was pushing against him a bit, so he let her put a little space between them. "I think there's more. I can't imagine it, but I think there's more."

She lifted those large dark eyes to his. He could hear the tears in her voice, but she wouldn't let herself cry. Her eyes didn't even cloud with tears. "I loved him," she said. "I really did."

"You must have."

She nodded. "Very much. It was completely crazy how much. From the second I saw him."

Cooper frowned darkly. There was a great deal missing from this explanation and he was a little afraid to hear it, but he knew it better come out. "I want to know everything," he said. "I want to understand this."

She took a breath. "It feels very strange. We're so . . . naked."

"Better to keep from covering up, I think. You can trust me with it, Sarah."

"I loved him," she said again. "I met him at work. One look and I was attracted and then he asked me if I'd go out with him. Of course I'd go out with him — he was so hot, so sexy, so beautiful. But I had Landon,

447

I explained. And he said, 'Let's all go out.' He took Landon and me to a great restaurant. Then he went to watch Landon play football twice before we even had a private date together. Does any of this sound familiar?"

"Like us?" he asked.

She nodded. "Can you see why I'm not letting anything like that happen to me again? Derek even lavished Landon with gifts, went to every game, stayed at my house while I had to sit alert . . ."

"I don't care," he said. "I'm not him." He lifted her chin with a finger. "Sarah, you know I'm nothing like him. Besides, you didn't love me on sight." He grinned lamely.

"Cooper, I was really just a kid when I lost my parents. I had a little brother to raise and he was so small, so vulnerable. I don't mean to sound like a baby myself, but it was hard. Sometimes I was so isolated, so afraid I'd never get the hang of this — like a single mom, thrown into the deep end of the pool. And then along comes this man I thought was wonderful and just having him there for us, for the first time in so many years I thought we could be a real family. I thought maybe I'd have a normal life, after all. I was thirty the first time I had a glimpse of a normal life. I was sleeping with a man I loved. Not only was I in a stable relationship, so was Landon. We were finally safe. I started to have hopes and dreams for the first time since I was in college. I started to fantasize about a family of my own — not only a safe place for Landon to grow up and thrive, but maybe a child of my own someday. And I had that for a year, Cooper."

"Sarah . . ."

"Cooper, I know how to lose a guy — I've had brief relationships here and there that didn't make it and I survived, Landon and I survived. But this time I had dreams. He didn't just let me down. He let Landon down, too. He didn't just break my heart, Cooper. He killed all my dreams." She shook her head. "I can't go through that again."

He looked into those dark, liquid eyes for a long moment. Then he pulled her closer and kissed her lightly. "You won't have to."

"I'm not taking that chance, you know. I'm not letting myself love anyone."

"I understand," he said. "I don't blame you. But I'm not him."

"I know, and it's not your fault that you're stuck with this. It's his fault, the bastard. He probably screwed this up for you. I apologize. But that's how it is."

# TWENTY

January was a cloudy and wet month, typical for the coast at this time of year. Sarah had a weeklong training class to attend in Florida. She was hesitant to allow Cooper to be in charge of Landon because of the way it resembled her relationship with her ex. But Cooper made a good case. "He's going to want to be on his own," Cooper said. "And he's definitely capable. But I can at least make sure he eats and doesn't use your house as a sex shop."

After a brief shudder, she said, "All right. But don't get any ideas."

"God forbid," he said.

Unlike her ex, Sarah *was* monogamous. She was just afraid of commitment, and for good reason, it seemed. There was no practical reason for her to trust a man, especially a man like Cooper, who could admit women had in the past complained that he just couldn't stick. There were no more proclamations of love, but the passion hadn't weakened.

While Sarah was in Florida, she called him daily. He spent his time at the renovation or his trailer. Rawley was still coming by most days and had taken to wearing a tool belt. Building was something he could do with minimal interaction. He did break down and ask Cooper if he might work on that old pickup in the shed, rather than taking it to his father's house where there was limited driveway and garage space. Ben had left an impressive collection of tools.

"Makes no difference to me, Rawley," Cooper said. "Just leave me enough space in there for the toys. I'll put the Jet Ski on the water when the weather gets warm."

The bait shop was officially gone and the bar/deli was looking damn good. They'd managed to kill the mold, reinforce the struts, lay down new floors, put up new drywall, rewire, plumb and polish without tearing down the deck. Cooper and Rawley got to work on the stairs to the dock, but the new roof and dock were going to wait till spring. One of Cooper's favorite things to do was walk through the renovated structure first thing every morning. Every day he was more impressed than the day before.

One of the best parts of the day, if it was a

nice day, was watching Landon come to the beach in his Razor. Sometimes Eve was with him. Ham was almost always sitting beside him — and he wore a helmet. He looked so silly, sitting up tall with his small helmet latched under his chin. Then Landon would park in the center of the beach, let Ham get out, remove the helmet and run the beach after sticks and balls.

During that week that Cooper was spending nights at his house, Landon only gave him a wave. When Cooper wasn't the nanny, Landon might come up to the shop and look around at the progress.

When a new stove top, oven, warming trays and industrial-size ice maker were delivered and installed, it was virtually done. There was still enough finishing work to keep him busy, new tables and chairs to be delivered, bar stools to be ordered, but the contractors would be moving out and taking their Dumpster, trucks and equipment with them.

The two rooms above the bar were also finished, though vacant of furnishings. It was basically just a bedroom, sitting room and large bath with shower. He had installed a fireplace downstairs that extended to a second-floor fireplace in his sitting room. Drawers were built-in. If Cooper chose, he could move into the bar. If he wanted to, he could find storage space for the toy hauler and have something under his feet that didn't move in the wind.

Mac's involvement in any case against Jag Morrison had been limited to the battery charges, but it was the link to all other things. The first hurdle had been to convince Puck that he must press charges. In the end, Mac was able to convince him that Puck might be able to escape large sums of payment for his third son's education by stipulating that the boy had assaulted him.

"What's the difference?" Puck had asked. "It's not like there's any real money left."

"The difference is, the court could attach your future earnings to benefit the person who beat you up," Mac told him. "And all you have to do to attempt to prevent that is file charges. Besides, eventually Jag needs to bear responsibility for his actions."

Puck, though in his seventies, had seen many fortunes come and go in his lifetime and fully expected to hit it big again any second. He was divorcing Effie while he had no visible means of support.

The next step for Mac was to charge Jag and send him to court. If the judge put him in jail for as little as forty-eight hours, that could be enough. The judge gave him a week in the county jail and two hundred hours of community service to add to the time he was already assigned for attacking Landon Dupre.

If there was one thing Mac knew about criminals, particularly young criminals, it was what idiots they could be. As Jag was taken into custody by an officer of the court, the homicide detective working on Ben's case told him, "Just so you're aware, Mr. Morrison, we'll be interviewing your mother, father, brothers and friends about your relationship with the late Ben Bailey at the approximate time of his death."

"What for?" he asked. "I didn't know that guy at all."

"Just the same," the detective said. "Anything you want to tell us before we start that process?"

"Do I look worried?" he asked with his usual insolence.

That was all that was needed.

When Jag was booked, he was told the same thing as every prisoner — that they have use of the phone in the jail, but that all calls will be recorded. When any prisoner picked up the phone and accessed an outside line, a recording restated that warning. And yet, Mac knew from experience, it was the rare inmate who believed anyone had time to listen to all those recorded calls.

They did.

Morrison called his mother, his father, his three friends who made up his little high school posse, and warned them all they'd better not say anything about his involvement with Ben Bailey.

Those people were already on the list to be interviewed, but not right away. What was done immediately was a review of the phone tapes. And there was one conversation that was the most revealing.

Jag's buddy Kenny Sinclair said, "You said you offed him! You expect me to lie about that?"

"There's no evidence!" Jag said. "We burned the two-by-four I hit him with! And I was alone! There aren't any witnesses!"

And there it was. It was admissible. He might have burned the forensic evidence, but his recorded statement was now in the hands of the D.A. They hoped to use that to sweat a confession out of him, as well.

It might not have been premeditated, it could have been manslaughter, but they knew who did it. And Jag Morrison knew he was a suspect. It might take months to bring it to trial, but they knew the truth.

This all caused Mac a great deal of reflection. He had brought his family to this little town to be safe and comfortable. And the scariest person in town turned out to be a seventeen-year-old kid.

Cooper was using a razor blade to scrape some of the paint off a pane of window glass, shining it up. He was on the deck, working on the outside, when the deputy's SUV came down the road from the highway. He dropped the razor into the open toolbox that sat on the table and wiped his hands on a rag.

"Why didn't you come across the beach?" Cooper asked when Mac stepped onto the deck.

"I had business in Coquille at the Sheriff's Department. Place is looking pretty good, Cooper," he said with a nod. "Better than it ever looked while Ben was here."

"Look around the inside," Cooper said, opening the door. "There's some cleaning and deliveries left, but it's close to finished. Rawley and I are still working on the stairs to the dock, but we're close."

Mac whistled. "I could live in this. That fireplace is just the touch."

"I'll sell it to you," Cooper said with a laugh. "You'll have to leave the kids and aunt behind, but the dogs can stay here with you."

"Funny," he said. "Maybe I could be a cop during the day and wait tables at night."

"Hey, it bears thinking about. How long do you intend to be a cop?"

"Long enough to make the pension worth my time. But seriously, Cooper, this place looks fantastic. I had no idea it was going to end up looking this good."

"Did it all without totally gutting the interior. Mold is gone, plumbing doesn't talk to you all day and night, sits still in the wind, keeps out the rain. And done in around three months' time." He chuckled. "Amazing what you can do with a ton of money."

"Will you get your investment back when you sell it?"

"No telling," he said with a shrug. "It mattered to Ben. I couldn't just sell off the land. I wanted to do something to deserve what he left behind. I wanted to leave it better than I found it, something that would make him happy. That's about all there is to it."

"Well, there might be one more thing. Jag Morrison was arrested this morning for the murder of Ben Bailey."

Cooper was shocked into silence, his mouth hanging open. It was a long moment before he whispered, "Oh, Jesus."

"I don't know how it's going to shake out. It's still under investigation. The prosecutor is alleging that Morrison's father, Puck, paid multiple visits to Ben, trying to entice him to sell his land. Puck wanted to develop it and there were plenty of investors on board for that idea. But Ben wasn't interested at any price. They believe Jag Morrison caused the fall that killed him."

"Why would he do that?" Cooper asked in a breath.

"Money," Mac said. "Puck's business was suffering with the recession and he had been asking the family to cut corners. According to Puck, he'd told them the house was going into foreclosure. That house — it was like the Morrison anchor, announcing them as the richest family in Thunder Point. That could all have been stopped if Ben considered even a small portion of his land for sale."

"He was rooted here," Cooper said. "It meant more to him than just land. It was home. He wouldn't have wanted to start over, find a new home at forty."

Mac nodded. "He wasn't about to budge. But a lot of people around here thought he had no family, no next of kin, no one who would step in and take care of it. Then you came along."

Cooper ran a hand around the back of his neck. "Did Jag's father have anything to do with Ben's death? Did he put Jag up to it?"

"I doubt it, but there's still an ongoing investigation."

A sardonic laugh shot out of Cooper. "The big house behind the gate was the evidence they were the richest family in town and the gentle giant in the crappy little bait shop was, in fact, the man with all the money."

"That about sums it up. I just wanted you to know. I can keep you posted, but I think until there's a court date, we're not going to have access to any more information. So — you came here to find out what happened. It wasn't an accident, Cooper. That's what happened."

"He was a good man," Cooper said. "Why should good men die?"

"If I could answer that, there'd be no reason to have me in this job. Now, what about you? You were supposed to be here for a week. A little over three months later, you're still here. What's next for you?"

That brought a melancholy smile to his lips. "Pretty soon I better work for a living."

"What about Sarah?" Mac asked.

"She's already working for a living," he said with a smile.

It was the following afternoon that Sarah came across the beach with Ham. Cooper chose not to tell her over the phone about the arrest. He hadn't been told to keep anything about the situation confidential, but he'd be damned disappointed if they failed to convict the little motherfucker.

After he told her the news, she said, "Are you making this up?"

"I'm not. He's been arrested. Investigation and hopefully a trial to follow."

"My God," she said. "He might've killed Landon!"

"And now he's arrested." He put his arms around her waist and pulled her near. "Want a cup of coffee? I should rinse off the dirt and grime."

"I'm just a little blown away by the news."

"So was I. I didn't want to tell you on the phone. Let me know how Landon takes it. I'm not surprised by this, but it's still shocking. I knew he was bad but hell, Sarah, I underestimated him. Come on," he said, taking her hand and leading her — and Ham — to the trailer. He used the rag from his back pocket to wipe Ham's mouth and feet, then he fixed up his water in the saucepan. He tore the hoodie off over his head.

"Feel like a shower?" he asked her.

"I do," she said, smiling. "Lock the door."

"You know, these little interludes are very nice, Mrs. Robinson," he said with a grin. "It's naughty and sneaky and I like it." And he pulled his T-shirt over his head.

"No funny business," she said. "I know you think this place is a mansion, but that shower is not really a two-person shower."

"Fine," he said with a smirk, as he removed his boots and socks. "All funny business begins when you're dried off." And he dropped his jeans, revealing an erection.

She laughed. "Cooper, you're not the least bit coy, are you. Can you hold that thought?"

"I can. But let's not waste time."

She went to the bedroom to remove her clothes, folding them in a pile on one of his built-in dressers, walking naked to the shower. When she got in, he was soapy and he pushed her up against the wall. He kissed her deeply, holding her against his soapy body. "Sarah, you are beautiful. Have I told you that lately?"

She ran her hands over his chest. "You're beautiful, Cooper." She traced his tattoo on his right shoulder. It was a globe and ocean.

461

Fitting. "Are you clean enough yet?"

"I think I could manage to make you happy right now . . ."

"Not right now, Cooper," she said, laughing. "This shower is worse than an airplane bathroom."

"Have you ever done it in an airplane bathroom?" he asked.

"No. Have you?"

"Well, no. But with you, I could." He lifted the showerhead from its bracket and rinsed them off. "Come on." He turned off the water and pulled her out of the shower, but instead of drying off, he grabbed and carried her, slippery and squealing, to his bed.

"Cooper," she said and laughed. "I'm cold!"

"You won't be cold for long," he promised, covering her with kisses until she relented, put her arms around his neck and opened her legs for him. "That's what I'm talking about. . . ."

It took only a few moments for both of them to explode in the ultimate satisfaction, then melt into laughter once more.

"Do you know what I love about being with you?" she asked. "You're fun, you know when to be serious, then you're fun again."

"Do you ever feel like there are eyes on you?" he asked.

Her eyes grew very large, then she turned her head to see Ham sitting patiently at the side of the bed near the foot, waiting for attention.

Cooper pulled on her chin, bringing her gaze back to him. "Please don't talk to him," he whispered. "If you do, I'll have a Great Dane on my back."

She started to laugh and he covered her mouth.

"Laughing at him could do it, too. Shh. This is good, my hand over your mouth. I have to tell you something." He was smoothing the damp hair off her brow. "Remember when I told you that I'd been accused of being emotionally unavailable? Afraid of commitment?"

"A couple of months ago," she said, and nodded.

"I didn't understand that at the time, but I think maybe the woman who said that was right." He shook his head. "I'm not that way with you. With you, I'm mentally, emotionally, physically in the moment. All in. All there. All yours. I can tell. I feel different with you than I've ever felt before."

"Why are you saying this, Cooper?"

"Because I want you to know. It's important that you know."

"Why? You already told me you love me."

"Love is easy," he said. "The other stuff is even more important."

She smiled and rubbed her knuckles along the hair over his ear. "You're awfully good to me when I'm the one who's emotionally unavailable and afraid of commitment."

"I'm not worried about that." He grinned at her. "Do you want food?"

"You always make me hungry," she said, sitting up and wiggling to the other side of the bed so she wouldn't have to wrestle her way around Hamlet.

"This has been fun, these afternoons when Landon is at school and you're not at work."

"And Rawley isn't here," she said.

"Rawley is here. He's working on that old car of Ben's in the shed. One of these days soon, I'm going to have to actually work, too." He pulled on his jeans and gave Hamlet a pat on the head.

"The bar is done, then?"

"It's as close to done as it needs to be."

"Have you been sending out résumés?" she asked quietly.

He shook his head. "But I've gotten a couple of offers without applying. An old friend from Texas is giving up a news chopper job in San Francisco and he said they'd hire me on his recommendation. ASAP. And Colorado really needs firefighters — that was another personal recommendation. Last year's fires charred the state. They're ready to gear up for summer. Both positions are open immediately."

She looked down to fasten her pants.

"What would you do, Sarah?" he asked her.

She gave a shrug. "News chopper," she said. She looked up. "Cooper, do you think we'll stay in touch?"

"I hope so, Sarah. You could beg me not to leave," he suggested with a patient smile.

"You know I can't do that."

"I know you can't do that."

"How soon on that news job?"

"They'd like someone right away. I assume that means within the week. But —"

"You wouldn't leave without saying good-bye, would you?"

"Of course I wouldn't do that. Would you?"

She shook her head. "Wow. The idea of you leaving. It hit me. Even though I knew all along, since that first day I caught you surfing the net, looking at potential jobs."

"You wouldn't like that? Me leaving?"

"I'd hate it."

"Yet you wouldn't ask me to stay?"

"You know I can't. I explained about that. The best I could."

He gave her a little kiss on the forehead. "Yes, you did. Let me take you out to dinner at Cliff's. Text Landon and invite him. Tell him Eve can come. Take your horse home and I'll pick you up in an hour."

Sarah assumed one of Cooper's reasons for taking her out to dinner with Landon along was to explain to her brother that he'd be leaving. But of course Landon brought Eve and the conversation around the table didn't leave room for any kind of serious discussion about Cooper's next move. Instead, it was all about Jag.

"Everyone in school is talking. People say Jag shot him or stabbed him, but that can't be right," Eve said. "The police would've known if that happened."

"What about his friends?" Cooper wanted to know.

"Only Wormitz and Pickering were there. They said they didn't know anything, except that Morrison lied so much all the time, bragged so much, no one really took him seriously," Landon said. "Except Sinclair didn't come to school and someone said he isn't coming back. He's going to stay with his aunt and uncle in Seattle for a while. He might be afraid of Morrison."

"Did either of them try saying they were

sorry for backing him up? For picking on you?"

Landon shook his head. "I don't see that happening, man. But around school, they're treated like they have typhoid fever."

When Cooper took Sarah home, he didn't go inside. Landon and Eve had followed them home in Landon's little truck, and they walked past them to go inside. Sarah told him she had to go to work early and probably wouldn't see him until late tomorrow, so he spent delicious moments at the front door, kissing her stupid.

Landon snapped open the front door. "Get a room, guys," he said, then laughed at himself.

"He's a pain in the ass sometimes," Cooper said.

"Will you promise me something, Cooper? Will you please not leave town without explaining to Landon what's going on? Where you're going, what you're doing, all that? Because even though he's a pain in the ass, I think, in his way, he depends on you."

He rubbed a knuckle down her cheek.

"Sometimes you really act like you don't know me," he said, giving her a brief kiss. "Or maybe you think I'm someone else? Of course I would never leave without saying

467

goodbye, without talking to Landon. Is this going to keep you awake all night? Because you have work early tomorrow and you need sleep."

"No, I'm fine," she lied. "Thank you for being so understanding. About Landon and everything."

"I'll talk to you tomorrow," he said.

*Why can't I say it,* she asked herself. *Why can't I say I love you, don't go?* "Good. Tomorrow."

Sleep came hard. She heard Landon leave to take his girlfriend home, heard him return, saw the time on the clock every hour. The next day at the station dragged so much she found herself almost wishing they had a training day or an inspection.

She did talk to Cooper, but somehow managed not to ask him if he was packing. It hung like a pall over the conversation. The only thing that filled her mind right now was giving him up, an unfathomable notion. And yet she didn't want their relationship nailed down.

The sun was setting by the time she got home. Landon and the dog were gone, as was the Razor. She changed into spandex, rubber boots, turtleneck and her red slicker and headed across the beach. She suspected Landon and Cooper were having a talk about his leaving. But then she found Landon on the beach, throwing the ball for the dog, his ATV parked nearby, Ham's helmet in the seat.

"Hey," Landon said.

"Hey," she answered. "Did you see Cooper? Talk to him?"

"Not yet," Landon said. "I'm wearing out this big old moose. Hey, I'm going over to Eve's tonight. That's okay, right?"

"Sure. They aren't getting sick of you over there, are they?"

He grinned his heart-stopping grin. "They love me."

She looked up toward the bait shop. Cooper and Rawley were both there, working on something, though it was getting dark. "I'm going to go see Cooper. Are you having dinner at Eve's?"

"Probably. Mac is starting to refer to me as his oldest son." He made a face. "Creeps me out."

She laughed at him and that was all it took to remember they were a team. Invincible. Hard stuff had happened to them, but together they were up to it.

Well, today Cooper wasn't packing up. It appeared he was putting some sort of finishing touch on the bar. He and Rawley had ladders against the wall, one on each side of the double doors that opened onto the deck. It looked to be a sign, covered with a sheet or piece of paper. They lifted the sign just as she started up the stairs and while she climbed, they fastened it into place.

They were coming down as Sarah reached the deck. "What are you guys doing?"

Cooper looked at her over his shoulder, smiled at her and tore off the cover. The sign read BEN & COOPER'S.

Rawley lifted his ladder and took it around the corner, leaving them alone on the deck.

"What is that?"

"A sign, Sarah," he said, laughing at her.

She took a step forward, looking up. "You're going to sell it with your name on the sign?"

He shook his head. "I'm not going to sell it."

"Rent it?" she asked.

He shook his head. "Run it. I hope I can figure it out."

"But, Cooper, what about that flying job?"

He shook his head. "Nah. I think I'm done working for other people. I'm too judgmental, for one thing. Now if I pick apart the way things are being run I have no one to blame but myself. Sarah, I'm not done with us. We're just getting started."

She was shocked for a moment. Then she

said, "You let me believe you were leaving!"

He shook his head, then he put his hands on her waist. "I didn't correct your assumption. It's true, I was contacted about a couple of flying jobs. I turned them both down. Even though dropping flame retardant on a big nasty fire does sound like fun."

"Why didn't you say so? Why didn't you tell me?"

"I told you I loved you. I told you I was all in, that you could trust me. Do you think I'm the kind of guy who can say something like that and then leave you?"

"Yes!" she said. "I thought that! Not because you're a bad guy, but because you said you had to work."

He chuckled. "There's no doubt in my mind, I'm going to have to work. I bet this place only looks simple. I bet it turns into a giant pain in the ass."

"Oh, Cooper, what are you doing?"

"I'm staying, Sarah. I'm not going to push you, crowd you or worry you. I'm just going to love you. I'm going to hang around here, close to you, until you trust me enough to get your dreams back."

She stared at him for a moment. Then she put her hands on his cheeks and pulled his mouth onto hers, kissing him so deep and so hard it knocked him back a step. But he hung on to her. Then, against his lips, she whispered, "I do love you, Cooper. I do."

He smiled against her lips. "I know, baby. I know."

# ACKNOWLEDGMENTS

Special thanks and deep appreciation goes to the United States Coast Guard, and especially to Lieutenant Commander Russell Torgerson, for arranging a wonderful tour of the U.S. Coast Guard Group/Air Station North Bend, Oregon. Thanks to Lt. Cmdr. Torgerson for answering a million questions and giving me an up close and personal view of the mission. Of course any mistakes or artistic license for the sake of story and drama are entirely mine.

My personal gratitude to the men and women of the USCG for your service. Too many lives to count have been saved because of you.

And special thanks to my husband, Jim Carr, for shepherding me around the coast of Oregon with camera in hand. What a fabulous way to research — a trip to one of the most beautiful regions in the U.S.

Thanks to my editor, Valerie Gray, and

my agent, Liza Dawson, and my most fabulous Harlequin publishing team for giving me the opportunity to have all the fun of writing.

# ABOUT THE AUTHOR

**Robyn Carr** is the *New York Times* and *USA Today* bestselling author of over forty novels, including historical romance, series romance, and a thriller. Originally from Minnesota, she and her husband, Jim, live in Nevada. They have two grown children. Visit her website at www.RobynCarr.com.